Leslie Leaned Against Ryan, Her Hair Beginning to Blow in the Wind . . .

She smiled up into his hazel eyes.

"You will be my cabin boy," he said, his voice suddenly husky, his hand tightening on her arm. Even in the darkness she could see the desire in his eyes. Then he released her and turned swiftly away to lean on the rail. "We shall have to remain in Nassau for close to a month," he said. "But then we'll go in at Wilmington and you'll be able to search for your so charming father."

For a moment, Leslie wondered what she had done to so displease him, and then she understood. The demon he was fighting was his desire for her. Well! As far as she was concerned this wonderful, warm and natural feeling was no demon, it was love. Only a month, or less, to prove to Ryan that they belonged together . . .

Dear Reader,

We, the editors of Tapestry Romances, are committed to bringing you two outstanding original romantic historical novels each and every month.

From Kentucky in the 1850s to the court of Louis XIII, from the deck of a pirate ship within sight of Gibraltar to a mining camp high in the Sierra Nevadas, our heroines experience life and love, romance and adventure.

Our aim is to give you the kind of historical romances that you want to read. We would enjoy hearing your thoughts about this book and all future Tapestry Romances. Please write to us at the address below.

The Editors
Tapestry Romances
POCKET BOOKS
1230 Avenue of the Americas
Box TAP
New York, N.Y. 10020

The Golden Lily

Jan McGowan

A TAPESTRY BOOK
PUBLISHED BY POCKET BOOKS NEW YORK

Books by Jan McGowan

The Golden Lily
Silversea

Published by TAPESTRY BOOKS

An *Original* publication of TAPESTRY BOOKS

A Tapestry Book published by
POCKET BOOKS, a division of Simon & Schuster, Inc.
1230 Avenue of the Americas, New York, N.Y. 10020

ISBN: 0-671-54388-1

First Tapestry Books printing November, 1985

10 9 8 7 6 5 4 3 2 1

The Golden Lily

Prologue

IN CENTRAL FLORIDA, NORTH OF THE WIDE SWEEP OF undulating golden grass known as the Kissimmee Prairie, lie nine hundred square miles of thick hardwood forest and subtropical growth that in its heart is impenetrable. A bowl of fertile muck and dark water, it breeds thick undergrowth cabled with tangled vines of smilax, thorn and wild grape beneath the huge magnolias and oaks. Pools, shadowed by pale green willows, rimmed by the fragile white swamp lilies, are visited only by the snowy ibis that slant great wings between the trees and drop to feed in the shallow water. From the tops of tall pines which grow in the occasional dry spot of sand, the sharp rap of pileated woodpeckers echoes though this wilderness known as the Green Swamp, but most of the denizens of its deep woods are quiet and secretive.

Quiet, too, have been the desperate men who have sought shelter through the centuries in the fringes of the forbidding land. Seminole Indians hid there from their white enemies before they drifted further south to the Everglades. And, in 1861, another hunted man found refuge from his own kind in its forests.

Harry Gordon, a gentle schoolmaster sickened by the bloody carnage of the Civil War, had left Wilmington, North Carolina, and slipped south with his young daughter, Leslie. Traveling with forged papers and well aware of the certain death that awaited an army deserter in wartime, Gordon found a spot in the outskirts of the Green Swamp on the bank of the Hillsborough River. He knew from his studies that the Hillsborough, its headwaters in the swamp, ran southwest to the Gulf of Mexico and a settlement on the shores of Tampa Bay. The settlement meant nothing to him, but it might, in case of his capture, be a haven for his daughter. Satisfied, he settled down to wait for the war to be over.

Chapter One

ON A FINE AFTERNOON IN APRIL OF 1864, LESLIE GORDON kicked her old horse gently onward through shady, open spaces in the outermost fringes of the Green Swamp. She was wearing a pair of her father's trousers rolled up past delicate ankles, and a linsey shirt of his that ballooned like a tent around her thin shoulders and small, rounded breasts. Honey blonde hair, streaked a pale gold where the Florida sun had touched it these past three years, hung to her waist in rippling, damp profusion. Beneath the enveloping clothes her too slender body was also still damp from her daily bath in the crystal springs that bordered the great swamp on the west. Behind her saddle was a bundle of old but freshly washed clothes, and tied on the side of the saddle where she could reach it in a hurry was her father's one reminder of the war, his Enfield rifle, loaded.

Riding the bank of a river that began in the swamp and ended, her father had told her, in the Gulf of Mexico, Leslie was heading for a hidden shack in a thick woods of magnolia, oak and pine just ahead. It was near time for sunset, and the shack, poorly constructed and beginning to rot, was still some protection against the roaming panthers that haunted the woods at night.

The old horse seemed anxious to get home. In sight of the thick copse of trees, he pricked his motheaten ears forward and broke into a shambling trot. Leslie laughed and patted his neck. She hadn't laughed in weeks, but this morning she had made a decision she should have made long before, and it had given her courage.

Tomorrow, she had decided, she would leave. She would gather her few possessions, pack them into the old dugout canoe her father had found in the swamp, and head down the river until she came to a town. There was no use pretending any longer that her father would return. This time, taking the few last coins they had hoarded to buy food, he had reminded her of their plan in case of disaster.

"Each time I leave, the chance of my capture grows greater," he had said. "If I'm not back in two weeks, you must make your way downstream. In any town there is some charitable family and you can make yourself useful." He had seemed more despondent than ever as he added: "I have failed not only in my duty to my country but also in my duty to you. Thank God you are sensible and well educated. Perhaps it won't be too hard for you to make your way."

Leslie had nodded silently. She loved her father dearly but had never understood him. Why an honorable man would desert the army that was trying to free them from the rapacious Union was beyond her. She had listened with pity to his explanation that he couldn't bear to kill another human being. An enemy was an enemy to Leslie. In a case of kill or be killed, she was sure that she could pull a trigger. In any event, she now felt strongly that it was her duty to find him, to aid him if he was still alive, and if not, to mourn his death properly.

Turning from the bank of the river, she headed for the trees, thinking with an almost erotic pleasure that tonight, for once, she would eat her fill. For the past month and a half she had been living on short rations, measuring out the cracked corn in tiny amounts so it would last until her father got home. Tonight she would boil it all, and the meat from the fox squirrel she had shot in the morning would go in the pot as well. Tomorrow, paddling on the river, she would need her strength, and there was little strength left. She knew from the way her own clothing hung on her that she had lost too much weight, and the attacks of dizziness were becoming more frequent. But food would fix that.

Nearing the trees, she pulled the old horse to a stop, twisting in the saddle to take a long, close look along the sunny river. Here the banks were bordered with the tall plumes of dog fennel, its bright green waving in the breeze. In the past three years there had been only two occasions on which there had been a solitary hunter on the river swale, looking for the wild pigs that abounded there. Still, she and her father had always scanned the area before entering the woods. Neither of those two hunters had come near the woods that held the hidden shack, which was lucky for them. Her father's rifle shot true, and she had held it trained on them as long as they stayed in sight.

Now, though there was an agitated movement going

on in the chest-high fennel further east, Leslie shrugged and went on. It could only be the wild pigs, rutting and fighting now that it was spring. Riding through the thick underbrush toward the clearing, Leslie's mouth watered at the thought of wild pork. But with so little powder and shot left for the Enfield, she couldn't justify killing one. The meat spoiled quickly, and the smell of slaughter brought the panthers to growl and claw at the bottom of the rickety shack, which proved unnerving in the middle of the night.

Once dismounted, with the saddle put in the shack and the clothes distributed to dry along the long limb of a magnolia, Leslie stood back with her rifle and surveyed them. A skirt and two blouses, all that remained of her always skimpy wardrobe. But she would wear the skirt and the best of the blouses tomorrow. She had no idea how soon she might come to a town, but she didn't intend to arrive in men's clothing. The skirt was patched, the blouses thin from wear, but they would have to do. Trembling now from hunger and weakness, she turned to the flight of steps that led up to the shack, stilted high above the damp, mucky ground.

Halfway up, she heard a shot.

The day had begun with high hope for sea-weary Captain Ryan Fitzsimmons of the *China Pearl*. For the first time in years he intended to indulge his love for hunting wild game. Today and tomorrow he would explore this Florida backwoods and forget his varied problems.

A full day's ride behind him, one of his problems was being solved. His ship lay securely hidden on the Hillsborough River, six miles upstream from Tampa Bay. The fastest blockade runner that ever brought supplies to the Confederate Army, the *China Pearl* was once more undergoing repairs. Speeding back from the Bahamas with a full load of supplies and luxuries aboard, the ship had been headed for Mobile. But, rounding the Keys, she had been badly holed by a lucky shot from a surprised Yankee cruiser.

Ryan had been forced to bring his leaking ship into Tampa Bay, running her stealthily past the Union blockade in the middle of the night. He had been aided considerably by First Mate Ralph Tudbury, a native of Tampa who knew the channels by heart. Tudbury had taken the wheel later and run the small ship up the Hillsborough on the high tide, letting her ground near a sandy bank as the tide went out. It was a perfect spot for repairs, hidden by tall trees on high banks, and Ryan had congratulated Tudbury warmly.

Tudbury, overcome by joy at being home with a chance of seeing his family, was moved to brag further about the glories of the Hillsborough, pointing out that where they lay was the last of the brackish water; that upstream they could fill their barrels with the sweetest, freshest water this side of Heaven. Furthermore, he had added, a day's ride would take a man where he could down a wild pig or bear and have fresh meat enough for the whole crew of twenty.

Immediately, Ryan had put the unfortunate Tudbury in charge of repairs, instead of meat. Borrowing a horse from Tudbury's brother, who farmed near the river, he started off.

Ryan now regretted listening to that brag. There was no trouble in finding the place; he had only to follow the river. There had been no trouble in finding a wild pig, either, but the pig had brought trouble by the barrelfull. Riding along in a high stand of dog fennel, the horse had almost stumbled over the beast, which started up practically beneath his hooves.

Startled, Ryan had dragged his already primed muzzleloader from its sheath and given chase. Within seconds he was flying through the air, his gun spiraling away, the horse turning a somersault. He had time to hear the solid thump as the horse landed before he landed himself and the sunny world went black.

Ryan had no means of knowing how long he lay there before consciousness returned. Not long, he judged, for it had been afternoon when he arrived and the slanting rays of sun were still making his face sweat. He sat up slowly, testing for broken bones, grateful to find no more than a bump on his head from a rocky outcropping and a few assorted bruises and aches.

Sitting there, smelling the sharp, soapy odor of the fennel waving over his head, he looked through the thick stems and saw with a sinking heart that the horse was still down, thrashing weakly. He rose, looking around instinctively for his rifle. Picking it up, he thrust through the tall growth to the horse's side and found what he had known he would find. A flying hoof had found a deep hole on the bank, and the horse's leg was broken.

Ryan's clear hazel eyes filled with pity. Leaning, he soothed the frantic horse, stroking his neck, gradually pressing the straining head gently down to the soft ground. Easing, the horse rested, his big rib cage heaving. Quickly then, Ryan dispatched him with a merciful shot and turned away as the big body shuddered once and was still.

His eyes blurring—a thing he wouldn't have wanted his crew to see—Ryan stood with his back to the horse and reloaded his gun. He never hesitated to kill for food or in self-defense, but the horse was fine and willing, trusting in man. He hated to think of having to tell John Tudbury what he had had to do. There was

8

gold enough hidden on the *China Pearl* that the cost of a fine horse and saddle wouldn't make a dent, but finding a horse like that one wasn't easy. All in all, it was a bad end to a day that had begun so promisingly.

Sighing, he turned back and pulled his bulging saddlebags loose, slinging them over one broad shoulder. Thoughtfully, he stared at the saddle. Well made and comfortable, but too heavy to drag back the thirty or forty miles he had traveled. He would pay for it, but Tudbury might still think it worth a trip to retrieve it. Squatting, he unbuckled the girth. He would hang it in a tree and blaze a few trunks to lead Tudbury to it.

Standing, Ryan looked around. The sun was beginning to set and he would need a shelter for the night. Considering the boggy ground, he figured on using the long rope on the saddle to weave a hammock of sorts from a couple of limbs, and that would take a large tree. Fortunately, a bit to the west and close to the river there was a large stand of oaks and magnolias, either of which might offer exactly the configuration he needed. Purposefully, he started off toward them, his lean, whip-strong body relaxed, the last rays of the sun bronzing his bright chestnut hair, highlighting his rugged features.

"Stop right there, Yankee!"

Ryan froze in midstride, the curling hair on the back of his neck rising. Ahead, right on the edge of the trees, he could see the dull glint of a rifle barrel. But what scared him was the voice. Hard to tell from a sudden shout, but he would swear it was either a woman or a young boy, either of which was notoriously nervous with a trigger. He waited a moment and then answered calmly.

"I'm not a Yankee, son. Just a hunter, looking for a place to spend the night."

Hidden behind a tree, Leslie grimaced. *Son?* Couldn't the man tell a woman's voice when he heard it? She knew she ought to tell him to move on, say she and "her family" wanted no strangers around. But, whether it was the chance to talk to another human, or maybe those bulging saddlebags that must hold food, or even just the calm, deep voice, she said something entirely different.

"Then keep that gun pointed at the ground and come over here where I can get a look at you."

This time Ryan identified the warm contralto as the voice of a woman. With a grunt of self-disgust, he pointed his gun barrel at the ground and walked forward. Ryan Fitzsimmons, ambushed by a female! It was enough to make a dog laugh—and, by God, so was the small figure that stepped out from behind a tree. His eyes swept it, top to bottom, in disbelief.

An old felt hat, pulled low to hide the face and jammed down over the thickest mop of tangled yellow hair he had ever seen. A formless, patched and worn linsey shirt above baggy men's pants, tied with a length of rope at the waist and flopping around broken shoes at the bottom. His eyes narrowed as he got closer. Even though he couldn't see her face or any line of her body in those Godawful clothes, still there was something about the small, shaking hands on the Enfield that told him she was young and frightened. He got about a dozen feet from her before she spoke again.

"Stop there, mister, and come up with a name." Inside, Leslie was shaking a lot worse than her hands. The man was big, even bigger than her father. Maybe she ought to run him off. But there wasn't anything to keep him from sneaking back after dark . . . and he didn't look mean. In fact, he was about the best-looking man she could imagine. He actually looked like a gentleman, as well as she could remember. Never realizing that the tilt of her head now revealed her young chin and tremulous lips, Leslie watched him slowly smile.

"Captain Ryan Fitzsimmons, ma'am, of the ship *China Pearl*. At your service."

Leslie gasped. Everyone in Wilmington had known of the *China Pearl* and the mysterious man who owned her. Some said he was a Yankee in sympathy with the South, others said he was a Britisher out for a profit. But all thought him a hero for the supplies he brought their army. Fitzsimmons, they had said, was the most daring of all the runners. But she didn't dare to mention Wilmington. . . . She stumbled over words:

"Then—then you're a gentleman, Captain Fitzsimmons! I mean, as a master of a ship, surely you're—you're honorable." Her gun wavered away as he moved closer. "I was afraid. . . ." She gasped again as he grabbed the barrel of her gun and jerked it away from her hands. "Wha—what are you doing?"

"Making sure that I stay a live gentleman," Ryan said roughly. "I'd rather face a Federal gunboat than a nervous woman with a rifle." His other hand whipped out and snatched her hat off. "Now, let me see you, my lady, and hear a name." Staring down, he was sorry he'd done it. Her enormous blue eyes looked terrified; the thin face was pitiful. In his life Ryan had seen enough to know the blue-veined pallor of near starvation, the hollowed eyes and pinched look, and he was looking at it now. She was only a young girl and she was *hungry*. She was also angry; the terror in her eyes was changing gradually to blue fire. "Sorry," he added lamely, "but I don't like a gun pointed—"

"I am Leslie Gordon," she spat out, snatching her hat out of his hand and jamming it back on her head.

11

"And I only shoot what I want to shoot!" She tilted her head back and glared at him from under the dark brim of the old hat. "You'd best mind your manners if you're planning on having dinner with me."

Staring at this bundle of old clothes topped by a small, angry face, Ryan managed with great difficulty to keep from bursting into laughter.

"I accept your gracious invitation," he said solemnly, and handed over her rifle. "Just keep this thing pointed away from me, if you don't mind."

Leslie took the gun triumphantly and slung it over one thin shoulder. "That's better, Captain. Now, just follow me." She marched off into the woods without a backward glance.

Grinning, Ryan followed the bundle and the fall of tangled hair that glowed in the shadowed depths of the woods like a patch of sunlight. She might be ragged and comical, but that hair was beautiful and clean. Even the thin little face had been scrubbed until it shone. Her mother, whom no doubt he was about to meet, must set high standards for the girl.

Leslie couldn't believe her luck. She had read correctly what had happened to Captain Ryan Fitzsimmons. The saddle in his hand, the earlier shot, had told her. He had lost a horse, no doubt a fine one, and now he needed a way to return to his ship. The trip in that old dugout canoe down an unknown river had held a certain terror for her, but now, with a large, strong man—a gentleman, no less—to accompany her, the terror receded. She felt quite warm at the thought. Arriving at the shack, she turned and gestured at the steps hospitably.

"If you'd care to rest while I start the fire," she said grandly, "please make yourself at home." She unslung her rifle and leaned it against a tree, picked up an armload of wood from beneath the shack and started toward a circle of rocks and an iron spit. "It's late," she added, half to herself, "but once the fire's roaring there will be light to cook by."

Standing still, Ryan gazed around at the tiny clearing in amazement. His eyes scanned the rotting box of a shack, the rickety steps that led upward. He looked at the ragged clothes spread neatly to dry on the limb. Then he watched Leslie as she worked industriously at the fire pit, building a pyramid of dead logs and stuffing dried moss between them. In a moment she had it blazing and had turned back.

"Now to get the pot and some water," she began, and then stopped, staring at him. "What's the matter, Captain? You can put that saddle in the house if you like, with mine."

"Where's your family?" Ryan put the question abruptly, afraid of the answer.

"I haven't . . ." Leslie began, and stumbled. Gentleman or not, perhaps she hadn't better let him know she was all alone. "I haven't any mother," she amended. "She died some years ago. And my father is gone, on . . . on a hunting trip."

Ryan relaxed. "Well, he'll be back soon," he said, glancing at the gathering night, "unless he has a lantern."

"He has a lantern," Leslie said quickly. "Yes, a very good lantern. At times he comes in very late. Now, let me get our dinner started."

Ryan yawned and slung the saddle up over the limb that held the drying clothes. Propping his gun with hers, he ambled over and sat on the steps, watching her frantic activity. She was up and down the steps, bringing an iron pot, rushing to a pool to fill it, hanging it on the iron rod over the fire. Then she was up again to

13

fetch a small, half-empty bag of corn and a cleaned and dressed fox squirrel. When Ryan realized that was all, he picked up his saddlebags and sauntered over.

"I will feel more welcome if I can supply part of our meal," he said, and brought forth a bag of sandwiches that his galley cook had made for him. He watched her shadowed eyes fasten on the thick slices of meat inside the chunks of bread and held one out to her. "Try it," he said casually, "and tell me if the meat's too salty."

There was more meat in that sandwich than Leslie had seen at one time in months. She took it in careful hands and bit a tiny crescent out of one side. She chewed it thoroughly before she spoke.

"It's just right," she said politely, and forced herself to hand it back.

"You may as well eat it," Ryan said, evading her hand. "I've three more just like it." He squatted by the fire and took another sandwich, beginning to munch.

In the end, there was corn and squirrel left over, though it was tastier by far than Ryan had expected. They had had apples and cheese and strong, hot coffee, topped off with generous amounts of brandy. Sitting on the steps with Ryan on a large block of wood beside her, Leslie was pink and replete, sipping the last of her coffee and brandy. When Ryan rose and began looking for branches where he could string his rope hammock, she shook her head.

"My father's bed is clean, and it will suit you much better," she said, "and I will not mind. You are a real gentleman, Captain Fitzsimmons, and, in any event, I shall sleep in my clothes." The brandy, she thought with mild surprise, had loosened her tongue. She could have phrased that much more subtly.

Ryan's lips twitched. But not for the world would he have let her know how little she tempted him. "Thank you," he said gravely, "but your father will feel quite differently when he comes home. I'll stay out here, Miss Gordon."

"I will be very much surprised if my father comes home," Leslie said, throwing caution to the winds, "since I haven't seen him in over two months." She looked up, seeing the firelight flickering over a rugged face stony with shock. "I've given him up, Captain. I was leaving here tomorrow. And I want to ask a favor."

It was over an hour before Ryan slept, but he slept in Harry Gordon's bed, cursing the man silently and listening to the soft, even breathing across the tiny room. How could any man, no matter how degraded, leave a young, defenseless girl in a place like this? Half starved, yet with a courage and spirit a man might envy. Even now, he had learned, she felt she must find and help the scoundrel!

He jumped and then moved restlessly as a panther screamed in the distance. Damn the man! She must have been terrified at times, though she stoutly denied it.

Well, he would see her safe in Tampa before he left.

Chapter Two

Morning in the Green Swamp began with silence. With the first faint light the creatures of darkness ceased their hunting and the startled cries of victims died away. In another half hour the small birds would begin to twitter sleepily, but now, as Ryan Fitzsimmons opened his eyes, he decided that what had awakened him was the absolute quiet. There wasn't a sound.

Sitting up, he reached for his shirt. He had slept in his trousers in deference to his female roommate, but as he glanced across the tiny space he discovered the gesture had been unnecessary. Her bed was empty. Ryan frowned. He didn't like knowing that anyone could move in a room where he slept and not awaken him. That could be dangerous, considering the various situations in which patriotic Yankee spies or jealous husbands might figure.

Standing, he put on his shirt and moved toward the door on silent bare feet. Outside, the scene held an eerie beauty often found in swamps. Mist shrouded the tops of the huge trees, dewed the shrubs below with glistening droplets like diamonds, softening the reality of the rough terrain. Yawning, he slowly swept the scene, his eyes stopping and widening, startled, as he caught sight of Leslie Gordon standing beneath the limb that held her laundered clothes. She was completely nude, engaged in extricating her feet from the baggy, worn trousers.

Caught by the grace of the bending figure, Ryan couldn't tear his gaze away. Too thin, the young body still retained a touching femininity of tender curves, of small, high breasts with pink rosettes tightened by the chilly dampness of the air. Mist swirled around the slender legs and glistened on the small triangle of dark gold curls at the apex of her thighs. The thick mass of her golden hair flowed down a white, tapered back that seemed too frail to support it, touched the line of a waist that Ryan could have spanned with overlapping fingers. Then he noted, with a fresh burst of anger, that he could count her delicate ribs even at this distance. Half starved, indeed. She was close to a dangerous condition.

He stepped back as Leslie shook out a pair of clean but patched drawers and began to dress. Ashamed of his peeping, Ryan welcomed the new anger at her neglectful father. Taking off his shirt again, he crawled back into the bed to feign sleep. Behind his closed eyes he could still see the delicate, curved body of warm ivory and gold with the ghostly mist swirling around it. A picture, he realized suddenly, that he would probably remember for a long time.

Below, Leslie dressed with care, making herself as neat as possible. She was breathless with joy, infinitely grateful for both food and human companionship. She rushed to fill the shiny coffeepot that Ryan had brought and put it on the renewed fire. She hung the pot of mush and squirrel to warm and then, hesitantly, she climbed the steps again.

"Are you awake, Captain Fitzsimmons? I've put your coffeepot on to boil."

Ryan affected a long, drowsy yawn and opened his eyes. Sitting up, he reached lazily for his shirt and then smiled at her, standing in the doorway. She seemed newly shy, dressed in the patched skirt and old blouse, her hair neatly combed and braided, pinned in a coronet around her head.

"That sounds wonderful," he said, discovering with alarm that his memory could see pink rosettes beneath the blouse even though they were certainly not discernible to his eyes. "I'll be with you in a moment." He listened to her scamper back down the steps and gave himself a short lecture. That pitiful, small creature deserved respect.

It had been decided the night before that the two of them would journey down the river in the canoe. Over breakfast, which included, besides the warmed-over corn and squirrel, a slice of ham which came from Ryan's seemingly bottomless saddlebags, they discussed the details of the trip.

"Are you sure the canoe will hold us both?" Ryan hadn't yet seen it. "You might be better off riding your horse." He glanced at the old nag, which had wandered into the clearing and was grazing on fiddlehead ferns. "Then you would have him to ride in Tampa."

Leslie shook her head. "I must ask for charity for myself," she answered, "and that is hard enough, even though I intend to earn whatever I receive. There is plenty of pasture here, but in town the horse would have to be fed. I'll leave him." She looked at the horse with obvious affection. "He'll not wander far. And, if my father should return . . ."

"Extremely unlikely," Ryan said grumpily. "Any rascal who would leave his daughter in a place like this without even sufficient food . . ."

Leslie interrupted in turn, instantly defensive. "That wasn't his fault. He told me if ever he was gone over two weeks, I should go down the river and find help. I dallied a month and a half after I should have gone, hoping for his return. The fault is mine."

Ryan admired loyalty, but in this case he felt it undeserved. "He should have taken you with him."

"He couldn't!" Thoughtless in her ardent defense, Leslie brought forth the reason. "It was known that I left with him, and, if the two of us were seen together . . ." She flushed, the blood rushing up her slender neck and staining her cheeks with red. "Anyway," she added in a vain attempt to cover what she had said, "I didn't want to go." She could see the sharp understanding in Ryan's clear eyes. Now, Captain Fitzsimmons knew her father was a wanted man. It might not take him long to check a list of deserters for the name Gordon. Even if he said nothing or didn't care, she felt shamed by his knowing. She admitted to herself that in the short time she had known Captain Fitzsimmons she had—well, she had conceived a great affection for him. Not only was he very handsome and so, well . . . so nicely formed, but he was also a man of tender feelings and thoughtfulness. It would be hard indeed to part with him when they arrived in Tampa. She glanced at him shyly and found the hazel eyes dwelling on her, sweeping her figure with a long, fascinated gaze. When the gaze reached her face and found her watching him in surprise, Ryan spoke rather hurriedly.

"You might be better suited by the clothes you wore

yesterday," he said, thinking that the baggy pants and linsey shirt might also be better for his own peace of mind. "There are rapids in several places and one or two I think we shall have to portage around. Your skirt will get wet and dirty."

Leslie frowned. "I will not arrive at a town in men's clothing."

Ryan shrugged, rising to begin his packing. "In that case, you will arrive in a skirt wet and dirty to your knees." He picked up his saddlebags and glanced back at her woebegone face. "Where is this dugout?"

"Hidden beneath the cut of the bank where the fennel is highest," Leslie told him, and jumped up, gathering the tin plates to scrub in the nearest pool. "I shall be ready in a quarter hour."

The dugout was indeed large enough. Too large, for it was thick and ancient cypress and far too heavy for portage. But sound. Heart cypress, Ryan thought gloomily, never rotted. He almost wished it had. Undoubtedly its weight was the reason the Indians had left it behind. It would have to be dragged over the stretches of rocky outcroppings where the river widened and the water became too shallow to float a canoe as it rushed over the rocks. Leslie could have never made the trip alone; no woman's strength would be sufficient. It was easy enough for her father to say, "Just go down the river." A man who didn't care for anyone. A wanted man. Ryan had a shrewd suspicion of the charge against Gordon. A lot of inferior men were too fainthearted—or too wily—for battle. Sighing, he went back toward the clearing to get John Tudbury's saddle. At least, the canoe provided a way to return it.

At the clearing he was greeted by an amazing sight. Leslie had compromised. She had put on the baggy trousers over her skirt and they were baggy no longer.

With the long, full skirt tucked around her hips, her tiny waist rising from the rope tied at the top, Leslie was a child standing in a khaki-colored barrel. Ryan turned aside, hiding laughter.

"Laugh if you like," Leslie told him. "They'll take the wet, and I can throw them away when we arrive."

She was truly a unique female, Ryan thought. The first he had met without a trace of vanity. The women he knew would have preferred ruining everything they owned before appearing before him in that ludicrous get-up. On the other hand, she was too proud to show herself in town in men's clothes. Perhaps it was only that she didn't care how she looked to *him*. The thought was disquieting. Captain Ryan Fitzsimmons had always been extremely successful with the ladies.

Later, watching her waddle down the bank and climb awkwardly into the canoe, Ryan burst into helpless laughter. Climbing in himself and poling away from the shallows, he saw her blue eyes twinkling beneath the old hat, her thin face alive with silent amusement. Still smiling, Ryan relaxed, settling back to paddle in mindless contentment. Somehow the green ribbons of banks, the fragile crinum lilies on their long, graceful stalks, the sudden spreads of yellow daisies along the way were more noticeably beautiful than they had been the day before. Silvery mullet, far from the brackish water they usually preferred, leaped and fell back on the placid surface, the slap startling in the quiet. The river was slow-moving, here in the swamp, and it was possible to hear the many creeks that burbled into it to add to its size. Later, Ryan knew, he would be frantically guiding the canoe, not paddling it. Some of those rapids had looked quite dashing.

Leslie was inexpressibly happy. Even when they arrived at the first set of rapids. She followed Ryan's directions exactly, kneeling low, facing forward, holding on with both hands as he paddled furiously to keep them in the winding, tortuous passage between the bigger rocks. When they reached calmer water she turned around with her hat dripping and went back to watching him again.

It was fascinating to see how skillful he was. He had rolled his shirt sleeves as high as they would go and a thin dew of perspiration beaded his arms, gleaming on the rolling muscles as he swept the paddle in sure strokes. He sat on his heels, the soft nankeen trousers he wore shaped tight over powerful thighs, his narrow waist twisting as gracefully as a dancer's as he paddled. He seemed the very epitome of masculine beauty to Leslie, and as she raised her gaze to his, she saw he knew she had been examining him. He looked faintly amused, his hazel eyes gleaming and the firm mouth quirked up at one corner. She decided she didn't care, and smiled at him. Taking off her hat, she lay back and closed her eyes, enjoying the sun. It seemed only minutes before he spoke to her.

"More rapids, Miss Gordon."

She sat up, maneuvered her immensely padded bottom around so she could kneel, and heard him chuckle. Then they were again careening over a rocky stretch of white water while Ryan alternately paddled and poled. Not that they had much to fear; when the dugout finally hit one of the bigger rocks it bounced off serenely and plunged on.

All in all there were perhaps seven or eight sets of rapids, and when they reached the last of the rocky outcroppings that Ryan remembered they were both sweating and tired. Two of the stretches had been too shallow to float the canoe. There, they had stepped out into wet rocks and rills of water to pull and heave the canoe along. Now, in calm water that ran easily to the southwest, Ryan pushed the canoe to the nearest bank.

"We'll share that last sandwich," he said, "and have a pull at that water jug. It's an easy run from here, except for the mosquitoes."

Collapsing gratefully on the sandy shore, Leslie accepted half of the sandwich and chewed thoughtfully. It was apparent now that she couldn't have managed the trip alone. Either she would have overturned in the deeper rapids or failed to get the heavy canoe across the shallow ones.

"I owe you a great deal," she said soberly. "I couldn't have done it." She had left off her hat and the short hair around her face lifted in curling strands, blowing against the thick braid in a sunny halo. Beneath it, her enormous blue eyes were close to adoration as she looked at him.

Ryan was shaken. "You owe me nothing," he said, looking away. "If it hadn't been for your canoe, I'd be walking." He glanced back and added gruffly, "I find it hard to believe your father would even allow you to attempt a trip like this."

"He didn't know about the rapids," Leslie countered, leaping to her father's defense again. "He never tried it." She lapsed into silence, wishing Ryan would leave the subject of her father alone. How could he despise him so, when he had never met him?

Back in the canoe, they ran through a maze of dark, tangled creeks and back out into a main stream again. Watching the high banks, Leslie suddenly sat up and pointed.

"Look!" A man on the top of the bank was waving wildly. "He is trying to attract your attention." She clutched the edge of the canoe as it swerved and turned to look at Ryan. His face was grim.

"John Tudbury," he said shortly, "the man who owned the horse I had to shoot. He'll not like my news." Paddling hard against now fast-running current, he brought the canoe to the shore and grounded it firmly. "Stay here. I'll see what brings him looking for me."

Leslie watched him stride rapidly up the bank toward the square bulk of the waiting man. They talked, the other man making excited gestures, and even at this distance Leslie could see Ryan's lean body grow tense, his jaw jut forward. Then they both came walking back down to the shore and suddenly Leslie was badly frightened. Ryan's face was dark with anger, his body like a coiled spring. And the other man so sweating and anxious, barely acknowledging her polite greeting. Both men got into the canoe and Ryan pushed off with vicious thrusts of the paddle.

"We'll go down another mile or two and wait until dark," he growled, "and then we'll see who runs the *China Pearl* out of the river."

"I tell you you're mad," the other man spluttered. "The Yanks have fifteen armed men on the ship, waiting for the high tide."

Leslie froze, looking past the bulky back of the man Ryan called John Tudbury, staring into the hazel eyes that were now red with rage. She felt faint, her heart clutched with terror. The war was no longer a faraway thing, a nameless horror of blood and tears for others. The war was *here*. And Ryan was in danger.

"The top of the flood isn't until midnight," Ryan was saying, "and in spite of the whole Union Army I'll have her back by then."

"Man, you *can't*," Tudbury protested. "You're well away, Captain. Ralph took care of that by pretending to be you! He did it so you could escape them and find another ship."

"I *have* a ship," Ryan roared, "the *China Pearl!* I own her . . . the Confederacy doesn't! I'll not have her taken by the Yanks." He had stopped paddling to glare

24

and yell at Tudbury, and now he subsided, looking past the man at a white, frightened face. He spoke again, gently.

"You'll not be hurt, Leslie. I'll put you ashore well east of the ship. If all goes well, John here will find you a way to town, and, if not, well . . . it isn't a long walk."

Leslie didn't notice his use of her first name; it wasn't important. "I'll stay with you," she got out through a tight throat. "Maybe I can help."

After an instant of startled silence both men laughed incredulously, a strange sound that seemed to break the tension.

"You'll go ashore," Ryan said, "but I'll be grateful for your Enfield." He gave Tudbury a direct look. "If you want to keep your brother out of a Federal prison, you'll use it."

Tudbury was still sweating, but he nodded. "If we've got a chance at all, Captain, I'm willing to try." He brightened suddenly. "They do feel secure, thinking they've got the famous Captain Fitzsimmons and his whole crew in irons below. They were breaking out the liquor to celebrate while I was still watching from the woods."

"Celebrating the capture of my ship with my store of liquor," Ryan said dryly, "but I'll gladly give it to make sure of drunken guards. You say the whole town is under siege?"

"The whole town is overrun," Tudbury corrected dourly, "and all the home guard and rangers tucked away in Fort Brooke under guard. The Yanks came ashore this morning while the home guard were rounding up cattle and took the fort without a fight. Threw the cannon out on the beach to rust." He looked disgusted. "After all this time of sitting out there doing nothing, there they were, marching around like heroes.

If some of them hadn't wanted to swim in fresh water, they would never have found your ship."

Ryan laughed bitterly. "A comedy. Well, it won't be so funny tonight." He began paddling again. "I suppose I'm lucky they didn't burn it, like they did McKay's *Scottish Chief.*"

"McKay's boat was loaded with cotton they didn't want," Tudbury pointed out. "They'll take yours north for the gunpowder you have on her."

"They'll not," Ryan promised. "Given a moment of distraction for those bluecoats, the *China Pearl* will be running free in the gulf by two o'clock in the morning."

"But how will you get her past the blockade?"

Ryan laughed, genuinely amused, his white teeth a slash in his dark face. "Why, John, that's the easy part. That's my trade. If they shoot at all, which I doubt, they'll be shooting each other in my wake."

To Leslie's fascinated, terrified gaze, Ryan Fitzsimmons in that moment looked precisely like a pirate.

In late afternoon the canoe was grounded again, well east of the ship, though by looking carefully through the trees one could see the top of the tallest mast in the distance. Leslie found shade in a small grove of pines near the shore and the two men left quietly to go through the woods and reconnoiter.

Leslie watched Ryan out of sight, wondering at her own terrible fear. *She* was safe. In the southwest sky she could see the wavering plumes of cooking fires from homes in Tampa, and John Tudbury had told her the names of two matrons she could ask for help and receive it. Good women, he had said, glad to help any needy stranger. And her part in the adventure seemed to be over. Ryan had brought everything of hers and piled it in the grove. Everything but the rifle, which lay with Tudbury's saddle off to one side. She didn't mind losing the rifle in a good cause, but what possible chance did two men have against fifteen? Even drunk, the Union men were trained and able. Her throat was dry with fear. She didn't mind losing the rifle, but she did mind losing Ryan Fitzsimmons.

When the men came back and squatted near her in the shade they were as tight as bowstrings with excitement. Leslie listened carefully to their talk, piecing together what they had seen and what they planned. The Yanks, she learned, had warped the ship up to the south bank and made a gangway to carry off the things they wanted. The northern troops weren't to get it all. And most of them, according to Tudbury, were drunk as lords.

"They'll sober up quick enough if they hear a shot," Ryan warned. "They're soldiers. We'll accomplish what we can by stealth and let the guns speak last." He stared off at the river worriedly. "I wish we could count on something to draw their attention to the south bank without alarming them. I must get over the starboard side in the dark and slip below." He shrugged. "I'll manage. It's only a step to the hatch of the hold. That's where they will have shackled my men."

"I could do that," Leslie said timidly, and flushed as Ryan gave her an annoyed look. "Create a distraction, I mean." Fanning herself with the old hat, she brushed away a mosquito and forced a smile. "A woman wouldn't alarm them."

"You'll stay out of it," Ryan said roughly. "Bullets have a habit of going astray in a melee. In fact, you'll stay right here, and if you haven't heard from us by dawn, you walk." He rose, his muscular body tense, and came to her to grasp her arms and lift her to her feet. Turning her, he marched her to the edge of the pool of shade and pointed. "That way. See the smoke?"

Leslie nodded, breathless. It was the first time he had

touched her and his hands were strong and warm. He was close, still holding one arm as he pointed. She was very conscious of the broad shoulder level with her eyes, of the masculine scent and the warmth that came from him. Looking down at her, Ryan misinterpreted the excitement in her eyes.

"I suppose you're anxious to get settled," he added, somehow reluctant. "If you want to go now, John could escort you part of the way."

"I'll wait," Leslie said hastily. "I—I'm curious, I suppose." Her lips trembled. "I want to be sure you have your ship back." Not for anything would she leave him while there was still a faint chance of staying together.

Going back to the shade, they found John Tudbury pacing restlessly. He had decided to go through the woods and see if his farm was guarded. If not, he said, he'd bring back food for them all. It was a long time until midnight.

John was scarcely out of earshot when Leslie burst forth.

"If you succeed in recovering the *China Pearl,* could you take me with you? I could go home! You'll be putting in at Wilmington again."

Ryan looked at her curiously. "So, that's where you're from. Do you have family there?"

He hadn't refused. Her hope rose sharply, almost choking her. "No, but many friends! And it's where I must start if I hope to learn my father's fate. I—I could earn my passage, Captain Fitzsimmons. I could clean, or cook."

Looking at the thin, intense face with the blue eyes much too large for it, Ryan smiled gently. "If I succeed in recapturing my ship, I will give you gold enough to make your way there with no trouble. I am sure John will find some trustworthy person to aid you.

But a blockade runner is no place for a woman, Leslie."

Hope faded, leaving her pinched and sad. "I don't want money given to me," she said stiffly. "I will make my own way." This time she noticed the use of her first name, but it seemed no friendlier. It was more as if Ryan was speaking to a child, where formality was not needed. She moved restlessly, uncomfortable in her bulky attire, and then stood up. "Since I'll not be on the river again," she added, "I'll rid myself of these trousers." She stalked off, a still ludicrous, lumpy figure, to seclude herself in the trees for the unveiling.

The afternoon and evening wore on, agonizingly slow. Tudbury returned with a loaf of bread and a half gallon of milk, cold meat and cheese. There had been no one at the farm but his family.

"The Yanks fear nothing," he reported. "There has been no resistance and they expect none. Most of the garrison has gone back to Egmont Key, my wife has heard. They say the commander feels it has been a useless effort since nothing of importance was taken except for your ship. They are glad of that unexpected prize."

"I hope to disappoint them later," Ryan said quietly, "helped by their foolish confidence. And let me say now, to you, how much I value your help and the loyalty of your brother. If it hadn't been for First Mate Tudbury's quick thinking and his claim of being Captain Fitzsimmons, they would be combing these woods for me now."

Leslie listened and watched, a slim figure again in the wrinkled skirt, silent and fearful for Ryan's safety as darkness came on. She could feel the tension building in the lean, muscular body as if some current between them communicated it to her. He was like one of the panthers she had seen in the swamp, beginning his stalking. Hungry and watchful, with every muscle in his powerful, coordinated figure poised for action.

As the time neared, the men spoke seldom. The plan had been devised. Tudbury was to mask himself to prevent later identification and creep through the woods: ready, if necessary, to create a diversion. Ryan was to drift down on the river side of the ship and wait his chance to board her quietly, slip below and release his own twenty men. Most of the Yanks, he had said, would be sleeping. With no attack expected there should be few guards.

"Thank God," Ryan added, "there's wind tonight. The noise in the rigging will cover mine."

Still worried, Tudbury wagged his head dolefully. "Your men will have no weapons and the soldiers are all armed."

"With surprise on my side," Ryan answered shortly, "I'll pit my men with their belaying pins against any pistoled Yank. You'll see fast action, John."

John subsided. Leslie, a pale blur in the darkness in the light skirt and blouse, was full of confused thoughts. She would never be able to simply sit and wait out the results of this battle. The suspense would kill her, she was sure. But there was no use in asking for a part in it; they would only laugh again. And what could she do? Her mind whirled with possibilities, each more bizarre than the last.

When the time finally came nothing was said. Ryan rose and disappeared into the black night, going toward the river. Tudbury, breathless, tied a dark cloth over the lower part of his face, pulled his hat low and reached for the freshly loaded Enfield. He struck off along the shore, moving silently in spite of his bulk. Leslie waited only a moment before following Tudbury. She was as silent as he, having learned in the three years past that a noisy hunter stayed hungry. She knew the light color of her clothes was against her, so she stayed well behind. John Tudbury was perfectly capable of escorting her back to the trees.

It seemed a long way. Twice Leslie slipped on a steep stretch of bank, once into a dry rustle of leaves that made her stand motionless for several minutes as the dark bulk ahead of her paused to listen. But, all in all, the wind that was to help Ryan helped her also, covering her few mistakes, and finally they came separately within sight of the ship.

Lanterns in profusion flared and smoked around the decks, and Leslie caught her breath at the first sight of the *China Pearl*. It was no wonder Ryan would risk his life to keep her. Small for her task, perhaps, a bit less than a hundred feet long. But low, rakish and built for speed. Low masted, also, but three masted for maximum canvas, and the funnel and side wheels that proved her to be steam-and-sail. What a prize for the Yankees.

Her heart pounding, Leslie shrank into deeper shadows and waited. One thing seemed certain—with those low sides Ryan would have no trouble going aboard if only those two men leaning on the starboard rail would move. Leslie stared at the dark river and strained her ears for the dip of a paddle.

The men on deck wandered, pistols gleaming in their belts. One, on the landward side, leaned against the side of the stern cabin, slipped slowly downward into a sitting position and yawned. A bottle appeared out of nowhere and was passed around. There was a spate of sudden laughter and then a harsh, sleepy command from the stern cabin that quieted it. But still the men wandered; not as if they were watching for anything, only bored with the night.

It was past time for Ryan to make his move. Somewhere on that black water he held his dugout immobile and waited. With the brightly lit decks he could easily see the men that passed back and forth and he must be growing impatient. Slowly, a plan grew in Leslie's mind. If John Tudbury tried to divert them, the men would be put on the alert. A man, especially a masked man, appearing, or a shot heard, would make them suspicious. But, a girl? A perhaps outrageously idiotic girl?

Her hands went swiftly to her hair, unpinning, unbraiding. She must look as crazy as possible. Combing frantic fingers through the long, springing mass of hair, rubbing dirt on her cheeks, Leslie knew she must run down the bank and into the circle of light before John Tudbury caught sight of her. Shaking the hair loose into a curtain around her, she leaped downward, crashing through brittle shrubs and not minding the noise now. Into the light, almost to the foot of the improvised gangway, she tilted up her dirty face.

"Toss me a bit of bread, you men," she cried out to the startled faces, "and a bottle, too, if you have it to spare. You've plenty, I know, and poor Mary has none." She made her voice a high, singsong plaint to go with a mad appearance, and was gratified to see every man on deck come crowding to the rail. Seven of them, and she had only counted six.

Several of the men laughed, and one growled at her.

"Get away, woman. We've nothing for beggars."

"Just like the others, ain't you?" Leslie whined, drooping in the bright light, sad and woebegone. "Not a soul in Tampa but what scorns poor little Mary. . . ." Her frantically pounding heart stopped as a shadow slipped over the far rail behind the group of men, and her voice rose. "Mean and selfish, every one of you Southerners . . ."

"Southerners?" A fresh-faced boy on the end

sounded insulted. "We're Union men, you fool! Can't you tell blue from gray?"

"I ain't saying you lie, mister," Leslie was desperate now to keep them listening, "but if you say true, then you Yanks have been here too long. You done learnt their selfish ways."

One of the older men laughed suddenly. "She's witless," he told the others, "but under that dirt she's not bad looking. Bring her on board and I'll see that she's fed. Why, with all of us here, we could send her back full." The innuendo in his tone was unmistakeable and most of the men laughed with him.

"Better take another look," one man said humorously. "There might be nits in all that hair."

"Or worse than nits, somewhere else," another man interjected, and there was a rumble of chuckles.

Leslie could have killed them. She paced back and forth as if confused and then shrank toward the shadows, pulling at her hair. "You're making fun of poor Mary," she whined. "Cruel and heartless, you are. . . ."

A half-full bottle landed on the soft sand at her feet. "There you are, Mary. Drink it all. And don't say the Yanks never did anything for you. That's Captain Ryan Fitzsimmons's liquor, and it's the finest. But he won't be needing it now."

That did bring a laugh, rippling heartily along the line before it died away and a calm voice spoke behind them.

"Aye, and she's welcome to it, boys."

The line of men whirled as one, to stare at the tall figure and long rifle behind them, and the flood of men pouring from the hold, grabbing belaying pins from the rack at the mast, running forward.

Bursting from the shadows behind her, John Tudbury grasped Leslie and swept her roughly behind him. Mask in place and Enfield in one hand, he ran up the gangway.

Leslie landed solidly on her bottom in soft sand and sat there in the shadows, blinking at the scene of confusion, listening to the incredible noise of hoarse yells and scuffling, the solid sound of belaying pins meeting skulls. Neither rifle spoke; there was only a single shot from a struggling Yankee who managed to get his pistol out, and it must have gone wild for no one fell. Dazed and disbelieving, other men appeared in their smallclothes from the companionway and were knocked on their heads for their pains, pistols snatched from their hands. The men of the *China Pearl* swarmed over the outnumbered Yanks and in minutes it was over, the bluecoats tied to the rails. John Tudbury, the Enfield still clutched in his shaking hand, ran back down the gangway and came into the shadows where Leslie still sat, faint and exhausted.

"For God's sake, Miss Gordon, you liked to scare me to death when you run out there! But you pulled the trick, girl, it worked like a charm!" He got her to her feet, brushing sand from her with a rough, careless hand, still too excited to know what he was doing. "The captain wants you aboard, ma'am."

A sudden silence and then a harsh command behind them turned them both around. Tudbury sagged.

"Oh, God, no," he whispered, "we missed one."

On deck there was a frozen tableau. Inside the open door of the stern cabin stood a Yankee officer with a drawn pistol aimed at Ryan's chest, not a dozen feet away. Ryan's rifle hung from a sinewy hand as he stared at the officer in a fury of surprise. His men, frightened for him, were statues on the deck. As they watched, the officer stepped forward, his pistol gleaming in the light.

"Now," he said evenly, his voice as calm as Ryan's had been, "one of you seamen start freeing my men."

"Shoot!" Leslie's frantic whisper startled John.

"I can't," he whispered back miserably. "I could miss, and Fitzsimmons would die."

Leslie's small hands moved in a blur of speed. Snatching the rifle, she aimed it and pulled the trigger. At the blast the pistol spun up crazily into the black night, whirled downward through the flickering lantern light and splashed in the river. Ryan leaped like a tiger, swinging his rifle like a club, and the officer fell heavily to the deck. Leslie burst into tears and handed the Enfield back to John, who took it in nerveless fingers, staring at her.

"Don't cry," he said through dry lips. "Please don't cry, Miss Gordon." He patted her shoulder helplessly. "That was the finest piece of shooting I ever saw, and now that's twice you liked to scare me to death."

Leaping down the gangway, Ryan strode over to them in the shadows, banging John heartily on the back.

"Right in the nick, John! My God, I thought we'd lost it all." He turned to Leslie. "As for you, little rebel, you've earned the gold to pay for your trip home, twice over. I advise you to seek a career on the stage."

"It was her that shot, too," John said, stumbling over words in his haste to give Leslie the credit. "I'm no shot, and I was scared to try, but she grabbed that rifle away from me and sent that pistol flyin'. Did you ever see anything *like* it, Fitzsimmons?" He was positively burbling in his praise.

Ryan's mouth dropped open. He stared down at Leslie's dirty, tear-streaked face in disbelief.

"Well, where in God's name did you learn to shoot like that?"

Wiping her eyes on her sleeve, Leslie smiled up at him. "It wasn't any harder to hit than a squirrel," she said. "They're about of a size."

"My God," Ryan said softly, "I owe you."

It was her best chance yet to stay with him. "Yes, you do," Leslie said firmly. "You owe me a trip to Wilmington—on the *China Pearl*."

Chapter Three

"THIS SHOULD BE EASY," RYAN SAID, MAKING A BRIEF statement to his crew. "They expect the ship to join them at precisely the time we will be steaming out. But they will wonder as we near the blockade, and we will be challenged." He shouldered into a blue coat and grinned at them. "We shall all be Yankees at the time." The several men already wearing blue coats grinned back at him self-consciously. "We'll pass, even if they use their Drummond lights. If they then suspect something has gone wrong, they still aren't likely to fire on these uniforms until we pour on the coal. Then it will be too late."

There was a carefully subdued cheer. Ryan guessed his men were still shaken by the sudden appearance of that Yankee officer. He watched them scatter to their posts and turned to his own, standing beside the pilot with his speaking tube to the engine room handy.

The soldiers, minus their coats and securely bound, had been put ashore, lashed in a line between trees. After the alarm was raised when the *China Pearl* slipped into the gulf, they would shortly be found by more searching soldiers. John Tudbury, still wearing his mask, carrying enough gold and more for a new horse, had melted into the darkness. The Yankees hadn't found Ryan's cache of gold coins, nor had he expected them to. It was too well hidden.

Leslie had been ordered below, with a burly seaman in charge of her safety.

"Take her to the hammock deck," Ryan had said tersely, "and see that she stays there."

Leslie supposed he was very angry. She had forced his hand, and a man like Ryan Fitzsimmons didn't like to be forced. Following the seaman down the ladder of the companionway, she was conscious of a heavy feeling in her chest, a prickle of tears behind her eyes. It was only that he was the first friend she had had for three years, and, very likely, the most prized friend she had ever had. If she had stayed behind, she would never have seen him again.

The hammock room was small, and, with the hatch closed for safety, airless. Leslie found a small stool and sat down, disheveled and sandy, to wait for the freedom of the open gulf and a chance to wash up. A rumble amidships and a vibration that shook the ship's timbers signaled the preparations for departure. Her mind raced ahead, thinking of the blockade, which in her imagination was a line of huge ships, waiting like lions with open jaws for their victims. She shuddered and glanced up, seeing that the burly seaman had placed himself in the doorway with his back to her, more effective a blockade than any ship of the line. She was jailed, there was no doubt about it.

Slowly, the ship's engines built up steam as the witching hour of high flood tide approached. And then, finally, Leslie felt the movement and heard the thrashing of the paddle wheels as the ship floated free.

Six miles, Ryan had said, and then across the bay and past Egmont Key before they met the blockaders. She shifted uncomfortably and, without turning, the seaman spoke.

"If you'd like a hammock unrolled, Miss, I'll be glad to oblige."

Leslie stared at his broad back. He had sounded kind, and for the first time she understood why he faced away from her. He was giving her as much privacy as he could.

"Thank you," she said with her usual warmth, "but I'm entirely too sandy. The next man who tried to sleep in it would be miserable."

He gave a surprised chuckle and came in, reaching up to untie and let fall a hammock. "Make yourself comfortable, Miss. By the time the captain allows us sleep, the men will be too tired to feel a little sand."

Leslie was not inclined to argue, since the hammock was too inviting. She dragged the stool over to it and managed to climb in. The rough canvas cradled her small form with hardly a sag, rising in great walls on either side, and she lay back gratefully to relax in its cocoon. In minutes she was fast asleep, rocked by the gentle swaying.

Two hours later, Ryan Fitzsimmons stepped up on the stool and stared down, his tired eyes softening as they gazed at the pale face cradled in tangled hair, the long, glistening golden lashes lying on blue hollows of fatigue, the soft lips relaxed in sleep.

"Hard to believe she could shoot the pistol out of that Yank's hand," he commented to the seaman, "but she did it. We owe her the ship, Bosun." He thrust both arms beneath her and tilted the hammock, rolling her against his chest. Stepping down, he carried her up the ladder, clutching the side with one hand, and started toward the stern.

Cool air woke Leslie. With a surprised gasp she fastened both hands on Ryan's shoulder, looking first at him and then out at the sea. The ship was rising smoothly over gentle waves, stars wheeled above in a clear, cold sky and a pale, dying moon showed nothing but water around them.

"We're . . . we're out!" Leslie stammered, "and I never heard a thing."

Ryan sat her down at the door of the stern cabin. "Nothing to hear," he said, quietly, "by the time they caught on we were out of range. They sent a cruiser to chase us but we showed them our heels." He smiled, rather coolly, she thought. "You may hear battle sounds enough to satisfy you when we arrive in Mobile." He ushered her into the cabin, which, by her standards, was luxurious. A large bunk instead of a hammock, a washstand with a set-in basin and a half barrel of water beside it. And a comfortable chair beside a desk.

"This must be your place," Leslie protested. "I don't want to put you out."

Ryan smiled, his hazel eyes momentarily amused. "You won't. We'll share it."

Leslie's eyes flew to the bunk. "There's only one bed." She glanced at him, bewildered. "When we shared before, there were two."

"Do you mind?"

Leslie blushed furiously. "Of course I mind!" Actually, the idea of lying beside him was lovely and warm, except that it sounded outrageous. The thought was distracting, and she was afraid he was reading it, since he looked more amused than ever. "Don't you?"

Ryan laughed and gave up his teasing. "What I meant," he said gently, "was that you would use it during the night, and I will sleep during the day. Most of my pressing business is accomplished in the dark."

"Oh." Leslie turned away, conscious of a slight disappointment, and for the first time she noticed the pair of nankeen breeches and a soft blue flannel shirt draped neatly over the end of the bunk.

Ryan followed her gaze. "That will be your apparel while you are on board," he said casually. "I promise the men will treat you with the courtesy due you no matter what you wear. And trousers are more practical on a ship."

Leslie knew he was only saving her pride. Her bundle had been left behind, the filthy clothes she wore were all she had. She fingered the nankeen and nodded, her lips compressed.

"Thank you. They seem close to my size."

"As close as could be found aboard. Part of the wardrobe of a cabin boy who sickened of the sea and went home to his mother. You will find more like them in that small chest." He came close to her, lifting a handful of her tangled hair with sinewy fingers. "There is also a comb in the chest, for this golden treasure."

It was the first compliment she had heard from those firm lips, and, along with his gentle touch, it made Leslie warm. Delightfully warm.

"A bothersome treasure," she answered awkwardly, "and difficult to hide. Perhaps I should cut it."

"Never," Ryan said sharply. "There are knit caps. Wear one. When necessary, you can tuck your hair into it." He stood looking down at her for a long moment and then added softly: "You are very like one of the

41

crinum lilies in that swamp of yours, Leslie. Your skin so fresh and pure, your hair as golden as their stamens. A fragile, golden lily . . ." The memory of her in the morning mist was strong in his mind, dissolving the wrinkled, sandy clothes into a transparency no more solid than the mist. The delicate ivory and gold body seemed to glow through the clothes. He dragged both his thoughts and his gaze away with an effort and turned to the door. "You'll want to wash and sleep," he said abruptly. "I'll not keep you."

A day and a half later, Leslie was on deck as they came within miles of Mobile Bay and then silently withdrew. The lookout in the crow's nest had spotted the large and dangerous U.S.S. *Brooklyn,* pride of the Union navy. A ship, she was told, whose hail of fire could sink the *China Pearl* in seconds.

Ryan now employed a favorite ruse. Turning out of the regular sea lanes that ships took to the port, he had the sails tightly rolled and tied to the spars. Placing the ship at right angles to the lanes, he shut off the engines. In the heaving seas the low, rakish ship was difficult to see at any time, her masts mere thin black lines without the glory of her sails. Now, end to, the *China Pearl* was hiding, unseen in full view.

"We'll go in tonight," Ryan told Leslie. "With luck, we'll thread through to the protection of Fort Morgan before the blockaders know we're here. Though I have heard that they have increased the size of their Mobile fleet."

Leslie, still an exotic sight to the seamen in her nankeen breeches and blue shirt, her hair in a thick gold braid hanging down her back from a knit cap, was excited by the promise of adventure. Happily unconscious of the way the soft cotton nankeen shaped the tender curves of hip and thigh, outlining the delicate femininity of her form, she pattered around the clean decks in her bare feet. The cabin boy's feet, alas, had been huge.

Ryan was well aware of the eyes that followed Leslie, but he knew he'd have no trouble with his crew. All had heard of her acting on the shore of the Hillsborough; all had seen the pistol fly away. She was a heroine, small but mighty.

Now, standing with Ryan on top of the paddle box, Leslie gazed off at the faint spiral of smoke on the horizon that spelled the presence of the mighty Union warship. Her blue eyes sparkled as she turned back to Ryan.

"Shall I see it, Captain, or will I be imprisoned again in the hammock deck?"

Ryan laughed indulgently. From the eminence of his thirty-two years he told himself Leslie was still a child, though quite charming. No matter that he had to conquer sudden and almost irresistible impulses to touch her. He put that down, so far, to nothing more than the affection of an older brother, or perhaps even a father. His sexual preferences had long been for experienced older women, women who knew how to please a man thoroughly and then let him go. His dangerous life admitted no other style of living. But still Leslie touched his heart in an entirely new way. At times, he found it distinctly frightening. Times, for instance, when he thought she might be in danger. Now, he answered carefully.

"You may stay on deck and watch if you promise to go below at the first sign of danger," he said, and listened with pleasure to her delighted gasp. "And you must not make a sound during the run."

"I promise!" Leslie wanted to hug him in gratitude, but in full view of the men on deck she contented herself with a touch of slim fingers on his hand. "Thank you. I shall be absolutely quiet."

Leslie remained on the paddle box long after Ryan had gone to the stern cabin for his sleep. She watched the distant smoke and tried to imagine the thrill of slipping past the formidable guns of the *Brooklyn* and the other ships that must ring the harbor entrance. She had not the slightest doubt that Ryan would succeed. She stood dreaming until one of the "jacks"—ordinary seamen—came to tell her respectfully that food and drink would be served for her in the ward room.

The wind dropped at sunset and Leslie saw the mood of the ship change.

"If you still wish to stay on deck," Ryan said, "you must stand by the companionway, ready to drop down inside. With no wind, the splash of our paddles may give us away."

Leslie nodded silently, watching the ship prepared. The glowing fireroom hatch was tented with a tarpaulin, the glow of the binnacle hooded, with only a peephole left for the pilot to see the compass. Every lantern was extinguished. Lookouts were posted on the bow, on the paddle boxes, and crouched behind bulwarks. Orders were given in whispers as they coasted toward the harbor. Leslie's fingernails bit into the wood of the companionway entrance as she strained to see through the darkness ahead. The blockaders, Ryan had told her, pulled in close to the land at night, converging in a semicircle the *China Pearl* must penetrate. Leslie watched the tall figure standing near the pilot, a shadowy blur with his nightglasses raised to peer through the murk. Then his sharp whisper:

"Two gunboats, dead ahead! Dive between them."

Leslie heard the pilot's involuntary groan, and then, across the water with every word icily distinct, someone barked a harsh command.

"Heave to, or I'll sink you!"

Ryan's voice answered immediately, smooth and

easy. "Aye, aye, sir! The British merchantman *Vixen*, sir. Out of Nassau and needing repairs. Sorry we missed you in the dark."

Leslie's mouth dropped. How could Ryan hope to fool the Union captain with a tale like that? She saw him grab the speaking tube to the engine room, heard the harsh whisper.

"Full speed ahead! Give her all you've got or we're sunk!"

The *China Pearl* surged ahead like a scalded cat, her paddle wheels beating the dark sea into white foam. Ryan's lie had gained him a full minute, but now there was a harsh oath, startlingly close from one of the gunboats, and a shout:

"Fire!"

Jetting upward from both gunboats with incredible speed, rockets blossomed above them like red flowers, lighting the sea with their brilliance, and on came the Drummond lights, glaring white, to expose every inch of the small ship. With a roar and a shock the thunder of artillery began.

Leslie swung her bare feet down, hanging by her arms as her toes caught and held the rungs of the ladder. She scurried to safety from the pandemonium above, her hands tight on the steel ladder below as she listened to the crash of exploding shells, the sound of splintering wood on the decks. Watching the flaring lights sweep the ship, she prayed for Ryan Fitz-simmons, her heart stopping at the sound of a hoarse scream of pain from the afterdeck.

The ship shuddered and rocked from the blows, from the convulsing water around them, but her speed never slackened. In minutes instead of the hours it seemed the lights that had swung and flared above them faded behind. Shells still screamed through the air, but now they were falling behind the stern of the *China Pearl*, not on her. Leslie went up the ladder like a monkey, her bright braid flying as she twisted to look forward.

"Oh-h-h, thank God," she breathed, shuddering, though no one could hear her except the Deity she addressed. The tall blur still stood easily at his post beside the pilot.

They were flying through the darkness, and the funnel above was trailing a thick pall of black smoke, covering the ship's wake. Leslie leaped out of the way as seamen came from the aft deck bearing a wounded man to take him below. Shrapnel had riddled his right side and blood poured from the wounds as the men eased him down the ladder and disappeared in the darkness below. Leslie drew a deep breath and went forward, noticing a sudden blue glimmer appear on the foremast and a skinny male figure slide down and away. A signal, she supposed. She went on, quietly, to touch Ryan's sleeve. He turned sharply and looked down at her, his face invisible beneath the visor of his cap.

"Worried, Leslie? We've lit the blue light to announce we're clear and coming in," he said, "and barring accident we'll be under Fort Morgan's protection in another quarter hour. The ships pursuing aren't fast enough to catch us." He put an arm around her shivering shoulders. "As I told you," he added remindingly, "a blockade runner is no place for a woman."

His warmth drew Leslie irresistibly. She leaned closer, her own arm crept beneath his cloak and around his muscular middle. "I only wished to ask if I could go below and help with the wounded man," she said quietly. "I have had experience with the wounded in the Wilmington hospital."

"No!" His arm tightened. "We have a surgeon aboard. And our men, unfortunately, have more experience with wounds than any nurse. You should be in bed. Once we're under the fort's guns, I'll light you back to your cabin through the wreckage." Still holding her to his side, Ryan drew his long, dark cloak around her and fell silent, watching the night ahead.

Leslie was utterly content. The heat of their bodies mingled in the confines of the cloak, her head rested against his broad shoulder. The cold night air that swept the deck and made the pilot hunch deeper into his pea jacket was only a caress on her warm cheek. Her arm and hand that clasped Ryan's waist were sensitive to each tensing of the hard muscles as the ship rolled, and that was a strangely exciting pleasure. It was a very short quarter hour to her thinking when Ryan spoke again.

"There are the range lights, pilot. The fort has seen our signal. Take her in while I see Miss Gordon to her cabin."

Ryan lighted a lantern, its flare exposing tired lines in his lean cheeks, the strain in his eyes. He took Leslie's arm, holding her close to him as they made their way toward the stern. They skirted shell holes and splintered planking, and Ryan stopped to examine one. "Fortunate for both us and the gunboats that it didn't penetrate the hold," he commented as he went on.

"Why fortunate for them?" Leslie winced as her bare foot touched a splinter, and Ryan, looking down, handed her the lantern and swept her up in his arms. "There's two hundred barrels of gunpowder down there," he said. "They would have joined us on the bottom in that explosion. Now, hold that lantern so I can see where we're going."

Grasping his strong neck with one arm, holding the lantern high in front of them with the other, Leslie knew she was foolhardy to be on this ship, and also that she wouldn't be anywhere else. In the circle of light thrown by the lantern she could see how the deck had been pitted and scarred by bursting shells. There were bulwarks smashed, tangles of severed rigging. But Ryan's booted feet moved through the damage steadily, his knee pushed the cabin door open. Stepping inside, he put her down and lit the gimbaled lights on either wall.

Leslie looked around in the flickering glow. Miraculously, there had been no damage here. She smiled up at Ryan's intent, shadowed face. "As cosy as ever, in spite of them." Now she could see the lines of fatigue in his bronzed cheeks, and she reached to smooth them away, her fingers soft and light. "I wish you could stay and rest with me."

Her touch released a wild mixture of emotions in Ryan that he couldn't have explained. He caught her hand and turned it, kissing the small palm, drawing her close. His arms went around her and tightened, crushing her soft warmth against his hard and hungry body.

Leslie gasped as his mouth covered hers. Her softly parted lips were irresistible, her yielding body tantalizing. For long moments time stood still while Ryan gave in to temptation, his tongue probing her mouth in a tenderly sensual exploration, his loins swelling in hot arousal against her. Then, panting and breathless, they drew apart, staring at each other in the shadowed cabin.

"I—beg your pardon," Ryan said, struggling to regain his poise. "I shouldn't have done that." He fought hard against a wish to gather her up again. "Please forgive me, Leslie."

Leslie hardly heard him. She had just discovered a strange and wonderful fact. "I love you," she said with amazed certainty. "I think I've loved you since the moment we met."

Ryan groaned. Turning away, avoiding her eyes, he was desperate for a way out of this predicament. "You don't love me, child. That's only a romantic illusion, brought on by the excitement and danger of the moment."

"I am not a child," Leslie said intensely, "and I do love you. You're the most wonderful man I've ever known."

Confounded by her utter frankness, Ryan decided he'd better clear this up in a hurry. "You're mistaken in both statements," he said harshly. "And, in any event, it would be useless for a decent woman to put her hopes on me. I will never marry. And for a woman like you there is only marriage. You were born to honor a home."

Leslie smiled. "I was born for you, married or not," she said softly. "I will be yours now, if you want. I could never belong to anyone else." Her voice was caressing, warm, her face full of an eager, innocent sensuality. Desire pulsed through Ryan, hot and full, almost impossible to resist. He turned on her savagely.

"Don't offer yourself to me like some slut, Leslie! You are innocent and pure. You have no idea what you're saying." He caught her head between his palms and looked into her enormous blue eyes, so soft, so full of young passion. "You were in that swamp too damn long, held away from the world by your criminal father! What you are feeling is no more than an animal instinct, a primitive desire to mate. It isn't love!"

Leslie stared up at him, at the glazed look in his hazel eyes, the muscles twitching in his jaw. He was trying to convince himself as well as her.

"Then . . . what is it you feel for me, Ryan?"

His hands dropped away. "Lust," he said harshly. "What else could it be? Forgive me, Leslie." He grabbed up the lantern and stormed out the door, striding rapidly away along the riddled deck, the lantern silhouetting his tall figure, his black cloak flying out behind him. He looked like a man possessed, the cloak a demon that clutched his throat and refused to let go.

Trembling, Leslie shut the door, a mixture of anguish and joy filling her to the bursting point. She was sure of her love for him, and, in spite of what he had said, almost sure he loved her. Somehow, before they reached Wilmington, she must make herself necessary to Captain Ryan Fitzsimmons.

Chapter Four

IN MOBILE, HASTY REPAIRS WENT ON WHILE THE BARRELS of gunpowder were rolled away, the boxes of shells piled on the docks. Men swarmed the masts to replace the rigging and nets while Mobile merchants waited in the shipping offices to claim the bolts of silks and satins, the cases of French wine which had traveled cheek by jowl with the grim armaments of war. Any scarce commodity meant gold to the runners, and these luxuries brought more profit than the powder and shell. Gold clinked continually in Ryan's strongbox while he drove the men hard to finish the repairs. Only two nights of darkness remained, and if they missed this dark of the moon, they would have almost a month to wait for the next.

By noon of the second day, the hold of the *China Pearl* was full again, stuffed with bales of cotton—the "white gold" of the Confederacy. In Nassau, men waited as anxiously for cotton as these beleaguered Southerners waited for gunpowder. All Europe was a hungry market willing to pay through the nose for the white fibers their mills needed.

The famous Fitzsimmons' luck held. Back from a hurried trip to the city's center, Ryan sniffed the first stirrings of a northeaster. A gale to fill his canvas and raise the mountainous seas that would hide his small ship from the *Brooklyn,* now his chief worry. Reports from lookouts at Fort Morgan had been that the warship had moved in to augment the circle of blockaders, its mighty guns ready to sink the impudent runner that had escaped two Federal gunboats.

Ryan was smiling as he strode up the gangway with his arms full of bundles, which he thrust into Ralph Tudbury's arms.

"Take those to the stern cabin," Ryan told him. "I've augmented Miss Gordon's wardrobe." He laughed at Tudbury's startled look. "I thought she might tire of looking like a cabin boy. And she'll be going ashore in Nassau in a few days. We sail tonight."

First Mate Tudbury grinned, happy to see his captain in such a merry mood. With his thick arms wrapped around the bundles, he turned toward the stern with a hoarse yell:

"Prepare to cast off!"

In the cabin, reading one of the books that lined a shelf above the bunk, Leslie heard the yell and jumped up, opening the door in time to take the bundles from Tudbury with an astonished look.

"What are these?"

"New duds, Miss, for wearing in Nassau." Tudbury was still grinning. "We're off to the fort to wait for the night and the storm. They'll not see the *China Pearl* in the rampage coming!" He hurried away, shouting enthusiastically at the crew.

Leslie lifted her face to the gust of cool air that swirled through the door and knew what he meant. An odd thing to be grateful for on the eve of departure—a howling gale. Wondering, she took the bundles to the top of the bunk to open.

There were thirty miles of bay to travel before the ship reached the opening into the gulf, and during the time they sailed half the distance, Leslie tried on all the clothes. From one package came camisoles and dimity pantalets, all lace edged and dainty, and pairs of lisle stockings. There were slippers of soft leather with tiny heels, and a pair of quite high boots that would serve with her nankeen breeches. From a round box came a darling blue bonnet that set back on her head, and a full dozen taffeta petticoats. She wondered why so many until she held up the gowns and saw how tremendously full the skirts were.

Looking carefully at the gowns, Leslie smiled wryly. Of the finest quality and very well made, the gowns reflected Ryan's picture of her as a child. Loosely fitted, and with such neat, high collars, ruffled bodices and long sleeves, they would have been most appropriate for a schoolgirl. One blue, one white and lacy and trimmed with golden ribbons. Still, everything fit, and she was touched by his generosity.

Back in the breeches and shirt, Leslie pulled on a pair of the stockings, thrust her feet into the boots and stalked out proudly to find Ryan. Locating him in the ward room, she stuck out a foot for his inspection.

"I owe you," she said soberly. "You were overly generous."

They were alone in the ward room. Ryan examined the boots and then ran his eyes slowly over the newly rounding figure in the revealing breeches and shirt. Raising his gaze to her face, he also inspected the healthy pink color in her cheeks, no longer thin and white, and the sparkle of sea-blue eyes beneath the golden hair. A sudden, intense jealousy filled him as he thought of the lucky devil who would eventually possess her. A young man, no doubt, untouched by danger, with some profitable business ashore. A man who would wed her and bed her with enthusiasm. He could almost see the man's feverish hands eagerly grasping those pink-rosetted breasts, imagine his humping back and straining loins between the slender, white thighs. . . .

"You owe me nothing," he said savagely, turning away, grasping the squat-bottomed brandy bottle from the table. He poured himself a stiff drink and downed it. Then he turned back, meeting her puzzled blue gaze. "Except," he added, trying to smile, "the pleasure of seeing you in something more feminine than that outfit you're wearing. We'll be having a festive dinner tonight under the protection of Fort Morgan, as we wait for the storm to build. Wear one of your gowns for me."

He was trying to hide some unhappiness. Leslie wanted to put her arms around him, make him forget whatever it was that bothered him. But she didn't dare. Instead, with her characteristic gesture, she laid cool fingertips on his hand for an instant and then withdrew them. "I will," she said and smiled. "Just for you. In honor of the successful Captain Ryan Fitzsimmons!" She was gone, out into the passageway, and he heard her booted feet tapping quickly up the ladder. She was as agile as any cabin boy he had ever had on the ship.

That evening, anchored at the mouth of the bay, Leslie dressed with care, putting up her freshly washed hair in a golden coil that left a wisp or two curling against her nape. She had used the sewing kit provided for alterations by the store, and had taken a few tucks in the waistline of the blue gown, improving it a little. Wearing several of the beruffled taffeta petticoats beneath the full skirt, she had to pause in the companionway to force the fullness into the narrow space. But it was worth it just to hear the swish and rustle as she entered the ward room.

The dinner was a gift from the merchant who had ordered and received the French wines, and it was indeed festive, as Ryan had described it. Smoked turkey and roast quail scented the air, and there was wine and fruit, fresh ground coffee and tiny cakes with pastel frosting. All in addition to the usual corn pudding, vegetables and homemade bread. There were wide smiles around the table as they all took their seats.

Only the highest-ranking of the men ate with Ryan and Leslie—the mates, the bosun and the quartermaster. But Leslie had always enjoyed the friendly give-and-take of their conversation with her, though it had occasionally raised a frown on Ryan's face. This evening she was at first puzzled and then disappointed. Instead of their usual lively talk, the men treated her with a stilted gallantry that she hadn't known they possessed. They actually deferred to her, their eyes admiring but wary. Nor could she shake them out of it.

Glancing at Ryan's satisfied expression, Leslie understood. He had armored her! The soft blue cambric linen of her gown was a steely declaration of propriety. She was now a lady, and must be treated like one. Even by Ryan. Especially by Ryan! After dinner, strolling the deck, he was excessively polite and distant. After a few moments, Leslie excused herself and went to the cabin.

It was not to be tolerated, she thought, opening the small chest, rummaging furiously. Pulling out a clean pair of breeches, a shirt, and a small pea jacket to ward off the rising wind, she changed quickly, hanging up the gown with a sigh of relief.

Night had fallen and the engines were rumbling, building steam, as she came out again. Noting Ryan's look of surprise and amusement, she smiled brightly.

"More suitable for running a blockade, don't you think?"

He laughed, reaching for her hand and drawing it through his arm again. "My golden lily retains a bit of the swamp's wildness," he said softly. "Was I wrong, Leslie? Do the gowns make you feel uncomfortable?"

She leaned against him, her hair beginning to blow in the wind, and smiled up into his hazel eyes. "They will be lovely for sweeping along Nassau streets. But on the ship . . ."

". . . you will be my cabin boy," he finished for her, his voice suddenly husky, his hand tightening on her arm. Even in the darkness she could see the desire in his eyes. Then he released her and turned stiffly away to lean on the rail. "We shall have to remain in Nassau for close to a month," he said. "But the next trip, we'll go in at Wilmington and your ordeal at sea will be over." He glanced back at her with a twisted smile. "You'll be able to begin your search for your charming father." Straightening, he strode toward the bow to give the order that would bring up the anchor and begin the night's run.

For a moment, Leslie wondered what she had done to displease him so, and then, for the second time that night, she understood. The "demon" he was fighting was his desire for her. Well! As far as she was concerned this wonderful, warm and natural feeling was no demon—it was love. Jamming on the knit cap she had been carrying, she buttoned the pea jacket and went to stand at what she now considered her "post," the entrance to the companionway. She had only a month or less to prove to Ryan that they belonged together. It might not be enough. If the time came to go to Wilmington before she was assured of keeping his love, she wouldn't go. Once Ryan was certain she was safely at home and among friends, she would never see him again. Suddenly it seemed that her life's happiness depended on the next four weeks.

"All hands, up anchor!"

The terse command sent the men running, eager now to meet the challenge of both storm and warships. Blacked out, the *China Pearl* was soon moving, slowly at first and then sprinting for the gulf as she reached the channel. Above, the jacks clung to the ropes and balanced on the spars, ready to loose sails at an order from Ryan's trumpet. They clung the harder as the ship began rising and falling abruptly in the choppy seas near shore.

"Sail right ahead, sir!"

A lookout's sharp whisper brought Leslie's head around, her eyes widening at the black bulk towering on the starboard side, her feet slipping as the ship veered in answer to Ryan's order to port the helm. An instant later, the ship veered again, this time to starboard as another hulk loomed on the left. Thus they worked their way, in and out, hidden by the heaving seas and the spume from the waves that flew half-mast high. Salt spray stung Leslie's face and dampened the hair that had fallen down her back; her fingers were cramped and stiff on the companionway rails. Staring into the night, she kept Ryan's tall shape, swathed again in the dark cloak, in the corner of her vision. He seemed to her to be more tense than ever; the quick way he turned his head at the sight of another hulk too nervous and wary. It was natural, she thought, to be afraid of the *Brooklyn*. Not only could the eleven-inch shells of the warship sink this small ship with one broadside, but the warship was the only blockader fast enough to catch the *China Pearl*. Everything depended on keeping out of sight of the giant.

They were away from the lee of the land behind them now, and the waves grew mountainous. Deep in the valleys between them the lookouts held their breath, wondering if the next topping would reveal a gunboat beside them. Falling and rising, the small ship went steadily on, threading through six menacing dark shapes without a challenge. The thrashing of the paddles blended with the noise of the storm, and below, using the last of the precious, smokeless coke for fuel, the men in the engine room kept the steam whistling through the safety valves. Soon they would have to use coal, and the smoke from the funnel might give them away.

Suddenly, so suddenly that all saw it at once, there was the massive shape. And beside it another, smaller ship like a greyhound with its master. The smaller ship was under power, moving in slow, tossing circles.

"I see their plan," Ryan whispered to the quartermaster at the wheel. "They mean to take us one way or the other. If the *Brooklyn* misses, the other ship is ready to chase." He stared forward and then gave his orders. "Slip behind the *Brooklyn*, pilot, as close as you can. Right under the old hen's wings." His white teeth flashed in a taut grin. "If they look down, they'll see us. If they don't, we're away."

Swiftly, the small ship ran close, disappearing in the shadow of the warship, veering away as they passed the bow to miss the huge anchor chain that held her. On they ran, without a light coming on, without a bellowed trumpet call, until, looking behind, they could see nothing but black night. Relaxing, laughing with a great gust of breath, Ryan ordered the men aloft to lay on every rag of sail the ship possessed. As he walked back to Leslie, the storm wind filled the canvas with sharp snaps, seeming to make the long, low hull fly over the water. Ryan looked at Leslie's upturned face, the gleam of starshine in dark pools of eyes, the glint of small teeth as she smiled at him. Picking up her hand, he held it against his cheek for a moment, watching her hair fly like a whipping banner.

"Wild as the night, sweet as the freedom we have gained," he said softly. "Go to your cabin, Leslie. Stop torturing me."

"You are torturing yourself," Leslie said, and withdrew her hand. "Needlessly. Come with me." She watched him turn on his heel and go back to his post. A few minutes later he sent the pilot down for a mug of coffee and took the wheel himself. Sighing, Leslie made her way along the heaving, windswept deck to the stern cabin. Ryan Fitzsimmons was a very stubborn man.

The blue, open-ended bowl of the Gulf of Mexico was an arena crossed furtively but continually by blockade runners, their ports of call ranging from Mobile Bay to New Orleans, Galveston, and the neutral port of Matamoras in Mexico. And crossed also by the Union ships, bristling with guns and challenging any ship they met to search for contraband. It was necessary to be watchful and fast for the forty-eight hours it took to traverse the gulf and then run the gantlet around the Florida Keys and past the bulge of Cuba. But the seasoned crew of the *China Pearl* could be trusted to do that, and Ryan caught up on his sleep. He was in the cabin in the morning as soon as Leslie was out, and never emerged until time for his watch at night.

They did share dinner. But, with the letdown of tension and the long days of sun and tossing seas, Leslie could hardly keep her eyes open at the table. Nor did there seem to be any reason to stay awake. Ryan was withdrawn and silent; bent, she thought, on proving there was no future for them together.

But there was one occupation that kept her from boredom. The release of tension had affected the crew differently. Now they sang as they worked the sails, sang the same songs sailors had always sung, the chanteys with the rhythm of the turning sails, the twisting capstan in them.

Leslie listened with an ache of longing for her father. Harry Gordon had loved the chanteys, the ballads of old countries and new. The songs took her back to the time when her father's pleasant voice was the sound of her childhood. She had learned all his songs, and learned to sing with him in harmony. But that had all been over when they came to the Green Swamp.

At first, Leslie was content to listen. Perched on the top of a paddle box, she let the deep voices flow over her in healing memory. But the evening shifting of the sails brought the swing of her father's favorite, and when the lead voice stumbled and hunted words near the end, Leslie sprang to her feet. Her voice rang out, clear and true.

"And, as soon as that packet was out on the sea . . ."

There was an instant of astonished silence, and then, grinning, the men boomed back:

"To me way, hey, blow the man down!"

And back came Leslie, her arms flung wide:

"'Twas devilish hard treatment of every degree . . ."
"Oh, give me some time, to blo-o-ow the man down!"

Leslie laughed with pleasure, her eyes shining. It was the first time she had ever heard the song the way it should be sung, with the deep male voices booming the chorus. She went on with the next and last verse with them, though it wasn't at all necessary. The sails were set and the men doing nothing but singing, looking as pleased with her as she was with them.

Later, the bosun, whose name, she had learned, was Harold Finney, stopped and spoke to her. He was the burly seaman whose back had blocked her way out of the hammock deck that first night, and he had always taken a sort of proprietary interest in her since, feeling more easy than the others with her.

"It's rare to find a woman who knows the chanteys," he said. "You sang that well, Miss Gordon."

"Thank you," she said, "I enjoyed it. I must know dozens of chanteys and ballads, but I had never heard a chantey sung by men together before. Only my father's voice. . . ."

"Ballads, you say." Finney's heavy face lightened. "Would you know this one?" He hummed a few bars and Leslie smiled.

"You're a Scot, Mr. Finney? That's 'Loch Lomond.'" She sang it for him, nostalgia for her father prickling behind her eyes and lending an even more authentic tone to the Scottish lament. Her voice floated out on the faint evening breeze, each note round and crystal clear, with the unconscious warmth of her nature coloring the sound.

"A concert, Leslie?"

Leslie turned, seeing Finney fade quickly away toward the wheel to take over from Ralph Tudbury, and Ryan's clear, hazel eyes waiting for her answer. Discomfited, she scrambled down from the paddle-wheel box and stood in front of him defiantly.

"Hardly a concert, Captain. Only a song from the past."

Ryan smiled slowly. "I meant no criticism." His eyes roved the small figure with the boots planted firmly, the hands on her hips, rose to her indignant face and lingered on her soft, sensuously curved mouth. The look melted down through her, almost as potent as a kiss, and Leslie's defiance melted with it as Ryan added in a half whisper: "Your voice is as beautiful as you are. . . ." Then, forcing his gaze from her face, he turned away. "Your talents seem endless, in fact. Perhaps I wasn't far wrong when I advised you to seek a career on the stage. Shall we go down to dinner?"

The change in his tone made Leslie feel cold and desolate. "I'm not really hungry," she answered. "I think I'll read awhile and then go to bed." She left him, her emotions inextricably mixed, and went along the deck toward the stern cabin, her booted feet striding, her small, curved hips swinging in the soft nankeen breeches. Ryan muttered a curse and swung down the companionway, angry at himself. There was no reason to hurt such a small and helpless adversary.

On the evening of the second day there was a rise in spirits as they entered the straits between Florida and Cuba. What ships they spotted were merchantmen. No threatening silhouettes had appeared on the horizon by the time Leslie went to bed.

"By tomorrow noon," Ryan told her, "we'll have passed the worst of it. With our speed it should be clear sailing for Nassau after that." Standing at his usual post, he was looking down at her with a stiff air of reserve that made her heart ache. Rested, his clear eyes and rugged features were more handsome than ever; the air of vitality in his lean, muscular body drew her relentlessly. Yet he seemed impervious now, a solid wall of resistance. Leslie's confidence was at a low ebb. Shivering slightly, either from the brisk evening breeze or the chill in his manner, she nodded lifelessly as she turned toward the stern again.

And again, Ryan watched her out of sight. This time when he turned forward he caught the flicker of Finney's wondering glance.

"Watch the compass," Ryan commanded abruptly. "There are times when staying on course becomes important."

Leslie woke at dawn to a strange silence. There was no splash of paddle wheels, no slapping of waves against the hull. Only an occasional lazy flap of sail and a feeling of nearly motionless drifting. Rising, she went to the small, high windows and stifled a frightened gasp. Lying a hundred yards away, on a mirror-smooth, opalescent sea reflecting the dawn colors of the sky, was a warship close to two hundred feet long and armed with deadly pivot guns. Behind closed gun ports there must be at least six more cannon. And, between the lethal, lead-gray invader and the little *China Pearl* was a boatload of men rowing purposefully toward them. Surely, Ryan hadn't surrendered without at least trying to escape! It took her sleepy eyes several more minutes to search out and identify the flag on the mizzenmast, drooping in the calm air. The Stars and Bars of the Confederacy!

Laughing at her own cowardly fright, Leslie rushed to wash and dress, braid her hair, push her small feet into the commodious boots. A rendezvous at sea was exciting, and she wanted a closer look at the first Confederate Navy ship she had seen.

Bursting from the cabin, Leslie ran to the rail, grasping the cool metal with both hands and leaning forward as she surveyed the big ship. Her heart swelled with pride. A year ago her father had described the Confederate raiders that preyed on the Yankee merchantmen, and now she was seeing one with her own eyes. Her father had heard of them on one of his trips and had been pleased to know that while they accosted and burned ships carrying supplies to the Union, they were careful to first remove the people aboard and bring them safely to port. Saving lives was important to Harry Gordon.

Oblivious to the small boat now lying against the *China Pearl* and the man who climbed up from it, Leslie examined the raider from one end to the other. Three-masted and bark-rigged, with two big funnels and huge paddle wheels to push the weight she must carry. British-built, her father had said, and none finer.

"Leslie."

She whirled, coloring slightly at the frown on Ryan's face. He had approached with another man while she gawked—a man in a gray, box-coated suit and a captain's hat cocked on tan, tousled hair, the visor shadowing slanted green eyes that seemed both admiring and amused. Leslie was suddenly conscious of her unconventional attire. On ship, it had been easy to forget that ladies didn't wear breeches.

"Captain Spencer Burdette of the Confederate ship *James Bulloch,*" Ryan said, formally, "Miss Leslie Gordon, of Wilmington." His frown deepened as the other man's green eyes ran over Leslie expertly and then glanced up at Ryan in undisguised envy.

"I see there are certain advantages to owning your own ship and choosing your own crew," he said, smiling. "Miss Gordon is quite the most charming cabin boy I have ever seen." He bowed over the hand Leslie had offered him and dropped a light kiss on her fingers. "I could wish myself one-tenth as fortunate in my attendant."

Leslie was well aware of his conclusion, and didn't mind at all. She smiled at him openly. What if he did think they were lovers? She wished it true.

"Miss Gordon is a passenger," Ryan said, his frown black as thunder. "You are being objectionable, Spence."

Captain Burdette's smile disappeared as he straightened. Looking at Leslie apologetically, he turned red with embarrassment. "Miss Gordon, if I've been offensive, I humbly beg your pardon."

"Your mistake was perfectly understandable," Leslie said cheerfully. "What else could you think? I am dressed scandalously, I know, and since I came from Ryan's cabin . . ." She looked up at Ryan's furious face and added, rather shakily: "I suppose I should have put on one of those gowns you bought me in Mobile."

Ryan wondered if she could possibly know how much worse she was making the situation with every word. "Please do," he gritted, "and meet us later in the ward room for coffee. In the meantime, please excuse us. Captain Burdette is an old friend of mine and we've much to discuss." Deliberately, he took the arm of his friend and turned him around smartly. There was, Leslie decided, something almost overbearing in the way Ryan marched Burdette to the companionway.

Returning to the cabin in a much less ebullient mood, Leslie hastily removed the offending breeches and shirt and put on the blue gown. After the sameness of the days aboard ship, she didn't want to miss what might be a very interesting conversation. Captain Burdette must know the latest news of the war. Unbraiding her long hair, she swept it back into a knot on her neck and went quickly along the deck to the companionway. Except for a faint rustle of taffeta, her approach to the ward room door was soundless. The soft slippers didn't click on the polished floor like her boots, a fact she afterward regretted. Once more, it was proven that eavesdroppers hear no good of themselves. . . .

Not that she had intended to listen. But Ryan's deep voice caught her attention too quickly to resist.

"She was like a wild creature there in that swamp," he was saying. "You wouldn't credit the conditions in which I found her, Spence. Living alone in a rotten box, half crazed by loneliness and almost starved. Three miserable years she had been there—hardly a wonder she has no sense of propriety even now. I pitied her, and I still do, yet I admit . . ."

Leslie whirled and left, almost tripping on the annoying gown as she went up the ladder with blurring eyes. Pity! Pity and passion, those were the only emotions she woke in Ryan Fitzsimmons. A wild creature, indeed! With no sense of propriety. A *gentleman* like Ryan would find the thought of mating with a wild creature distasteful, of course, no matter what the temptation. She rushed toward the stern cabin, unsure whether she suffered more from anger or grief, fury or unrequited love. *How* could he speak of her like that to a stranger?

Ignoring not only the sight of the proud Confederate ship but even the soft and beautiful morning, she entered the cabin and slammed the door. Taking a book from Ryan's shelf, she flung herself into the chair and opened it on her lap. If he bothered to come to the cabin, he would find a very model of propriety. A lady, unconcerned with the affairs of men, reading to improve her mind.

The book lay neglected on her lap as she struggled to calm herself. It was close to an hour before the knock on the door came, plenty of time for her to acknowledge that Captain Burdette was obviously no stranger to Ryan; to acknowledge also that Ryan had not exaggerated the conditions in which she had been living. And, to admit that propriety wasn't her strong suit. But that "pity" still rankled, a thrust in her heart.

"Leslie?"

She rose, the book in one hand, swept to the door and opened it with a polite smile.

"Captain Burdette would like to make his adieus,"

Ryan said frozenly. "We expected you in the ward room."

Leslie stepped out, offering her hand to Burdette. "Good-bye, Captain. I am very happy to have made your acquaintance, and to have had the opportunity to see your ship. It is wonderful to know we have such staunch defenders of our Confederacy."

Ryan looked surprised and uneasily gratified at the pretty speech, but there was a glint in Burdette's slanted green eyes as he again kissed her hand. Leslie had a feeling that he saw right through her to the roiling emotions within.

"I look forward to my return to Nassau next week," Burdette said gallantly, "and my extended leave, time to make a friend of my newest and loveliest acquaintance." He stepped back, smiling at them both. "Now, if I am to scourge the Yankee traders, I suppose I must return to my ship." With another warm sweep of green eyes that covered Leslie leisurely, he clapped a hand on Ryan's shoulder. "Fitz, you will be more popular than ever when you arrive in port with this golden angel."

Ryan's parting glance at Leslie was dark and unreadable as he walked away with Burdette. Leslie shrugged. Going to the rail, she watched Burdette go lithely down the short length of rope ladder and drop into the waiting small boat. Glancing up at her as he sat down, he caught her gaze and smiled, a quick, amused gleam of white teeth beneath the shadow of his visor. Warmed, Leslie smiled back and waved as the men rowed Burdette away. Joining her at the rail, Ryan was frowning again.

"If you wished to flirt with Burdette," he said caustically, "you would have had a better chance if you had joined us at coffee. Why didn't you?"

Hiding her hurt beneath an even more brilliant smile, Leslie tried to answer carelessly. "Somehow I thought there would be a certain restraint in my presence," she said. "I was positive, in fact, that there would be thoughts you would want to . . . to share with your friend . . . that—that you wouldn't want me to hear." The last of the statement was neither careless nor steady. Blinking back tears, she left him, hurrying to the cabin again, furious with herself. More furious as she heard his quick stride behind her. Coming in before she could shut the door, he caught her arm, turning her toward him.

"I thought I heard a rustle in the passageway," he said, and he seemed as angry as she was. "You were listening, weren't you? Did I lie, Leslie?"

She jerked her arm from his grasp, her huge eyes full of blue fire. "No! Even your opinion of me was correct. I must be a wild creature, for at this moment I could kill you for your *pity!*"

Ryan growled and reached for her, his long fingers closing painfully tight on her shoulders. "Would that pity was all I felt for you," he muttered, and dragged her toward him, sweeping her up into his arms, her feet off the floor, her newly rounded body welded to him by his crushing strength. "I could have killed, too—when Spence dared to look at you like that." Staring into her flushed face and the blue flames in her eyes, his own eyes flared and darkened, his mouth descended savagely.

The hot sweetness of his invading tongue turned the fire of Leslie's anger into a passionate response. She clung to him with a growing fierceness, her hands pushing his cap away to be buried in the crisp chestnut hair, her eyes closed, her attention blissfully concentrated on that flaming point where their mouths met.

It was something neither of them would forget, a seeking, demanding, surrendering kiss. If their first kiss had hinted, this one told them clearly that the force between them could consume their wills, bend them to its purpose, never let them go. Swept dangerously close to the edge of his control, Ryan forced himself away and set her on her feet. "I apologize," he muttered. "That was—entirely my fault. . . ."

Leslie looked at him, dazed, suddenly cold without his arms around her. "Ryan . . ." It seemed so simple, so clear to her. "Can't you tell? We belong together. . . ." She had never been more sure of anything in her life.

Ryan turned away, his mouth twisting, his body as tense as a bent bow. "I will belong to no woman, Leslie! I need no dutiful chains to bind me to shore." He was gone, striding through the door of the cabin, slamming it behind him. A moment later she could hear him telling the crew roughly to get the ship underway.

Miserable, Leslie flung her full length on the bunk, her body aching with longing, her heart pounding insistently. Maybe pity and passion were all Ryan felt for her, but in that moment it would have been enough.

Chapter Five

SPENCER BURDETTE HAD BROUGHT A WARNING, TELLING
Ryan there were two Federal cruisers lying in wait near
the Berry Islands, northwest of Nassau, looking for
blockade runners. Accordingly, as soon as the *China
Pearl* was into the Northwest Providence Channel,
Ryan ordered the engines stopped. He went to bed
while the ship lay to, waiting for darkness.

"We could outrun 'em, unless they be some of the
new craft the Yankees have built," Harold Finney told
Leslie later, "but a shame to take a risk now with the
cotton aboard. The Lancashire mills in England need
it, and we need the dollar a pound it brings."

Leslie gasped. Dressed again in the cabin boy's garb,
she was leaning against the forward rail, watching the
clear blue water below. Now she glanced at the bosun,
awed. Ryan had paid but eight cents a pound for that

cotton and there were tons aboard. It was no wonder he was willing to risk his ship running the blockade for a profit like that. She gazed at Finney thoughtfully.

"I know Captain Fitzsimmons isn't a Confederate," she said, "and he doesn't speak quite like a Britisher. Where is he from, Bosun?"

Finney grinned. "The sea, you'd have to say. A wanderer, like his father before him. Old Captain Fitz put him ashore once in a while for schoolin', and it was one of those times, around the Liverpool docks, that I met him. When he went back aboard his father's ship I went with him. And I've stuck with him ever since."

"Still," Leslie said impatiently, "he had to be born somewhere. Was it Ireland?"

"He was born on the *Sea Lord,* Miss. His father's ship. Old Captain Fitz took his wives with him."

"Wives?"

Finney blushed. "A slip of the tongue. In truth, Ryan's mother was the only wife the old captain ever had. After she was gone, he never married any of . . . he never married again." Finney turned quickly toward the companionway. "I'd best be rousing the next watch. These men have been on duty long enough."

Leslie knew the bosun was only escaping her questions. She smiled wryly as he disappeared down the ladder and then turned her attention again to the blue depths. It was as clear as the water below her what Ryan's heritage had been. "Old Fitz" had undoubtedly been a privateer—a pirate, to put it plainly. A master of a ship when a captain was his own law. A generation ago these islands and the Indies below them had sheltered an occasional freebooter who preyed on other ships and wrecks, some with frayed letters of marque that made their piracy seem legal. A wild, free life, and, after his mother's death, a few wild, free women in his father's cabin. She wondered suddenly where Ryan had gotten his own strict moral code—or was he so strictly moral with other women?

She shrugged. Ryan was a trifle more civilized perhaps, but he had been raised in a simple tradition. Own your own ship and make a fortune any way you can. The War Between the States was a great opportunity for such an adventurer. An adventurer with no dutiful chains to bind him to shore. . . .

The afternoon sun was blinding hot and Leslie soon left the rail for the shadow of a drooping, loosened sail. Sitting on the edge of one of the piled bales of precious cotton, she pulled off her knitted cap and let the faint breeze cool her heated forehead. I'm not a chain, she thought rebelliously, and if Ryan's mother could live on a ship, so could I. She lay back, closing her eyes and dreaming of sailing these sunlit seas forever with an Irish adventurer. . . .

At dusk, Ryan emerged from the stern cabin looking cool and refreshed. He wore light nankeen trousers, boots, and a white shirt open over his bronzed chest. His sleeves were rolled up, exposing the thick muscles of his upper arms. He stood sniffing the rising night wind and looking over the gentle roll of the sea, with the last light of day limning his powerful figure against the background of deepening blue.

Leslie, sitting up again with her slender arms wrapped around her knees, watched him quietly. Everything about him drew her like a magnet—from his rugged features and air of command to the tiny detail of curling dark hair in the vee of his open shirt. She had only begun to know the depth of her feeling for him and yet she could no longer imagine a future without him. There had to be a way to break his resolve. . . .

Spotting the brightness of her uncovered hair in the shadows, Ryan came striding toward her.

"Have you eaten yet, Leslie? If not, come have a bite with me. The last dinner aboard for some weeks, once we sneak past those cruisers."

Leslie grimaced, counting on the dim light to hide her expression. Ryan's confident tone told her that he was again completely in control of his feelings, his reserve firmly in place. She rose, evading the hand he stretched out to her, and jerked the cap down over her head again, frowning.

"Mr. Finney kindly brought me sandwiches and tea an hour ago," she said, "and if we are to land in the morning, I have packing to do. I'll bid you good night, Captain."

"If you prefer," Ryan said casually. "But please remember that I shall be taking you to the Royal Victoria Hotel when we arrive in Nassau. I'm sure I don't need to tell you that you are to be properly clothed."

Leslie gritted her teeth. "I'll not shame you. Even a wild creature of the swamp knows better than to appear in society as a cabin boy." Head high, she stalked away with her golden brows in a scowl. In the morning, Ryan would reckon with a new Leslie Gordon!

That night, remembering the waiting cruisers, Leslie covered the windows of the stern cabin with thick blankets, stuffed cloth around the door to hide any hint of light, and proceeded to try on both the blue and white gowns, studying them critically from all angles. She did indeed look like a female—a fifteen-year-old female, all eyes, ruffles and shapeless fabric.

Seeking out the sewing kit again, Leslie reached for the scissors. It was close to dawn before she put the gowns away and crawled into the bunk, satisfied. The gowns had lost their girlish look along with the high collars and a good bit of the fussily ruffled fronts of the bodices. Low, rounded necklines now exposed the tops of her high breasts, the bodices clung to her tapered ribs and tiny waistline. And the long, full sleeves had been transformed into airy puffs that covered only the tops of her shoulders. She went to sleep dreaming of Ryan's startled look when he saw her new image. Properly gowned, yes—but not as a girl. As a woman!

The sound of the engines slowing awakened Leslie just after dawn. Even after only an hour or so of sleep, she felt refreshed, delighted as her eyes fell on the gowns. Leaping from the bunk, she dipped water for a bath. Ryan would soon discover he had no cabin boy on his hands.

Later, the white dress on and smoothed into place, her freshly washed hair in a golden coil that released a halo of tiny springing curls, Leslie climbed on a stool and tilted the small mirror by degrees, inspecting herself thoroughly. The full skirt swung like a bell, supported by layers of whispering taffeta, and above . . . she drew a deep breath and watched the ivory swells rise above filmy white lace. Then she frowned. The lace tended to stretch, the soft lining not stiff enough to hold it. Climbing down again, she found a length of the gold ribbon trim and began threading it through the low-cut top. Fetching, she wished to be, but not shocking. One more deep breath and she would expose far more than she had intended.

She was tying a tight bow in the ribbon as the *China Pearl* slowed again, proceeding now at dead-low speed. Leslie rushed to strip the blankets from the windows and lean out, gasping at the beauty of the scene. They were coming into Nassau Harbor from the northeast and the water around them was a deep clear blue.

Flying fish skimmed the surface, bright enough to rival the small butterflies that fluttered on board to perch on the cotton bales.

The ship cut through the Narrows, a squat, brilliantly white fort on the headland to her left, and then a trio of small islands. Past them, she could see the port, with numerous ships of every size crowded near the docks or anchored out in the calm waters.

But it was the island of New Providence that drew Leslie's gaze. Low, with a gentle slope upward from the sea, it was like an illustration in a fairy tale. Verdant with trees and shrubbery, colorful with pink and white, pale blue and green houses, it was beautiful. A more peaceful place she couldn't imagine, yet as they neared the ships moored at the seawall, she saw their decks were filled with frantic activity. They were loading mountains of cotton bales into their cargo space.

British ships, she thought, and stared at them curiously as the *China Pearl* thrashed slowly past to a berth of her own. Then, from a nearby deck, a pair of British tars caught sight of her at her window and began yelling endearments, clutching their hearts in grandiloquent admiration of her low-cut décolletage.

Hastily, Leslie left the window and tightly wrapped a shawl around herself, securing it with knots in the fringe. It was one thing to impress Ryan with her mature femininity, another thing entirely to expose herself to others.

As the ship shuddered and slid along the sheer, rocky wall, there was another shout outside.

"Fitzsimmons, by God! We heard you were holed and the Yanks captured you!"

Ryan's laugh rang out. "Old news, Pierson, but true at the time. We still have the rascals' blue coats to prove it."

There was a thumping rain of booted feet on deck, loud talk and laughter, a bit of ribaldry. Hesitating at the door of the cabin, Leslie turned and went back to a chair. She would wait like a lady for Ryan to fetch her.

It was an hour before Ryan knocked and came in, to gaze with approval on the modestly shawled and skirted figure. Hiding her impatience, Leslie glanced past him and saw there were still men on the deck. But not the ones so full of enthusiasm and welcome. These men were somberly clothed and quiet, fingering the fluffy white bolls from a split bale of cotton.

"Don't bother about me," she said quickly. "Those are your buyers, aren't they?"

Ryan's eyes gleamed. "You've a quick eye for business, little one. But this is the proper time to take you up and settle you in the hotel. Those men will be hours judging the fiber." He grinned at her. "You're my excuse for leaving. By the time I return, they'll be ready to outbid each other." He picked up the seabag Leslie had packed with the rest of her new clothes and hefted it. "Your first business will be adding to your wardrobe. We'll be here for three weeks and I'll want no one thinking me unwilling to provide the best for my ward."

"Your *ward?*" Leslie's voice was incredulous, and Ryan laughed, thoroughly amused.

"I knew you wouldn't like the role, but I'm afraid it's necessary. The Royal Victoria has guests from every layer of society—from the most dignified of Southern dowagers to the most blatant prostitutes—and one must make his or her position known from the beginning. You are the daughter of an old friend of mine, recently deceased, and I am your appointed guardian, returning you to your home in Wilmington. Fortunately, you look very young."

Leslie opened her mouth to protest and then closed

it. For the first time she realized how dependent she was on Ryan. It hadn't mattered on the ship, but now, with no money, not enough clothes and no prospects, she was forced to agree to anything he planned. Her face burning, she swept from the cabin into the noisy world outside.

Bay Street was clamorous and bustling with roustabouts, clouded with pulverized limestone dust as drays from the warehouses banged along, heavily loaded. Dockworkers and sailors from other ships dodged between the drays and shouted at the drivers, who shouted back through the screech and rumble. Ryan took Leslie quickly across the thoroughfare and found the offices of Frazer, Trenholm and Company, the Confederate government agents. Inside, he briefly reported his ship in and secured, and then took Leslie back outside. Walking up Bay Street now, they were in a different sort of crowd, one composed of native women and children selling exotic fruits and seafood, and a number of shoppers. There was, Leslie noted, far more laughter, yelling and chattering than business. Here the crowd parted magically before them, in seeming deference to a captain from a blockade runner. Admiring glances swung from Ryan's towering body to Leslie's blonde, shining hair.

Her head suddenly high, blue eyes sparkling, Leslie felt a thrill of pride. On the arm of Captain Ryan Fitzsimmons she felt every inch a lady. She walked along confidently with every misgiving forgotten.

Ryan's lips twitched, as he watched her take on a new role. That blue shawl matched her eyes and accented the high color of her cheeks and curved lips, and her hair was a golden crown for her innocence. She had a natural flair for becoming exactly who she wanted to be, be it gamine in boy's clothes or sedate young lady. He thought of that crucial night on the Hillsborough when she had thrown herself wholeheartedly into another kind of acting. Poor, mad Mary, begging for a bit of food and the dregs of a bottle! In that ragged skirt and blouse, her hair a wild thicket, she had indeed looked the part. And she had saved the *China Pearl*. As he gazed down at her, his hand tightened on her arm, unconsciously possessive.

"It isn't far to the Royal Victoria, but we'll take a carriage and be comfortable. I see one now. . . ." He flung up an arm and shouted. "Gabe! Over here!"

An old horse was easing an open carriage through the crowd, an elderly black driver on the high seat. The driver spread a wide, white grin in Ryan's direction. "Yes, *sah*, Cap'n Fitz! Soon as I drop me fares. . . ."

Leslie stared. His fares were two voluptuously curved and outrageously painted ladies, their hair in elaborate curls, their gowns sensational, their red mouths stretched in provocative smiles as they leaned forward and waved wildly at Ryan.

"Welcome back, Fitz! We're playing at the Prince John."

"Come see us, darling—we'll see you have a good table."

Leslie's startled eyes sent a glance at Ryan's face and found a fatuous grin and a gleam in his hazel eyes. He was waving back in extremely friendly fashion.

Her soft lips tightening, Leslie watched the conveyance move on toward a rawly new, unpainted frame building with a large sign—"Lodgings, Bed and Board." There the two women alighted and pushed their way through the throng to disappear into the entrance.

"Who were they?" Disapproval dripped icily from Leslie's voice. "Friends of yours, I take it."

Ryan laughed. "Friends to all. They call themselves Dolly and Belle." He looked amused as he watched the varying expressions flitting over her small face. "They are well-liked entertainers who made their name in London and came over here to make their fortune. They sing and dance quite well, and since entertainers are in great demand in Nassau, they will undoubtedly leave here rich. But they are just getting home now from a hard night—you've no reason to envy them."

"Envy them?" Leslie exploded. "Who would envy women like that? Why, they looked like . . . like . . ."

"Like a good many women you'll see here," Ryan supplied. "But Dolly and Belle are decent women. Here's our carriage."

Subdued, Leslie allowed him to help her up into the comfortably padded seat and then settled her full skirts around her gracefully. The sun was only now riding up the eastern sky, yet the square in front of them was bustling with action. Not only the food vendors shouting their wares, or the screaming, laughing children who darted about and climbed the teetering piles of cotton bales, but merchants who buttonholed customers and argued with energy and enthusiasm. She saw a fight break out and end almost immediately as men dragged the two apart. The noise was endless, the odors assailing her nostrils, rich and varied. Shops along the street had merchandise spilling out in front of their doors, barrels of gunpowder and crates of rifles, chained to prevent thievery.

Leslie's excitement rose as she realized suddenly that she was seeing the lifeblood of the Confederacy flowing in front of her eyes. These supplies brought from England to this small island were so desperately needed at home, and she was suddenly and profoundly grateful. They would be loaded on those gray ships floating on the blue bay, taken through the blazing jaws of the enemy by men like Ryan. She gave him a brilliant smile as he settled down beside her.

"I'm going to love Nassau," she said. "It's beautiful!" It was, what she could see of it. There was a dignity and charm completely English in the city: the squares so well kept, the public buildings graceful yet solid. She gestured toward a square in the distance. "I could believe I was in North Carolina. I would swear I've seen those very buildings in New Bern."

"And so you have," Ryan answered. "Those were built by English Loyalists who came here after your American Revolution. New Bern had been their beloved home until you drove them out." He laughed and took her hand, looking at her quizzically. "Now there was a war when your North and South worked together, fighting your present ally, England. But perhaps you don't like thinking of that now."

"That was entirely different!"

"Are wars different?" Ryan's deep voice was laconic. "Is one war better than another? It seems odd to me that former enemies can be friends in a fight between brothers."

Stung, Leslie looked at him mutinously. "You sound exactly like my father. He hates wars."

Ryan stiffened, dropping her hand. "I am not at all like your father. I hate wars, yes. But if my country were at war, I would defend it. And, if I had a daughter, I would take care of her."

Leslie's temper flared at the scorn she heard in his voice for her father. "Possibly. But since you have neither country nor daughter, that would be difficult to prove."

Ryan stared at her icily. "You, of all people, should know I pay my debts. Otherwise, you would be someone's kitchen maid in Tampa." He turned away, muscles twitching along his set jaw, and lapsed into silence.

His words cut Leslie like a knife. Her face burning, she pressed into her corner of the wide seat. She was no more than a duty to Ryan and she had been an utter fool to imagine that he had any real regard for her. Such harshness and scorn surely proved he didn't. She tried to fasten her attention on the passing scene, the gracious colonial residences, the churches in the distance with their soaring spires, and the lovely, shaded streets. The old horse was now trotting toward a large park and an imposing building that must be the Royal Victoria Hotel. She stiffened her quivering lips into a straight line and stared at her slippers, considering what Ryan was doing for her.

In that hotel she would be housed in luxury, given more clothes, fed, no doubt, on the finest of food. All *charity,* provided by this man who despised her father and would have gladly left her to become a kitchen maid had it not been that he felt indebted to her.

Pity, passion and duty. Of the three, she thought miserably, she resented the duty the most. As for the passion, it was no more than any virile man would feel when forced into close quarters with such a panting young female. He had been right in saying that she was acting like a slut that night, offering herself to him! And very likely he had been right also in saying that she had lived too long in the swamp, that she was like a young animal, wanting to mate. It was nothing more than instinct, no matter how her heart ached. How could she have been so stupid? Her thoughts ran on, drearily self-condemning.

Ryan glanced at her drooping head uneasily. As much as he disapproved of her father, he couldn't really disapprove of her loyalty to the man, no matter how undeserved. And he knew that much of his quick anger and sarcastic remarks were due to his own frustration. It was damned hard to maintain a cool and authoritarian attitude when he could hardly keep his hands off her! But there was no need to be cruel. He made his voice careless and cheerful.

"For Heaven's sake, Leslie, look up and tell me what you think of the Royal Victoria Hotel."

Leslie glanced up, surprised by the change in his tone and then fascinated by what she saw as the carriage drew to a stop. The gracious, English-style hostelry before them was huge. Four stories high, and surrounded on the lower three stories by three ten-foot-wide piazzas, which formed separate promenades more than a thousand feet long. And all of the promenades were alive with movement and action as the guests talked and laughed, walking in the fresh morning air. There were winding paths and many exotic, flowering shrubs on the lawn, along with shade trees.

"It seems crowded, Captain Fitzsimmons," she said stiffly. "There may be no accommodations left."

Ryan's thick brows quirked at her sudden formality. He laughed, jumping down to go around and assist her to alight. "Fortunately, I book a suite by the year. If someone is in it, they will be the ones looking for rooms." He reached up and clasped her waist, swinging her down playfully as if amusing a child. "Comfort at last, Leslie. You can forget the rigors of shipboard life and enjoy yourself." He reached in and picked up her bag of clothing. "Come along and meet some of my friends."

Leslie was amazed by his sudden change of mood, his apparent gaiety and good humor. She hated facing the crowd and meeting his friends now that she knew how he felt about her. And she wasn't at all sure she would know how to comport herself after so many years apart from polite society. Silent, she allowed Ryan to lead her up the path and the steps of the lowest piazza. There, a burst of welcome greeted him.

"Here's Fitz, back from the wars!"

"You lucky Irish pirate, you made it again!"

"Ryan! At last . . ." That was a woman's voice. Leslie's gaze went to her unerringly. Tall, darkly beautiful in emerald silk, the woman's black eyes danced with a diamondlike sparkle as she came forward. The crowd surged around them, giving Leslie the sensation of being buffeted by giants as the men clapped Ryan on the shoulders and the woman in green threw her arms around him and kissed his cheek. On the edge of the crowd an elderly man in a wheelchair slowly rolled toward them.

"And who is your lovely young friend, Ryan, who is in danger of being trampled by my wife?"

The woman in green flushed and stepped back as Ryan laughed. Extricating Leslie from the surrounding men, he turned to the elderly man and presented her. "This is my ward, Charles. Miss Leslie Gordon, the daughter of an old friend. I am to see her safely to Wilmington and her home on my next trip." He bent toward Leslie in a positively paternal manner and added: "This is Charles Rockwell, the manager of the Royal Victoria, Leslie, and . . ." His glance indicated the dark woman, "his charming wife, Wynne. And these buffoons are my rivals—Captains Thomas Farrell, George Latimer, Jeff Barclay . . ." He went on, but the names faded in the air as Leslie watched the dark eyes of Charles Rockwell's wife go from her to Ryan and back again, narrowed and considering. Perhaps, Leslie thought grimly, I am overburdened with instinct. How else would I know so surely that either this woman is Ryan's lover or would like to be? Was she the reason for his change of mood? He would have seen her standing on the piazza as they drove up.

"Please excuse us," Ryan was saying now. "I want to settle young Leslie and get back to my ship. I left several cotton brokers fingering my cargo."

Young Leslie. My ward. The daughter of an old friend. The lies slipped so easily from Ryan's tongue that Leslie decided she despised him. She pulled away from his arm and walked alone through the entrance of the hotel, thinking of Wynne's eyes and the way they had looked, traveling from Ryan to her. They had held a chill not even the balmy tropical air could dispel.

The large lobby was charmingly furnished with green wicker chairs and settees, their cushions covered with brightly patterned chintz. Potted palms sat around in a glassed-in court, and the walls of the lobby were hung with sporting prints of English country life. High ceilings and slowly revolving fans made the air pleasantly cool. Ryan received another hearty welcome from the desk clerk, John Rice, and then they were walking again, down a hall that led to the rear of the big building.

"You will like our quarters." Apparently still in a very good humor, Ryan strode along energetically. "We are on the ground floor with walled gardens outside our windows. A place for you to stroll during the long days here. And the bedrooms are as far as possible from the bar and dining room, so you will be able to sleep. This place is a madhouse every night with parties that go on until dawn."

He sounded, Leslie thought, more than a little pleased with the prospect. She didn't need to be told that his "ward" wouldn't be attending any mad parties.

Silent, biting her soft lower lip thoughtfully, she wandered through the suite of rooms at the end of the hall. Pure, isolated luxury. There were a lovely sitting room and two bedrooms, with a nice big bath between them. The furniture looked very comfortable, the decorating done in cream and green with touches of pale yellow. She thought about what it must cost a year to keep such a suite of rooms and felt more like an object of charity than ever.

Putting down her bag in the larger of the two bedrooms, Ryan insisted it would be hers, pointing out logically that the larger closet would be more suitable for a woman's wardrobe. He seemed, Leslie thought, a trifle distracted as he fumbled in his pockets and brought out what appeared to be an immense sum of money. He laid it on the top of an ornate chest of drawers.

"For your new clothes," he said, "and mind you don't skimp. I want you very well dressed. I'll ask Wynne Rockwell for the name of a good dressmaker."

"That will not be necessary," Leslie said stiffly. "I sew very well myself."

"But . . ."

"I prefer it," she snapped. "It will cost you less, and it will give me something to do while you—you attend wild parties. Now go back to your ship! Your 'ward' is settled." To her dismay, tears came sparkling to her eyes and she turned away to hide them.

Ryan's hands closed on her shoulders and turned her back to face him. In spite of everything she had been thinking, his touch thrilled through her as it always did, warming and weakening.

"You don't like this situation, do you?" His deep voice was infinitely gentle. "Neither do I, not the lies nor the pretense. But please believe me, it truly is necessary. If I wasn't so well known, I would have claimed you as a sister, which would have given you more freedom. But everyone knows I have no family."

"Why claim me as anything? Can't I just be myself?"

His hands tightened. "I brought you here, damn it! To my own suite! Without some legal relationship, everyone would instantly conclude that we're lovers. The decent women would shun you like the plague, and the men—good God, you'd receive a dozen insulting proposals every night. Every lightskirt is considered fair game by these woman-hungry men."

"Well . . ." Leslie faltered and looked away. "It's your decision." Ryan might be right, considering that suspicion in Wynne's face when they met, and that glint of speculation in another set of eyes—the blue ones belonging to that rakish-looking Thomas Farrell. But right now she was too distracted to think. Ryan's warm hands were almost caressing her through the thin shawl. She tried to pull away and they tightened again.

"Wait," Ryan said huskily. "I want to be sure you understand . . . I'm thinking of you, Leslie."

The tone of his voice made her suddenly more aware of his lean, strong body, the faint drift of his alluringly male scent. She could hear the change in his breathing, sense the growing tension in his muscles. He was as helpless as she was against the subtle magnetism between them. She looked up at him with intense blue eyes.

"I do understand. But I don't think anyone will believe you. I don't look like a child."

Suddenly conscious of his own feelings, Ryan dropped his hands hastily and stepped back. "Oh, but you do, Leslie," he said with an attempt at carelessness. "There's a lot in outward appearances. I took care to buy gowns for you that reflected youth. That's half the battle, and your acting ability will take care of the rest."

Her head came up, startled. Then it hadn't been a lack of judgment on his part—he had meant to buy those juvenile styles. He'd been planning this from the beginning.

"In that case," she said sharply, "you should have told me your plans earlier—before I used my sewing skills to alter the illusion you wanted."

"What do you mean?" He stared at her closely. "Is that why you're wearing a shawl on such a warm day?" His long arm shot out and captured her, dragging her closer. "What have you done, you minx?"

Leslie struggled, wrapping her shawl tighter, trying to escape his now enveloping arms. She gasped as he circled her waist and jerked her against him. "Let me go! I've done nothing wrong. . . ." Straining away from the iron grip around her waist only forced her lower body tighter against his muscular thighs. Helpless to stop the eager response of her body, she tried to twist away. "Please, Ryan . . ."

"Hold still! I want to see what you've done." His hand clutched the knotted fringe across her bosom and ripped it apart, jerked the shawl from her shoulders and let it drop to the floor. Then he simply stared.

Leslie shut her eyes to close out the sight of his face. His rough handling had torn loose the bow of gold ribbon and her struggles had done the rest. She could feel the drift of cool air on her bare breasts, feel the rosy tips tighten just at the thought of his gaze.

"Perhaps," Ryan said hoarsely, "I've misjudged you." There was a rock-hard immobility in the long body bending over her, a rough catch in his voice. "A woman who could plan this couldn't be altogether innocent . . . look at me, Leslie."

She shook her head, squeezing her eyes tighter shut, desperately fighting a wild desire to melt against him. "Just let me go. . . . I can fix it," she said faintly.

"*Look* at me, damn it!"

Helplessly, she complied, and the deep blue locked

with stormy darkness, sharing a knowledge as old as Adam and Eve. The current between them sang triumphantly. It had never been stronger.

"You know what you want," Ryan muttered. "You're no frightened virgin." His hand lifted to caress her breasts, shaping them slowly with his rough palm, his long fingers kneading. His hot eyes watched her mouth part in a soundless gasp, the tip of her tongue moisten suddenly dry lips. "What a fool I've been," he whispered, and covered the parted lips with his own, his tongue sliding within as if by sovereign right, searching the velvety softness possessively.

This kiss told Leslie that the fire between them had at last flamed out of control. Her tension melted in the flames as his tongue touched and stroked each tender hollow, thrust and withdrew, asking for surrender.

"Leslie . . ."

Only a muffled whisper, yet with a quick-drawn breath she gave in completely, pressing a breast tighter into his hand, swaying, moving sinuously against his hard heat, instinctively fitting her body to his.

A deep sound rumbled in Ryan's chest, half passion, half a surrender of his own. His hands moved, grasping the airy puff sleeves, the gaping neckline, peeling the lace bodice down to her waist. He picked her up, lifted her high, higher, until his face was buried between her breasts. Panting, Leslie grasped his hair and twisted in his arms, knowing without thought what she wanted. . . . She shuddered, stifling a cry as his hot mouth closed over her fiercely.

"Oh, Ryan . . ." Her trembling hands smoothed his hair, pressing him closer, her breasts on fire from his kisses. Leaning over him, she was limp with wanting. "Please, Ryan . . ."

His arms shifted, cradling her against his chest, her head dropping to his shoulder, her face pressing into his neck. They sank together into the softness of the bed, touching, kissing, struggling with their clothes in mindless haste. Awkward and desperate, they helped each other until finally they lay naked together, welded by the magnetism and murmuring incoherently.

"My love . . . my little love . . ."

"Darling Ryan, kiss me again . . . oh-h-h, yes, yes . . . there and there. . . ."

There was no rational thought, nothing but the driving force that had been denied too long. Ryan's skill took over as if his hands and his starving body knew exactly how to reach the utmost summit of what they both wanted. He shaped her slender body to his with strong, urgent caresses, covered her with kisses, coaxed and petted her into a fluid heat that had her writhing and moaning beneath him. Only then did he cover her, arch his powerful back and take her with a deep, inarticulate sound of primitive male triumph rising in his throat—a sound that cut off in midair as if sliced by a knife. He lay still, staring down into her eyes with a look of profound shock.

Leslie had cried out half in pain and half in joy. The hard possession was like a thunderbolt, changing everything she knew and making her somehow part of him. For a moment she gazed back at him in total surprise, panting, amazed and half frightened. Then Ryan shook his head hopelessly and moved again, slowly burrowing deeper, his body sliding tightly against the apex of her thighs. At that moment, Leslie's deeply sensual nature taught her surely and simply how to please them both. Clasping her strong, slender arms around him, she flowed into a sinuous rhythm all her own, softly demanding, incredibly sensuous, a rhythm that seemed to stroke every part of him, urging him on and begging for completion.

Lost in wonder, Ryan let her have her way, gentled

into her coaxing rhythm. He was fascinated by the languorous fire in her half-closed eyes, the warm sexuality of her curved mouth. She was breathing evenly, deeply, matching the smooth, silky movement of her caressing body. Watching, Ryan felt an intensity of emotion that he had never reached before, a deepness of desire that he had never imagined, a unity with this woman that soared past possibility. A dream, he thought hazily, a dream of how it should be . . . soaring higher and higher. Then all imagination, all wonder, was gone, rocketing away in a shower of bursting stars, a tremendous explosion of bliss that sprang from their throbbing loins and rushed through them in a tingling flood of glory, drumbeats that only gradually receded, leaving them limp and panting, clinging to each other.

Luxuriously contented, basking in the warm afterglow of lovemaking, Leslie opened her eyes to the sight of Ryan's face on the pillow beside her. The bronzed skin gleamed with a light film of perspiration, elflocks of bright chestnut hair tumbled on his forehead. His hazel eyes were clear again, shadowed only by his thick lashes, but in their depths was a look that worried her. A disturbing flicker of regret. Then he sighed and rolled over, shutting his eyes.

Ryan told himself that he should have known better than to touch her. He had been so close, so *close* to taking her before. He was too aware that he had let his passion convince him this time that it would be all right—that she must have had experience. He had known from the first that she was innocent, and he had *chosen* to ignore it.

Behind his closed lids he could see again the scene in the Green Swamp. The morning mist wreathing and drifting around her delicate, ethereal white body. She

had been half-starved then, but so brave, so stubbornly determined. An abandoned child whom he had
rescued and fed. And then seduced. God! Shame
twisted him. He had wanted her from the beginning
—wanted her more than any other woman he had
ever met. But that was no excuse. There was no
excuse.

"I will marry you," he said, his voice harsh with
self-disgust. "I won't desert you like your damned
father did. When we arrive in Wilmington we will wed
in the presence of your friends, so that they will
understand you are under my protection. And I'll find
you a home. Until the war is over, I expect you'd be
happier there in familiar surroundings."

Halfway through this terse speech, Leslie's eyes had
widened and then dropped away from his stern profile.
She lay quietly, listening to the strained guilt in his deep
voice. Inside, her sinking heart thumped heavily, blood
roared in her ears. For her, their lovemaking had
changed the whole world. She had felt filled with love
and a glorious happiness. But nothing had changed
for Ryan. Still only pity, passion and duty. A very
strong sense of duty now, filled with guilt. He would
make his sacrifice and marry her. *And he would hate
it.*

Silent and trembling, she slid from the bed on the
opposite side and stood, shaking back her loosened
hair, hearing the pins drop and scatter around her bare
feet, feeling the heavy hair slide down to cover her
back. There was only one honorable thing to do, and
she had better do it quickly before her courage failed.
Taking a deep breath, she looked back at his tense face
and forced a smile.

"Surely, Ryan, you know it's customary to ask a
woman if she wishes to marry. I—admire you greatly,

but . . ." She was searching frantically for a reason he would believe. "But while I am honored by your willingness to marry me, my first duty is to my father. Until I find him, or learn what has happened to him, I—I wouldn't tie myself down to anyone else." Glancing at him, she wondered painfully if the flicker in his eyes was surprise or relief.

"Ridiculous," Ryan growled. "You owe the man nothing." Sitting up, he eyed Leslie with amazed doubt. He had expected anything but a refusal. To be truthful, he had expected a loving assault, her soft arms around him, her kisses, her feminine excitement at the prospect of marriage. And, well, not gratitude exactly, but at least a wholehearted appreciation of his honorable intention. Now his eyes roved jealously over her nude body. She was so damnably beautiful, so unexpectedly passionate, so woefully ignorant on this island of reckless men. Rising, he strode around the bed and gathered her into his arms, his hold tightening as he felt resistance.

"Forget your father," he said gruffly. "You belong to me, now."

Tight against his bare, magnificently male body, Leslie knew she'd like nothing better than to be his—if he were hers. But she was miserably sure that he belonged only to himself and the sea. Oh, he wanted her, and she sensed that he always would. She didn't understand the force between them, but she knew it was there for them both. And it was very strong. But she wondered if it would be strong enough to carry her through the loneliness of being the one who loved and waited, and strong enough to make up to him for the feeling of being trapped and chained. She doubted it.

Sighing, she wound her arms around him, her slim fingers shaping and caressing the thick ropes of muscle in his broad back, reveling in his power and strength. Leaning her cheek on his chest, she let the curtain of her hair hide her damp eyes.

"I do love you," she said lightly, knowing it was not a light thing, knowing it was true and would always be true. "But I'm not yours, Ryan. I belong to myself. And I do not wish to marry."

Chapter Six

"YOU'LL HIRE A DRESSMAKER," RYAN SAID FIRMLY, "AND a good one. Ask John Rice at the desk. He has all that kind of information." Ryan was dressing—hastily, since he had remembered the cotton brokers waiting at the ship—and giving Leslie orders at the same time. Once over the shock of her refusal to marry him, he had regained his usual confidence. It was clear that he thought she would change her mind, once she reconsidered it. Leslie thought that he already sounded like a husband.

"Since I will be gone until dinner," Ryan continued, "you may as well begin by finding one today. And remember, the gowns must be of fine materials and in fashion."

Leslie nodded numbly. She knew his pride demanded it, but she hoped the clothes wouldn't cost too much. *Her* pride demanded that sooner or later she must pay him back, and she didn't want to starve doing it. There was, however, one thing to clear up.

"I will not order juvenile clothes," she said stubbornly, "and I will act my age. I'm not fifteen—I'm twenty."

His brows rose. "Nothing daring, then. Leave that to the jaded women who will be watching you." He came back to the bed and cupped her face in his hands, his eyes softening. "I know I should regret this," he added slowly, "but it's very difficult. I blame myself. . . ."

"There is no need for that, Ryan. If there was a fault, it was as much mine as yours." She accepted his light kiss and forced a smile as he left.

After she was sure he had gone, Leslie lay back on the pillow that still had his scent, knowing that in some mysterious way she was a thousand years older and much wiser than she had ever wanted to be. When Ryan had given way to his desire she had been sure that he loved her as she loved him, and he would want her with him forever. She had been wrong. What he wanted was to ease his conscience by marrying her, then tuck her into a house on shore and get on with his life. Oh, he would visit, undoubtedly. She might see him every four or five months if his cargo suited the port. He might stay for a week before he left and she was alone again. It was easy to visualize her life—there had been plenty of the wives of seafaring men in Wilmington. No one had ever envied them.

But it would be so easy to say yes. He might come to love her later. . . .

She considered it, concluding grimly that Ryan would be as likely to come to love her later as a prisoner would be to love his shackles after a year or two of wearing them. "I will belong to no woman," he

95

had said, and she was sure now that he had meant it. He would never share his life with her, and she couldn't settle for less.

Later, bathing in the huge, claw-footed tub with clouds of fragrant steam rising around her, the fine-milled French soap soft on her skin, Leslie's pride returned and brought her courage along. She had been strengthened by the years of enduring the hardships and real dangers of the swamp, and she was much more self-sufficient and proud than other young women. Beneath her fragile and feminine exterior was a steely determination to make the best of things and do it in her own way. She wouldn't pine away and mope over unrequited love. Climbing out of the tub, she toweled her newly awakened body vigorously until her skin was pink and glowing. Life, she decided, was for living. And everyone had to do that for themselves. She would make a life of her own.

Dressed in the blue gown, which even with its new fitting was considerably less daring than the lace had proved to be, Leslie took the money Ryan had left and set off. Stopping at the desk in the lobby to ask Mr. Rice for directions, she discovered that there was a very good dressmaker who lived only a few blocks away. Anxious to please Captain Fitzsimmons's ward, the clerk offered to send for a carriage.

Leslie smiled. "I shall walk, thank you. After days confined on the ship I will enjoy it."

Rice was horrified. "But the sun, Miss Gordon! If you insist on walking, you must take one of our parasols. We keep a number of them for guests who wish to stroll in our gardens."

Amused, Leslie left him beneath a pink lace parasol that cast a becoming glow on her ivory skin and shadowed her eyes into deep blue. Admiring glances followed her as she stepped out on the piazza, noting the tiny waist and provocatively curved bosom heretofore hidden by the modest shawl. Sitting in a swing with one of her cronies, Wynne Rockwell nudged her friend.

"Ryan's *ward,* Emily. Now do you believe me? Half the men in Nassau would line up to be named guardian of that bit of fluff, if only for a night or two. Ryan must be mad, to bring his latest bedmate here under such a pretense."

Her sibilant whisper came plainly to Leslie's sharp ears, and so did the friend's rejoinder.

"Now, Wynne, you aren't sure of that. Stop showing your claws. You'll have Ryan back, I assure you."

It was a double jolt, to both heart and pride. Pale, Leslie continued across the piazza and down the steps, pretending not to have heard. With her new knowledge of the intimacy of lovemaking, she couldn't bear the thought of Ryan with Wynne . . . or anyone else, for that matter. She told herself firmly that it had happened before she met him, and that it was inevitable that he would have had someone. Likely many someones. It helped very little. And it didn't help, either, to reflect that Wynne's remarks had been heard by others, including that reckless-looking Tom Farrell. His quick glance at her had been burning with interest. She could imagine what the listening men would think of her character, and at first she resented it deeply. Then, halfway to the dressmaker's shop, it occurred to her that their conclusions would be fair. She *was* Ryan's latest bedmate.

Shaken, she went on more slowly, thinking. For the first time she realized exactly what she had done. In this Victorian age, she was now what everyone called a fallen woman. And a stupid fallen woman, at that, since she had refused her seducer's offer of marriage. A moment later, her chin was in the air. They could think what they liked. She would follow her heart and her own particular sense of honor, and—and be damned to them! Another moment, and suddenly she was smiling defiantly, twirling the parasol, her feet lighter on the cobbled street. There was a very definite sense of freedom in being beyond the pale of respectability. There was nothing more to lose. If life was, as she suspected, for living to the fullest extent, she had the perfect opportunity. It might just be that the next three weeks would be the high point of her life.

Looking around, Leslie thought she could have never found a better place for such a purpose. The very air of this tropical island reflected the sense of freedom she felt. The streets were alive with color. Purple bougain-villea, pink and red hibiscus, sweetly scented flowers like gardenias and jasmine bloomed everywhere. Huge trees cast welcome pools of shade on the sparkling clean streets and the breeze was warm and caressing. There was nothing prim or disapproving about Nassau. Perhaps she would fit in very well.

Leslie was back at the hotel shortly after noon, with a bundle beneath one arm and a wonderful feeling of accomplishment. Mrs. Benneville, the dressmaker, had had a gown in stock that fitted Leslie exactly and it was now in the bundle. A lovely turquoise silk, with a belled skirt and the new, longer-length basque bodice that daringly outlined the beginning curve of slender hips. It also featured a canezou underblouse that allowed a dainty white frill to accent the scoop neckline and had huge, lace-encircled sleeves ending in tight wristlets to make small hands look delicate. Trying it on, Leslie had thought she had never seen anything so striking as those lacy sleeves bursting from the elbow-length pagoda sleeves of dark turquoise. She had ordered two more of the canezous, several morning gowns, an afternoon gown in leaf green, a brown tailored suit and an evening gown in white mousseline. The evening gown was to be made in the Empress Eugenie style, high-waisted and off the shoulder, with the wisp of tulle that circled shoulders and bosom caught in the middle by a flower. She smiled as she thought of what Ryan would say when he saw it.

Mrs. Benneville had thought a rose would be best, but Leslie, remembering Ryan's name for her, had chosen a tawny gold lily, a fragile bloom fashioned of stiffened silk.

The portly and pleasant Mrs. Benneville had given in gracefully. "It matches your hair," she had conceded, "and it will be different. Mostly, the ladies choose roses."

Leslie had been silent, thinking that the wearer would be different, too. And no longer a lady, by Victorian standards.

Now, hanging up the new gown in her closet, she worried about how much she had spent. Ryan wouldn't care—he had left twice that. But the money would be hard for her to replace, even though there were things in the Wilmington house she could sell. She must keep account of the money she spent and pay it back. If only she could find something to do here, some way to earn the funds needed.

At least she had thought how to repair the white lace. Getting out her sewing kit, she sat down to do it. The gown had more rips than she remembered. Due, she thought, to the haste in which it had been removed. Remembering that moment sent warmth spreading through her. She knew she could never have imagined the ecstasy they had created together, the pure pleasure of their joined bodies . . . Ryan's hands and mouth. . . . Oh, perhaps she should be both ashamed and regretful at being a fallen woman, but at this moment it seemed a most desirable state.

When she finished sewing the gown was both fashionable and proper, the neckline tightened and filled in with a rippling collar that she had made from the long sleeves she had discarded. In late afternoon she put it on and swept newly washed hair into a becoming topknot of deep waves and a few dangling curls. Ryan, she decided, would have no reason to be ashamed of his companion.

Dignified and serious in a dark blue suit with knee-length coat, Ryan appeared a half hour later. Opening the door for him, Leslie thought him more handsome than ever. A pristine white shirt and flowing maroon tie set off his bronzed skin; the suit was tailored precisely to his long legs and powerful shoulders. She waited expectantly for his arms to go around her.

"Will that neckline stay up?" The bronzed face still serious, the deep voice doubtful. Leslie laughed.

"It will, more's the pity." Her blue eyes invited him to laugh with her, but the serious look remained.

"I want no scandal about my future wife, Leslie. Not even with me as the guilty party. I've taken another room for myself in the bachelor wing. That should silence the gossips."

Leslie sighed. She wanted very much to tell him that the hotel gossips were not worth his concern. Bored and jaded they must be, to spend their time in idle, vicious conjecture about others. Why did he care so much? It seemed impossible that her ardent lover of the morning could be so stuffily conventional now. Had she been daring enough she would have also reminded him that she wasn't his future wife—only his present bed-mate. But none of it was important enough for an argument. She swept to the door, a small and resolute figure rising from the bouffant circle of white lace, her tawny gold head high and her pink-cheeked face sparkling with humor.

"I shall be very proper, Captain Fitzsimmons, while in your company. Now, will you take me to dine? Or do you intend to starve me into submission?"

Ryan laughed unwillingly and took her arm. "Why do I feel as if I'm trying to tame one of those panthers in your swamp? Life here has rules, darling. It's best to obey them."

Leslie smiled and was silent. Another stuffy remark, but that "darling" made up for it.

The Royal Victoria was transformed in its full, evening festivity. The huge lobby was overflowing, the bright lights no more glittering than the ladies in their silks and satins, the men in dress uniforms or full, formal regalia. On one side the double doors to the dining room stood open, and on the other a screen had been removed to expose a lounge. Inside was a long, shining mahogany bar and a set of gambling tables. Both men and women were grouped around the bar or watching the players, and a constant hum of conversation was punctuated by laughter and small shrieks of excitement.

Towering over most of the crowd, Ryan was stopped repeatedly as they made their way through the throng. Invariably, he introduced Leslie as "my ward, Miss Leslie Gordon." Leslie was aware of the disbelieving glances from many of the women. Amused, she smiled modestly and said very little. Truthfully, she was glad she wasn't expected to compete with them for attention. There was an amazing array of jewelry and outrageous fashion. She was sure that half the fortunes of the Southern aristocracy now dangled from the necks

101

and ears, the dimpled arms of Georgian and Carolinian matrons, most of whom were middle-aged or elderly. Even tiaras, encrusted with diamonds, were worn on masses of silver hair. And the gowns! The ladies were fit for an appearance at court. . . .

"Where have they all come from?" she whispered as she and Ryan gained the dining room and a small space to themselves. "Surely the hotel cannot hold them all."

Ryan laughed. "Half the town dines here for the entertainment after dinner. Charles Rockwell knows how to please his guests. There's an orchestra for dancing and often novelty acts—singers and dancers. Occasionally there's a small stage company from London. Then, of course, there are the townsmen—merchants and buyers. They come to bargain with us, though they are seldom successful."

" 'Us'? You mean the blockade runners?"

Ryan nodded. "Of course. We're their only link to their biggest market—the Confederacy."

"And why aren't they successful?"

"We prefer to bargain where we can see the goods," Ryan said. "Here, we huddle together and present a united front against them. . . ." He grinned down at her. "Deals made over a bottle tend to be lopsided in their favor."

He had been leading her through the small tables that filled the huge room, toward a group of men seated together near the east wall. Tables had been pushed together to make places for a dozen or so, with only two seats left. Charles Rockwell and Wynne presided, one at each end, and as Leslie glanced along the table she realized this was the "huddle." Tanned faces and the look of seafaring men identified them all. She recognized the three young captains that she had met on arrival in Nassau.

Pulling out one of the empty chairs for Leslie, Ryan glanced at Rockwell. "Still the same attention to detail, Charles. You remembered to make room for my ward."

"How could we forget?" Wynne Rockwell's voice was sugar over poorly concealed acid. "It isn't often one of our daring captains is quite daring enough to claim he stands *in loco parentis* to such a charming female."

Gathering her skirts, squeezing into the small space, Leslie wondered just how far Wynne would go with her sarcasm. Settling herself, she felt Ryan slide in beside her and heard him laugh.

"It may be the closest I'll ever be to being a parent, Wynne. I intend to make the most of it."

"I'm certain you already have," Wynne said, this time with more acid than sugar and more meaning than the words held. Her black eyes raked Leslie's face and moved away, dissatisfied. "How do you feel, Miss Gordon, about having such a handsome and attentive . . . ah, guardian?"

Leslie looked toward her in unwilling admiration. Wynne was gowned in carmine red silk that fit like a glove over her voluptuous figure and made her olive skin glow with color. She would have been extraordinarily beautiful if it hadn't been for that venomous expression.

"I—beg your pardon, ma'am. Were you speaking to me?" She made her voice soft and breathless.

Wynne frowned, irritated. "Naturally. I asked you how you felt about having Captain Fitzsimmons for a guardian."

"Very fortunate, ma'am," Leslie replied promptly, and subsided into silence. She could almost feel the relief flowing through the long, lean body beside her.

Ryan had been afraid of how she would react to Wynne's venom, but there was more than one way of taking the wind out of a gossip's sails. Wynne wouldn't question such a stupidly inattentive young woman again.

There was a decided disadvantage to having dinner with a group of sea captains, handsome though they were. The talk was technical and boring, since Leslie knew nothing of steam engines and very little of sails. Speed seemed the primary object now that the Yankees were building faster ships. Leslie addressed herself to an excellent dinner of roast lamb and ignored the conversation until it veered to the price of cotton and how successful the runners had been during the past two months. They had brought in a staggering fourteen thousand bales of cotton worth nearly three million dollars, and all of them seemed confident they could continue doing as well in the future—unless the new Yankee cruisers were much faster than the others.

"That's one problem," George Latimer said, "but we may have another. I heard there's a case of yellow fever in one of the rooming houses down by the docks. Most of our crews are billeted there."

There was a moment of silence as faces turned toward Latimer. Yellow fever was one of the least understood and most feared of tropical diseases, since it was frequently fatal and no known medicine cured it. Then Rockwell shook his head.

"The weather is too dry for an epidemic."

Relief swept the table, heads nodded. Yellow fever came with damp weather, though no one knew why. It was believed it sprang from the miasma of swamps, like malaria, floating through the air on the sickly odors.

Later, when the orchestra came in and began tuning up for the dance to follow, Ryan rose and escorted Leslie from the room. Wynne smiled sweetly as Leslie made her adieus, and then her black eyes went to Ryan with a hint of coquetry.

"You will return, won't you, Ryan? Your favorites, Dolly and Belle, are to sing tonight."

"I'll be here for a time," Ryan said casually. "I have an appointment in town later."

Leslie reflected that the role of a ward had decided disadvantages also. In the hall leading to the door of the suite, she gave Ryan a disappointed glance.

"I would have enjoyed listening to your Dolly and Belle."

Ryan smiled, his hand sliding down to enclose her fingers in his wide palm. "Some other night. Neither of them sing as well as you. And they live down there by the docks. Since no one really knows how yellow fever spreads, you'll be safer in the suite. I wouldn't want to lose you."

Leslie drew out her door key, feeling as if she were unlocking her own cell in a luxurious prison. It had been years since she had been to a party or listened to music that she hadn't made herself. Besides, she was sure Ryan was using the threat as an excuse. And—an appointment in town? She reminded herself that she had no right to question him.

"If you lose me," she said dryly, "it won't be from yellow fever. I had it years ago." She opened the door and slipped in, closing it partially, turning to peer out at him. "Good night, Captain Fitzsimmons. Enjoy your evening." Shutting out the sight of his handsome, surprised face, she closed the door and locked it.

Hours later, in spite of the long, eventful day and the lack of sleep the night before, Leslie lay wide awake in the big, lonely bed. Images of Ryan and Wynne kept waltzing through her imagination, accompanied by the faint, distant strains of music that she could barely hear from the other side of the hotel. They would make a handsome couple, she thought bleakly, both so tall and self-possessed, so sure of themselves. And Ryan in that beautiful blue suit, Wynne in her carmine red, with the full skirt sweeping around her long legs. She tried not to think of Wynne's friend, saying: "You'll have Ryan back. . . ."

She sat up, startled, stifling a gasp as the wide window that led to the gardens slid slowly upward and admitted a tall, agile figure whose long legs made nothing of the step inside. Straightening, Ryan shrugged off his coat and crossed quickly to the bed, sitting down beside her and gathering her into his arms. Leslie sighed softly and leaned into his warmth, breathing in his scent, caressing the smooth, hard flesh beneath the thin shirt. Her head dropped naturally into its place on his wide shoulder. After her lonely, painful thoughts, this was heavenly.

Ryan's hands were kneading the supple muscles of her back, slipping around to enclose her breasts hungrily. Leslie could hear his heightened breathing, feel the heavy beat of his heart increasing. A wild desire to be closer yet made her pull away, grasp the lacy shift she wore and take it off in one smooth motion. Naked, she curled into his lap and arms, reaching to pull his head down to her seeking mouth.

Moments later, Ryan's clothes were on the floor, and he was pressing her back into the softness of the bed, his big hands savagely possessive, his mouth open and hot on the ivory satin of her belly. His strong, dark face moved to her quivering breasts, then her panting mouth as he flung himself on her, crushing her with his weight. With a deep, erotic sound he entered her, fully and completely, as if nothing less could fill some primitive need. He lay still, his face in her neck, his hands buried in the mass of tawny hair.

"I couldn't stay away," he whispered hoarsely, "knowing you were here . . . knowing I could have you. . . ." His hard buttocks contracted, tightening, making sure of his possession, pinning her down. Breathless, Leslie stroked his back with trembling fingers, wriggled helplessly.

"Let me move," she gasped, "let me breathe . . . give me the freedom to love you. . . ."

Ryan's held breath gusted out in a long sigh, his weight eased as he raised his head and looked down at the pale oval of her face. He moved his hands, cupping her cheeks, his thumbs caressing the corners of her sensuously curved mouth. "Then love me," he whispered, choked, "love me. . . ."

Sliding together, their bodies swung freely into the age-old rhythm of mating. Their eyes closed as they found the unbelievable unity, the matching desires and perfect attunement. They breathed together, hearts pounding in unison as they neared the impossible peak, their cries blended as the peak was reached and reached and reached again in a series of delicious aftershocks. Tears of ecstasy ran from beneath Leslie's golden lashes when they finally lay still, clutching each other. Ryan kissed her tears away, stroking her gently, calming the still passionately trembling young body.

"I was going to wait," he said softly, "but I couldn't. We'll not wait for that wedding in Wilmington. We'll marry here."

Leslie sighed soundlessly. It would be so easy just to give in. She pushed the thought away and wriggled out of his arms and out of the bed, answers running through her mind, none of which were good enough. It was impossible to ask it—to demand that he love her completely, that he share his whole life with a woman. At this moment he might agree, just to satisfy her wishes. But unless he wanted the closeness himself it would never be right. Despairing, she went back to the reason she had first given him, even though she thought he would undoubtedly resent it.

"My father first, Ryan."

Ryan gave a grunt of disgust and swung from the bed, grabbing up his discarded clothes and beginning to dress, his rugged face impassive in the dimness. Then he surprised her.

"All right. If it means that much to you, I'll help. If we don't find news in Wilmington, I'll ask Spence Burdette to find him for you."

Leslie gasped. "You can't! Spence is in the service— he would turn him in. . . ." She stopped, miserably aware that now Ryan would be certain that Harry Gordon was a deserter. "In any event," she added weakly, "what could Spence do? How could a naval officer do anything? He's never on land long enough."

"Burdette has connections," Ryan said tersely, "trust me." Fully dressed, if a trifle disheveled, he came to put his arms around her, his shadowed eyes serious. "If that's what it takes, then one way or another, I'll find out what happened to your father." He kissed her, a kiss like a promise, and turned to the window.

Leslie followed him, watching as he dropped soundlessly to the ground, crossed the patch of moonlight and leaped upward, catching the top of the garden wall. Then he was over and gone.

The air from the open window was cool on her heated skin; the scent of night-blooming jasmine drifted faintly from the garden. It was late; only a few lights glowed over the small city, though she could see the silhouettes of church spires and tall trees against the lighter sky. Nassau. She would remember this place forever. Maybe, some far future day, she would come here again. She would walk, she thought, through the flower-laden streets, breathe in the soft air and sigh, remembering the short weeks of happiness she had shared with the dashing captain of a blockade runner . . . a man she had loved too much to marry.

Chapter Seven

BY THE END OF A WEEK, LESLIE AND RYAN HAD WORKED
out their public roles of ward and guardian, never
showing by word or glance that Ryan's regard for her
was more than paternal; that Leslie's affection for him
was more intimate than proper. Leslie had realized, to
her surprise, that Ryan had been right. In spite of
Wynne's gossip, she had been gradually accepted by
the staid matrons and the wives of Navy officers who
lived in the hotel, and she had seen the way the
demimondaines—who had their own suites or shared
them with a benefactor—were quietly ignored. The
"ladies of the night" wore gorgeous Parisian clothes
and many jewels, their faces were expertly enameled
and colored, but they were not accepted. She often
wondered why it mattered, but it was plain that it
mattered to them. They laughed too hard, flaunted

their clothes and jewels, but their eyes were restless and dissatisfied.

In addition, Ryan had also been right about the men. Leslie was sure of that, for one of them still wasn't convinced of her purity. Tom Farrell was in pursuit of her, in spite of Ryan's icy disapproval. Tom took every opportunity to be near her, to touch her hand or arm in a caressing manner, and he was full of whispered compliments that bordered on audacity. Leslie steadfastly refused his invitations to ride or walk together and hoped he would do as the other young captains did—seek out a more accessible woman. She had discovered that, even among some of the supposedly honorable women, there were furtive affairs, and that from time to time there were surreptitious duels between the cuckolded husbands and the reckless lovers, but they were mostly a sop to so-called honor, resulting in a few wounds but no deaths.

"It's the atmosphere," Ryan told her. "War, money and excitement. Men hungry for women, and women bored by their husbands, wanting a fling. And, over all, a sense that it may soon end and their chances gone."

They were riding in Gabe's carriage on a breezy afternoon, a very proper ride. Captain Fitzsimmons was taking his ward on a tour of the city and then to Government House to tea. They and the other runner captains had been especially invited to attend in what Ryan told her was a purely businesslike gesture. The governor was well aware of the prosperity brought to the island by their ships.

They sat well apart on the wide seat and conversed in low tones, their words made inaudible even to Gabe by the loud clip-clop of the old horse's hooves, the squeaks and rattles of the carriage. Leslie glanced at Ryan from beneath the sun hat he insisted on her wearing.

"Wynne Rockwell doesn't bother to hide her affairs

from others," she said daringly, "even her affair with you. I heard one of her friends tell her that she'd soon have you back."

Ryan gave her an astonished frown. "I wouldn't have had an affair with Wynne even if I found her attractive," he said stiffly. "Charles is my friend. If Wynne put that news out, it was sheer fabrication."

"Or hopeful anticipation," Leslie said, feeling much better. "I'm glad to hear it. I feel sorry for Mr. Rockwell; he seems both kind and intelligent."

"Charles doesn't mind Wynne's affairs," Ryan said wryly. "She's more his nurse than his wife, and she never neglects him. He's an extremely wealthy man and Wynne is his second wife. When he dies, most of his fortune goes to his children, and Wynne knows it. Believe me, if Charles feels the least bit ill, Wynne's latest lover will be the one neglected."

Leslie grimaced. "I begin to see why you never wanted to marry."

"I do now," Ryan pointed out instantly, "and, since I have promised to help you find your father, I fail to see why you want to wait longer."

Fortunately for Leslie, they were drawing up to the entrance to Government House, an imposing white-limestone two-story structure with wide porches and high frontal steps on George Street, up above the harbor. She took it as an excuse not to answer. The subject of marriage had now become an almost constant argument between them. Ryan, she had decided, was stubbornly intent on doing the honorable thing. She had caught herself wishing occasionally that either she hadn't been a virgin or that he hadn't noticed. It seemed deplorable to be so sought after only to ease a man's conscience.

Inside, joining the governor, Sir Wickham Beane and his wife, Lady Beane, and the other guests in an immense drawing room, Ryan presented his ward, Miss Leslie Gordon, with obvious pride. Leslie was wearing the turquoise silk and white canezou with its voluminous ruffled sleeves and looked beautiful and shy. As a matter of fact, she felt shy, still uncertain of exactly how to give the tiny, bobbing curtsy due her exalted hosts. She managed, her dozen taffeta petticoats whispering encouragement, and then smiled brilliantly with relief.

After that, the rest seemed easy. She was seated and given a cup of tea, then plied with tiny sandwiches and remarks about the weather. Ryan had told her that it was considered rude to talk of anything controversial, such as the war, or of anything unpleasant, such as the reported second case of yellow fever on Bay Street. All that was left, after careful mental elimination, was weather, fashion and flowers. Simple enough, Leslie thought, and chattered away cheerfully with the other guests. Still, she couldn't help noticing across the room a very bored Tom Farrell, a neglected teacup in one hand, watching her with brooding blue eyes. She suspected that handsome Tom was not accustomed to having a girl he fancied denied to him.

A half hour later, the conversation turned to ladylike talents. The governor's daughter, Miss Annabelle Beane, had appeared to entertain the assemblage on the piano with a selection of English folk songs and ballads. She had no sooner finished the first tune and been politely applauded when Leslie heard Ryan remark smugly that his ward had a lovely singing voice and was also fond of ballads. Naturally, Lady Beane immediately suggested that Leslie be heard, and Ryan promptly agreed.

Darting a disgusted glance from beneath golden lashes at Ryan, and a gracious smile toward Lady Beane, Leslie joined Annabelle at the piano. Thin, nervous but excessively polite, Annabelle asked in a soft, breathless voice what Leslie's choice would be. "Since your name is Gordon," she added timidly, "perhaps a song from Scotland?"

"Since your name is Annabelle," Leslie said, smiling, "I choose 'Annie Laurie.'"

Annabelle turned red with pleasure. "Oh, good! I love that song. . . ." Her thin fingers unerringly played the introduction.

Leslie took a deep breath and faced the assemblage. If she were to sing, she would *sing*. In this large room and with so many present she knew any attempt to hold back would leave some of them straining to hear. From the opening line she let her voice roll out, each note round and clear, dropping like pearls into the attentive silence.

> *Maxwellton's braes are bonnie,*
> *where early fa's the dew . . .*
> *And t'was there that Annie Laurie,*
> *ga'e me her promise true. . . .*

She was furious with Ryan for getting her into this, but as she went on, giving the song the full tenderness of its meaning, she saw, to her surprise, that she was also giving the audience a great deal of pleasure. They were listening, smiling, nodding their heads at one another. She was suddenly happy, even proud, her heart warmed by their appreciation. At the end, her rich contralto voice—so unexpected in a small, slender woman—was full of emotion as she softly repeated the lover's extravagant vow:

> *Oh-h, for bonnie Annie Laurie,*
> *I would lay-ay me doon, and dee. . . .*

There was an explosive sound of clapping. Ryan, Leslie noted with some amusement, looked slightly stunned. Lady Beane came hurrying over to the piano, beaming. "How lovely, Miss Gordon! And how thoughtful! Half of us here are from Scotland, and you've put a tear in many a homesick eye. Please, favor us with another."

They kept her singing for another half hour, and then, as she and Ryan finally made their escape, one of the many listeners who took her hand and thanked her said something that stayed in Leslie's mind.

"My dear Miss Gordon, I have heard no better singing on the London stage! Why, you could make a fortune with that beautiful voice."

In the carriage, Ryan gave her a look that mixed admiration and disbelief. "I expected a simple song or two from my shy young ward," he said wryly. "Not a concert from a poised and beautiful woman. You continually amaze me, Leslie."

Leslie laughed. "I was angry when you put me in that situation," she admitted, "but later I liked it. It felt lovely to know I pleased them."

There was a flicker of jealousy in Ryan's eyes, and then he smiled slowly. "You please me, too," he said in a low tone. "Does it make you feel lovely, then?" His intimate look left no doubt as to his meaning.

Leslie promptly blushed. It was positively embarrassing that even now, after their constant lovemaking, she reacted like an eager virgin to the slightest hint of his desire. Her eyes met his and suddenly the wide space between them was vibrating with the current that ebbed and flowed and was always there for them both. "Very lovely," she whispered, "always . . ." She would have liked to slide over into his arms, but that was impossible in public. She contented herself with a featherlike touch of fingertips on his hand, hidden on the seat. "But that's entirely different. Today, I felt at home in Nassau for the first time. I really enjoyed it."

Ryan's intense gaze moved over her hungrily. "Then marry me. I'll find a place here for you if you like Nassau so well. After the war I will be trading down through these islands again and I could see you more often. Every month or so I'll be bringing the ship in here."

Leslie's smile faded. In peacetime there would be no need to wait for the dark of the moon. It would take only two or three days to load a ship and leave again—for another "month or so." She straightened, staring ahead.

"It appears we have the queen of the gossip set and her cronies waiting for us on the piazza," she said lightly. "We'd be wise to fall into our usual roles."

Ryan shrugged. "I'm beginning to tire of our roles," he said flatly. "Perhaps, if I compromise you thoroughly, you will be more willing to consider my proposal."

Leslie glanced at him as he stepped out of the carriage and came around to assist her. He had sounded angry and he looked it. He was tiring of her excuses. Her heart sank as he took her arm almost impersonally and helped her down. Only two more weeks out of the rest of her life to be happy with him, and his temper could spoil it. But she could never explain to him that he hadn't offered her enough to make her consider marriage. A house was nothing. What she wanted was half of his cabin aboard the *China Pearl* . . . and all of him.

They ran the gantlet of inquiring eyes and questions on the piazza, proceeded through the quiet lobby and down the hall. Ryan left her at the door of the suite with a short remark about seeing to his crew's health and added that he might be late for dinner.

"If you tire of waiting," he said, "order a dinner sent in." Then he left, striding away without a backward look.

Leslie ordered dinner sent in. From the way Ryan had looked as he walked away, she was certain he wouldn't be back in time for dinner, if indeed he came back at all that night. He was very angry.

Later, eating her dinner in a solitary state, Leslie considered for the first time what her life without Ryan would be. She knew the chances of finding her father alive were slim, and except for some distant cousins she hardly knew, she had no other family. She would be on her own. Her plan to repay Ryan for her expenses here suddenly seemed ludicrous. How? Her chances of finding employment in war-torn Wilmington were also slim, and even if she did, the money she could make as a maid or seamstress would barely pay her living expenses. It would take years. . . .

Leslie finished her dinner without tasting it. There had to be a way. There was always a way if one could manage to find it. . . .

Charles Rockwell stared in silent bewilderment at Leslie the next morning. Or perhaps it wasn't bewilderment, Leslie thought. Perhaps he was embarrassed. She had come to his office very early, dressed in one of her new morning gowns, a pale green silk with a soft, draped skirt and a circle of rosebuds embroidered around the neckline and rose grosgrain bows on the tiny sleeves. She looked fresh and pretty, and Rockwell had greeted her with pleasure. But now, after she had broached the subject of entertaining his guests with her singing, he was very quiet. Leslie leaned back in the chair in front of his desk and smiled at him.

"Of course," she said, with more confidence than she

felt, "I wouldn't expect you to agree without hearing me. For all you know, I might have a voice like a frog."

Rockwell laughed, his lined face breaking up with humor. "That isn't what's bothering me. I heard nothing but your praises last night at dinner from the men who attended the governor's tea party. Tom Farrell said your voice would put Dolly and Belle to shame. But . . ." He looked at her frankly. "I am wondering what Fitz would think of it. He seems quite intent on . . . well, on keeping you in the background. Have you discussed this with him?"

Leslie was ready for that question. "Captain Fitzsimmons has advised me more than once to seek a career on the stage," she said calmly, "and I have good reason to try. My family—like so many other Southern families now—had nothing to leave me."

Rockwell waved a careless hand. "With Fitz as your guardian, that doesn't matter. He's very well-to-do. I'm sure that he'll provide for your every need, including a handsome dowry when you wed."

"Possibly," Leslie said, her voice flat, "but it doesn't suit me. I would rather make my own way." She picked up her drawstring bag and stood. "I do understand your reluctance, Mr. Rockwell, considering both Captain Fitzsimmons and my inexperience. So, I shall go elsewhere. I hear there's quite a demand for talent in the taverns."

"My dear Miss Gordon!" Shocked, Rockwell sat straighter. "Surely, you wouldn't! Those taverns are a challenge for the most seasoned performers."

"I'll meet the challenge and gain experience," Leslie said carelessly. "If necessary, I can hire a protector."

"Just a moment," Rockwell said hastily, "I haven't refused to hear you, you know. Nor have I turned down your offer. Let me see . . . John Rice is an excellent piano player, and we can use the lounge for an audition. At this time of day no one is in it." He wheeled himself rapidly away from the desk and toward the door.

Leslie followed, half ashamed and half triumphant. She had counted on just this reaction from Charles when she mentioned the taverns. Charles wouldn't like admitting to Ryan that he had allowed Ryan's ward to go down and try her luck on Bay Street. The audition, Leslie was sure, was only a maneuver to keep her at the hotel until Ryan appeared. But still, if she sang well enough . . .

In the lounge, John Rice shuffled through the printed sheets of music on an old piano near the bar. "Some of these songs are a bit risqué," he said doubtfully, peering at Leslie over the tops of his spectacles. "Do you have a favorite, Miss Gordon?"

"Any ballad," Leslie said cheerfully, "English, Scotch or Irish. Just begin playing and I'll join in." She felt quite at home with these two men, both so gentlemanly and kind. The lounge, though stale with cigar smoke and echoing with emptiness, was large enough to give her voice range, yet small enough for the intimate quality that the ballads demanded. She turned and looked at Rockwell. She knew the power of her voice and he was too close to her.

"If you'll position yourself at the back of the room," she suggested, "you can tell if all of your guests will be able to hear me."

Amused, Rockwell wheeled himself away. Behind her, John Rice faltered over the keys, recovered himself and slipped gently into the beginning of "Bendemeer's Stream." Leslie smiled. The soft, flowing rhythm was a wonderful start.

The two men kept her singing, one request after

another, until Rice had played all the ballads he knew. Leslie thanked her lucky stars for a father like Harry Gordon, who had known all the folk songs of the British Isles. She could see by Rockwell's expression that he had enjoyed every minute of it.

Dismissing Rice and sending him back to the neglected front desk, Charles told Leslie that she would have his full support in convincing Ryan to allow her to sing for his guests.

"I have often wished for a bit of genteel entertainment during the luncheon hour," he added, "and your ballads would be a lovely offering. And Fitz may take kindly to the notion. I doubt that he would want you to entertain during the evening."

Leslie looked at him curiously. "Why?"

"Tastes change," Rockwell said uncomfortably, "when the wine and liquor begin to flow. The audience is different, also. The men from town expect a certain daring . . . a bit of fun. In any event, your ballads will fit in beautifully during the day." He smiled at her. "You haven't mentioned what you would expect in compensation, Miss Gordon."

Leslie colored. She had no idea what entertainers were paid, but she knew what she wanted. "My presence here has added to Captain Fitzsimmons's expenses," she said, "and I wish to repay him. If the cost of his extra room and my board could be defrayed by my salary, that would please me very much. If it's too much, please tell me."

Charles laughed, his thick white brows rising. "I believe we can manage a bit more than that, Miss Gordon. You are more accomplished at singing than you are at business. If you mean to make a career of this, you must learn to strike a hard bargain."

Behind them, the door of the lounge opened and

Ryan came striding in, his thick brows lowering and drawing together as his gaze went from Charles to Leslie's startled face.

"Rice said you were in here," he said harshly, without bothering to greet either one of them. "Why? This room reeks of stale wine and cigar smoke."

Leslie was shocked by his appearance. Ryan still wore the suit he had worn the night before, now badly rumpled. He hadn't shaved, and his face was lined, his eyes reddened. Her heart sank. He wasn't himself. He was teetering on the edge of anger and it wouldn't take much to push him over. The very worst of times to tell him her plans. She forced a smile.

"Mr. Rockwell and I have been discussing a small matter of business," she said brightly, "and this was an appropriate place." She made herself go to him and take his arm. "If you'd like, I can tell you about it in more pleasant surroundings." She could feel the tension in the thick muscles of his arm, see the suspicion in his eyes as he searched Rockwell's genial face and then looked down at her.

"What possible business could the two of you find mutually interesting?"

"The business of the hotel," Rockwell said blandly. "Your ward is a very intelligent and talented young woman." His faded eyes went to Leslie with a look of guarded warning. "Later, perhaps, we can all get together and discuss it at length. At the moment, I should be getting back to my office." He swiveled his chair toward the still open door and wheeled slowly away, leaving Ryan staring after him.

A strategic retreat, Leslie thought, and a very wise move. She let go of Ryan's arm and sniffed the air delicately.

"I do believe you are right," she said, with an air of

making a discovery. "It truly is unpleasant in here. I shall go back to the rooms." She sailed rapidly toward the door, her soft skirt fluttering around her slender form, her chin in the air and her heart pounding. She could hear Ryan's quick stride behind her.

"And I with you," he said grimly, catching up with her in the doorway. His hand fell on her wrist with an iron grasp. "I'll hear about this business you've been discussing with Charles."

Going along the hall, Leslie caught a whiff of smoke and rum from his rumpled suit, which made her wonder how he could have objected to the lounge. Wherever Ryan had spent the night, it hadn't been in a boudoir! He had spent it, she would wager, in one of those "low taverns" the bosun had mentioned. In the arms of Bacchus, god of wine and drunkenness, not some other woman. At the door of the suite she paused and gave him a look of clear blue innocence.

"I'll be happy to tell you anything you want to know," she said sweetly, "but perhaps you would like to rest first. You look . . . tired, to say the very least."

Ryan growled and flung open the door. "You will tell me now. And don't be impertinent. You are quite right in what you're thinking. I drank too much last night and I haven't been to bed, none of which should concern you. But *I* am concerned. You are up to some new trickery and I want to know what it is."

Leslie pulled away from him and went in, a flare of anger burning away her uncertainty. Trickery, indeed! She waited while he shut the door and came to stand in front of her. His feet were spread, his hands shoved into his pockets, and he looked both powerful and aggressive in spite of his fatigue. Leslie lifted her chin and looked him in the eye.

"There has been no trick, Ryan. I went to Mr. Rockwell in search of employment, and we were in the lounge only because there is a piano there and he could hear me sing. He has been kind enough to hire me—"

"What?" Ryan roared the word, and Leslie looked at him impatiently.

"He has been kind enough—"

"I heard that! But I don't believe it! Charles wouldn't dare—"

"—to hire me to sing for the luncheon guests," Leslie finished hurriedly, frightened by the noise he was making. "You needn't worry. I won't be entertaining at night."

"You won't be entertaining at all," Ryan said dangerously. "I absolutely forbid it."

Leslie's heart sank. She knew that now she would have to make a stand. She would have preferred to beard this lion some other time—almost any other time—but it wouldn't wait.

"You can't, Ryan," she said quietly. "You can't forbid me to sing. You can't forbid me to do anything."

"What do you mean?" He was furious. "As your guardian, I have every right—"

"You are not my guardian," Leslie said unevenly, fighting a hysterical wish to laugh. Was Ryan beginning to believe his own lies? He looked suddenly baffled.

"Not legally, perhaps." He was struggling to be reasonable. "But the effect is the same. You asked for my protection."

"I did not," Leslie said firmly. "I bargained with you. A trip to Wilmington aboard the *China Pearl* in exchange for the help I gave you. Nothing was ever said about taking over my life or making my decisions."

Ryan stared down at her, knowing she was absolutely right and hating it. All he wanted to do was keep her safe, keep her as far away as possible from the seamy, ugly side of life here. The thought of her offering her fragile beauty and lovely talent to these hungry men was unbearable. If one of them touched her . . . A red mist rose before his eyes and he reached down, snatching her up and shaking her savagely.

"This is why you won't marry me. Your father is just an excuse! What you want is an exciting life—more lovers to satisfy that hot little body! I knew you had a deeper reason for refusing me. Admit it!"

Leslie was terrified, more by the fury in his dark face than by what he said. The hands gripping her arms were holding her up, not her helplessly weak legs. "It's—it's true that I have another reason," she stuttered incoherently, "but it isn't what you said. It's just that I m-must live my own life, because you—you don't really want to—"

"Don't tell me what I want," Ryan raged. "Let me tell you what you're asking for." He dragged her close, wrapping her to his lean length with arms like iron bands. "Any man who sees you on a stage will think he can have you—if he pays enough." Ryan's eyes were wild and strange, staring at her. "Old men or young," he added roughly, "dirty or clean, they'll be reaching for you, offering you money."

Held against him, Leslie was in a mad roil of conflicting emotion. She was angry, indignant, frightened beyond reason, and still her traitorous body reacted to his with a blind, glad passion. Her throat was constricted, her heart pounding wildly as she fought to think. "No! I will not let them touch me!"

Ryan growled. "How will you stop them, when they manage to get you alone? Scream? The others will laugh at you and tell you to charm the customers, not drive them away." His hand moved, hot through the thin silk, following the tender curves of her back, pressing her closer to his loins. "How will you like it when some stranger does this to you?" he asked hoarsely, and cupped a rounded buttock in his palm, squeezing impudently. "Or this?" He pushed his scratchy, unshaven face into the curve of her slender neck, his hot mouth closing roughly on soft flesh.

His words and his roughness made it all too real. He *was* the stranger; he was no longer Ryan. Wildly, Leslie kicked him and jerked away, her slender arm swinging, her small hand meeting his cheek with a crack like a pistol shot.

"And how will the stranger like that?" she shouted, her voice rising and breaking in tearful outrage, and swung again, accurately, with the other hand. "Or *that?*"

"Leslie!"

Panting, she stared at the matching red prints on his stubbled cheeks, at the shock and amazement in his eyes, and then crumpled back into the chair, her hands over her face.

"Go away," she whispered, "and leave me alone. I will manage my own life."

There was nothing but silence, and then uneven footsteps and the sound of a door closing.

Chapter Eight

CHARLES ROCKWELL LOST NO TIME IN CAPITALIZING ON his newest attraction. Discreet notices went out:

"The Royal Victoria Hotel Is Proud to Announce that Miss Leslie Gordon, Ballad Singer, Will Entertain Monday through Friday during the Luncheon Hour."

Leslie thought the announcement hardly promised excitement. But as long as her debt to Ryan was being paid, she was satisfied to make a modest beginning.

She hadn't reckoned on the reception that she received from the bored Southern emigrés and the others who were confined by business and war to this small island. In less than a week the luncheon trade at the hotel had doubled and Charles had added a salary to her benefits.

"It proves," Rockwell said on the first Saturday

morning after her debut, "that no matter how jaded or worldly, everyone is sentimental about their homeland and the songs of their youth." He smiled across his desk at Leslie. "I should add that everyone is also appreciative of beauty and talent. That's a lovely suit, my dear."

"Thank you." Leslie smoothed the tailored brown silk and remembered Ryan's stiff face when she told him that she had paid for her new clothes herself. She had thought he would be relieved, but he had seemed to resent it. She glanced at Charles and smiled. "I paid for it with the tips your patrons send along with their requests for certain songs." She laughed a little. "However, I do wish they wouldn't ask so often for 'Dixieland.' I'm as loyal as any, but I am tired of singing it."

Rockwell grinned sympathetically. "Still, as my theater friends would say, it always brings down the house. Patriotism seems to burn hotter as the war news worsens. A desperate hope, I'm afraid."

Leslie nodded her bright head reluctantly. As an Englishman, Charles hoped for the South to triumph, yet he could accept the possibility of defeat calmly. She couldn't. She hated to admit even to herself that the South was losing. She pushed the thought away.

"I didn't mean to complain. You've been very kind to hire me, and very generous with your pay. With my salary and tips, I'll have a good sum to tide me over when I go back to Wilmington."

"*If* you go back," Rockwell amended quickly. "I hear the ports are no longer safe." He had been studying the shadowed look that came and went on her young face. "Tell me, Fitz hasn't been objecting to your singing, has he?"

Leslie shook her head, avoiding his eyes. "Not at all. Of course, I see very little of him now, since he is busy arranging for his next cargo." She rose, closing the subject. "If I'm to have my early morning walk, I should be starting. Thank you again."

It was very early. Leslie swept across the deserted piazza, breathing the clear morning air. She felt very mature and proper in the tailored suit, its severity softened only by a cream-colored jabot of ruffles beneath her chin, ruffled cuffs at the wrists of the long sleeves. Her rounded breasts were outlined enticingly by the tight bodice, but the suit itself, Leslie was sure, was the very soul of propriety. If Ryan happened to see her, he would have to approve.

The sweet taste of success turned bitter when she thought of Ryan. Since that awful moment when she had slapped his face—twice!—Ryan had been a mountain of icy reserve. Oh, he kept up appearances in public, taking her to dinner each evening and maintaining his role as her guardian. But alone he was as silent as possible and never touched her, not even to take her arm. But he had come to luncheon at the hotel dining room and clapped politely after her singing. Also, she supposed, to keep up appearances. And last night he had come close to admitting that her decision hadn't been entirely wrong. Leaving her at the door of the suite, as he always did now, he had spoken of it.

"I give Charles credit for his good sense," he had said stiffly. "He presents you much like a father presents his daughter at a private party. All very genteel and proper." His clear glance down at her had been faintly ironic. "You've become quite a pet with the elderly Southern aristocracy."

It wasn't an apology, and the compliment was for Charles, so Leslie had only nodded and gone in, shutting the door. It had become so painful to be with Ryan these days that she was almost relieved each time they parted. Of course, she thought now, she could have told him he hadn't been entirely wrong, either. Tom Farrell had become much bolder. Twice now, Tom had waited at the door of the suite, hidden in the long hall, and Leslie would have wagered that only the close proximity of John Rice in the lobby had prevented Tom from acting precisely as Ryan had so cruelly demonstrated. Tom had invited her to go with him to his private club, where he promised that her singing—and perhaps a bit of acting—would earn her more in one evening than she made in a week at the hotel.

"Don't waste yourself on Ryan," Tom had wheedled. "I can show you a part of life in Nassau that's really exciting." He had put his arm around her and she had had to push hard to dislodge it.

Anyway, she had told him coldly that she wasn't interested in either his club or his ideas of excitement and had returned to the lobby to sit in solitary dignity until he left. She had felt sure he would try to force himself into the suite if she had entered it. She had thought of complaining to Charles, but her pride had intervened. If she was to be an entertainer, she would have to learn to handle her problems by herself.

Breathing deeply of the fresh morning air and walking down toward the harbor, Leslie reminded herself that this part of her life would soon be over. Another week, and the *China Pearl* would be sailing for Wilmington with her aboard; and when the trip was over she would never see this island or Ryan again. Gazing out over the blue water, she blinked away sudden tears. How could she still love such a stubborn, unfeeling man? There, right in front of her, was all that Ryan Fitzsimmons had ever really wanted—his sleek little ship and the freedom of the sea.

Her gaze sharpened. There was a huge newcomer in the midst of the ships. Gray and battle-weary, it lay tied to the rugged breakwater, its decks splintered and one of the heavy masts blown away. It looked very familiar. Shading her eyes, Leslie searched along the huge hull until she found the name. The *James Bulloch!* So, Captain Spencer Burdette had indeed returned to Nassau for his leave, as he had said he would. A trifle late, but she could see why. A battle had detained him. She wandered closer, fascinated by the size and power of the injured giant. Even at this early hour, men were busy on the decks, removing the damaged rigging.

"Leslie Gordon!"

Hurrying down the gangway, Spencer Burdette looked exactly as she remembered him. The rumpled, shapeless gray suit, the captain's cap carelessly cocked over tan, tousled hair and green eyes, the same brilliant grin on his pleasant, angular face. Leslie felt a rush of pleasure, as if at the sight of an old friend; the same friendly rapport she had felt as she had waved him farewell from the deck of the *China Pearl.* She went toward him, smiling.

"Nice to see you again, Captain Burdette. Ryan will be pleased . . ."

Spence caught both of her hands in his. "Bother Ryan! Are *you* pleased?"

Leslie laughed. "Of course. But not pleased to see your damage. You must have been in quite a battle."

He grimaced. "The Yanks are turning out warships now at an astounding rate. Well armed and fast . . ." He stopped, staring at her, and then added simply: "I'm sick of war and of talking of war. Will you have breakfast with me?"

Without a moment's thought, Leslie took his arm companionably and nodded. "I would like that very much. At the hotel?"

"On my ship," Spence said, and turned her toward

the gangway. "And have no fear—our cook is even better than the one at the Royal Victoria."

If that was an exaggeration, Leslie decided later, it was a slight one. The ship's cook had evidently been up and out at daybreak, for there was fresh fruit and eggs to accompany the ham and hot, strong coffee. They ate at a small chart table in the cramped quarters of the wheelhouse, with Spence keeping an eye on the men working on the littered deck.

Spence still declined to discuss the battle or even the war on land, except to say the news was bad along the front and the Southern casualties alarming. He turned the talk to Leslie, questioning her about her life on the island and what she thought of the society.

Leslie chattered away without reserve, feeling completely at home with Spence. She ended by telling him of her bargain with Charles Rockwell, and her ambition to continue as a singer when she went back to the States. But she didn't mention Ryan.

"A singer?" Spence's green eyes flickered. "It isn't an easy life for a woman."

"So I've been told," Leslie said dryly, "but I prefer it to working as a maid or seamstress in someone else's home or shop. And it's decidedly more profitable."

Spence regarded her thoughtfully. "You've changed," he said. "You make it hard to believe Ryan's story of finding you in some swamp. Except that you still have that air of independence and daring." He chuckled at her look of surprise. "You didn't know it showed? It shows very clearly, Leslie. You don't mind me calling you Leslie, do you? Maybe I shouldn't dare, now that you look the very image of a proper young lady."

"I don't mind at all." Leslie was laughing. "As for looking like a lady, I suspect it's an improvement on the cabin boy costume I wore when we met."

"I'm not sure of that," Spence teased. "I found you charming that morning. How I envied Ryan!" He sat looking at her with those quizzical green eyes for a long moment before he added: "And how is Ryan these days? Has he discovered yet that he's in love with you?"

Leslie's eyes went blank and then shadowed over with deep pain. She was suddenly sorry that she had accepted Spence's invitation to breakfast. He was too wise, too all-seeing. With an effort, she made her voice light.

"If Captain Fitzsimmons has made any discoveries of that kind, he has managed to keep them to himself." She curved her stiff lips into a smile. "Truthfully, what he feels is a duty to deliver me to Wilmington, because of my help in recapturing his ship. It was a—bargain, Spence. And, of course, I'm grateful." The smile this time was real, but mocking. "He has been most proper. In order to preserve my reputation, I am known here as his ward."

Spence leaned back, laughing incredulously. "If Fitz has convinced those gossips at the Royal that his feelings for you are paternal, I give him full marks for his acting ability. Why, when I saw you with him on the ship . . ." His voice trailed away as he scanned Leslie's face. "Perhaps I was wrong," he added after a moment, gently. "I rather hope I was. It would give me a clear field to pursue the most attractive young lady in Nassau."

"You are very flattering," Leslie said unsteadily, and lapsed into silence. She thought it likely that Spence had guessed exactly how she felt about Ryan, but somehow she didn't mind. Spence was different. She thought that behind those sometimes cynical eyes there was a lot of understanding, as if he knew all the foolishness of a human heart and forgave it. Finally, she pushed aside her last cup of coffee and stood up.

"I've enjoyed this very much," she said, "and I hope I'll see you again before I leave. Are you staying at the hotel?"

Spence was on his feet. "Before you leave? Where are you going?"

"Why, back to Wilmington," Leslie said, surprised. "We'll be sailing soon."

"Surely not! Not even Ryan could risk taking you through that blockade," Spence said vehemently. "It's the worst on the coast."

Leslie's private opinion was that Ryan would be glad to take her through the jaws of hell to be rid of her and free again. And, in any event, she had complete faith in Ryan's ability to run any blockade the Yankees could devise. She gave Spence a faint smile and turned toward the open door.

"I must go, in any case. I must find my father, or at least discover what has happened to him. He may be wounded or ill, and need me."

"An impossible task for a woman," Spence said grimly. "Ryan must know that."

Leslie's faint smile grew. "Ryan knows *me*," she said lightly. "He knows that I must try. Good-bye, Spence."

Spence opened his mouth and then closed it, thinking better of arguing. He followed her out to help her across the battered deck and down the gangway. There, he took her hand and thanked her for her company.

"I'll be up around noon to check in," he added. "Tell Fitz . . ." He looked past Leslie as a carriage clattered to a stop on the street. "Never mind, I'll tell him myself." His angular face broke into a grin. "Here he is, now."

Leslie turned, feeling the inevitable jolt of emotion that twisted her heart and closed her throat. Swallowing, she watched Ryan's long legs step down from Gabe's carriage, his bronzed face turn, expressionless, from her face to Spence. He came toward them with his easy stride and clasped Spence's outstretched hand.

"I've been looking for you," he said to Leslie shortly. "I'm glad to find you in safe company."

"Safer than yours," Spence said immediately. "I wouldn't be fool enough to take her through the Wilmington blockade."

Ryan's thick brows arched. "Nor would I let you," he said condescendingly, "but she'll be safe with me. I know a few tricks that work in the shoals of the Cape Fear River."

Spence dropped his hand and shrugged. "You still have to get through. And there's a lot more pickets in the Yankee fence. A hundred and fifty ships now roam the sea from Charleston to Wilmington. You may yet find the *China Pearl* sunk and yourself in a Federal prison."

"That many?" Ryan looked disbelieving. "That's double the number when I was there last . . . are you sure?" At Spence's nod, his face clouded. "Then, that will take some thought. Tell me about these additions, Spence. Their size and speed . . ."

"I was just leaving," Leslie interposed hastily. "I'm sure you two have a great deal to talk about. Thank you for your hospitality, Captain Burdette. I'll hope to see you at the hotel." She turned away and felt Ryan's hand close on her arm.

"Gabe will drive you to the hotel," he said firmly, "and come back for me." He took her to the carriage and handed her up without waiting for an answer. Pink-cheeked and silent, Leslie settled the folds of brown silk around her and leaned back. She had wanted to walk. "Wait there for me," Ryan added quietly. "There's something I want to discuss."

Leslie stared forward rebelliously as the carriage jolted away, wishing she had refused, even at the risk of having a scene in front of Spence. If Ryan intended to begin ordering her around again. . . . She sighed, her slim fingers touching the place on her arm where Ryan's fingers had held her. It still tingled.

She hadn't long to wait. She had taken off the brown suit and put on the more comfortable morning gown because the air had become warm and humid, as if threatening rain. She had paced restlessly, thinking it would be hours before the two friends finished their talk, and Ryan's knock startled her. She let him in with her small jaw set stubbornly. If he gave her one order . . .

Ryan stood in the middle of the room, waiting for her to be seated. He was silent, as he always was now, his dark face unreadable, his eyes avoiding hers. Leslie swallowed, admitting to herself that she had actually been hoping for a quarrel. Something that would miraculously clear the air, give him back to her for these few last days. She sighed and went to a chair.

Ryan sat down beside her. "When I planned this discussion," he said without preliminaries, "I had only one problem on my mind. Now I have two, thanks to Spence." He glanced at her, his clear eyes flicking over her quickly. "I may as well tell you now that he has convinced me of the dangers waiting at Wilmington. I won't be taking you along."

Leslie's mouth opened in a soundless gasp. Recovering, she spurted words. "But you must! You promised . . . and if you can go, I can, too. I'm not afraid!"

"*I* am," Ryan said tersely. "It will be dangerous, and I will have enough to concern me without thinking about your safety. I know how you feel, and I promise I will make every effort to find out about your father. . . ."

"Ryan!" It was a desperate cry of disappointment. "Please! I won't get in the way or cause any trouble. I will obey you implicitly." She leaned toward him, her flushed face pleading. "I will stay below, I promise. . . ."

"You would be on my mind," he said implacably, "and if what Spence says is true—and I have no reason to doubt it—I will need all my attention for the ship. Later, perhaps, I can take you to a safer port." He got up and strode to a window, his back to her. "Don't beg," he said hoarsely. "It's settled."

Watching him, Leslie knew she couldn't sway him. The pain inside her chest twisted like a knife. "You're taking revenge," she said, choked, "repaying me because I wouldn't obey you. Because I slapped you. . . ."

"God, no!" Ryan turned jerkily, his bronzed face tight with intense feeling. "How could you think it? I deserved worse. I accused you unjustly, and treated you like a—a woman of the streets." He came back to sit tensely on the edge of his chair. "You were absolutely right to insist that I leave you alone, but I hope in time you'll forgive me."

Leslie couldn't believe what she heard. Ryan and humility didn't mix. But still, a tiny tendril of hope curled inside. Perhaps he didn't hate her, after all. She lowered golden lashes over suddenly shining blue eyes. "I do forgive you," she said primly. "I . . . well, I haven't always been right, either."

"You amaze me." Ryan's tone was grave, but glancing up, Leslie was sure she caught a twitch at the corner of his mouth. She waited, her heart lighter by far than it had been for a week.

"That brings me to the other part of the discussion," Ryan went on, serious again. "That day I condemned you without reason, and I won't have anyone else making the same mistake. I'm sure what I heard was only gossip, but I think I should mention it."

Leslie nodded, not caring but anxious to be agreeable. Ryan, she thought, looked very uncomfortable. "Was it about me?"

"It was." He chose his words slowly. "A member of an unsavory club I visited last night spoke of you. He said they'd soon have a new young singer to replace the tired old acts, a singer whose beauty and daring promised real excitement."

Leslie gazed at him in surprise. "But perhaps they will," she said reasonably. "There must be other young singers."

"He used your name, Leslie. And described you as the ballad singer at the Royal Victoria. And," Ryan added reflectively, "I hit him. It caused quite a stir."

Leslie gasped and then struggled with shock and an insane desire to laugh. "You were right," she managed finally. "It was only gossip. I haven't applied for any new positions. But—why did you hit him?"

Ryan frowned. "Because he implied—no, I'll be honest—because he said plainly that Tom Farrell was your lover."

Leslie felt the heat of blood climbing her neck, spreading hotly over her cheeks. She looked away, shamed, knowing she should have told Ryan immediately when Tom had made those unpleasant advances. Much as she hated to admit it, Ryan was her natural protector here in Nassau, and he would have taken that idiot aside and scotched any chance of such bragging lies. She looked back at Ryan humbly.

"I suppose I should have told you," she began.

"WHAT?"

Leslie flinched. He was roaring again, just as he had before. What a noise he made!

"Don't *do* that," she said, trembling. "It frightens me. And, anyway, there's no reason for yelling. I haven't any lover but you, and . . . and, well—*you* haven't been m-much of a lover, lately. . . ."

Ryan stared at her, at the pink cheeks and quivering mouth, at the tears welling up in the clear blue eyes. The angry set of his jaw softened, his strained expression changed into something else entirely. He leaned forward and picked her up, settling back with her in his lap.

"Then what was it you should have told me?" he asked gently. "What a fool I've been?"

Leslie sat stiffly on his muscular thighs, bewildered and hardly daring to hope that this meant their estrangement was over. "No-o. . . I meant I should have told you that Captain Farrell was acting like a conceited idiot. He wanted me to go to that club and sing— among other things."

"What other things?" Ryan asked sternly.

"He said he'd show me the—the exciting part of Nassau." With Ryan's warmth around her and his mouth so close, Leslie was having trouble explaining clearly. "It was very annoying," she added indignantly. "He lurked in the hall to catch me, and was so insistent that I—I had to go sit in the lobby until he left! But, why on earth would he *lie* about me?"

Ryan sighed. "Farrell claims a lot of conquests he never made. But he won't lie about you again, and he's left the hotel." Reaching, Ryan's long fingers deftly removed the big pins that held the knot of tawny hair and let the silky coil slide down over his hand. He tossed the pins on a small table and smiled at her. "I hit him, too. In fact, I gave him quite a sound trouncing."

"You *did?*" The blue eyes were penitent. "What a lot of trouble I've caused you." She was not altogether sad; Ryan had *fought* for her. He must care, at least a little.

"It was a pleasure," Ryan said, almost too carelessly. He was running his fingers through the gleaming coil of hair, spreading it out and letting it fall smoothly around her. His gaze traveled slowly from the hair and studied her shining eyes and the softly parted lips. "But nothing compared to the pleasure I am hoping to have now," he added huskily, and eased her closer. His firm mouth closed over hers, his tongue nudging her lips further apart and entering the velvety interior very slowly, as if not quite sure of a welcome.

"Oh-h-h . . ." Muffled by his mouth, the sound Leslie made was still heartfelt. Her arms slipping around his neck were infinitely reassuring to his doubts. His tongue went deeper, probing delicately into soft corners and shattering beyond repair what control she might have had. She burrowed sinuously, flaming against the growing heat of his body, breathing in the musky scent of desire that drifted up between them. She hardly recognized as her own the urgent sounds that rose from her throat and then changed to a pleading insistence as Ryan pulled away.

"First," Ryan said unsteadily, "I must know what your intentions are, and exactly how you feel about me."

Leslie stared at him, dimly comprehending that he wasn't being humorous. The question was important, though she didn't know why. She tugged impatiently, but the strong neck resisted.

"I love you," she whispered, "and I want you, now."

Ryan's arms tightened convulsively. "That isn't enough. Will you marry me?"

She suddenly knew that if she said no, she would lose

him. He would put her down and walk away and she would lose these last, few, all-important days.

"I—I will. As soon as we find out . . ."

". . . about your father," Ryan supplied grimly. "All right. I'll settle for that, since I can't seem to do better." Gathering her in tightly, he stood up and walked toward the bedroom.

Chapter Nine

EVEN IN RYAN'S WARM ARMS LESLIE FELT A RUSH OF cool, damp air as they entered the bedroom. The room was eerily dim, the curtains billowing and flaring as wind gusted in through the wide windows. Outside, the sky had darkened alarmingly and thunder rumbled and rolled.

Ryan set her on her feet and went to adjust the windows, closing them partially. As he turned back to her a splatter of heavy raindrops drummed on the outside wall. His white teeth flashed in the gloom.

"Perfect weather for making love." Wrapping her close, he let his hands run hungrily over the slender contours of her back, his palms warm through the soft, thin silk of her gown. "We have all the time in the world. No one will be looking for either of us in this storm." His voice grew husky, his lean body arched over her, bending her yielding softness against the thrusting heat of his loins.

All the time in the world. Leslie sighed with happiness, letting her hands slip down from his neck to open his shirt, slowly baring the bronzed skin. Now there was no hurry, no urgency. Only a slow pleasure in touching the corded muscles, the crisp, thick mat of dark hair. Threading her fingers through the curls, she touched the flat nipples delicately, first with her fingertips and then with her tongue. She could feel the beat of his racing heart, his shallow, uneven breathing. Her own heart pounded. There was nothing that excited her more than his desire.

"I want to undress you," Ryan whispered. "I want to see my own hands taking off your clothes, I want to know that exquisite body is mine."

Leslie stood still, thrilled by the erotic sight of his long-fingered dark hands slowly unhooking her soft gown, lifting it gently from her smooth shoulders and pushing it down over her hips. When it whispered to the floor she stepped out of it unsteadily and stood still again, watching the fingers untie the ribbons of camisole and petticoat and remove them. Ryan unhooked the band of her short pantalets and let them fall. In the dim light of the room he could almost see the mists wreathing her, drifting around the slender legs.

Leslie could stand still no longer. Lifting her slim arms to his neck, she pulled him close and coaxed the firm lips open with a flickering tip of tongue.

"You're torturing me," she whispered.

Ryan laughed huskily, lifting her to the bed. "Such sweet torture . . ." He pressed his face into the satin curve of her belly, tonguing the tiny navel, laughing again as she wriggled and gasped. Sitting back on his heels, he pulled off her sagging stockings and soft slippers. Then he stood up and began removing the rest of his clothes.

He was fully aroused, something Leslie had never before seen clearly. She gazed at him, astounded both by the sight and the primitive way her body responded to it. Some deep reaction made her thighs quiver and move apart involuntarily, made the swelling ache inside grow sweetly painful. Perhaps he had been right, she thought, dazed. Perhaps I *am* overburdened with instinct, like some young animal.

But, moving aside to let Ryan lie beside her, it seemed a problem easy to bear. A lovely problem. She opened her arms to him, felt his hotly passionate body straining against her. Then, pressing her face into his neck, tasting the warm, salty skin with the tip of her tongue, she let instinct take over. Before this, she had always followed his lead, submitted gladly to his practiced skill. But now her hand roved sensuously over his broad back and tight buttocks and was drawn inexorably to move around for an intimate exploration of the phenomenon of male desire that she had just witnessed. Groaning luxuriously, Ryan eased slowly over on his back. It was the first time that he had ever moved away from her in bed, and for a moment her hand faltered.

"Oh, God," Ryan whispered, "don't *stop*."

Then he didn't mind; he liked it. Leslie sat up, surveying the dim outline of the long, powerful body stretched out full-length beside her. She examined the broad, jutting rib cage above the narrow waist and muscled flanks, the pure masculinity of every part from shoulders to feet. She decided to explore it all.

At her first touch, Ryan relaxed, loving the feel of her warm, slender palms moving over him and touched by the mixture of shyness and sensuality that guided her. He could have guided her himself, showed her what he wanted, but somehow this was better. Her face was so soft and dreaming, her breasts beautiful, round and shining in the half light, her slender back hidden by that golden torrent of hair. He felt mystically exalted, both by his desire and by a strange tenderness that pierced his heart and thickened his throat. He felt his body move involuntarily as her caresses became more intimate, saw her mouth curve as she realized she was pleasing him, and the tenderness he felt came close to choking him. Lord, she was beautiful. There was nothing to pity now—not in that healthy, exquisite body and tantalizing sexuality. She could drive a man wild. . . . He held his breath as she leaned over him, her mass of hair sliding silkily over his heated loins and tight, quivering erection, her mouth pressing through the dark patch of hair on his belly, to flick his navel with the warm wetness of her tongue.

Ryan's held breath gusted out sharply as he lunged upward, wrapping his arms around the slender, bending body, pulling her down across his chest and then rolling, pinning her beneath him, growling deep in his chest. This woman was his, and he had a primitive desire to prove it, not only to her but to himself.

Half smothered, startled, Leslie was close to fear. She had never seen Ryan like this nor felt the full strength of his unleashed power. Gasping for breath, she twisted and wriggled, only arousing him further. He was kissing her fiercely, his hands sliding beneath her to grasp a rounded buttock in each broad palm, then forcing her trembling thighs apart. But his first thrust drove fear far from her mind. She had been well and truly taken, completely possessed, and it was suddenly exactly what she wanted. Ryan's whole muscular length trembled with the force of his desire. He lifted her hips to clench her tightly against his heaving loins as if he couldn't get enough of her.

Flaming, Leslie closed her eyes and let it happen, let her body be his, gave him every atom of her heart and will. Truly part of him at last, she felt his passion and strength as if it were hers, mounting and mounting with each plunging thrust, each achingly sweet withdrawal, building and then drawing out the final, exquisite yearning. Then came that shattering moment when sensation flowered and burst into a glorious ecstasy of fulfillment. This time she was so sensitive to their joining that she felt her inner flesh tighten and lock, coaxing and rippling along the hard length within, radiating that intense pleasure that spiraled throbbingly through every vein. She felt Ryan's last, rushing thrust, heard his erotic moan as he reached the peak of rapturous release. Gentling, no longer fierce, he sank into her softness with a long, gusting sigh, rubbing his loins against hers slowly and luxuriously, sending new, tiny darts of delight tingling. He muttered, his face buried in her hair, the words muffled.

"I will remember this day until I die, darling."

Holding him, stroking his tousled hair, Leslie closed her eyes and refused to think of dying. "It was perfect, Ryan."

Later, Ryan wasn't so sure. He sat up in the rumpled bed and lifted her into his arms. "I was carried away. I didn't—I mean, I wasn't too rough, was I?"

Leslie laughed, her breath catching. She was still limp from her utter surrender to his male dominance. She felt beautifully ravished, thrilled to her depths by his driving passion.

"You carried me away with you, I believe. At least, I think I caught glimpses of another world." She knew Ryan could never really hurt her. Not with that innate gentleness he carried inside, that tenderness that had made him bring a half-starved waif down the Hillsborough and take care of her ever since. She put up a hand and touched his cheek gently. "I love you, Ryan."

He stared down at her, cradled in his arms, naked and beautiful and completely contented. His wild, golden lily . . .

"And I love you, my own darling."

She thought her heart might burst. It had swelled enough to fill her chest. There had been both conviction and a faint surprise in his deep voice. *"Do* you?" Her voice broke a little, tremulous. "Do you truly love me, Ryan?"

"I do," he said, the conviction growing, the surprise fading away. "I suppose I always have. . . ."

Leslie closed her eyes, overflowing with a happiness she could never have believed. Perhaps shouldn't believe, even now. "You've never wanted to love anyone," she said slowly. "You wanted no dutiful chains to bind you to shore . . . remember?"

Ryan stared at her, his eyes startled and then softening. "I did say that, didn't I? I knew I was fighting a lost cause. From that first morning in the Green Swamp, when I saw you naked in the mist . . ."

"You saw me *what?*" Wriggling from his arms, Leslie sat up and looked at him indignantly. "You—you spied on me? Ryan Fitzsimmons, you are no gentleman. . . ."

He lunged at her, laughing, pushing her down and pinioning her beneath him. "I never said I was. Anyway, you were too scrawny to tempt me."

"Scrawny and pitiful, I suppose!"

"And beautiful," he added softly. "Fragile. Ivory and gold, like one of the wild lilies that grew around you. The way I felt about you frightened me. I wanted to save you from everything, keep you from any harm, find your damn father and beat him within an inch of his life. I should have known what was happening to me."

She looked up at his bending head uncertainly. "What was happening to you?"

"I was being bound," Ryan said gravely. "Bound tighter than any chain could bind me. If I had left you there on the bank of the Hillsborough, I would have gone back for you. I would have had to."

Watching his eyes, clear and vulnerable and completely open to her at last, Leslie felt her own eyes fill with tears, her throat thickening. "You do love me," she said, choked. "You really do."

"Yes, of course," he said and kissed her. "In spite of all my good intentions, I really do love you. With all my heart and every inch of my body. And, when I come back from Wilmington with news of your father, you will marry me."

"Oh, I will!" Leslie began to cry, tears running freely from sparkling blue eyes. "I really will! And I'll be *glad* to." She put her arms around him and drew him down, close . . . very close, and let him kiss her tears away. Then she began a new, subtle caressing. After all, it was still raining. . . .

"I'm starving." Leslie sat up in the wide bed and looked at Ryan accusingly. "I've had nothing to eat since breakfast and it's nearly time for dinner. It's dark outside."

Ryan stretched luxuriously and smiled at her. His rugged face was relaxed, the light hazel eyes as clear as mountain air. "It has to be dark," he said reasonably, "if I'm to leave here without making it clear to John Rice that I've been with you all day. I can't climb out a window in broad daylight."

Leslie glanced at the window curiously. "Where do

you go when you leave? Over the wall, I know . . . but then where?"

Ryan laughed. "Do you have to know everything? Around the back wall, down to the street, and then I walk casually up to the entrance, a man-about-town coming home from a strenuous evening."

Leslie chuckled and fell on him, threading her fingers through the thick chestnut hair. "From a strenuous day, in this case . . ." Dreamily, she traced the shape of his mouth with a fingertip. "You pleased me very much," she said softly. "Did I please you?"

Ryan's arms tightened around her. "You know you did, angel. I'm looking forward to a lifetime of being pleased by you. . . ."

Leslie smiled and wriggled down to lay her cheek on his chest. The strong, steady beat of his heart was soothing. "Then . . . you'll be taking me along on the ship, won't you?"

His hand stroked her hair, tenderly brushing it away from her face. "No, darling. I can't risk it."

She had known what he would say, but she had to try. Pulling away from him, she sat up again. "You are risking *you*." She had always been so confident of his ability, but now she felt a curl of cold fear in the pit of her stomach. "If it's that dangerous, Ryan, why are you going?"

His face was almost indistinguishable in the darkness, but she could see the dark line of his brows move up in their characteristic fashion. "Because that's what I do. Everyone is going—but none of them is taking along a woman."

"If they had a woman who was willing to go," Leslie said with asperity, "maybe they would."

Ryan laughed aloud. "I doubt it. Latimer's light o' love stowed away on his ship last year. He found her just as they left the docks and threw her overboard. She had to swim to shore."

Leslie sat in utter silence. Then she shrugged elaborately and slipped from the bed. "You could leave now," she pointed out. "The rain has stopped, at least for the moment." She was profoundly grateful for the darkness that hid her expression. Her heart was pounding; she was breathless with excitement as she watched his shadowy figure rise, the long arms reach for his clothes. If he knew what she was thinking, he would roar louder than ever. . . .

Ryan kissed her lightly as he left. "Hurry into that hot bath, darling. This damp air is making you shiver."

"Oh, I will . . ." She closed the window behind him and took a deep, exultant breath. She wasn't shivering —she was trembling with a new, wild hope. She knew every nook and cranny aboard the *China Pearl*, and once the ship was brought to the docks and loaded, it would take only a bit of luck for her to slip over the side unnoticed. It was just as she had thought—there was always a way if one could manage to find it.

Sitting in the fragrant warm mist and soft water of her bath, Leslie erupted in breathless laughter. Ryan would be furious when she appeared on deck after he sailed, but he wouldn't throw her overboard. She was sure that she was doing the right thing, because that cold fear was gone entirely. As long as the two of them were on the *China Pearl*, the little ship would be invincible. That had been proven in the Hillsborough River, and again under the blazing guns of the Federal cruiser outside Mobile. Maybe that was superstition, but then all sailors were superstitious, and she was a sailor. That was another thing she hoped to prove to Ryan—that she could be as happy on a ship as in a house ashore. She could hardly wait to get out of those bulky gowns and back into those breeches and a shirt. . . .

Later, Leslie was sure she would always remember that week before the *China Pearl* sailed for Wilmington. It was filled with excitement. Not only the hidden, fearful, hopeful and breath-catching excitement of planning to stow away on Ryan's ship, but also the sudden and unexpected jolt of becoming a "noted entertainer."

The Guardian, Nassau's biweekly newspaper edited by Londoner Edwin Charles Moseley, printed a story about the ballad singer at the Royal Victoria Hotel that was so full of extravagant praise that it made Leslie blush. Describing her as ethereally beautiful, enormously talented and charming, the article also included a pen-and-ink sketch of her done by the famous Frank Vizetelly, an artist sent to Nassau by *The Illustrated London News*. But to Leslie the most striking feature of the report was the title: *The Golden Lily of the Confederacy*.

Ryan brought the newspaper to her in the suite Wednesday morning, handed it to her silently and sat down to wait for her to read it. She gave it only a shocked glance before turning to him.

"Why—this is your idea, Ryan! I wouldn't have believed . . ."

"It is not my idea," Ryan said somberly. "I thought it was yours. Who else would know my name for you?"

"No one! But I knew nothing of this. No one has even asked for my permission. . . ." At another time, Leslie might have welcomed recognition to favor her career, but not this week! This week she preferred to be unnoticed. "I wouldn't have allowed it," she added indignantly, "and certainly I would never have mentioned such a—a personal thing."

"The newspaper wouldn't need your permission," Ryan pointed out. "You are a public figure." He didn't sound as if he thought being a public figure was desirable. He sat staring at her thoughtfully. "I wouldn't put it past Charles."

"But the name! Charles wouldn't know that."

"It was Spence," Ryan said suddenly. "It can't be anyone else." He stood up and paced back and forth angrily. "In fact, I saw him sitting and talking with Vizetelly in the dining room while you were singing."

"But the *name,*" Leslie repeated impatiently. "Are you sure you haven't . . ."

"Spence would remember my story of finding you in the swamp," Ryan said reluctantly, "and, damn it, I probably mentioned how you reminded me of those lilies. . . ." His face was Indian red beneath the bronze.

"Spence should have known you spoke in confidence," Leslie said loyally. "I can't imagine him talking so freely." She was wondering just what Ryan had said to Spence that day. She wished that she had eavesdropped longer. It would have been much nicer to hear herself compared to a lily than described as a pitiful waif.

Ryan dropped back into his chair with a disgusted sigh. "He would do it, if he thought it would further your career. Spence believes you have a wonderful future in singing. He told me I'd be selfish indeed to hold you back."

"Well," Leslie said uncertainly, "I suppose that's nice of him." She looked at the article again, both fascinated and repelled at the thought of being a "public figure." In truth, she felt like two people, one the familiar Leslie Gordon, and the other a pen-and-ink sketch named the Golden Lily. It wasn't a comfortable feeling. She folded the paper and tossed it aside.

"It will soon be forgotten," she said carelessly, and smiled at him. Her future in entertaining no longer seemed very important, only her future with Ryan. "Have you begun loading your cargo yet?" she added, very casually.

"Most of it is aboard," Ryan said, making her heart skip a beat, "but I'll have to wait a day or so for the rest of it. There's a ship due in from England." He looked at Leslie rather grimly. "I understand the need for morphine and chloroform is desperate. And quinine. The camps are full of wounded and ill troops."

Leslie looked away from him. "We're losing, aren't we?"

Ryan nodded. "I'm afraid you are. If either of your 'secret' allies, England or France, would throw the weight of their full support to the Confederacy, the South would still have a chance. But I doubt they will." He stood up, looking tired and cynical. "Unfortunately, I'm afraid the rest of the Southerners are as stubborn as you, my sweet. They'll fight to the last ditch. There will be very little left of the world you remember when this is over."

She knew that he was right. No one discussed it, yet it was in everyone's eyes these days. The South was dying. Ryan was like Charles Rockwell—he could accept the idea, though he didn't like it. She looked up at him curiously.

"What is your country, Ryan?" she asked softly. "What place do you consider your native land?"

His clear eyes slanted down at her in surprise. "I have no country, darling, as you pointed out to me once. But," he laughed suddenly, "I suppose you could say I'm a native of the Atlantic Ocean. That's good enough for me."

A wanderer, like his father before him. After he had gone and Leslie was dressing for her appearance in the dining room at noon, she thought about that deeply. She was more than willing to make her life aboard Ryan's ship in fair weather or foul; she never wanted to be parted from him for more than a few hours. But . . . wasn't there a need in everyone for a place to call home? Some small place with earth and green, growing things? She sighed. With Ryan Fitzsimmons she would have to be satisfied with the sea.

There was standing room only in the dining room of the Royal Victoria that day. Charles hurriedly ordered tables set up in the lounge and at the end of a half hour had Leslie escorted across the lobby to sing to the patrons in there. The applause was deafening. Leslie smiled and bowed with a sense of unreality. It was as if the article in *The Guardian* had created an instant appreciation, as if people who normally cared nothing for ballads were now forced to enjoy them because it was the fashion! Leaving the small podium that held the piano, she glanced across the room and caught Spence's green gaze. He was leaning against the wall with a quirk of smile on his angular face and clapping with the best of them. He followed her out into the lobby and took her arm to lead her down the hall to the suite.

"You were wonderful, as always," he told her warmly. "You're on your way, Leslie."

"Thank you, Spence." She wondered what he would think if he knew she *was* on her way, very soon, to Wilmington. Her career, if one could call it that, would be in abeyance, at least until she returned. She smiled at him rather coolly. "It's the effect of the article in *The Guardian*, that's all. The crowds will thin out again."

"But that doesn't need to happen," Spence said eagerly. "Keep your name before the public, Leslie, and you'll be a great success. Don't waste your talent! I'll help you . . . why, with proper costuming and a bit of direction, you can be a sensation."

Leslie laughed, warming to his eagerness. He was so sincere, so anxious to help. "I'll think about it," she promised. "But I'm not exactly sure I'd like being a sensation. In any event, I have other plans for the next week or so."

"But you shouldn't wait. Strike while the iron is hot, and all that sort of thing. . . ." He took her hand again. "Come walk in the garden and let me tell you what I've been thinking."

This time Leslie did laugh. "If you'll look outside, Spence, you'll see that it's pouring rain again. I'm afraid the garden doesn't tempt me. But I really will think about it."

She breathed a sigh of relief when she finally was able to leave him and close the door of the suite behind her. Yesterday she had managed to find time away from Ryan and her duties, enough time to visit a certain store on Bay Street that carried the rough, seaworthy clothes worn by the ships' crews. She had bought an outfit for her "brother" who was going to sea as a cabin boy. Of course, there were plenty of breeches and shirts aboard the *China Pearl*, but it would be much easier to sneak on unnoticed in the proper clothes. A properly gowned lady sneaking around the docks at night would cause a sensation to rival the one Spence was planning for her! She had hidden the bundle in the back of her capacious closet, but she wanted to try them on. If she had sewing to do, she barely had time for it.

Chapter Ten

THURSDAY EVENING, AS THEY ENTERED THE SUITE AFTER dinner, Ryan spoke with studied casualness.

"We leave at midnight tomorrow, darling. Tonight will be our last night together until I return."

Leslie, taking the pins from that hated knot of hair, turned away and shook her hair down vigorously to hide the surge of excitement she felt. Tomorrow at midnight! She was ready. Her final plans were made, her letter to Charles written to explain her absence. All that remained was to determine the right time to leave the hotel. If she boarded the ship too soon, Ryan might discover her empty room. She turned and looked at him, biting her lip thoughtfully.

"Why, then—if you don't leave until such a late hour, what prevents you from spending an hour with me before you go?" She waited, hoping desperately that something—anything—would prevent that final meeting.

Ryan frowned. "A tradition, silly as it sounds. The Rockwells always give us a bon voyage party. After dinner, everyone making the trip gathers in the lounge for last-minute plans and information. The Rockwells provide rounds of liquor to toast our success, and then we all leave together for the ships. No one misses that meeting, and my absence would be noticed." His frown faded as he looked at her. "Perhaps I could slip away for a moment or two."

"No," Leslie said hastily, her mind reaching for reasons. "We would have only a hurried kiss, a few words, and a sharper sadness in our parting." She went to him and put her arms around him coaxingly. "I would rather take leave of you properly tonight. With all my love and time enough to express it. Tonight is mine, Ryan. Tomorrow night your thoughts will be on the ship and the trials ahead of you." She was almost, but not quite, ashamed of pretending such unselfishness. She needed that time between dark and the midnight departure. And, in any event, Ryan looked very pleased with her.

"You're a lovely romantic," he said, smiling, "but I do agree. My mind should be on my ship then. But tonight isn't yours, my sweet. It's ours, and I'll make sure that we have all the time we need." His kiss promised that and more. "I'll go back now so I can slip away early."

Leslie watched him leave, half amused at his skill in preserving the guardian-and-ward myth. She was sure that some of the women in the hotel suspected their real feelings, but Ryan never gave it away. None of the men—since Tom Farrell had left after his beating—seemed to have caught on. Even Spence, though appearing puzzled at first, had accepted their indifference to each other. Accepted it too well, she thought ruefully. Spence's attentions to her were never crude or importunate, but recently they had been marked by unusual warmth. Those slanted green eyes were no longer cynical when they gazed at her.

She shrugged, turning toward the bedroom. Spence might soon know. If there was news in Wilmington about her father, then she and Ryan would marry. If there wasn't, she had a long search ahead of her. She was ready, if necessary, to travel anywhere to find Harry Gordon, and she was wise enough to know that Ryan Fitzsimmons would never let his wife start out alone on such a journey. It was reason enough to put off marriage. It was simply something she had to do first. And then . . . well, then she would have to make sure of a place for herself on his ship. There would be no loving and waiting, lonely in some port.

But still, she thought as she began undressing, there must be advantages to being married, or it wouldn't be every woman's goal. She must remember to ask . . . later. Right now, the night ahead was enough. She turned down the bed and then put out the lights, darkening the room to a glimmer from the starry sky. Then she went to the window to raise it high.

"This will be a night to remember," Ryan said softly from outside. There was laughter in his low voice. "You have never greeted me at the window before. I do like an eager woman."

Leslie laughed, startled. She hadn't seen him at all in the shadowy garden. As he stepped inside and took her in his arms, she could only hope that tomorrow night she would be as invisible to his eyes.

It was, indeed, a night to remember. Ryan made sure of it. Leslie had never known him to be so inventive, so openly erotic. She willingly learned the ways to draw out the singing tension between them, to approach the ultimate ecstasy with feather touches of lips and tongue, to wait trembling on the ragged edge, flaming with need, and then withdraw. Skillfully, subtly, Ryan taught her the many ways of love, brought her quivering body to a sweet, sharp agony of desire over and over, and only when she thought she could stand it no longer, swept her past the edge into tumbling rapture.

It was close to dawn before Ryan dressed again and made his farewell. Sitting on the side of the bed, he took her hands and held them between his broad palms.

"Remember, I love you. Remember, you're mine. And keep yourself safe for me."

"I will." Leslie felt a twinge of guilt that gradually built into worry. Until now, her plan to stow away aboard the *China Pearl* had been a secret but glorious game. A serious game, since she felt she must go, but a game, nevertheless. A game Ryan must lose if she were to win. But, what if it was wrong? What if his fear for her safety did distract him? She began to wonder if she should go through with it.

Still holding her hands, Ryan sat with his head bent thoughtfully, his face hidden in the darkness.

"Leslie, are you positive that you have had yellow fever?"

"Why, yes." Surprised, Leslie wondered why he had asked. "My mother and I both had it when I was only a child. I survived, but—she didn't. Why?"

"I believe there will be an epidemic here," Ryan said slowly. "There are a half-dozen cases on the west side of the city and with this constant rain it's almost inevitable. If you hadn't been sure, I've been thinking of taking you along after all, and leaving you in Wilmington. The dangers of the trip might be less than the danger of leaving you here. But, since you are sure . . ."

"I'm sure," Leslie said crossly, "but I wish I hadn't told you. I would gladly flee an epidemic on your ship!"

Ryan chuckled and gave her a last, tender kiss. "I prefer you safe, my love."

The first faint light of dawn outlined the garden wall as she watched him swing his lean, muscular body over it and drop from view. Then her eyes ran along to the espaliered branches of a small tree against the wall and she smiled. All her doubt was gone. If Ryan could even consider taking her, she would go. That tree would be her ladder tonight. She couldn't reach the top of the wall as he did, but there was always a way if one could manage to find it.

Leslie rose early in spite of the nearly sleepless night. In midmorning, neatly dressed in her brown suit, she walked down to the harbor and the dock where the *China Pearl* lay snugged up for the final loading. It was necessary to discover any difficulties that might meet her when she came down in the dark.

Neither Ryan nor First Mate Tudbury were in sight, but the bosun spotted her and came, grinning, to help her aboard.

"Wish you was shipping out with us, ma'am. You brought good luck on the last trip." His grizzled hair blew in the light breeze, his heavy face shone with undisguised admiration. "You do look fine, Miss Gordon. Nassau agrees with you."

Leslie laughed. "And I agree with you—I wish I were going." If only she could ask for his help! But Finney would never go against Ryan's wishes. She pretended an interest in the cargo and Finney immediately offered a tour. He took her below to show her the magazine room, crammed with gunpowder, saltpeter, sulphur; to the cargo space that held the cases of medicines, bolts of uniform cloth, boots. There were also boxes of tea and sack after sack filled with hams. Leslie raised her brows.

"Food? I should think it less needed than armaments."

"People are starving, ma'am," Finney said shortly, "and the poor will go on starving, lucky to get cornmeal. Those hams there will bring fifty dollars each, and the tea will sell for over a hundred dollars a pound. Only the wealthy eat good in the South, now."

Leslie's heart sank, thinking how much worse the war had become in her homeland. People in the cities were no better off than she had been in the Green Swamp before Ryan found her. Back on the decks, she glanced along at the chained crates that held rifles and wished that they, too, held food. But, in any event, the spaces between them would give her a place to hide tonight if necessary.

"I suppose you mount a guard at night," she said casually. "There are valuable things here to steal."

Finney shrugged. "Little need for that, with the chains and lanterns. We leave one man on deck to keep an eye open." He laughed grimly. "An intruder is shot and then questioned, ma'am, so most of them stick to stealing on land."

"Shot?" Leslie paled. "What if he's innocent?"

"Someone who slips aboard a ship in wartime isn't innocent," Finney said firmly. "He's up to something." Noticing her frightened face, he turned genial again. "Nothing to worry about tonight, ma'am. When the ships' crews come out of those rooming houses and head for their bunks aboard, there'll be a crowd of honest men on the docks all evening."

"Of course," Leslie said slowly, "I hadn't thought of

that." She forced a smile and said a few more words about the cargo, wished him a fine trip and good luck. Then she turned to leave and met Ryan coming up the gangway. But she had prepared herself for a possible meeting. She smiled brightly and hurried to him.

"I hoped to find you here," she exclaimed, and took a package from the capacious bag she carried. "I have a gift for you, and I couldn't wait to see if it pleases you."

Caught off-guard, Ryan's strong face reflected exactly the way he felt about her. Love shone from his eyes. Then, as Finney coughed and moved away, the usual mask of authority fell into place. Taking the package, he turned it over curiously and then opened it, exposing a leather case with a long strap fastened to each side. Unsnapping the case, he took out a pair of binoculars.

"The best of German made," he exclaimed. "You know the gift pleases me. I have nothing nearly as fine as these. Where did you find them?"

Leslie sighed with relief. "Then you do like them. I bought them this morning from an impoverished English officer who needed money to pay his gambling debts." She laughed a little. "I know I could have given them to you later, but I simply couldn't wait, even though I knew you'd be busy. But I won't keep you, Captain. I'll see you at dinner." She pushed past him hastily and left.

Glancing back as she reached the end of the gangway, Leslie saw both Ryan's and Finney's heads bent over the binoculars. The excuse had worked well; Ryan wouldn't wonder why she had been on the ship today. But what in the world would she do about that crowd of sailors tonight? They would be straggling along the docks and up the various gangways all evening. Someone would be sure to notice her.

She was halfway up Parliament Street before the

solution came to her. Then she turned and went back, hurrying now, to the shop where she had bought the breeches and shirt.

That evening, Leslie wore the Eugenie gown to dinner. Standing in front of the looking glass while she tied the ribbon tightly below her breasts and adjusted the froth of tulle that swept around her bare shoulders and outlined the low cut of back and bosom, she was struck again by the grace of the gown. The sheer mousseline fell in an unbroken line from the ribbon to the floor, swirling as she turned, revealing and then concealing again the lines of her slender figure. Her back and shoulders, the line of her delicate neck, all rose from the graceful tulle in creamy perfection. Her upswept hair with its springing, rebellious curls, matched the tawny lily at the cleft of her bosom. She stared at her image with a sense of unreality. Could that tall, poised stranger actually be Leslie Gordon? She could hardly wait for Ryan to arrive.

Later, she rushed to open the door when the expected knock came, and then stood still in surprise.

"Spence!"

Looking extraordinarily neat in a well-pressed gray uniform, Spence stared back at her. "You are absolutely beautiful, Leslie," he said reverently. "No one else could wear that gown with such grace, such style. I give Ryan credit. He recognized that quality when he spoke of you as a golden lily."

Leslie hardly heard him. "Thank you. You're very kind. But—what has happened to Ryan? Is he ill?"

"Indeed not. Only late getting back from his ship. He told me I might take you in to dinner and he will join us later."

Relieved, Leslie smiled to hide her disappointment and took Spence's arm. "Nice of you to bother, Spence. I could have waited."

"It's hardly a bother." Spence tucked her arm closely against his side, his green eyes adoring. "It's a privilege. One I hope to keep. Ryan has asked me to look after you while he's gone. Seldom has duty been so pleasant a prospect."

Moving slowly toward the lobby, Leslie couldn't help laughing. "Spence, I believe you would flirt with a wall if no woman was near."

"And I believe," Spence said quietly, "that you will discover in time that I'm quite serious."

This time, Leslie pretended she hadn't heard, a deception aided by a fulsome greeting from one of the Southern matrons.

"My dear Miss Gordon, what a lovely gown! A Eugenie, I believe? And Captain Burdette—why, has Miss Gordon's fierce guardian relented at last? What a lovely couple you make."

Leslie could have killed the silly, simpering woman. She could have killed Spence, who was looking fatuously pleased by the woman's romantic assumption. But then she looked up and caught Ryan's gaze as he came toward them, caught the sweeping look he gave her, the faint smile as his eyes rested on the golden lily at her breast. She knew that smile, and it made up for everything. Her heart high, she went in to dinner between them. If she failed in her attempt to stow away tonight, at least Ryan would have a memory of her looking her best.

For once, Ryan had trouble maintaining his paternalistic role. He looked at Leslie too often, leaned too close, his attention wavered from the general conversation. But tonight no one noticed. For one thing, Wynne was absent. "Indisposed," Charles had said calmly. For another thing, there was a great deal of tension among the younger captains. Keyed up, they talked too loudly, argued and bickered, laughed it off. Spence eyed them quietly and, as the dinner ended and the orchestra came in, he rose from the table and went to speak to the leader. Turning back in a moment to the roomful of diners, he asked for their attention.

"In honor of the brave men leaving tonight to take desperately needed supplies to our nation, I suggest a song from the Golden Lily of the Confederacy!"

There was instant applause. Spence's grin beamed at Leslie across the room. "How about 'Dixieland,' Miss Gordon?"

Leslie gritted her teeth. She should have killed him, there in the lobby. Rising, she smiled and bowed and then made her way gracefully through the tables and up on the podium. She hated Spence. She was tired, with a strenuous night ahead of her. But, as the room quieted, she looked at the table full of men who would be risking their lives in the Federal blockade and her resentment melted away. They deserved something, some accolade, some notice from these Southern emigrés who waited in luxurious safety for the war to end. She nodded to the pianist, and as he began to play the spirited song her voice rang out with enthusiasm.

Oh, I was born in the land of cotton
And old times there are not forgotten . . .

Leslie got no farther alone. The whole room joined in, the men standing, the women looking toward the table of young captains and the clapping for them started even before the song ended. Leslie smiled forgivingly at Spence and took his hand as she stepped down.

"I never would have thought of it," she said. "I'm glad you did." She looked up at Ryan as he came toward her through the throng.

"Spence will see me to my door," she said hastily. "I know you must be with the others. I wish you the best of trips and a fast run home." Their eyes met and Ryan nodded, a muscle moving along his tight jaw.

"I will remember you standing there," he said quietly. "That gown moves around you like drifting mist." His faint smile reappeared as he watched her cheeks turn pinker. Then he clapped Spence on a shoulder. "As for you, you'll be welcome in the lounge. We can always use some advice from a raider captain."

Leslie left Spence at the door of the suite with a simple: "I'm very tired." Closing the door, she knew it wasn't a lie. The tension and excitement had taken a toll along with the sleepless night. But she had no idea how long the session in the lounge would last and it was already dark. There was no reason to delay. This was the moment, and, thank God, it was raining again.

She dressed quickly in the breeches and shirt, the knitted cap for her long hair. Then she put on the extra articles she had bought today—a long, dark oilskin coat and a hood, a pair of dark boots. She would be the best-dressed cabin boy or powder monkey in the whole fleet. She looked at the shining cleanliness of the new clothes dubiously. Something would have to be done about that with the dirt in the garden.

Rushing, she laid the letter to Charles on a table in the sitting room and left, dropping from the window as silently as ever Ryan had. There was something to be said, she thought triumphantly, for three years of hunting in a swamp. She paused long enough in the pelting rain to gather dirt and smear her boots and dull the gleam of the oilskins. The rain might wash off most of it, but it would be doing the same for the others. And everyone would be head down and hurrying in this weather.

The espaliered tree had sharp twigs; the drop on the other side of the wall was much longer than she had thought, with the ground below uneven. When she picked herself up and started around the back wall her hands were bleeding and an ankle hurt, but she was far too excited to care and surging with new energy.

The tree-shadowed street offered good protection for a dark figure darting from trunk to trunk and there were few people out. Only once she had to avoid a clattering carriage, then went on, stealthy but quick, calling on all the skill she had learned in those three years.

A half hour later a small, hooded figure slipped quietly between two chained barrels in front of a darkened store and fell in behind a noisy group of similarly clad sailors heading for the docks. Shortly afterward, another group caught up with them and Leslie was slogging along in the middle, head bent against the rain, ears scalded by the language they were using.

None of them were heading for the *China Pearl*. She passed the gangway with them and then melted into the shadows of another store, retracing her steps, startling nothing but a cat. She joined three groups before five or six men broke off at the *China Pearl*. By then, she had thoroughly studied the decks, which were lit by smoking lanterns and filled with shadows as the rain and wind swept them. She followed the men up the gangway unnoticed and disappeared like a puff of dark smoke behind a crate of rifles.

She lay there, panting, knowing that now she would need more luck than skill. Somehow, she had to get to the captain's cabin in the stern. With all the cargo hatches battened down, that would be her only refuge. But she would have it to herself, for most of the night.

That was the great piece of luck the rain and wind had brought. Ryan would never trust anyone else to take the *China Pearl* out on a night like this. Now, to get there.

She watched and listened intently. The men who had boarded had gone below, out of the weather. The man on watch was quiet, shuffling his feet and sighing. She raised her head cautiously. He lingered near the gangway, staring along the dark street for the rest of the crew, his back toward her, his face obscured by the dripping hood. The noise of the storm would hide the rustle of her movement. She began, quite calmly, to move from crate to crate.

Twenty minutes later the last of the men appeared, two of them dragging a limp, drunken form between them and shouting for the guard's help in getting the man up the gangway. Grumbling, the guard went down to help, and at the stern the door of the captain's cabin opened and shut silently.

Inside, sagging against the door in relief, Leslie was sure that Fate meant for her to succeed. Why else the wild night, the drunken sailor? She couldn't have managed without such help. Now the only danger was Ryan himself, surely the very worst danger she could face. He wouldn't use the cabin, that was true, but he would be entering it to put down his seabags. And that could happen at any moment now. She looked around as her eyes became accustomed to the darkness. There was space beneath the bunk, but he kept his seabags there. If he shoved them under and felt resistance, he would find out why. There was the desk, but the legs were slender, the space open. Even in the dark he could see her crouching there. She glanced at the open closet. On the floor was the trunk that held the cabin boy's clothes and there was room behind it, beneath the hanging cloaks and oilskins belonging to Ryan. A dangerous choice, for the oilskins would be the first thing Ryan reached for on this stormy night.

A sound outside—a familiar quick footstep. She sprang for the trunk and was over it, huddled behind it with her hooded head down, her hands curled beneath her so no glimmer of skin could show. The cabin door opened, banged sharply in the wind, a sound followed by footsteps. A heavy weight hit her slender back, she felt another thump on top of it and heard the rustle of oilskins snatched from a hook above. Then another quick stride and the door banged shut.

Good Lord! He had thrown his seabags on top of her! How careless! She was half smothered, gasping under the weight, utterly indignant. If she had known that he would do such a thing, she could have been comfortable under the bunk, stretched out and relaxed. This was terrible, the more so because until the situation became safe, she couldn't move. The noise those heavy bags would make thumping around! Gritting her teeth, she reached through a small opening and grasped the rough material, conscious now that her hands were stiffening around the cuts and tears from the tree. Holding the bags carefully so she wouldn't dislodge them, she wriggled until her nose found a faint current of air. Then, fearful of doing more, she settled herself to endure the cramped limbs, the stifling oilskins and the weight of the bags. Soon the *China Pearl* would move out with the rest of the ships and begin the long and dangerous trip to Wilmington. If her luck held, Ryan wouldn't find her until it was too late to turn back. She would be home in less than three days.

The shouts of the crew outside came dimly to her ears. The planks beneath her vibrated to the running feet on deck. Then the whistle of escaping steam shrilled faintly from the boiler room and the ship swung out, caught by the tide.

Leslie's excitement rose. She was almost ready to heave the ponderous bags up and over the trunk when she remembered Ryan's tale of Latimer's stowaway, caught as they left the docks. Maybe that woman had thought herself safe, too, and had given herself away. Leslie subsided again into a miserable heap. The thick oilskins were an impermeable blanket around her; perspiration ran down her cheeks, between her breasts. She closed her eyes, listening as the slow clack of the paddle wheels gradually increased, feeling the rise and fall as the small ship nosed into the wind-tossed water. She would, she thought, give it an hour or two to be safe.

At dawn, Ryan stood motionless in front of the hanging closet, his gaze fixed incredulously on a small, filthy hand, crisscrossed with red streaks and lying, palm up, on the bumpy side of one of his seabags. Whoever owned that hand could be smothered under there, and no one, not even a stowaway, deserved that. Galvanized by the thought, he grabbed both bags and jerked them away. Tossing them behind him, he reached down and dragged up the oilskin-covered heap, pushing the hood back hurriedly. He stared at the revealed face with shock so profound that it left him speechless.

Leslie stared back at him, every bit as silent as he was. To be wakened by rough, clutching hands had frightened her badly and the expression on Ryan's face was hardly reassuring. He looked so completely blank that she had no idea what to expect. She waited fearfully to find out.

"Good God!" Beginning to breathe again, Ryan released his grip on her and watched, stupefied, as she crumpled down and disappeared again behind the trunk. Then two hands appeared, both dirty, and clutched the top of the trunk as she pulled herself up to look over it.

"You could at least help me out of here," Leslie said pettishly, "my legs are numb."

Without another word Ryan picked her up and sat her in the heavy chair by the desk. Then he stepped back and crossed his arms and stared at her. Beneath the perspiration-streaked dirt there were circles of fatigue around the huge blue eyes, her curved mouth drooped like a tired child. How fragile she looked, he thought, and what a deception that was! She was not only strong, but damnably determined once she set her mind on something. She had just proved that once and for all.

"Who helped you stow away?" His deep voice was intentionally harsh and cold.

Leslie sighed. It had been useless to hope that he'd be glad to see her. She drew her arms from the heavy oilskins, stretched her whole body with a groan of relief and settled back in the chair with her booted feet stuck out straight in front of her. Reaching, she pulled the knitted cap from her head, releasing a flood of tangled gold.

"No one."

"Don't try to protect the man who got you aboard," Ryan said warningly. "I'll find out, and it will go the worse for him."

She sat up, blue eyes snapping in spite of fatigue. "You know I don't lie, Ryan! No one helped me. I did it alone, from beginning to end." Her lips trembled. "It was very hard, too. And most uncomfortable, especially after you threw those heavy bags on me. That was—was very careless of you."

"I apologize." Ryan was heavily sarcastic. "I should

have looked first. I wish the hell I had!" The enormity of what she had done was finally sinking in. "My God, Leslie, what possessed you? Not only have you put yourself in grave danger, but Charles—and Spence also—will be combing the island, thinking you've been kidnapped or worse!"

"I left Charles a letter, saying I decided at the last minute to make the trip with you." The words were right, but her voice kept breaking. It was too much. Her hands hurt, she ached all over and one ankle was paining her badly. Besides, Ryan wasn't taking this at all well. "I should think you'd give me credit for having a little sense," she added tremulously, and began to cry, silently, tears running down her cheeks and making more streaks in the dirt.

Ryan reminded himself that she wasn't a child—she was a grown woman, opinionated and stubborn, full of feminine wiles. She deserved no pity or consideration. Then he let out his breath in a disgusted sigh and squatted on his heels, pulling her boots off and eliciting a yelp of pain.

"My ankle . . ."

He peeled down the heavy hose and looked. One slender ankle was slightly swollen and pink. "At least," he said drily, "your feet are clean." He felt the ankle carefully. "Only a sprain. When you finish your bath you can bind it." He looked at her hands, one by one. "Scrub these scratches and put ointment on them." Then he looked at her face.

"Leslie," he added quietly, "why did you do this to me?"

She felt terrible. There was so much pain and worry in his clear eyes. "I couldn't stand you leaving me behind," she blurted. "I wanted to be with you. And, I'll be fine, really I will." She gave him a sudden, tearful smile. "With both of us aboard, the luck is good, remember? Like when the Yanks had her in the river, and then at Mobile Bay?"

Ryan stood up. Maybe she was a child, after all. He loved her, but right now that fact couldn't be allowed in his calculations. His face gradually hardened as he stared down at her.

"Do you swear to me that there's no man aboard who knows that you stowed away?"

Leslie brightened, seeing pardon ahead. "No one knew, neither on the ship nor ashore, and no one saw me, I swear it!"

"Then you didn't stow away. We will say I brought you aboard. I'll not be a laughingstock to my men. And we go right back to the way we lived on the ship before. I'm going down to breakfast and you are going to take a bath, change into clothes from that trunk and be on deck when I come back. I need my sleep and we can't share a bunk. Now get started."

Leslie watched him storm out the door with a catch in her throat. He was Captain Fitzsimmons again, stern and dour as ever. But, well . . . it could be worse. She struggled to her feet, wincing a little, and began to undress. Beneath the exhaustion and pain there was a small, warm feeling of pride. She'd never get the credit, but she'd stowed away on the *China Pearl*—successfully!

Chapter Eleven

LESLIE WAS SITTING IN THE SHADOW OF A SAIL, PERCHED on a crate of rifles, when Ryan came up the ladder from the ward room. There had been startled grins from the men working the sails, but there had been a wholehearted welcome from Harold Finney at the wheel.

"Glad you changed your mind, ma'am," he had added, making it evident that Ryan had talked to him.

Now she looked up and smiled as Ryan stopped beside her.

"The weather looks good," he said casually. "We'll make a fast run." His tone was light enough, but under the shadow of his cap his face was brooding and serious. "Enjoy the fresh air while you can. Tomorrow night you'll be swinging in a hammock below."

"I've swung in one of those hammocks before," Leslie said carelessly. "I expect there's still sand in it."

Perhaps he thought he should warn her, but he didn't need to be overbearing. She stood up. "Excuse me, Captain," she added. "The fresh air also makes me hungry."

Ryan stared after her morosely as she went toward the ladder, the thick, bright braid tossing on her slender back, the rounded buttocks outlined by the soft nankeen breeches. Except for a slight limp and faint lavender smudges around her eyes, there was no sign left of the miserable night she must have spent. She had reverted completely to the gamine she had always been aboard the *China Pearl,* and damned if he didn't think she was happier in the role than she was in any other, including the role of the noted Golden Lily. He went on toward the cabin, an unwilling smile breaking the stern, tired lines of his bronzed face. Trouble she was, but worth it. He would tell her so once he had her safely on land again.

Back on deck after wolfing a breakfast of ham, eggs and biscuits accompanied by cups of hot, strong coffee, Leslie stood on the paddle-wheel box and scanned the horizon curiously. There was no sign of the other ships, unless that faint drift of smoke to the rear came from one of them. She questioned Harold Finney.

"Once away from the island, they scatter," Finney told her. "It's safer. And this time some are making the long trip to Bagdad and Matamoros in Mexico. Unloading there and waiting weeks to collect a third of the profit don't tempt Captain Fitzsimmons. But there's no blockade at a neutral port." He went on, explaining that while Matamoros was just across the Rio Grande from Brownsville, Texas, still it was an expensive haul to take the supplies to where they were needed, and Mexico collected fat landing fees.

"It's the new Yank cruisers," he ended, "that scared some of the captains into trying it anyway."

Leslie smiled. Here, with the fresh breeze blowing, the waves slapping the sleek sides of the ship, dark, gleaming dolphins playing in the bow wave alongside, she couldn't imagine the menacing black shapes, the vicious bursts of shells that she had seen in Mobile Bay. She leaned on the circle of railing that enclosed the paddle box, watching the dolphins with their perennial smiles and dreaming of the days ahead when the war would be over and the *China Pearl* would sail in peace. With her aboard, naturally. She looked back at the bosun.

"Could you teach me to handle the wheel, Mr. Finney?"

He laughed, his bearded face creasing with merriment. "It's no job for a lady, ma'am. There's plenty of men aboard who can handle her."

Leslie ran down the steps of the paddle-wheel box and stepped up beside him. The spokes of the huge wheel reached as high as her chin, but she could see over it, well enough. She watched the needle of the compass quiver and move, saw Finney's gnarled hands move in answer, keeping the course. She glanced up at him with her blue eyes sparkling and her mouth curved in a winning smile.

"Still," she said, "I'd like to learn. It would pass the hours pleasantly."

Several hours were passed pleasantly, both that day and the next. But during the afternoon of the second day, Finney spotted a ship ahead, hove to and apparently waiting for them.

"From the look of her," he told Leslie, "she's George Latimer's ship, the *Nassau Belle*. But we'll have Captain Fitzsimmons up to examine her through those binoculars you gave him." He sent a man to fetch the captain and took the wheel from Leslie.

Ryan confirmed Finney's guess a few minutes later.

"Latimer left hours ahead of us, and he's empty," Ryan said, lowering the glasses, "but the speed he gained did him little good. Now he has to wait for darkness." He looked at Finney grimly. "He was a little ashamed to make the trip without supplies, but the foreigners who own his vessel care nothing for the needs of the South. All they want is the cotton."

Coming up on the *Nassau Belle* later, Ryan stopped long enough in an easy sea for a short parley with Latimer. They were close enough to shout across the intervening space.

"They know we're coming," Latimer shouted. "I've seen three cruisers on the horizon since I stopped here." He gestured vaguely northwestward. "They're widening the search. I'm going in at Charleston once it's dark enough. You'd do well to follow me." Perspiration shone on his wide forehead, and his gestures seemed nervous.

Ryan nodded and thanked him. Latimer was a native of Charleston and knew the difficult channels there. His offer was friendly and well meant. But still Ryan shook his head. "We've reason for going to Wilmington," he called back. "We'll stick to our course."

Listening, Leslie was struck by guilt. She turned away and went to sit amidships, staring out over the heaving sea and thinking that if it weren't for her presence and her desire to find her father, Ryan might have chosen a less dangerous port. As the ship got underway again, she watched him worriedly. He was heading down the ladder for coffee. He'd not go back to bed, not after Latimer's sighting of those cruisers. Which meant he'd be up until the ordeal was over. She shook her head and got up, heading for the stern. She might as well have a few hours in a comfortable bunk before she went below to swing in that hammock.

That is, she thought, if her suddenly active imagination would let her.

Taking off her boots and the breeches and shirt, she left on her camisole and short pantalets and climbed into the still warm, rumpled bunk. Her fears receded as she sank into the pillow and caught the faint scent of shaving soap and male skin. Drifting in a flow of warm memories, she closed her eyes. Nothing truly bad could happen as long as they were together.

A feather-light touch on her cheek awakened her. Opening her eyes, she caught a look on Ryan's face that brought her arms up, open to embrace him. The look disappeared, replaced by sternness. He took her hands and pulled her into a sitting position.

"Time for dinner, and then you can pick your hammock. The sun is setting." He turned away quickly and left the cabin as she slid from the bunk, his long legs striding along the deck as if that same old demon was chasing him. While she dressed, Leslie reflected that more than one demon tormented him tonight. His desire for her could have been easily solved, but his fear of taking her through the blockade was her fault entirely. She went out on deck in a sober mood that deepened rapidly into apprehension.

The *China Pearl* lay motionless in the water, no smoke wavering up from her funnels, and the sails wrapped tightly to the spars and tied. Looking south, she saw the reason. A half-dozen warships paced each other, their shapes ominous as they maneuvered against the darkening sky. They were far enough away that she could only see them as the ship rose on the tops of the waves rolling beneath her, and she knew that they couldn't see the *China Pearl*. Ryan was again "hiding" in full view of his enemy. His slender gray spars and low hull would be indistinguishable against the dull northern sky. But why were they north of them? There was no entrance to Wilmington from the north.

"That's the northernmost end of the blockade," Ryan explained at dinner. "We mean to circle them once night falls, and creep back south along the shore inside. The sound of the surf will drown out the thrashing of the paddle wheels. God willing, we'll make New Inlet and be over the bar before they see us."

Leslie nodded and was silent. She knew Wilmington's shores well enough to know the chance he was taking. He could go aground by the slightest miscalculation and be a sitting duck at daybreak. She ate little, and went back up the ladder. She meant to stay on deck until ordered below.

The crew gathered for orders. Ryan sent the most steely nerved of the men to the quarters of the ship to handle lead lines and give him bottom soundings. He put Finney on the wheel. He reminded the whole crew that any man showing an open light would be shot, and then saw to the fitting of the tarpaulins that covered every opening. Finney put the canvas funnel over the lighted binnacle and adjusted the tiny opening to show the compass reading. Leslie had stuffed her bright braid into the dark knitted cap and made herself as small as possible on a midship crate, hoping to be invisible.

She had wasted her efforts. Once finished with his orders, Ryan turned and came straight to her in the dark. She had the feeling that he had known every move she made. He reached down and took her arm and led her to the darkened companionway. Pausing there, he looked down at her sternly.

"This time I require a solemn promise. Will you stay below or shall I set a guard?"

"I will stay below." She touched his hand briefly with her fingertips. "You can trust me, Ryan."

For a moment more he stared down at the pale oval of her face, serious now, not the slightest glimmer of a smile in the darkness. "Then I will," he said gruffly, and released her arm. "I hope to God you can trust me."

Leslie went down the ladder into total darkness and the reek of coal gas from the engines, hearing Ryan's soft tread on the decks above. Then she made her way in the blackness to the ward room and sank down in a chair. She had had enough sleep, and the thought of swinging in a hammock while being bombarded seemed ridiculous.

The night was long. At times, Leslie thought they had stopped. The roar of the surf drowned out the sound of the paddle wheels even to her. It was strange to find that her fear, which at times choked her, came and went irrationally. Once the hull of the ship scraped bottom and she shot upward in her chair. Then it slipped off easily and went on, and she slumped in an equally unreasonable relief. She hadn't thought that she would sleep, but she did, huddled in the chair. Her head ached from the coal gas, which could escape no longer from the covered hatches and swirled everywhere. She bitterly regretted her promise to stay below. What she would give for just one whiff of the clear night air. She slept again and dreamed that she was walking the deck, they were far at sea and safe, the sun was shining. . . .

She sat up suddenly, every sense alert, straining to hear. The sound of the surf had receded, the clack of the paddle wheels increasing, increasing every second. She jumped up and felt her way to the ward room door and braced herself with a hand on each side. They were making their run, heading for the bar at New Inlet!

The ship had never gone faster. The sound of the paddles increased with speed; the vibration of the engines racked the flying ship until timbers screeched and trembled. Leslie was filled with a wild hope. Surely, no one could catch the *China Pearl* now. She'd be over the bar and safe in a half hour. . . .

Someone shouted on the deck, a loud, hoarse warning that echoed down the companionway and struck utter fear into Leslie's heart. The blackness above her exploded into a white glare streaked with the red ribbons of flares. Cannon boomed, the burst of deafening sound startlingly near. Shells screamed overhead and detonated with an ear-piercing crash. Cowering back against the ward-room door, Leslie dug her fingers into the frame. Then the ship shuddered and a cacophony of yells and harsh orders sounded from the decks. Ryan! Leslie threw herself forward and grasped the ladder, starting up, her feet climbing surely as the ship shuddered and shuddered again, veering sharply. Those shells were finding their mark. *Oh, God . . . Ryan!*

She was halfway up before she remembered her solemn promise to him. Clinging to the ladder, she wept. He could be hurt, and she couldn't go to him; killed, and she wouldn't know. Shells were bursting now on every side. She heard the shrieking groan of wood breaking and then a crash as a mast toppled. The tortured ship listed to one side with the weight. Fragments of wood showered down around her as she slid from the ladder and sat on the planks, hopelessly listening to the continual roar of the big guns. The slanting planks that she sat on told her the ship was listing badly even though it still traveled forward. *Drove* forward, though surely they would soon sink— or burn. She could see the flicker of flames dancing above her, smell the burning wood. If only she could go to Ryan . . .

She would be of absolutely no use up there. The

thought hit her like a pail of icy water. Ryan had been right. This was no quick dash through fire like the one in Mobile Bay. This was no encounter with a group of drunken soldiers in a river. This was a hell, a baptism of fire. Oh, God, what was *that*? A tremendous boom that shook the very air, and then another, splitting the still vibrating sound of the first, rolling on and resounding like thunder. She clapped her hands over her ears. Surely no ship's cannon could . . .

The fort! Fort Fisher! She was on her feet exulting, listening as the big cannons boomed again and again and the only sounds coming from the Federal gunboats were from their racing engines as they fled out to sea. Feet pounded on deck, lights flared, water splashed down the companionway as men above her doused the fire, cursed and ran on. It was over. *Over.*

She was halfway up the ladder again as Ryan started down. She slid to the bottom quickly and stood still, staring at him in the light of the lantern he carried. His face was blackened by smoke and there was blood on his wrist, blood that ran slowly from beneath his sleeve. He held the lantern high and examined her.

"You're all right," he said gruffly. "I hope you weren't too frightened. We were lucky."

Lucky? She looked at his wrist. "You're bleeding."

"It's nothing. A piece of a spar jabbed my arm as the mast came down." He handed her the lantern. "Hang this in the ward room and make coffee. I'm needed on deck."

She stumbled through the ward-room door, hung the lantern up and made coffee, tears of relief running down her face. Ryan might think it luck, but she considered it a miracle.

There were four wounded men, one groaning with pain, but as Ryan had once told her, the crew took care of its own. Morphine was given, the wounds cleansed and bandaged with expert speed. She could have helped, but she wasn't needed. She poured coffee instead.

Finney came down for a cup. He looked exhausted, his grizzled head drooping. "The *Pearl*'s hurt," he told her, "but she'll make it. Moving the mast leveled her off, and so far the pumps are taking care of the leaks. But we'll not anchor off Smithville. We're going on upriver to Wilmington." He sipped from his mug and grinned at her. "Those two gunboats were right where the Captain said they would be. A good thing he was going so fast when he got between them. Kind of spoiled their aim."

Leslie had thought their aim quite good enough. When no one else wanted coffee she went up on deck, dreading the sight of the destruction. Not as bad as she had feared, but the loss of the mast gave the ship an odd, naked look; the littered decks with their burned spots were ample proof of the danger. A corner of the stern cabin was smashed in, a window broken. Leslie picked her way through the litter to Ryan's side. His wrist was clean, a bandage bulked under his sleeve. He glanced at her and smiled.

"I have a man cleaning up in the cabin," he said. "He'll fasten a tarpaulin over that corner. Then you can go to bed."

She ignored that. She was suddenly furious. "Why haven't you guns?" she asked passionately. "Why don't you fight back? It isn't fair! They are firing on unarmed men!"

Ryan laughed. "I think too much of my neck. There's always the chance of being disabled and taken prisoner. As it stands, we're imprisoned for a time and then paroled. But if one man on the ship so much as fires a pistol at those Yanks, we come under the piracy law. Every man on the ship would be hanged."

Leslie gasped. "You can't even defend yourselves?"

"We defend ourselves," Ryan said gently, "with skill and speed. Usually, it's enough. That was a bad ten minutes, I'll grant you. But we slipped the whole fleet except for those two small gunboats near shore." He chuckled. "They ran quick enough when the fort opened up on them."

Ten minutes. Leslie had thought it an hour at least. She stared ahead at the smooth glimmer of the black river that led to Wilmington.

"I'll not be as frightened," she said slowly, "the next time."

"There will not be a next time," Ryan said grimly. "I'll not take you through that blockade again. We'll be in Wilmington making repairs long enough to find out what you can about your father. You'll be my wife and standing on the dock where I can see you when I leave. As I have said, I prefer you safe." He grinned at her fleetingly. "And I prefer you married. To me."

Once again, Leslie knew that she couldn't sway him. Nor, this time, trick him. She would be what she had never wanted to be—a seafaring man's wife in Wilmington.

The *China Pearl* was given a hero's welcome at the Wilmington docks the next morning by a crowd of bystanders who had come down to gawk at the daring ship that had come in through that Yankee barrage the night before. Luckier yet, the port officials told Ryan, were the two ships that followed him in, undisturbed by the gunboats which had preferred to stay out of range of the alerted fort.

The piers were overrun by the busybody officials, Confederate agents, clerks to check the ships' manifestos, burly black stevedores stacking bales of cotton and tierces of tobacco. Leslie had been raised in this town, but she would never have recognized it now. The staid, drowsy little village she remembered had been nothing like this. In all the faces she scanned, there was not one that was familiar.

She stayed out of the way, her braid tucked into her cap and a jacket flapping loosely around her to hide her feminine form. She watched from a distance as Ryan took the senior boarding officers into his cabin for a celebratory round of brandy and then for a look at the cargo. Arrangements were made for a quick auction so the ship could be emptied for repairs. By afternoon, Ryan had ordered a carriage, left the ship in Tudbury's hands and, taking along his "cabin boy," set out for the home of William and Helen Lockwood.

"They'll be glad to take us in," he told Leslie. "It's impossible to find decent accommodations here. And we can't stay alone in your house until we're married."

Leslie wondered if his confidence in his old friends might be misplaced. By now, her opinion of herself was at a low point indeed. It had occurred to her that Ryan would again have to provide her with a wardrobe. She thought him very kind not to mention it, but surely he knew that she wouldn't be welcome in a lady's home in what she was wearing.

She grew even more uncertain as they entered the section where the Lockwoods lived. Well away from the noisy port, the homes were still well maintained and elegant. They stopped at a high, white-painted gate in a stone wall and Leslie quailed at the sight of a lovely colonial home. Surely, they would never accept her.

Ryan climbed down, tossed a seabag over one shoulder, picked up the sacked hams and boxes of tea he had brought as gifts and looked back at her, still sitting and looking.

"Come along," he said gruffly. "In those clothes, you can climb down as well as I can."

Leslie flushed and did as she was told, trailing him through the gate and up to the door in a state of miserable apprehension. The Lockwoods, she thought, were likely to kindly tell her the direction to the servants' quarters.

They had been seen from the windows, and two portly figures met them at the door, greeting Ryan with genuine pleasure, nodding pleasantly at Leslie and exclaiming over the hams and tea. William Lockwood was tall and distinguished-looking, his wife Helen plump, silver-haired and still possessed of a beautiful, kindly face.

Ryan introduced Leslie, beginning by tweaking off her cap and letting the heavy braid escape down her back.

"This is my fiancée," he said calmly, "Miss Leslie Gordon. I brought her through the blockade, which accounts for her odd appearance."

"Mercy!" Helen Lockwood's tone was full of shocked sympathy. "I thought you a young lad! What an ordeal for a woman to endure. And without proper clothes!" Her look implied that the ordeal would have been infinitely easier to bear if fashionably attired. "Men! What were you thinking of, Ryan? Come, my dear, I'm sure we can find something suitable among our daughters' clothes. Both of them have been sent to the country since the town has become so rough and wicked, but among the things they left there must be something that will fit you." She was leading Leslie through a spacious entry hall and to the stairs while she talked, bustling her along as if she must be removed as soon as possible from the company of the men.

Leslie never looked back. She could easily imagine Ryan's expression without seeing it. And she was perfectly willing to follow this motherly creature anywhere.

"Something suitable"—in fact, the only garments that fit—turned out to be the uniforms that daughter Amy had worn to a strict finishing school in Baltimore before the war. After a hot bath and a bowl of soup to ward off "ships' fevers," Leslie dressed and surveyed herself in a mirror. It could have been worse. The uniforms were long, navy blue silk skirts with old-fashioned bustles, white tailored blouses with high, lace-trimmed collars and long sleeves. In spite of the severity of the style, they were surprisingly becoming to her slender, subtly curved figure. Ryan, she thought, would be very pleased. His wild creature certainly looked proper.

"How wonderful you can wear them," Helen enthused. "They are much too small now for either Amy or Mary Ann. You may have them all, though it may be wearisome to wear the same style and colors every day; still in Wilmington now it's impossible to find either material or gowns. And everything is so expensive! What a blessing Ryan has been with his gifts of food. We haven't tasted tea in months, and very little meat. We had a small flock of chickens, but they were stolen. . . ." She went on chattering as they went downstairs to join the men.

Leslie listened in wonder. If people who lived in a house like this were deprived, then the bosun had been right. The poor must be starving. She thought of the neighbors in her own section of town. Like her schoolmaster father, they had been comfortable but not wealthy. Artisans and clerks, bricklayers and shipwrights, living happily within their modest means. But now? Suddenly, she dreaded the trip to her home tomorrow.

The news was no better in the drawing room. Ryan was listening to Lockwood in frowning disbelief. The *China Pearl* hadn't put in at Wilmington in over three months and Ryan was seriously disturbed at what he was hearing.

"We're flooded by dishonest profiteers," William said, "and decent people can't walk the town streets even in the day for fear of the rogues and desperados who kill and rob for pennies."

"There is nothing to buy on the streets in any event," Helen chimed in, settling her comfortable bulk in a chair and motioning to Leslie to sit beside her. "Or money to buy it with if it was there. Why, one must now give two thousand dollars in our Confederate currency to buy one dollar in gold. And only gold will buy the scarce items."

Ryan glanced at Leslie uneasily. He could leave her plenty of gold; she could live as well as any profiteer. But, looking at the delicate figure in the proper clothes, he still could remember only her foolhardiness. What trouble would she get herself into, once he was gone?

"The authorities—" he began, and was interrupted by William's bitter laugh.

"Do nothing! There are uncounted murders, bodies found floating and mutilated in the river each morning. And deserters by the hundreds, paying blockade-runner crews to hide them in the cotton bales for a trip out."

"Not among my bales," Ryan said grimly. "I'll see to that."

"The military will do it for you," Lockwood said. "Every loaded ship leaving must submit to a search. They use smoke and long, sharp poles to root the poor souls out and then drag them away to shoot them."

Leslie's face was suddenly as white as her blouse. Ryan changed the subject. "Surely, food can be brought in from the farms, William."

"There are no able-bodied men to work the farms. They are all in the army, starving." His angry bitterness was fading into resignation. "Without a miracle, I see no way that we will win this war."

Thoroughly depressed, Leslie leaned her golden head back against the handsome but shabby wingback chair and was silent, her thoughts going back to Lockwood's story of the deserters. She and Ryan were to go to the provost marshal of the town garrison in the morning and ask for news of Harry Gordon. The prospect was frightening.

"Your young lady is exhausted." Helen Lockwood's voice was gentle as she spoke to Ryan. "This is too much for her. Come, Leslie. A nap before dinner is what you need."

Leslie started to protest and thought better of it. She rose meekly and followed again as Helen led the way up the stairs and into a small but comfortable room. She was yawning as Helen turned down the covers on the bed. Dropping off to sleep, Leslie thought drowsily that if she were to stay in Wilmington, it would be as well not to hear any more of the troubles and atrocities that went on. Peace, even the uneasy peace of the vanquished, seemed more desirable than ever.

Chapter Twelve

As always, Leslie's spirits rose with the sun. Leaning on the sill of the window in the small bedroom, gowned in a voluminous, borrowed shift, she watched the sunrise in the blue Carolinian sky, heard a mockingbird sing from a magnolia tree below, and felt at home at last. In the distance she could see the steeple of the church that she and her father had attended, and the bell tower of the school where he had taught. Surely, today she would see a friendly face, hear a surprised greeting.

Leaving the window to dress, she told herself that things couldn't be as bad as the Lockwoods had pictured. Perhaps it would even be a pleasure to be here for a while. But only for a while. There was warmth in coming home again, in remembering her childhood and youth, but still it was like remembering another world, another life. She could close her eyes and see the scene from her window in Nassau—the garden wall, the tropical beauty beyond—and remember the happiest days of her life. During her first year in the Green Swamp, she had been terribly homesick for Wilmington, but not nearly as homesick as she was right now for Nassau and the Ryan she knew there.

The Ryan she knew here was a stranger. He was sleeping downstairs and the light kiss he had given her as they parted last evening had only increased her longing to be in his arms. Yet, in spite of that longing and in spite of his calm assumption that they would soon be wed, she was still determined to know Harry Gordon's fate first. When she gave herself to Ryan it would be with a whole heart.

There was no hurry in dressing for the trip to her old neighborhood. Ryan planned to visit the ship first, alone, and make sure of the shipwrights who would be repairing the *China Pearl*. He wanted it finished, if possible, before the moonlit nights.

Still, she dressed carefully, anxious to make a good impression on her old neighbors. She smoothed the wrinkles from her skirt and coiled her hair high and neat above the stiff collar of the blouse. Then she went downstairs to be greeted by voluble Helen Lockwood.

"It's so nice to have a young woman in the house. I miss my daughters terribly," Helen said, leading her in to breakfast. "I do hope you'll consider staying with us when Ryan leaves."

Leslie didn't know what to say. Ryan had avoided mentioning either her father or the fact that she was a native of Wilmington. She smiled and thanked Helen for her invitation and then told her that she didn't know what plans Ryan had made.

Ryan was late returning. Somewhere, he had found a

quarter of lamb and some late peaches to contribute to the Lockwood larder and they left Helen exclaiming over them as they walked out to the carriage. Once they were in it, Ryan explained his delay.

"I went to the provost marshal alone," he said soberly. "I wanted to spare you if the news was bad. But they know nothing, Leslie. There has been an extensive search for all the deserters who went south, but for over a month there has been no news of Gordon. They are sure he is dead."

Leslie's bright face went pale for a moment, but then she rallied. "I am sure he is not," she said firmly. "He is not really old and he has always been strong. And he is very clever. If by some chance he were hurt or ill and knew he were dying, I know he would have gotten word to someone here so I would hear of it."

"It's possible," Ryan admitted reluctantly. "Perhaps one of your old neighbors will know something. Give me directions."

Leslie laughed. "Give me the reins. I love to drive, and I know the way."

She took the horse through the streets at a fast trot, her excitement rising as she saw old landmarks along the way. When they turned at last into the tree-shaded lane she remembered and began passing the modest houses her cheeks were bright pink, her eyes a blazing blue, straining to see the gray and white cupola that had always been the first sight of her home.

"I should be able to point it out to you from here," she said uncertainly, slowing the horse, "unless the trees have grown to hide it." At the slower pace she could notice the cracked windows and blistered paint on the houses, the weed-tufted lawns and signs of neglect. Her heart fell a little and she pulled the horse down to a walk.

"I suppose it's natural, with this war," she said slowly, "but it doesn't look like the same place. Most of these houses are empty."

"Very natural," Ryan said, hiding a sudden pity. "Families broken up, sons and fathers gone." Watching her, he saw her hands tremble on the lax reins. "How much farther is it?"

"Right here," Leslie said, her breath cut short, "or it was. . . ." She pulled the horse to a stop and sat staring, her eyes filling with tears.

There was nothing but an empty lot, the remains of a wide fireplace, a tumble of blackened timbers. Ryan knew immediately what had happened. It was common in the South for patriotic Southerners to burn the house of a deserter, to leave him homeless and, in their way, repudiate his cowardice and show their contempt. He put an arm around Leslie's shoulders.

"Never mind, my darling. We'll have our own home."

"It's not so much the house," Leslie whispered, "but what was in it. My mother's picture, my father's journal . . . I wanted to see them, to hold them in my hands again."

Ryan took the reins from her hands and held her. She was crying in earnest now, snuffling on his shoulder like a heartbroken child. Over her head, he saw an old woman come out on a sagging porch next door and stand staring at them, one hand shading her eyes. As Leslie's sobs died away, the old woman stepped down and came toward them, her slippered feet scuffing up tiny clouds of dust from the dry street.

"Is that you, Leslie?"

At the sound of the cracked voice, Leslie turned, wiping her eyes unashamedly. "Mrs. Lowery!"

"I thought I knew that streaky gold hair," the old woman said and smiled. "I'm glad to see you're still alive, my girl. And sorry to see you cry over that bad job there." She gestured with a gnarled finger at the blackened ruins. "When I saw you looking I had to come out and say that not all of us felt it was right. Some of us still remember Harry with kindness. He was always awful good to me."

"Thank you, Mrs. Lowery." Somehow, in spite of her tear-stained face, Leslie spoke with dignity. "I'll remember you for that. It was kind of you to come out and tell me."

The old woman nodded, staring at Ryan curiously. "That your beau, Leslie?"

"Yes," Leslie said firmly. "Captain Ryan Fitzsimmons, Mrs. Lowery."

"Oh!" The old face brightened. "The blockade runner, eh? Well, it fits, I reckon. You were always a daring, reckless little sprite, even as a child."

Driving away, Ryan was deep in thought. He glanced at the pale, set face beside him and could almost hear the wheels turning in the inventive brain. What his "daring, reckless little sprite" might be planning now was of greatest interest to him, but he thought it better to wait than to ask. He had decided this morning after viewing the town and docks that he would take her back to Nassau after all. She would be better off running the blockade with him than staying in a nest of crime and violence.

"I will stay with the Lockwoods," Leslie said suddenly. "Helen invited me this morning." She was sitting straight as a ramrod, her head high and eyes burning blue. "While I'm there I can help around the house. They seem to have no servants, and the work is too much for one woman."

Ryan frowned. This was unexpected, to say the least. He had been sure that before he left, Leslie would try to persuade him to take her along. He had planned to give in gracefully. Why did she always surprise him? He glanced at the small, determined face.

"That will not be necessary. I've decided to take you back to Nassau. The dangers of the blockade seem no worse than the dangers here."

"Oh, no." Leslie shook her head. "You were right, Ryan. My place is here, where I can continue my search for my father. I shall stay until I have exhausted every chance."

"Ridiculous!" Ryan exploded. "What can you do that hasn't been done? Believe me, when the army searches for deserters, it does a thorough job. You're only a woman. . . ." Belatedly, he realized that that was the wrong thing to say to Leslie. She was giving him an icy stare.

"I have a plan," she said coldly. "I shall find out from the provost marshal the routes and extent of their search. And then I shall continue from there. They may want him badly, but they don't know my father as well as I do. Besides, in those little Florida towns, there may be some who will talk to me who wouldn't say a word to an army sergeant."

Ryan's temper flew away into the upper atmosphere. The thought of her daring to travel alone in this war-torn and stricken country was impossible.

"That will take money," he said harshly, "and while I am willing to support you anywhere, I will not finance so foolish a venture. Your cowardly father can rot in his hiding place as far as I am concerned."

She hated him! What a cruel and unfeeling man he was! She drew her small body away from him, revolted. "I have money enough and more," she said sharply, "in Charles Rockwell's safe in Nassau. If you will not give me the equivalent in exchange for a note to Charles, I shall ask one of the other runner captains to do so. I am sure they will oblige me."

Ryan was also sure they would. They all carried gold, more than enough for their cargos. And gold in Rockwell's safe was a surer thing now than gold in the endangered ships. And, with the gold, Leslie could buy enough Confederate money to take her anywhere in the South. Enough money to tempt the first dishonest man she met to kill and rob her. His temper cooled rapidly in the chill of his fear for her. He drove on for some moments before he spoke again. Carefully.

"If you feel so strongly," he said, his voice cold and distant, "I will give you the gold before I leave. The less others know of your search the better."

Even choked by her anger, Leslie knew that was true. Talk could lead to her father's arrest. She was silent and withdrawn, her heart aching as her temper faded away. She couldn't turn her back on her father, but she was losing Ryan.

During the next few days, while Ryan busied himself at the docks overseeing repairs, Leslie made her inquiries about the search for Harry Gordon. The provost marshal, a fatherly man of good will, was open with her. He understood her concern and saw no reason why he should hide any information, particularly now that he considered it useless.

Incredibly, Leslie found that the searchers had traced her father into Florida, had found out several of the small towns he had visited for supplies, though they had never discovered where they had settled. One of the reports, she noted, had been made after he left the Green Swamp for the last time. He had been spotted then in a tiny settlement near Jacksonville, Florida. But there the reports ended.

"He dropped out of sight," the marshal said, then added kindly: "I hate to discourage you, Miss Gordon, but we find that when a man disappears completely for such a long time, it's generally because he, uh . . . has met with an accident. If my trained men can't track him down in Florida's sparse population, I'm afraid you would be wasting both money and effort."

Leslie agreed with him, thanked him and left. She still intended to try, but it was better to let the provost marshal think that he had convinced her. Certainly, she didn't want to lead his men to Harry Gordon.

The relationship between Leslie and Ryan grew steadily more distant. In the presence of the Lockwoods they were cordial, but that was all. The strain told on Leslie. She appeared more fragile than ever; her body looked pencil slim in the navy skirts and stiff blouses, her brilliant blue eyes huge above thinning, high-boned cheeks.

Helen Lockwood put it down to Leslie's worry about Ryan and tried to comfort her.

"I know how you must feel, seeing him ready himself for another trip, after you know how harrowing they are," she said. "But trust in God and his skill. He will come back to you."

Leslie prayed that he would, in more ways than one. But no matter how she searched for a sign that Ryan had relented, his bronzed face showed no flicker of feeling, no sign of softening. She felt he would never forgive her for putting her father first, nor certainly would he ever understand why she must. He probably hated her. Under the circumstances, she found it difficult even to ask him about the transfer of gold. But it was one thing she had to do, and soon. Only Jeff Barclay and one other, older captain whom she knew only slightly, had come into Wilmington, and in truth, she hated to ask them.

Finally, the evening came when Ryan casually mentioned at dinner that the *China Pearl* would be ready for sea in another day.

"She'll be faster than ever," he told Lockwood. "I

have had the steam engines overhauled and the boilers strengthened while the other repairs were being made."

"But you've too much moon," Lockwood objected. "You'd better cool your heels and wait." He glanced at Leslie and smiled. "You've plenty of reason to enjoy a bit of leisure ashore."

Ryan smiled but didn't answer. It was plain to Leslie that he could hardly wait to leave. That night she wrote out a note to Charles Rockwell instructing him to give her savings to Ryan, and the next morning she arose very early to follow Ryan out into a wet morning. The summer rains had begun in the Carolinas as well as in the Bahamas. It had evidently rained all night and was still misting.

"Please, wait . . ."

Ryan was already in his carriage, but he waited, watching Leslie as she came toward him. Droplets of mist were diamonds in her golden hair, her eyes startlingly blue in her white face. But he noted that the set of her slim jaw was as stubborn as ever.

Leslie hated this, but she had to do it. She stopped at the side of the carriage and looked up into the stern face with as much poise as she could muster.

"About the gold," she said, and reached into a pocket in her skirt, handing him the slip of paper. "There is the note to Charles. I—I hope you haven't forgotten your promise that you'd do me this favor."

Ryan's eyes slid away as he stuffed the paper into a pocket. "I haven't forgotten," he said tersely. "If you'll accompany me to the ship tomorrow morning, I'll give you the gold and send you back with a guard."

Leslie stared at him in surprise. "Why not bring it back with you tonight?"

Ryan's brows arched. "I can, of course. But I thought you might enjoy seeing the ship once more, now that she's repaired and refurbished. She's quite a pretty sight."

It was the first time he had said anything even remotely friendly in over a week. "I would like that very much," Leslie said tremulously. "I'll be ready tomorrow whenever you are." She turned and almost ran back into the house.

Leslie was happier that day. She sang around the house as she helped Helen with the chores, and Helen listened and thought with pleasure of the days ahead. Leslie had agreed to stay with them, though she had been vague about how long. Leslie had thought it better not to mention her plans until they were completed. There were many arrangements to be made for the arduous trip ahead.

The next morning was even wetter. Leslie hurried through her dressing and, at the bottom of the stairs, snatched an old cloak from a hat rack as she followed Ryan out. Ryan helped her into the carriage, his hand stiffly on her elbow.

"More rain," he commented. "It promises to continue all day. Miserable weather."

"Perhaps it will clear," Leslie said. She almost smiled, her heart lifting. At least they were talking!

In this weather, and at this hour, the docks were almost empty, with only a few men standing around, huddled in their cloaks. But there, swinging in the river current, the *China Pearl* glistened in the misty rain, bright with new varnish on the decks, her rakish hull sleek with a new coat of pale gray paint. She looked new, reborn, ready to skim lightly over the waves and show her heels to any enemy. For a moment Leslie was racked with longing and jealousy. *If only* . . . She pushed the thought away without finishing it and turned to Ryan resolutely.

"She's beautiful," she said. "I know you must be

proud of her. Now, if we could conclude our business . . . ?" She didn't want to be brusque, but she had just discovered that she couldn't stand this. It was tearing her apart to think of Ryan leaving without her.

Ryan nodded abruptly and helped her up the gangway as Harold Finney approached, grinning from ear to ear, and greeted her. Then he turned to Ryan.

"They've finished with the engines, sir. Shall I test them now?"

"Certainly." Ryan's deep voice was irritated, as if Finney should have known. "Be sure that you build a full head of steam. If one of those boilers won't hold it, I'd rather find it out here instead of in the ocean."

Perhaps, Leslie thought, Ryan was irritated with everyone these days. She allowed him to lead her into the cabin, which had also been improved, with a new window, new carpeting and even curtains. It looked, she thought, very lovely. She sat down on a small stool as Ryan seated himself at the desk and drew a ledger toward him.

"I keep careful records," he said coolly, "and I will write down this transaction in full. Then I will ask you to sign it."

It took a very long time. Ryan wrote slowly and neatly, dipping his pen often in the ink bottle, shaking it carefully, going back to the paper with deliberation. Leslie sat silently, listening to the rumble of the engines as they built up steam. It seemed to take much less time than usual before the hissing of the escape valves began. Usually, cold engines took much longer. She sighed as another wave of longing swept her. If only her search was over and she could go. She glanced at the bright chestnut head bent over the ledger and then forced her gaze away, looking out a window.

"We're moving!"

"I imagine," Ryan said, still writing steadily, "that

Finney will test the paddle wheels with a trip in the river. One of them has had extensive repairs."

Leslie subsided, listening to the click-clack of the paddle blades, which began when they had drifted out from the docks. For a moment she had wondered—but that was silly! Ryan wouldn't leave with an empty ship. There was no profit in that. She watched Ryan and listened. Ryan was pausing longer between the phrases he was writing, dipping the pen thoughtfully, taking more time to make sure it wouldn't drip. He seemed, she thought, to be thinking of something else. He might be listening to the paddle blades, too. Finney was giving them a real workout. The *China Pearl* was flying down the rain-shrouded river, passing beyond the final buildings and old, rotting docks that marked the southeast outskirts of Wilmington. Then Ryan leaned back in his chair and shut the ledger with a snap. His clear hazel eyes met her gaze openly for the first time since their quarrel. They were full of amusement and some other, deeper emotion.

"Can you think of a more fitting revenge against a stowaway, Leslie? You have just been shanghaied."

For a moment the huge blue eyes simply stared back at him blankly. Then Leslie leaped to her feet with a strangled cry and threw herself at the door of the cabin. It was locked and the key missing. She turned back, raging.

"You'll not get away with this, Ryan Fitzsimmons! I'll not keep my mouth shut this time! It's a crime to take me against my will. . . ." She stopped, choking, knowing very well that she was making no sense at all. Every man jack on this damned ship would swear that she came aboard willingly, even Finney. How could she persuade him? "The Lockwoods," she added, her voice trembling, "they know I didn't plan to go. They will worry about me."

"I left them a note," Ryan said, "saying we couldn't bear to be parted." He grinned and gave her her own words back again mockingly: "I should think you'd give me credit for a little sense."

Leslie groaned and dropped back down on the stool. The shock was wearing off and she was beginning to think again. "You're doing this only to frighten me," she accused. "I know very well that you're not really leaving, not with an empty ship and during the day."

He laughed at her. "But I am, my darling. For one thing, a loaded ship might have warned you. For another, I wanted no weight to slow my speed if I'm to run the blockade in daylight. Think of the fame! I'll not be the first man to challenge the Federal fleet during the day, but surely I'll be the first to leave a Confederate port without my profit aboard."

His wry humor was convincing. She believed him. "Why?" she whispered, "why are you doing this to me, Ryan?"

He stood up, his bronzed face sobering, and pulled her up from the stool, his broad palms tight around her slim shoulders. "Because," he said quietly, "I couldn't bear to leave you to face such danger. I planned this from the first day we quarreled. I have no excuse for ruining your plans, my own darling, except for one. In case you've forgotten, I love you very much."

Some stronger woman might have been able to resist the look in Ryan's eyes, the tenderness in the deep voice, but not Leslie. Not entirely. She wavered, the blue of her eyes deepening, her sensuously curved lips beginning to soften and quiver. "But," she said weakly, "you shouldn't have . . ."

Ryan's hands slipped down her back; his arms drew her close as his faint smile appeared. "Let me try to persuade you," he said softly, and bent to kiss her.

Leslie sighed, her lips parting involuntarily, her

slender body seeking his hard warmth. They both trembled with the fierce flush of long-held desire that swept them; their hands fumbled hungrily for warm, bare flesh. Clothes fluttered to the floor like autumn leaves in a gale, and they were in the bunk with no clear idea of how they got there, only a deep satisfaction in sharing it. In minutes, their bodies were joined tightly.

"My love," Ryan whispered, covering her face with kisses, "my wild little love. How I have wanted you. . . ." He reached desperately for a control that was rapidly slipping away, looking down into eyes that mirrored a desire as great as his own, feeling her soft hands caressing his back, her body rippling beneath his. He groaned, knowing the control was gone, and took her panting mouth with a deep kiss as their soaring passion reached its peak, catching their trembling bodies in a mighty, thunderous beating of rapture that united them completely.

Afterward, Ryan pulled the pins from Leslie's still knotted hair, and, lying beside her, combed through the shining mass with his fingers, spreading it out over the pillows.

"This is the way I see you in my dreams," he said softly, "tender and beautiful, and so willing to be mine." He began again to caress her, shaping the rounded breasts with his long fingers, teasing the pink rosettes and slowly stroking down the curve of waist and hip. Leslie felt the pulse of her body begin to quicken again, to glow beneath his palm. She twisted her head and looked at him with a smile.

"Won't you be needed on deck?"

Ryan kissed the smile. "It's a long river, darling. And the men know what they're doing."

"I suspect," Leslie said, quirking a golden brow, "that they also know what we're doing."

Ryan frowned. "It's my ship and my crew. And I've

discovered something that I think you've always known. Some things are more important than propriety."

Her blue eyes widened and began to sparkle. "Now that's a concession," she acknowledged in a whisper, and put her arms around his neck, her fingers ruffling the bright chestnut hair. "Life aboard ship sounds better and better, Captain. I may forgive you for shanghaiing me." She thought about that for a moment, her face sobering. "And I may not. I truly do wish I could have stayed. I won't be able to find my father now until the war ends. That may be too late."

"You've forgotten my promise," Ryan said quietly. "I will ask Spence to help. If anyone can find him, Spence will."

"But how? I still can't believe . . ."

"It's Spence's secret, not mine. Just believe me. He can and will do it."

Looking into his clear eyes, so strangely light in the dark face, Leslie believed him. She sighed and snuggled closer. "Then it was foolish of me. . . ."

"It was," Ryan said, and crushed her against his length, his hands running hungrily over her again. "At times your foolishness is overwhelming. Tell me, are you foolish enough to love me?"

"I am," she said, her words muffled by his neck. "And I always will be."

"Then show me," he commanded huskily. "Show me again and again." He rolled until she lay over him. "It's your duty to convince me."

Leslie gazed down at the strong, dark face, the sensual, wide mouth, and smiled. "Seldom," she said softly, "has duty been so pleasant a prospect." The words were faintly familiar; she remembered them from somewhere, but she had forgotten who had said them. It didn't matter. Nothing mattered but the love and the hunger between them. She wriggled upward until her hair hung like a shimmering gold curtain around them, shadowing their faces, and began what she hoped would be an endless task by kissing Ryan's eyes shut and then trailing more kisses down his cheeks to the corners of his firm mouth. There was a lot of Ryan, but she didn't intend to miss any of him.

Chapter Thirteen

IT WAS A LONG RIVER, BUT LIKE ALL RIVERS, IT ENDED AT the sea. By noon, Ryan was on the deck and taking command again. Leslie, wearing the usual breeches and shirt, covered today by her oilskins and hood, stood at the rail and watched the tiny fishing village of Smithville, the looming majesty of Fort Fisher on its promontory, emerging from the murk. Once again she realized how deep and far-reaching Ryan's knowledge of his trade really was. The sea and the heavy rain blended in a thrashing medley of gray, and the Union ships would have a very hard time of it seeing the low, gray *China Pearl*. In fact, the danger of running aground on some unseen obstacle was now much greater than the danger of being fired upon. She knew that Ryan knew the channels well; she hoped that he knew them well enough.

Men had been posted again on each quarter of the ship, swinging their lead lines. Lookouts stood on each paddle-wheel box, their anxious faces continually moving, sweeping the gray walls that seemed to enclose them. Faintly, the noise of the sea buoy at the inlet came to their ears, softened by the heavy and constant sound of rain.

Ryan cursed softly and changed course as the bottom of the ship scraped along a bank. Leslie left the rail and went to him. They must be nearing the bar.

"Will the gunboats be there?" She was whispering.

"No." He smiled, the red-brown face beneath his cap shining, wet from the rain, the light eyes as soft as mist as he looked down at her. "They only come in at night when the gunners at the fort can't see them."

"They can't see them now," Leslie pointed out, and Ryan laughed.

"True. But they don't expect a runner to try a daylight break, and they don't know these waters. They would run more risk of getting grounded than we do. And, grounded, they'd make a pretty target for the fort when the rain stopped." His gaze roved over her. "Still, you might be better off below. You're wet enough, and once we're over the bar there will be a rough sea to contend with."

"I'll stay," Leslie said stubbornly. "I wouldn't want to miss anything."

An hour later she was back in the cabin, removing the oilskins. There had been nothing to miss. Nothing but the crossing of the bar and passing the noisy, plunging sea buoy. They had turned north to run again along the shore, the ship rocking awkwardly in the humping waves, the roar of the surf wild today. This was the long, necessarily slow beat up into the wind, and Leslie didn't mind missing uneventful discomfort.

Tudbury spelled Ryan on the wheel, and Leslie joined Ryan for lunch in the ward room. He was wet, tired and chilled to the bone, glad for the hot stew and coffee.

"The rain will lessen in late afternoon, I believe," he told Leslie, "which may be a help. We'll be near the northernmost horn of the fleet and ready to make a run for it. But if it changes to intermittent, heavy showers, it will be no more our advantage than theirs."

Leslie didn't understand that, but she didn't bother him with questions. She poured him another cup of coffee instead and smiled.

"You'll get through," she said confidently. "You always do." They both jumped as the ship's bottom ground over sand and came free again. Leslie laughed. "Mr. Tudbury is yelling some choice words at the port leadsman," she added. "I don't have to hear him to know that."

Ryan grinned at her. "You're picking up quite a few bits of knowledge, aren't you? I'll have to hire you on."

Leslie grinned back at him wickedly, her eyes sparkling. "You don't know how true that is, Captain. You've shown me how nice life can be aboard ship."

In late afternoon, the intermittent showers that Ryan didn't want arrived. The *China Pearl* cautiously began her slow turn from the beach, with Finney at the wheel and Ryan standing by the engine-room tube. All lookouts were tense and alert as they moved through the erratic pattern of dense clouds of rain sweeping past and leaving surprising stretches of clear sky. The men spoke in whispers. Voices traveled like magic over water and were known to alert an enemy quicker than the watery thrashing of the paddles. Leslie found herself tiptoeing on the tossing, heaving deck. She could see now what Ryan had meant. They were completely hidden at times by the patches of heavy rain, but so were any other ships. And the Federal ships were anchored, waiting for the night. Moving, the *China Pearl* might run across any one of them before the lookouts could see it.

All hands stared south as they crept along. They were well north of where the fleet had been on the last trip, but in this weather the Yanks might have spread out, keeping away from each other. There was a dark blur to the southwest, and Ryan raised his glasses to examine it.

"Heave to in that steamer, or I'll blow you out of the water!"

They all whirled at once to the loud hail from the north. There, like a terrifying nightmare, lay a huge warship, clearly visible as the heavy rain blew away from its open gun ports and bristling cannon, the hooded men with rifles on the deck high above them. It was no more than two hundred yards away.

Leslie, rooted by fear, heard the seaman beside her whisper: "My God, the *Brooklyn.*" She saw Ryan step to the engine-room tube, his voice crisp as he spoke.

"Full stop!"

Then came the response through his horn: "Ay, ay, sir. Stopped and standing by."

Leslie groaned, and heard the same sound echo from the men around her. With those few words, the unbelievable, the impossible had happened. Ryan Fitzsimmons had been forced to surrender. She looked despairingly at a heavy shower northeast of them. Had they been in it, they would have been hidden and safe. But there had been nothing Ryan could do. One salvo from those guns and the *China Pearl* and all the souls in her would have been at the bottom of the sea. She had no idea what the Yanks might do with her, but the thought of Ryan in prison was heartbreaking. She moved to his side quietly and watched with him as the boats were lowered from the warship into the tossing sea. She had heard tales of capture that described the boarding men as laughing, cheering as they came, anticipating the prize money they would have. But these men looked grim, pulling doggedly against the high waves and silent as they came. She realized suddenly that they knew the ship was empty; they would have seen the decks from their vantage point above. There would be no prize money for them and she was perversely glad. It was bad enough without laughter.

The overloaded boats were having a hard time of it in the seas, but they were close enough now that she could see each individual face. None of them were smiling, though she was sure that the captain of the *Brooklyn* was grinning all over. Ryan stood tall and motionless beside her, his face as still as death. She slipped her hand into his and felt a sudden pressure as his fingers tightened in a quick squeeze. At that moment she saw the men in the boats rise with their long boat hooks and reach for the *China Pearl*'s tossing rail. Smoothly, Ryan bent his head again to the tube and, in the same crisp tone, spoke three more words.

"Full speed ahead."

Leslie gave an incredulous gasp and looked up. There was the cloud of rain that had been northeast of them, a great, gray wraith sweeping down on their bow as the *China Pearl* surged to meet it, plunging into the mass and leaving nothing in sight of the *Brooklyn*'s guns but a foaming trail and small, tossing boats full of yelling and cursing sailors.

Afterward, flying recklessly through the clear patches and meeting head on the dense clouds of rain, with the hysterically relieved laughter of the seamen around them, Ryan told Leslie that the ruse was not original. A daring Englishman, a younger son of the Earl of Buckinghamshire, who ran the blockade as "Captain Charles Roberts," had pulled the trick early in the war. He, like Ryan, had counted on speed, surprise and what he called "the natural reluctance of a captain to fire when his own men were part of the target."

"It was our only chance," Ryan ended. "Thank God it worked."

Leslie looked at him adoringly. "Thank God for your split-second decision," she amended. "Had you tried anything else, I do believe that monster could have done us some harm."

By nightfall the wind had swung around to the southeast, giving them a warmer breeze and a smoother sea. A pale moon rode the starry sky and for once it was welcome.

"A peaceable kingdom." Leslie leaned against Ryan at the wheel and spoke softly, her eyes on the sky. "This is the way the whole world will feel, once the war is over."

"My dreamer," Ryan answered, half laughing. "Only the sea is ever this peaceful, darling. And even then only at times. There are storms, you know. And, if we happened to run into the *Brooklyn* out here . . ."

"Sh-h-h," Leslie said indignantly. "Let me dream."

When Tudbury came up to take a turn at the wheel, Ryan went with Leslie to the cabin. Stepping inside, he shut the door and tossed his cap on the desk.

"As I said before," he said, unbuttoning his jacket, "it's my ship and my crew. Tonight we'll share the bunk."

"Ryan!" Leslie pretended shock. "Your stuffing is coming out."

He stopped undressing and stared at her. "Do you think I'm stuffy?"

Her laughter bubbled. "You *were*," she said, and began helping him with the buttons. "Darling, how can it matter what others think if you know that you're right? We've belonged to each other since the moment we met." Her laughter trailed away as she looked up at him. "And we always will," she ended softly.

"Wise sayings from a wild creature," Ryan answered huskily, and gathered her up. "But I still wish we were married. Tell me more about always belonging to me, and make me believe it. . . ."

Only the present mattered during the next long, beautiful day. There was no past, no future, only the water that grew bluer, the wind that grew warmer. Leslie laughingly swore that she could smell the flower scent of Nassau when she faced southeast, that it was as good as any compass could be.

"I can prove it if you let me take the wheel," she told Ryan. "Let me show you. I'll follow the scent and I wager that I'll be on course."

Grinning, Ryan let her have it. Watching, he was first amused and then incredulous as she held the ship on point. When he finally caught her glancing at the compass he turned and looked at Finney. Finney turned red.

"She does well," Finney said gruffly, "and it won't hurt her. She's stronger than she looks, sir."

"I'm well aware of that," Ryan said blandly, and took the wheel again. When Leslie wandered off, Ryan grinned at Finney. "Just don't teach her how to wear the captain's hat."

"She don't want the hat, sir," Finney replied, laughing. "Just the man under it."

It was, Leslie thought as the day wore on, the happiest day yet. Escaping the massive threat of the *Brooklyn* the day before had given them all a sense of being under a lucky star. Even the crew, who knew they'd get no extra pay bringing back an empty ship, felt fortunate to have escaped the prison terms that capture would have meant. They talked endlessly among themselves of the trick Captain Fitz had played on the Yanks and considered it worth the trip to have seen it.

They sailed through New Providence channel without incident, and as evening deepened, the lights of Nassau glimmered in the distance. Leslie thought of the huge, claw-footed tub in the suite at the Royal Victoria and could hardly wait to crawl in. She changed back into the navy blue silk skirt and tailored white blouse, ready to land like a lady even if out of fashion.

Ryan arched his brows. "For someone who doesn't care what anyone thinks, you've gone to a deal of trouble."

"That's true," Leslie said, her eyes glinting. "Perhaps I should change back, just to show them."

"No, no," Ryan said hastily, "you look lovely."

They tied up at midnight beside an English ship, having received permission from the guard onboard. Clambering over the railings of both ships, they made their way to the docks. On the way, the guard spoke to them idly, and to Leslie it was as if a beautiful melody had been cut off with a sharp, discordant sound.

"I hope that all of you have had yellow jack," he said, yawning. "If you haven't, you'd better get back on that fine ship and sail away. There was eleven funerals this morning."

Afterward, walking toward the hotel, Leslie shivered involuntarily. "You were right, Ryan. The rains brought it."

His arm tightened around her. "You're safe," he said cheerfully, "and most people recover. Perhaps the man exaggerated."

Leslie slowed her steps, looking up at his shadowed face. "Have you had it, Ryan?"

He shrugged. "No, but I've been exposed more times than I can count. I doubt that I'll get it." He tugged at her arm. "Come along, we'll be taken for thieves, lingering here in the dark."

The cheerful, beckoning lights of the Royal Victoria proved a false promise. No enthusiastic crowd greeted them, only a dour John Rice and a few elderly couples sitting in the lobby.

"It's the fever," Rice told them, "or rather the fear of it. The guests stay in their rooms, afraid of contagion. Fortunately, many of our guests were able to flee in an English ship last week. I say fortunately because we haven't the staff to run a full house. The natives and the boarders down at the rooming houses have been the worst stricken."

Ryan nodded. "Many deaths?"

"Close to fifty percent."

"That is bad," Ryan said sympathetically. "You've been spared?"

"I've had it, thank God. Now, is there anything I can do for either of you?"

"If we could have a light supper . . ."

"Certainly, sir. I'll have it sent to the suite."

"The bitter side of the tropics," Ryan said once they were in their rooms. "Fevers unknown and incurable. Yet the more medicines tried, the more deaths." He flexed his broad shoulders tiredly. "The two men I know who staunchly refused all remedies and treated their fevers with ice alone both lived and recovered in a surprisingly short time. Odd, isn't it?"

Leslie, on her way to the bedroom, stopped and looked back at him. "Very odd," she said thoughtfully. "The doctors treated my mother with large doses of quinine and emetics, and she died. I was considered hopeless, too young and weak to treat, but I lived. My father often told me that it was Fate, but perhaps it wasn't."

Ryan smiled. "If Fate saved you for me, I'm eternally grateful. Go take that hot bath you've been talking about for the last four hours and I'll meet you here for our supper." He hesitated and then picked up the seabag he had dropped. "But I'm not staying. I had thought I might, but I find I do care what people think—of you."

Leslie shook her head as the door closed behind him. She'd have to marry him to keep him around. But, as she turned on the hot, soft water that she liked so much, she was smiling again. It was rather romantic, at that, to have a lover who climbed in your window.

Charles Rockwell confirmed most of the bad news the next morning, though he put the death rate lower. Meeting Ryan and Leslie in the dining room for breakfast, he looked tired and worried. He gave Leslie a quizzical smile.

"You surprised me greatly," he said. "When the maid brought me your letter I was shocked at your impulsiveness. You ran away just as your career as a singer had truly begun. Your friend Spence, by the way, was terribly upset."

Leslie flushed at the note of criticism in his voice. It was quite deserved, she supposed, which made it worse. "How is Spence?" she asked, hoping to change the subject. "Not down with the fever, I hope?"

"Oh, no. Quite the opposite. In very good health and making ready to go back to scourging the seas." He turned to Ryan. "He'll be happy that you've returned before he leaves. He's mentioned your absence daily and has seemed more worried than usual. What delayed you? The usual repairs?"

Ryan had been staring at Leslie thoughtfully. "Oh, yes, of course. Isn't it always?" He seemed to collect his thoughts. "However, we also spent time trying to locate members of Miss Gordon's family. Since we were unsuccessful, I decided to bring her back here. Wilmington now is not the place for a young woman alone."

Leslie finished her breakfast hastily and left with a murmured excuse. Ryan had fallen right back into his role as her guardian. She told herself that she should have known he would when he had refused to stay in the suite. She would be expected to resume her role as his ward! No one in Nassau was to know their interest in each other. It was very disconcerting.

And what was she to do with herself? Ryan would be readying his ship for the next trip, now only two weeks away. And she would be expected to stay here and worry until he returned. There was no use in asking Charles for her job back; it was too clear that there would be no luncheon crowd to entertain.

She wandered through the lobby and down the hall, and then, thinking better of closeting herself in the suite, went outside into the walled garden. It was beautiful, full of morning freshness and pale sunlight. She was wearing a morning gown of white muslin, trimmed with a band of white lace around the low square of neckline, a wide blue satin ribbon threaded through an insert of the lace at her narrow waist. She thought the gown romantic and charming and pictured herself ruefully as a lovelorn maiden—well, perhaps not a maiden—a lovelorn young woman waiting in the garden endlessly for her lover to return. Her sense of the dramatic was fed by the loneliness. Normally, the garden was full of strolling guests, but today it was as empty as the lobby. She wandered, her bright head drooping, until she found a bush full of white roses. Leaning, she sniffed the fragrance and wished for company.

"Leslie!"

It was Spence, hurrying along the garden path. Tanned and fit, his green eyes bright, his crooked grin as humorously charming as ever. She ran to meet him, putting both of her hands in his, her smile brilliant.

"I'm so happy to see you, Captain Burdette! I was lonely and feeling very sorry for myself."

He glowed, the green eyes very soft. "A strange world," he said unsteadily, "where one so beautiful can be lonely. I've missed you terribly, Leslie." He released one hand and drew the other into the crook of his arm. "Walk with me. I'm leaving soon, and I have a great store of things to say to you."

"And I to you! You won't credit the adventures we have had—though I am sure Ryan will be better able to tell them." Leslie was not only happy for company, but the admiration in Spence's eyes was flattering. She chattered away, telling him of the bombardment by the Yankee gunboats, the rescue by Fort Fisher, with a great deal more enthusiasm in her voice than she had felt at the time. She ignored the growing horror in his face until he pulled her down with him to sit on a bench in a secluded corner.

"Leslie! Don't you realize the danger that you were in? Fitz was a reckless fool to take you along. Criminally reckless, and I shall tell him so."

Leslie was shocked out of her gay mood. Spence was genuinely angry, and blaming Ryan. "It wasn't Ryan's idea," she said uncomfortably. "I—well, I insisted on going."

"He shouldn't have listened to you! It doesn't excuse him. He knew the dangers—you didn't. No, I shall still have it out with him. He had no right . . ."

"Spence." Leslie gazed at him, upset by the breach she had caused between the two friends. "Can I tell you something in strictest confidence?"

"Anything," he said instantly.

"Ryan didn't listen to me. He never agreed to take me. No one knows, not even his crew . . . that I—I stowed away." She hesitated, seeing the shocked amazement on his face. "So you can't blame him, Spence. Only me. He was furious at first, but . . ."

"But it's impossible," Spence said slowly. "Ryan's crew is able, the ship well guarded. And you . . ." His eyes swept over the delicate form in the soft muslin gown, came up to the pink-cheeked, innocent face. "You *couldn't!*"

"I could and did!" Leslie said spiritedly. "I knew the ship, and . . ." She told him, beginning with the moment when he himself had left her at the door of the suite. She had never told anyone the full story before and she omitted no details, except, of course, some of the personal things that had happened after Ryan found her. Even though she knew now that it had all been very wrong, she was still secretly proud of her accomplishment. Her eyes sparkled, and she was breathless as she finished. "He was very angry," she concluded, "but he took it well. He let the crew believe that he'd brought me aboard himself."

Spence was fascinated by the dramatic story. His eyes never left her animated face, his hands still held one of hers tightly.

"What spirit you have," he breathed, "what courage!" He leaned forward and kissed the parted lips.

"Spence!" Leslie drew away. That kiss had not been merely friendly. It had been full of hungry ardor and she had not expected it of him.

"Leslie, please! Surely you know what you mean to me." Breathing hard, Spence tried to pull her into his arms. "This is what I wanted to say to you . . . it wasn't until you were gone that I realized how deeply I feel about you. Let me say . . ."

"Wait!" Leslie was trembling. "I'm in love with Ryan, Spence. Very much in love . . . hopelessly in love . . ." She was stuttering in her effort to keep him from committing himself, to prevent the embarrassment of having to refuse him. "I think you should know that," she ended awkwardly, "even though Ryan wouldn't want me to mention it."

Spence was white with pain and disappointment. "Then Ryan *is* a fool. A man who would not value your love must be jaded indeed. And he has made it plain that he has no romantic interest in you."

"It isn't that," Leslie said helplessly. "I'm sure that he, well, he does value my love, Spence. It's only that he doesn't want anyone to—to know about us."

"What do you mean? Why should he insist on secrecy? Any man should be proud . . . Leslie! He hasn't . . . surely, he hasn't *seduced* you?"

The horror in his voice made Leslie feel like a leper. Her face flooded with color; her eyes slid away from his miserably. "Of course not," she said weakly. "How—how could you think it?"

Her appearance made much more impression than her words. Spence got to his feet slowly, his green eyes as hard as jade. "No decent man would think of seducing a woman like you," he said hoarsely. "Ryan has gone beyond the pale." He turned on his heel and strode away.

He was going to find Ryan! Leslie leaped to her feet.

"No! Wait!" She set off after him. "It wasn't like that—it was all very natural. . . ." She stumbled in the deep grass and stopped. The charming, romantic gown clung and twisted around her legs. She snatched it up to her knees and ran.

The hall was empty. She shook down her skirt, smoothed her hair and went into the lobby.

"Can you tell me where Captain Burdette went?"

Rice gave her a bewildered smile. "I can, and I can tell you that he went in a hurry. He came rushing in here a few seconds ago and asked for Captain Fitzsimmons. I told him that he'd gone down to his ship. Burdette left as if his coattails were on fire. Something must be afoot."

"Very likely," Leslie agreed bleakly, and went back to the suite. Ryan would be furious. And Spence—what in the world possessed the man? One simply didn't go around kissing women without warning. Oh, Ryan would never understand any of this!

Before noon, Ryan arrived. He stalked into the sitting room and sat down. Leslie had been pacing the floor nervously but now she composed herself and sat down opposite him.

"I . . ." She was going to say that she could explain everything, which wasn't true. But Ryan cut her off.

"You amaze me," he said. "I leave you alone for an hour and somehow you persuade my best friend that I'm a rotten cad. Spencer Burdette challenged me to a duel."

Leslie gasped. "A *duel?* Oh, Ryan, you mustn't! He might kill you."

"Because," Ryan added, ignoring her completely, "I have dishonored you. He suggested that we meet on the hill above the town tomorrow morning. He was kind enough to say that I could have a choice of weapons."

"You mustn't kill him, either! I would feel terrible!"

"Since Spence is both an expert swordsman and a deadly shot," Ryan continued, "I hardly think the choice important."

Leslie burst into tears, rose from her chair and flung herself into his lap. "No! The two of you have always been such good friends. I shall tell Spence I lied!"

Ryan's arms closed around her. "He said you did."

"What?"

Ryan's lips twitched. "He said that you lied to save me. That you loved me to distraction and swore I hadn't seduced you."

Leslie sat up. "That's true," she admitted, wiping her eyes. "But he didn't believe me."

"Fortunately," Ryan said dryly, "he believed me. I told him the only reason we weren't married was because you wouldn't have me." He smiled faintly. "I also told him why. He has called off the duel."

"Oh, wonderful! But—why, then, you've only been torturing me!" She struggled to get out of his lap, but he held her firmly. "That was cruel."

"No more cruel than you," Ryan said calmly. "Spence is in love with you. When will you learn that you can't hang on a man's arm, hold his hand and show great pleasure in his company without giving him reason to hope? Spence thought that you returned his affection."

"I was only being friendly. I like Spence very much." She paused, staring at him thoughtfully. "Besides, he doesn't love me; he only thinks he does. He wouldn't, if he knew me well. Spence could only love a proper lady."

Ryan's eyes glinted. "But he could give you much more than I can. A beautiful home in Athens, an aristocratic background, plenty of money. Spence is a real Southern gentleman."

Leslie smiled. "I'll take a lucky Irish pirate and the *China Pearl*. As soon as I . . ."

"That will be soon. He has promised to find your father."

"Oh, Ryan! Do you truly think he can?"

"If he can't," Ryan said soberly, "then Harry Gordon is dead."

Chapter Fourteen

THE *JAMES BULLOCH*, WITH CAPTAIN SPENCER BURDETTE in command, sailed at dawn the next day, and Leslie felt a shamed relief at not having to face Spence before he left. Looking back, she could see that her actions, coupled with her apparent indifference to Ryan or any other man, could have been taken as encouragement. But she was still firm in her belief that Spence was only infatuated and would soon forget her. In the meantime, she hoped desperately that he wouldn't forget his promise to find her father, by whatever mysterious "connection" he had ashore. Ryan still adamantly refused to tell her any more about it.

The rains continued. Tropical rains, followed by bright sky and drifting clouds and then rain again. Leslie took to carrying an umbrella on her daily walks. The city was still busy; the crowds of cotton brokers and armament sellers as active as ever. Greed, she supposed, was stronger than the fear of yellow fever. But the air of reckless gaiety was gone from the Royal Victoria, the Southern emigrés subdued, the runner captains thoughtful as they discussed the new Federal fleet. Everyone in the hotel seemed changed by the epidemic or other dangers, but none seemed as changed as Wynne Rockwell.

Leslie came out on the lower piazza one morning and found Charles Rockwell and Wynne sitting as usual in the pale yellow sunlight after a shower. Wynne seemed glued to Charles's side, glancing often at his ruddy, lined face, touching his hand. She seemed to have forgotten her animosity to Leslie and talked to her freely.

"I am so afraid that Charles will take the fever," she confided. "He hasn't been at all well lately, with all the worries and problems of the hotel." Wynne's dark skin was sallow with fear as she spoke.

"She hovers over me like a mother hen," Charles said to Leslie. "I may smother." He looked at his wife irritably. "If you want to be a nurse, go down to the infirmary on Bay Street. They need help."

Wynne gasped. "Why, Charles! I wouldn't set foot in it. Besides, my duty is to look after you, not some ragtag beggars."

You and your fortune, Leslie added silently. She excused herself and went on, stepping down into the dripping, glistening world of Bahamian summer. People were dying all over the city, but the tropical beauty was as blooming, the birds singing as sweetly. Before she reached the end of Parliament Street, a funeral cortege passed her. She stopped respectfully to wait for it. The black horses shone in the sun, the silver decoration on the black coach sparkled. Among the solemn faces of those who followed were a few who still smiled and chatted as they went. Leslie thought it might be easy to pick out the ones who had already had the fever and were now safe.

Well, she was safe, too. But she didn't want to ignore the grief around her. In any event, she told herself, she needed something to do. When she got to Bay Street she asked a merchant for directions to the infirmary.

"You mean the pesthouse," he said dourly. "They've set one up in that warehouse over there." He pointed. "It's no place for a lady."

Leslie thanked him and went across the muddy street, picking her way carefully. The doors to the warehouse were closed, but her knock brought a harried-looking middle-aged woman to the door, drying her hands on a ragged apron.

"I came to see if there is something I can do," Leslie said. "I've helped in hospitals at home."

The woman laughed sharply. "This is no hospital, ma'am." She opened the door wider. "Come in and see for yourself. I doubt you'll want to stay."

Rough pallets and cots held men, women and children in communal misery in one big room. Many of the sufferers were yellow with the jaundice that gave the disease its name; others, pushed nearer to the door, had flecks of the dreaded black vomit that was known to mean death. A few of them looked at Leslie with vague curiosity in their dull eyes, but most of them seemed lost in some private hell. In one corner a child moaned and twisted restlessly. A woman moved toward him with a basin and towel.

Leslie conquered an impulse to turn and run back out of the door. "What do you do for them?"

The woman shrugged. "There's not much we can do. These people can't afford the medicines, so we just try to keep them comfortable. When the fever gets real high, we bathe them to cool it off, and when they get chills we put blankets over them. And we catch the vomit if we can—it's easier than cleaning it up." She gave Leslie a grim smile. "Most of them live, anyway. We lose a few, but so do the doctors." She left Leslie standing and hurried to the side of a retching woman. Leslie waited, leaning once to brush a mosquito from the cheek of a sleeping child. When the woman came back she was staring curiously, taking in Leslie's brown suit and tiny bonnet with the gold hair beneath it.

"Say, aren't you that singer? The one they call the Golden Lily? You surely do look like that drawing in *The Guardian*."

Leslie flushed. She hadn't thought of that story nor the name since the day she had read it. "Why, yes, I am."

The woman laughed again, the same sharp, cynical sound. "What were you thinking of doing for them, ma'am? Sing lullabies?"

"I can do much more than that," Leslie said firmly, "if you'll let me."

The woman stared at her questioningly. "Not in those clothes, you can't," she said finally. "You'd ruin them."

"I have other clothes," Leslie said, and turned away. "I'll be here this afternoon." At the door, she looked back and smiled. "My name is Leslie. What's yours?"

"Mary." She gave Leslie a sudden, genuine smile. "We can use the help."

Leslie wore the simple blue gown when she went back to the infirmary, and carried an apron that she had bought from one of the hotel maids. Noting her slight size, Mary put her in charge of the children.

"The fever rises fast in the afternoons," she cautioned. "You'll be kept busy washing them down. Watch for chills, too. There's a pile of old blankets in the back room. Oh, and give them plenty of water. We don't feed them until they're on the mend. It seems to work better."

It was twilight when Leslie tiredly trudged back to the hotel and found Ryan waiting impatiently in the suite. His bronzed face stiff, he listened silently to her explanation. Leslie braced herself for a fight that she was determined to win. Cooling and comforting those small bodies had given her the most wonderful satisfaction.

To her surprise, Ryan didn't argue. He said only that he would make arrangements for her safety on Bay Street and that he would trust her not to overdo it.

The next morning Leslie found Harold Finney waiting for her with a carriage.

"The captain says I'm to stay with you," Finney said, "and help out. I've had the fever."

Leslie gave him a brilliant smile. Ryan's choice couldn't have suited her better. The bosun was not only kind—he was strong. "You'll be a help with the men," she said, getting into the carriage. "Some of them are heavy."

That afternoon four of the British seamen who now formed most of the runner crews came through the door bearing a litter holding a woman past middle age, ashen-faced and in acute distress. The seamen looked a hard bunch, wearing outlandish clothes and gold rings in their ears, their faces scarred from fights. They stayed for a while, talking in low tones to Mary, and as they left, Leslie heard one of them say that if anything was needed, they would supply it.

"We'll take up a collection," he added. "We all owe her."

Outlandish but kindhearted, Leslie thought. She went to help Mary make the woman comfortable, wondering what had prompted the men to such generosity. Certainly, it was neither youth nor beauty. The woman's eyes were closed, her lined face sallow with jaundice, her carrot red hair showing a good inch of gray at the roots. A once plump body sagged in bulges as she and Mary bathed her. But there was something familiar in the lined face, and when they had finished and the woman was sleeping, Leslie asked in a low tone who she was.

"Belle," Mary said flatly, "the entertainer. She and her sister, Dolly, nursed a dozen or so of those Britishers through the fever, then Belle nursed Dolly until Dolly died. Their rooming house was one of the worst hit."

Shocked, Leslie remembered the day she had arrived in Nassau and had seen the two women in Gabe's carriage, brilliantly dressed and so full of gaiety.

"Why is she here? Surely, she could afford the hospital."

Mary grimaced. "From what the men said, she and Dolly weren't making so much, now that they're old. Hard nights and low pay. And then, they was always a good touch for the poor, and they had no family to fall back on. Old Belle will miss Dolly, I expect." She rushed off, harried, as another woman weakly called for water.

Going home, Leslie mentioned Belle to Finney. "It's a sad case," she told him. "She's worn herself out caring for others. Ryan told me once they were fine women."

Finney nodded. "Fitz knew them well. I guess most of what he knows about his mother came from them. They were the ones who told him where to find her."

Surprise and a queer sense of presentiment rushed over Leslie. "But—I thought that Ryan's mother was dead! You told me yourself she was gone."

"Gone don't always mean dead," Finney said gruffly. "She left, Miss Leslie. Once Fitz was born she went back to the stage. From what I hear, she was a popular actress. Anyway, she couldn't take the lonely life aboard a ship." He hesitated as if wondering if he should say more, then went on doggedly. "Fitz and I went to see her in Paris once his father died. I guess Fitz was about twenty and he was excited about his mother being a famous actress. It didn't work out very well. She didn't want the men she was seeing to find out she had a twenty-year-old son, and she made it pretty plain to Fitz. She was past her prime, and most of her money came from those . . . uh, gentlemen."

"I understand," Leslie said slowly. She did. Ryan's unreasonable actions weeks ago were now explained. And, she realized, it was a measure of his love that he had returned to trusting her afterward, had put his heart in her hands. Her eyes misted as she climbed down from the carriage.

"Thank you for telling me, Harold. I'll not mention it."

Finney snorted. "There aren't many secrets at the Royal Victoria. Rockwell's wife knew one of the men who kept Fitz's mother in funds. And she knows how Fitz felt about it, too. I was surprised when Charles hired you, but I guess it worked out all right with you, ma'am."

So Charles had known—and Wynne. Going up on the piazza, Leslie smiled sweetly at both of them and passed on. Gossips, it appeared, told you anything except what you needed to know.

Leslie sat with Belle the next day and watched helplessly as life flickered and died away in the raddled face. Belle was still conscious, the fever abating as death neared.

"I know you," she whispered to Leslie. "I saw you

the day you arrived with Fitz. I hear you have a lovely talent for song."

Bathing the pale face with a damp cloth, straightening the rough pillow, Leslie tried to smile cheerfully. "I remember you, too. You and your sister in a carriage, both so pretty and well turned out."

"Illusion." Belle's hoarse whisper was wry. "We were good at illusion . . . had to be." Her eyes followed Leslie as she moved around, pulling at the sheets to smooth them. "You keep on singing, love, and you'll find out. You have to keep up the illusion. It's all you have. . . ." She sighed, closing her eyes. "That's all I have to leave . . . a bit of advice. Dear Lord, I'm so tired. . . ."

"She wanted to go," Mary said later, pulling the sheet up over Belle's lifeless face. "She hadn't no one but Dolly, you know. It's a hard life, I guess. The clapping don't last."

Leslie couldn't bring herself to tell Ryan about Belle. He looked so tired these days, the strong bones of his face standing out from thinning flesh. The epidemic had hit his crew badly. Some of them were in the infirmary, with others being cared for by their women in the rooming houses where they lived. Ryan was working long hours and spending even more time looking for able seamen to hire for his next trip. Holding his ever-leaner body in her arms at night, Leslie worried about him. Finally, when there was only a night or two left before the dark of the moon, she spoke of it one evening.

"Wait," she said. "Most of your old crew are past the worst of it. In another few weeks you can sail with men you know and trust." She knew that she hardly looked the part of a capable advisor. Ryan had come in early and caught her in her bath. Her hair was in a tumble on top of her head and foam from the fragrant soap was all over her, even smudges on her face. Ryan had been looking at her in fond amusement, but now his smile faded.

"The supplies are needed," he said soberly. "The Union is pushing them back all along the front. Without gunpowder, how can they fight?"

Leslie's face clouded with passionate anger. Her family, like many others in the South, had always been against slavery. But she had a firm belief in the right of the states to secede. "I cannot believe that Fate has chosen the Union to win!"

"I believe," Ryan said dryly, "that the iron ore, smelting furnaces and factories of the North have more to do with the success of their armies than some cruel Fate. Even the most glorious Southern pride can't make a bullet out of a cotton boll. Are you going to get out of that tub or am I going to get in with you?"

"In that suit?" Leslie laughed and stood up, turning on the faucets, pouring dippers of fresh water over herself until her skin gleamed like polished ivory. Then she held out her arms to the side so Ryan could wrap a towel around her. "I still say . . ."

"No more." Ryan lifted her into his arms and carried her into the darkened bedroom. "I need you very much tonight," he said softly. Putting her on the bed, he pulled the towel away. "I shall play lady's maid and see that this soft skin is treated tenderly."

The slow strokes of towel and his warm hands played havoc with Leslie's senses. It was clear that Ryan was enjoying his game, so she closed her eyes and lay still, lost in sensation, her tired body warming into a glow of pleasure. Fingers kneaded her breasts into aching delight; Ryan's mouth brought them to hard, glistening-wet peaks. His hands smoothed the curves of waist and hip, thigh and knee, and then moved slowly upward to the silky softness of her inner thighs. Leslie sighed. There might be disappointments in her world, but, oh, this wasn't one of them. The soft, urgent sounds that she could never prevent began rising in her throat as his mouth followed the path his hands had made. She could lie still no longer, game or not. She reached for him wildly and found only cloth. She sat up.

"You're still dressed!"

Ryan laughed and lay down beside her. "Play valet, my sweet. I think I'm too tired to take them off." Kneeling in the already rumpled bed, Leslie pulled off his silk tie and began on the buttons, her fingers flying. Then, as she touched the bare skin of his chest, her hand slowed and stopped, flattening. Ryan's flesh was always warm, but this warm?

"You feel feverish, Ryan." Her voice was a frightened whisper. "Are you ill?"

Ryan smiled and reached a hand to tousle the tangled golden hair. "Lovesick, perhaps. But feeling better by the minute. Stop teasing me."

"I'm not teasing. You do feel hot."

He pulled her down and kissed her. "You see specters in every corner since you've been working at the infirmary. I'm fine, I tell you. Only a little tired." He kissed her again, more passionately. "I need you," he repeated softly, "I need you so much."

Leslie's heart swelled to fill her chest. Ryan Fitzsimmons had never needed anyone, but he needed her. "You have me," she promised in a husky whisper, "for always." Slowly, she took his clothes from him with sensual caresses, delighting in the throbbing awareness, the flaring response of the big body. Then she sank down over him, taking him in her arms. "I need you, too," she whispered, and felt his arms close around her.

In moments, the heat of their bodies blended and her fears were forgotten in the fever of love, in the one perfect thing in a world of lost causes and tragedy.

At dawn, Leslie was already up and dressed, with her laundered apron and a basket of fruit for her small patients at the infirmary. Her thoughts went frequently to Ryan with a twinge of worry. He was sleeping these nights on the ship, now moored at the loading dock. He had said that he wanted to keep an eye on the cargo, but Leslie thought perhaps he was also avoiding the depression around the Royal Victoria. She didn't blame him. There still were no cases of fever among the guests, but they were more fearful every day. There had been complaints about Leslie going to and fro from the infirmary and bringing a chance of infection back to the hotel. But Charles Rockwell had told Leslie to ignore the criticism.

"If people carried it, the whole island would be infested," he had said, "instead of only the poor souls who live in the low-lying spots. At least you're doing something helpful."

Now, as she waited at the entrance for Finney, Leslie took hope from a cool breeze and a clear blue sky. If the rains ceased, surely the epidemic would subside.

Finney came clattering up Parliament Street in haste, and Leslie ran down to meet him with a laugh.

"You seem anxious to get to our work today, Bosun. Don't tell me you're beginning to like it."

Finney jumped down and helped her into the carriage. "I'll not tell you that," he said grimly, "and we'll be there just long enough to tell Mary that we're needed aboard the *China Pearl*. Fitz is down with it, ma'am."

Leslie gasped. Even suspecting his feverish temperature last night, she had refused to allow herself to believe it. Now the knowledge filled her with nightmarish fear. *Ryan!* Her lover, her strong protector, her fortress against the world. She stared at Finney's bleak face and her slim jaw tightened.

"Hurry."

At the infirmary she pressed the basket of fruit into Mary's hands with a brief explanation. At the dock she was over the ship's rail with a swirl of skirts before a hand could be offered to help her. Ryan's face, flushed with fever, turned toward her from the bunk as she entered the cabin.

"Finney's a fool," he said brusquely, "dragging you here. The men can take care of me."

Leslie laid a hand on his brow and then stripped the covers back. "Be grateful for the fools, Ryan. Two of us are going to see that you recover." She bent and laid her cool cheek against his hot face for a moment, blinking back tears. "I love you," she whispered. "You are my life. Remember it." She drew back and looked at him seriously. He was terribly hot, but his eyes were still aware; there was no confusion yet.

"I need to ask you something, Ryan. We've talked before, but without decision. Do you want the medicines given to you?"

"I do not. They do no good and may do harm." He reached and took her hand. "Nor do I want you wearing yourself out caring for me. Finney and the others—"

"Sh-h-h. You know I couldn't bear to leave you. I would be as sick as you are from worry alone. Finney will help me." She forced a smile. "Now we must plan. If you don't want the medicines, then we cannot have a doctor. He would insist on them." She went to the door. "Mr. Finney!"

Finney's heavy face was sweating and anxious as he came in, glancing fearfully at Ryan. Leslie shot questions at him.

"Is there food aboard?"

"We're supplied for the trip."

"Ice?"

"Only enough for the foodstuffs. It's hard to get."

"We will need food for perhaps two weeks, Mr. Finney, and all the ice you can find. Try the English ship that came in yesterday. Pay anything they ask. And once you've put the food and ice aboard, dismiss all but enough men to handle the ship in the bay. Send the rest ashore and take her out to an anchorage. We want no visitors."

Finney stared at Leslie's pale and determined face with incredulity and then turned to Ryan. Ryan gave him a crooked grin.

"See what you did?" he asked hoarsely. "You taught her to steer the ship and she's grabbed the captain's hat. Do as she said, Finney."

That was Ryan's longest speech and one of the few coherent ones for over a week. His fever rose rapidly, frighteningly high, his clear eyes grew glazed and dull. Leslie stripped him and bathed him with cloths wrung from a pail of ice and water. He was shaken by violent, thrashing chills that sent her rushing for blankets. He moaned in his uneasy sleep, his muscular body twisting with the cramping pains of the disease, but when awake he was silent, his eyes following Leslie.

Leslie talked to him continually, soothingly while she bathed his burning skin, commandingly when she held cool water for him to drink. When she had to move him she called Finney.

Finney was having his own troubles with Ryan's friends, who had heard of his illness from the dismissed crew members. They came out to the ship to insist that Fitz be brought into the hospital.

"When I tell them it's his orders that he stays here and has no visitors," Finney told Leslie, "they think he was out of his mind with the fever. Captain Barclay brought a doctor out yesterday. When I refused to let them board the doctor said the captain's death would be on my head." Finney's heavy face was lined with worry, his usually calm eyes now fearful.

"The hospital lost as many or more than the infirmary," Leslie reminded him. "And we're not going to lose Ryan."

Still she watched with dread as the yellow of jaundice tinged Ryan's dark skin, and when he retched she held her breath in fear of seeing the black vomit. At night, she took off her outer clothing and crawled into the bunk with him, holding him as she tried to sleep a little. Every night she was up to fetch the bucket of water to bathe him again, or to reach for the blankets to stop his chills.

"Take a turn on the deck for a breath of fresh air," Finney said often. "I'll sit with the captain. Have a decent meal below. I'll have two of you sick."

Leslie developed a positive love for the bosun. He was as gentle as any woman, his bearlike arms tender as he turned Ryan's pain-wracked body or held him for necessary toilet services. But his rough voice boomed out with authority when anyone approached the ship. In the middle of the second week, Charles Rockwell sent John Rice out to the ship in a small boat and Leslie heard the conversation from an open cabin door.

"No, sir, Mr. Rice. No one permitted aboard. Thank Mr. Rockwell for his concern, but Captain Fitzsimmons isn't receiving visitors. I'll tell him you called, sir."

Leslie stayed in the cabin, listening. She had long

since changed to breeches and shirts, and for Ryan's sake she wouldn't be seen in the unladylike costume. She gave Finney a tired but genuine smile when he came in.

"You sounded like the governor's butler, bosun." Her smile grew, making her blue eyes sparkle. "But I doubt you'll need to turn away friends much longer." She gestured toward the bunk. Propped up on pillows, Ryan was looking at them both, his face haggard but calm, his eyes clear and questioning.

"By God, Captain Fitz, you're going to make it!" The words burst from Finney's throat in pure amazement.

"Certainly," Ryan said in a faint whisper, and dropped off to sleep again.

It wasn't much, but it was wonderful after ten days of fear, after ten nights of lying beside a burning, restless body, ready to slide out and reach for the bucket and cloth. Leslie slept well that night, one arm draped carelessly over his chest, and woke at dawn to find him staring at her.

"How long?"

Leslie sat up, her tangled hair an unruly mass around her, her sleepy blue eyes searching his face. She drew a hand over his bared chest and found the flesh cool and moist.

"Thank God," she breathed, "it's over."

"How long?"

She smiled. Fever patients, she had discovered, often asked that question. They truly didn't know. "Ten—no, eleven days," she said, humoring him.

Ryan frowned. "I missed the trip." His faint voice was infinitely disgusted.

Leslie's jaw dropped. "Is that all you can say, you ungrateful ape? You're *alive*, damn it! Finney and I have worked like dogs . . ." She stopped, gazing down at the beloved, emaciated face, half hidden by a ten-day growth of red-brown beard. She gulped back a sob. "Oh, Ryan! You were so sick, so awfully sick." She fell forward on his chest and hugged him tightly. "I couldn't have borne it if you'd been silly enough to die."

Ryan, half smothered by her thick hair, put up a shaky hand and pulled the hair from his face, then buried his fingers in the silky strands. "I had no intention of dying of the fever," he said, "but I may starve."

Leslie threw on her clothes and went to the galley.

Chapter Fifteen

"I PROMISE YOU," RYAN SAID, "I WILL NEVER THINK OF you as a child again. You are a woman, a resourceful, talented, intelligent, devoted woman who probably saved my unworthy life some weeks ago. You are also tantalizingly beautiful and extremely charming. But you are not the captain of this ship. We are going back to the docks."

Sitting in a deck chair, Ryan looked pale in the brilliant sunshine, his long body still thin from the ravaging fever, but his hazel eyes clear and without the tinge of yellow that was usually the last sign of jaundice to leave. Leslie was standing before him with her hands on her slender hips, her booted feet apart, her blue eyes blazing. Beneath the booted feet she could feel the vibration of the engines as the ship prepared to leave the anchorage.

"And you are an unreasonable, foolhardy and stubborn man," she answered hotly. "You have less than two weeks before the next dark of the moon, and it will be another month before you are truly fit to sail. I didn't save your life only to have you throw it away."

Ryan grinned at her infuriatingly. "I am in perfect health due to your efforts. A week of decent food instead of oatmeal, boiled eggs and fruit, and I'll be ready to tackle the whole Federal fleet."

There was no use in argument. Ryan had missed two trips because of his illness and she knew that he wouldn't miss another. Behind her, Leslie could hear the creaking of the capstan as the men winched up the anchor. "Then I shall go with you," she said, her eyes daring him to disagree, "and keep an eye on you. Since I am both resourceful and intelligent, you can hardly object." She waited for the refusal that she was sure would come out roaring.

"We'll discuss that later," Ryan said, surprising her. "At the moment it might be wise to change your costume, since you are going ashore. For one thing, you're too tempting in those breeches for a man in my weakened condition."

Leslie stalked away in pretended indignation. Perhaps he was better, after all.

Later, in the privacy of the hotel suite, Ryan put his arms around Leslie and held her close. "You're as tired as I am," he said, "from the miserable days and nights of caring for me." He leaned back and looked at her with a deep tenderness. "I wanted to spare you that. But that first day when you stormed into my cabin and took over my ship, I knew I couldn't. You said something that has stayed in my mind and heart ever since—'*You are my life. Remember it.*'" Incredibly, there were tears in his clear hazel eyes as he went on. "It struck me then that it was true for us both, and I knew I had to get well. Our lives are knitted, my darling. One of us without the other would be only a torn and aching half. In sickness or in health, in danger or safety, we are still one. Therefore, the *China Pearl* will never sail again without you."

"Oh-h-h . . ." Leslie was not ashamed of her tears as she kissed him. Who wouldn't cry with such happiness? Ryan had discovered what she had known from the beginning. They belonged together in peace or war, in fair weather or foul. Nothing would ever part them again.

It seemed to Leslie during the next few days that Ryan's yellow fever had been replaced by a fever for action, for pitting himself against all odds. He regained his weight and strength rapidly and seemed bent on proving himself indestructible. Watching him, she felt that she understood. Ryan had never been conquered until that devastating illness laid him low; now he must become again the unconquerable Ryan Fitzsimmons. She worried that he might push himself too hard, and one night she mentioned it.

Ryan laughed. "How can you doubt my recuperative powers? You are in the best of positions to know how I feel."

Since at the time they were in her bed, she had just been in several of her favorite positions and it was certain that he had felt wonderful to her—it was difficult to argue with that. Or anything else. She looked at him adoringly. She had thought their love perfect before, had revelled in their closeness. But now she was awed by the new dimensions, the trust and rapport between them and the tenderness that marked their passionate lovemaking. Even thinking about it while she lay curled in the semicircle of his lean body made her desire rise again. She rose on one elbow and leaned over him, tracing his smile with an inquisitive fingertip and then the tip of her tongue.

"I'm still not sure," she said thoughtfully, "just how rapidly you recuperate. Perhaps I should make a few simple tests."

Ryan laughed huskily. Moonlight streamed into the room, but he didn't need to see to know that her breasts were nestled warmly in the mat of hair on his chest, that one slender leg was thrown carelessly over his thigh, that the satiny warmth of her loins and that tantalizing patch of dark gold curls were resting against his flank.

"By all means. Mount a thorough investigation and carry it to a logical conclusion. Otherwise, you'll never be sure." He stretched his whole length and then relaxed with a sigh of anticipation, flat on his back. Leslie glanced along his muscular frame and chuckled.

"That isn't fair. You recuperated before I started."

"Moonlight is deceiving," Ryan pointed out hastily. "That may be an illusion. Besides, it isn't scientific to depend on sight alone."

Leslie stifled a laugh. Ryan's playfulness was an endearing, surprising trait in such a stern man. "True," she said, and kissed him. "I shall use all my faculties to discover any solid evidence."

A few moments later, Ryan was dragging her away from his quivering loins and lifting her over him. "Now for the logical conclusion," he said raggedly, and lowered her gently on the point of the investigation.

Later, replete with love, yawning and sleepy but still unwilling to part, they talked.

"I have never before wanted a home ashore," Ryan said into the darkness, "but I want a home with you. One we can make together in some new and untried spot. A place near a good anchorage. Perhaps, after the war, we should go back to the Hillsborough."

"Back to the swamp?" Her soft, sleepy voice was incredulous.

Ryan chuckled. "I'd never risk that with a half-tamed woman. Who knows how wild you'd become? I was thinking of land near the river, a house to come home to between our voyages. There's good hunting there."

Leslie sat up and soared into a dream that she had thought impossible. "I *know* the place, Ryan! A green place, with huge, crystal-clear springs and lovely big trees and fertile land . . . everything. I used to bathe there every day and it's—oh, it's beautiful!" She flung her arms wide, embracing the dream. "I can plant a garden. . . ."

"With wild lilies?" Ryan pulled her down across his chest and stroked her hair. "It sounds right, my darling. New and untried, and only a day's ride from a good anchorage. Once the old South dies, we'll build a new South of our own." His voice was serious as he added: "I promise you that we'll sail peaceful seas and come home to your green place. It will happen."

Leslie moved, just far enough to lay her cheek over his heart. The strong, steady beat was comforting. The future had suddenly become so bright that she was fearful of losing it.

"I wish the war was over and done with," she murmured, "and the *China Pearl* sailing past Egmont Key."

"Soon," Ryan said, "a matter of months and the war will end. Nothing can save the South."

Leslie sat up again. It was the only way she could really think, since lying against his warmth was too distracting.

"Then why keep on running the blockade? You don't

need the money and the supplies you take only extend a war that cannot be won. Why risk your ship?"

"I don't know why," Ryan said with bleak honesty, and slid from the bed. "I suppose it's because the gallant fools are still fighting, against all odds, and I feel I can't let them down." He dressed quickly and then bent to kiss her good-bye. "They're like you," he added softly. "You never give up, my little love. Don't give up on me."

"I never did," Leslie said impishly. "That's why I have you now." She touched his cheek with tender fingertips. "And I never will, I promise you."

With Ryan busy with the ship, Leslie began going back to the infirmary. Her duties were lighter every day. The rains had stopped a month ago and there were no new cases. And, as the barnlike warehouse emptied, the Royal Victoria filled up again. Parties began and Charles Rockwell sought out Leslie and asked her to begin singing again at the luncheon hour.

"They are asking for you," he told her. "Even the new arrivals from England have heard of you because of Frank Vizetelly. He seems bent on making you a celebrity. He wrote an article about the young and talented singer who charitably worked amongst the poor during the epidemic. Your reputation is soaring."

Leslie laughed. "What nonsense! In any event, Charles, I'm afraid I can't amuse your guests. We're leaving in less than a week, you know."

" 'We'? Of course I know Ryan will sail, but I had no idea that you would risk it. Surely, you know the dangers."

Leslie wondered suddenly if Charles knew the dangers. If he knew how the shells screamed before they exploded, how the ship shuddered when she was hit. If he knew how it felt when a person you loved was

243

standing defenseless on deck. And, if he knew just how much worse it would be to wait and wonder and fear. But those were things she never would tell anyone.

"Of course I know," she answered carelessly, "but I like the trips. It's very exciting, Charles."

"Good Lord," Charles grumbled, wheeling himself away. "You young people are entirely too fond of excitement. You could get killed."

Of course the story spread, because Charles told Wynne. *The Guardian* came out with an article extolling the courage of the Golden Lily of the Confederacy, who found running The blockade "exciting." The story was picked up by the *Illustrated London News*, along with a new sketch by Vizetelly depicting Leslie in the Eugenie gown. But by then, the *China Pearl* had docked in Wilmington.

"The easiest trip we've ever made," Ryan told William Lockwood the next morning at breakfast. "We must have been invisible. I spotted three gunboats at the south inlet where we came in, but somehow they never saw us. We ran up the Cape Fear River with Latimer and Barclay right behind us, and considering the noise we all made clanging over Frying Pan Shoals, I was sure the gunboats at the bar would come down on us." He laughed, his newly tanned face shining. "We never heard a challenge or a shot."

William nodded. "Fort Fisher has brought in new long-range guns for the attack they expect from the sea," he said, "and those gunboats stay farther away from the bar. But you really were lucky not to be seen at the south inlet." He smiled at Leslie. "Perhaps your fiancée brought luck."

Ryan's eyes gleamed as he turned and put his arm across the back of Leslie's chair and closed his hand on her shoulder in a quick squeeze. She looked up, startled, and saw a look of deviltry in his eyes. "Not my fiancée," Ryan said, "my wife. We were married in Nassau a few weeks ago."

Leslie's mouth opened in a soundless gasp at this outright lie; her cheeks turned scarlet as Helen rose and came to kiss her excitedly. William was on his feet, shaking Ryan's hand and congratulating him, and in the general confusion, Leslie could have almost believed the lie herself.

"Why, we should have known," Helen was saying, "that you two would marry soon. When you left so unexpectedly the last time, Leslie, the note that Fitz wrote to us was so beautifully romantic! Well, now you will never be parted." She laughed, her eyes twinkling in her pretty face. "I had just been thinking I should run up and air out your room, Leslie. Now that's a chore I won't have to do."

"That's true," Leslie said hastily. The advantage of the lie had become apparent. Her cheeks still red, she stood up and began clearing away dishes. "And I will help you with the rest."

That night she shared the downstairs bedroom with Ryan. She lay stiffly in the canopied double bed, watching while he moved around the room, whistling under his breath as he took off his clothes and draped them carelessly on a chair. When he blew out the lamp, crawled in and reached for her, she felt positively sinful.

"Why did you tell that awful lie?" she whispered. "I feel terrible."

Ryan's hand moved beneath the covers with practiced ease and found the bottom of her shift. His warm palm moved up her thigh, curved beneath a rounded buttock and eased her closer. "I wanted you in my bed," he said logically. "Why do you feel terrible?"

"Because you *lied!* And because William and Helen were so charmed! All those best wishes for the bride and groom and those beaming smiles when we said good night. They think it's wonderful that we're in here, making love. But what would they think if they knew that we weren't married?"

The hand had crept further under the loose shift, sliding in and out of the curve of her tiny waist, curling around the contour of a breast. "They would think it was terrible," Ryan said gravely.

Leslie nodded emphatically, her head bouncing on the pillow. "That's what I mean. I *feel* terrible." She hesitated, fully conscious of Ryan's thumb brushing the tip of her breast. "At least, I did."

Ryan smiled in the darkness, his fingers beginning a gentle kneading. It seemed to him that Leslie's breasts were more tempting than ever, full in his big hand and taut with desire. All her contours were more softly feminine these days. "I think you feel delightful. But your gown is in the way." He stripped it off efficiently, tossed it aside and moved to fit himself around her. "Better?"

"Ye-e-es . . ." Her voice was barely audible as she snuggled closer. "But—what if they find out?"

"How would they?" Ryan began kissing her with sudden passion, kissing her eyes, her cheeks, ravishing her mouth, his lips trailing down her neck and over her shoulders. This new softness drew him irresistibly. He began kissing his way down her silky, sleek skin, pushing the covers away. "How . . . would . . . they . . . ever . . . find . . . out?"

"Oh, Ryan . . ." She could feel the force of his intense desire and it became her own, her body rippling against his questing mouth. She fought for reason. "They might . . . oh, who *cares?*" She thrust both slender hands in the rumpled chestnut hair and tugged until they were face to face again. *"You're* terrible," she whispered breathlessly. "You went too fast. Please . . . start over."

He started over, kissing the shining eyes closed again, exploring the panting mouth sensuously. Leslie could smell the musky scent of an aroused male; she breathed it in deeply and concentrated on the moving mouth. First the hot trail from her neck to the cleft of her breasts, then the slow ravishment of one aching peak, leaving it quivering while he moved to the other. Her fingers moved restlessly through his hair as he moved on, nipping at the curve of waist, circling with a warm tongue the softness of her belly. She squeezed her eyes tighter shut and fought to lie still; she wanted him to go on and on, to touch every part of her with that hot mouth, but she couldn't wait . . .

Ryan felt the slender flame of body arch suddenly toward him, heard the soft, pleading sounds that excited him so. His own control broke shatteringly, his hands reaching beneath her to grip her soft buttocks while he swung into the soft cradle of her thighs. He felt her slender hips tense and reach, begging for his thrust, and thought with dazed wonder what a glory it was to have her wanting him as much as he wanted her. At the last moment he eased and entered her slowly, listening to her small, erotic sounds, feeling the moist velvet of her inner flesh close around him eagerly. Then, there was no more time for thought, only the rushing blood, the exquisite sensation, the swinging rapture of true mating.

Waking in the morning with Ryan's face buried in her neck, his arm flung over her, Leslie lay looking at the bright sunshine that flooded the room and decided that there was quite a bit to be said for the married state. It was very pleasant to wake up together and to know that when they emerged from the room the fact that they had slept together would be taken as a matter of course. Ryan's lie no longer seemed so awful. When Ryan stirred, sat up and yawned, she smiled at him.

"We won't have to get married at all," she said contentedly. "When we go back to Nassau we can simply tell everyone there that we were married in Wilmington. It will work both ways."

Ryan burst into startled laughter. "For someone who felt so terrible last night, you've recovered admirably." He rumpled her silky hair and kissed her. "I still insist on a real marriage, my sweet. Once Spence has the news you want, we'll have the biggest wedding ever seen in Nassau." He kissed her again, lingeringly, and then dragged himself away reluctantly. "I'm late. I should be at the docks now, bargaining for cotton."

Leslie watched him with soft eyes as he swung out of bed, stretched like a great cat, and, yawning again, padded toward the bathroom. Not a sign of illness marred the masculine perfection of his muscular physique now, and she thought him altogether beautiful. That well-modeled head with the crisp, bright hair, the strong neck and wide shoulders, and all the rest of him lean and whip strong. She sighed. If he wanted a big wedding, so be it. But it did seem an unnecessary bother.

Leslie spent the day with an ecstatic Helen. Ryan had brought the usual gifts of food in plenty, but Leslie, knowing a woman's feelings, had brought bolts of material and trimmings by the yard. Silks and muslins, laces and braids, enough to make gowns for three women. She had known that Helen would think of her daughters first.

"I shall send for Amy and Mary Ann, and have a dressmaker in," Helen exclaimed. "My girls will leave the safety of the country willingly for a splendid new gown." She laughed and hugged Leslie warmly. "How generous and thoughtful you are, my dear. You seemed only a girl when you were here last summer, yet you are a woman this fall."

It *was* fall, Leslie thought. Drawing ever closer to the time Ryan had predicted the war would end. It gave her a feeling of foreboding. Surely, as the Union tightened its grip on the faltering South, it would tighten the ring of blockaders also. The incredible luck of the run through this time wasn't likely to be repeated. She was silent and preoccupied as she went about helping Helen with the household tasks.

Helen seemed to sense her feelings. As they set the table for dinner that evening, she brought the subject up.

"I still wish that you would stay with us, Leslie. In spite of the dangers here, I still think Wilmington is safer for you than running the blockade. I should think you'd be petrified with fear."

Leslie laughed at the term. "Not petrified, but at times very frightened. I'll be glad when the war is over." She looked up and met Helen's eyes. "Until then, as long as Ryan makes the run, I'll be with him."

Helen sighed. "I know. William urges me to join the girls in the country. He worries about the time coming when Wilmington will be overrun. He says there are always looters and outlaws to take advantage of a time like that. But my place is with him. While he stays, I stay."

It was sobering, though not surprising, that William had accepted the inevitable defeat of his town and Fort Fisher. When Wilmington fell, the South would fall, choked off from its vital supplies. None of the other ports could handle the huge amounts needed nor get them to the front as quickly. William spoke of it when they gathered at the table.

"We've heard that the Union ironclads are already moving down the coast and that it won't be a month until the bulk of the Federal Navy will be massing against our fort," he said, and glanced at Ryan grimly. "This may have been your last run, Fitz. I hope your trip out tomorrow night will be as safe as the one in."

Ryan shrugged and smiled. "We'll make it. And, as for next month, the Yanks may find Fort Fisher a tough nut to crack. Until the fort falls, the *China Pearl* will keep coming in. Maybe we'll spend Christmas with you."

"Oh, that would be wonderful," Helen chimed in, beaming. "And perhaps there will even be a truce! After all, it's the birthday of the Prince of Peace." She looked at Leslie and her smile faded. "Peace," she repeated softly. "We can no longer hope for victory or justice; we can only pray for an end to the killing."

Cotton bales were stacked high on the decks of the *China Pearl* when Leslie and Ryan boarded the next day. Only narrow corridors between the stacks allowed the men to move back and forth. Leslie's head was barely visible above the bales as she went promptly to the cabin to exchange her swishing skirts for breeches and her shawl for a pea jacket. It was chilly; fall weather had moved down to grip the South with a vengeance.

They made the run downriver and anchored off Smithville to wait for dark. Ryan scanned the ocean outside with his binoculars.

"From the lay of those Federal ships anchored offshore," he told Leslie, "there's a strong current from the south. The water will be warm and the air cold. We may have a cozy blanket of fog." He smiled, his clear eyes sparkling. "I expect they've got their glasses trained on us now, but if I'm right, we'll disappear shortly."

Their luck held. Fog set in thick and fast well before sundown. Ryan ordered the anchor up immediately, knowing the blockaders would never expect him to make a break that early. The fog was the thickest near land, muffling any sound as they made their way down the Cape Fear River and over Frying Pan Shoals. Slowly, Ryan threaded his way through the south inlet by soundings alone, crept on, veering sharply at the sight of a dark and shapeless mass he found outside. There were tense hours ahead, but by midnight they had traveled beyond the outermost of the four cordons of blockaders and were running free for Nassau under a clear and starry sky, the fog behind them.

"It couldn't happen twice, but it did," Ryan said jubilantly as he entered the cabin. He had turned the wheel over to Tudbury and Finney to join Leslie for the rest of the night. "If I were superstitious," he added, shaking off his damp coat, "I'd be worrying about the next time." He grinned at her, stripping off the rest of his clothes efficiently. "Fortunately, I'm not superstitious."

His flesh was cool and damp; he smelled of the sea. Leslie welcomed him into the warm cocoon of blankets with open arms. Her cheek in the hollow of his shoulder, she caressed him sleepily, warming the cool flesh with her soft palms. Nothing really bad could happen while they were together.

Chapter Sixteen

"MISS GORDON!"

Leslie, coming in from a morning stroll, looked up at John Rice, who was waving her over to the desk. His voice had sounded excited, his smile was wide as she approached.

"You have a letter," he added. "A packet arrived from Bermuda this morning."

Now she understood his excitement. Letters were rare and prized by the Southerners at the Royal Victoria. She had never received one nor expected one, for that matter. She took the envelope from his hand and examined it doubtfully. There was no mistake, her name was plainly written in the unfamiliar handwriting.

"Why, it *is* for me," she said, surprised, and turned it over. The seal on the back was also plain, the black wax firmly engraved by a seal. *James Bulloch.* Spence! Her heart turned over. There was only one subject that would bring a letter from him.

"Thank you, Mr. Rice," she said breathlessly, "thank you very much." Aware of curious glances from several guests and Wynne Rockwell, all seated nearby, she clutched the letter and darted down the hall toward the suite. Inside, gazing at the water-stained and crumpled envelope, she went slowly to a chair and sat down, a wild hope and a dreadful fear battling in her mind. Her fingers trembled as she opened and unfolded it. Then, as she read the first line, she burst into tears.

"The relative you have been seeking is alive and well." Her relief in knowing that her father was neither ill nor dead kept Leslie wiping tears away as she hurriedly read the rest of the short letter. Spence had been careful not to identify her father in any way. "My new chaplain has access to privileged information," he had written, and Leslie took that to mean information that could not be forced from the chaplain—like a priest in a confessional, she supposed. "But," Spence continued, "I have learned from him that your relative was ill and that following his recuperation he had a search made for you. He knew that you had left the country and is very glad to know that you are safe and well. The chaplain can tell you much more. It may be difficult to arrange a meeting between you, but be assured that I shall try. My very best wishes to both you and Ryan."

It seemed too good to be true, but Leslie knew Spence. It *was* true. Her heart soared as she allowed herself to again think of her father, to remember his gentle, humorous ways, his voice, the love that shone from the eyes as blue as her own. It had been agony to remember him when she feared him dead, but now she gloried in it. Memories that she had hidden away came rushing back. But she had to know more. How to find him, after the war, how to tell him where she would be. She knew what Spence meant by saying that it might be difficult to arrange a meeting. Now that the South's defeat was close, England had withdrawn her hidden support from the Confederate Navy. Spence's warship would not be allowed to enter Nassau Harbor again. But Ryan would know how to arrange a meeting! She leaped to her feet. Ryan would also be delighted to know Spence's news, if only because he could now arrange that silly big wedding!

Ignoring the fact that she was dressed in the white muslin morning gown she had thought so romantic, and which was hardly proper wear for Bay Street, Leslie stuffed the letter in her string bag and set off for the docks. In the fluttering gown and with loosened hair beginning to trail down her shoulders, her cheeks red with excitement, Leslie drew stares, a scattering of sharp whistles and a few ribald suggestions as she crossed the dusty street to the loading dock. Frowning, Ryan came down the gangway to meet her, his presence resulting in sudden silence from the other men.

"I take back my promise," Ryan said sternly. "You are a child. A ragamuffin who cares nothing for appearances. Explain yourself."

"I *am* a child," Leslie said unsteadily, "for the moment. A very happy child. But I may cry. Take me to your cabin so I can tell you about it in private."

In the cabin she sat on the small stool and leaned forward with her slim arms crossed on his knees and watched him while he read the letter. First the eyes sharpening, the brows rising, and finally the white flash of grin. Tossing the letter aside, he pulled her up into his arms.

"Wonderful news, darling, for both of us. Your worries are over, and I can begin planning that wedding." He kissed her and then added reluctantly,

"Perhaps I was wrong about your father. At least, he did make a search for you."

"Of course!" Leslie said tearfully. "I knew that he would if he could. When *you* are a father, you'll . . ." She hesitated. Even mentioning such a possibility unnerved her. During the past month she had been forced to consider it deeply.

"When I am a father I'll what?"

"Understand," she finished weakly, then added: "But I didn't mean, well—I'm sure I'm not pregnant. It's just this weather, so unseasonably warm, don't you think?"

Ryan stared at her, thinking of the delightful new lushness of her breasts, the new feminine curves that softened her slender figure, and thinking also of his own stupidity. His arms tightened. "How long has it been," he asked carefully, "that this—this unseasonable weather has been affecting you?"

Leslie was relieved by his calm tone. "Quite some time," she said, "weeks and weeks . . ." She frowned, counting back. "Perhaps a dozen. I was worried at first, but truly, I feel wonderful." She smiled and put an arm around his neck, nuzzling his ear. "There's no cause for alarm, darling. Other women have told me that when you're with child you feel perfectly awful."

"Oh, my God," Ryan said with feeling. "Almost three months! How could you possibly not know . . ." He stopped abruptly and leaned back in his chair with a muffled groan. It was just like her. The bewildering complexity of this woman he loved never failed to amaze him. She was so resourceful and able at times when other women would faint dead away, yet so utterly lacking in female wisdom. He reminded himself firmly that she had had no mother and that, during the years when she should have been learning from other women, she had been isolated in a swamp.

"Some women," he added almost gently, "feel wonderful. Like you."

Leslie drew in her breath sharply. "You think I'm pregnant!"

"I know you are." With his own words, the full meaning hit Ryan like a thunderbolt. He stood up, placing her on her feet with care. "I'll take you back to the hotel," he said sternly, "and then I will make every effort to obtain a special license and we will be married immediately."

"Wait!"

"Wait?" Ryan's raw emotion leaped headlong into rage. "That's all you've ever said to me when I mentioned marriage! By God, if it were up to you, my son would be born a bastard. I'll not *wait!* When that child appears, he'll have the Fitzsimmons name on him." Red-faced and furious, he strode toward the door.

"I only meant," Leslie said reasonably, "that if you go flying around arranging a hurried marriage, everyone will suspect . . ."

Ryan turned and glared at her. "No one will suspect! They will *know!* Three months! Three whole damn months and you didn't tell me. What else can I do but marry you as quickly as I can?"

Leslie sighed. This all meant so much to Ryan. He didn't want a breath of scandal about his wife. To her thinking, it made little difference what the gossips at the Royal Victoria said. Once the war ended, they would be somewhere else. But Ryan really cared.

"You could tell everyone that we were married in Wilmington," she said, and flinched as he opened his mouth for another roar. "The first time we were there," she added hastily. "That would be long enough, wouldn't it?"

"But we *weren't*, damn it!"

Leslie raised her chin and stared at him, a glint in her eye. "We weren't married in Nassau a few weeks ago, either."

Ryan's mouth opened and closed. He came back, flinging himself down in the chair again, looking a trifle sheepish. "We have no proof."

Leslie looked surprised. "Would someone ask for proof?"

Ryan knew that no one would dare. He sat looking at her, silently considering the problem. The solution was far from perfect, but still the best they could manage. In this case, their acquaintances might suspect, but they wouldn't know. It was a change for the better.

"All right," he said grimly, "I'll try to be convincing with that unlikely tale. But I have one question. Do you ever intend to actually marry me?"

Leslie smiled and sat down on his lap again. "Of course I do! And since, if we marry again in Nassau or Wilmington, we would give our friends reason to wonder, I have thought of a perfect place."

"Where?"

"Why, aboard the *James Bulloch*. With Captain Burdette to sign the papers, a shipboard wedding won't require a license. And his chaplain can marry us." Her blue eyes sparkled like diamonds. "All you have to do is arrange a meeting."

"You," Ryan said slowly, "are the most straightforwardly deceptive woman I have ever known. Have you been planning this ever since that letter came?"

Leslie's lashes fluttered down. "Not exactly, though I did plan to ask you to arrange a meeting. Then it occurred to me. . . ."

Ryan laughed suddenly, the stiff planes of his face breaking into merriment. "God help me if that child you are carrying is a girl," he said and pulled her close. "Two such devious females would undo me." He kissed her lingeringly, his hand seeking one of the breasts now so full and tight with promise. Cupping it, feeling the new weight, he thought of his seed growing in that delicate, ivory and gold body and his own body's pulse quickened, flaring into desire. Through the soft layers of muslin, the hardening tip of her breast pushed upward against his warm palm in instant response. He dragged his mouth away.

"In another moment I'll have you on that bunk," he said raggedly, "and this is hardly the time or place. Go back to the hotel and let me think. What in God's name am I going to give as a reason for keeping our marriage a secret?"

Standing, Leslie repaired her fallen hair, tucking it up neatly and pinning it again. Her eyes were still a dark blue from that kiss, her lips pink and soft. "You'll think of something," she said confidently. "You always do."

In spite of her confidence in Ryan, Leslie was nervous as she dressed for dinner. She chose the turquoise silk and lacy canezou, still her favorite gown, and made every effort to appear dignified in it. As she joined Ryan in the hall, she asked in a breathless whisper if he had thought of a reason.

"I've decided," he said thoughtfully, "to say that I was waiting until you grew up."

Silenced, Leslie took his arm and went with him through the crowds. He seemed completely relaxed and ready for anything, even Wynne Rockwell. She dreaded that woman's reaction.

Champagne arrived at the long table as soon as everyone was seated, and a smiling waiter set stemmed glasses at each place. Charles Rockwell looked at Wynne curiously.

"Did you order champagne? What are we celebrating?"

"I ordered it," Ryan said easily, "to celebrate a wedding last June in Wilmington. A belated gesture, I admit, but better than none." He rose with a brimming glass and grinned as faces turned toward him. "Please join me in a toast to the former Leslie Gordon, who has been Mrs. Ryan Fitzsimmons for the past six months."

There was instant uproar as the men stood to shake Ryan's hand, laughing as they congratulated him. There were appropriate remarks.

"You sneaky dog! No wonder you kept her to yourself!"

"Fitz, married? I don't believe it!"

There were toasts to the bride, to the groom, to their future children. Leslie blushed. Then, as the noise died down and the men resumed their seats, she looked toward the quarter where she expected a storm. Wynne's face was twisted in what might pass for a smile, her dark eyes narrowed as she watched them. There was no doubt in Leslie's mind that Wynne would say something. What it would be was anyone's guess.

It came soon enough. With her fingers twirling the stem of her champagne glass, Wynne fastened her eyes on Ryan.

"A secret marriage! How very romantic, Fitz. And how like you. But what possible reason could you have for keeping it quiet? Or perhaps I should ask why have you announced it now?"

"And perhaps you shouldn't ask either question," Charles Rockwell said harshly. "Pardon my wife's insatiable curiosity, Fitz."

"Perfectly all right, Charles," Ryan said comfortably. "I expect that everyone wonders. Leslie didn't want the marriage made public until she could locate some member of her family and let them know first. Fortunately, we heard today." He swept the table with a sudden grin. "As to why I announced it tonight, I have a very good reason. I'm looking forward to sharing the suite with her, as well as the captain's cabin. It's a long time between trips."

Leslie thought the laughter would never die down. She also thought Ryan had little reason to call *her* deceptive. What a tangled confusion of half truths and whole lies! Then she thought of waking with Ryan beside her in the morning and it seemed very worthwhile. She was still smiling when Wynne spoke to her.

"So, that's why you were so excited this morning about that letter. Actually, I was sure that it was from London."

Leslie looked at her, amazed. "Why? I know no one in London."

Wynne smiled her bitter smile. "But they know you, my dear. Frank Vizetelly has seen to that. By the way, he is coming here tonight to see you. He has asked me to introduce you to him formally. Do you mind?"

What was the woman up to? Leslie started to speak, then turned to Ryan. "Do *you?*"

The flicker of astonishment in Ryan's clear eyes changed to amusement. He smiled at Wynne charmingly. "We will be happy to meet such a talented man, if the meeting is early and short. Send him to the suite, Wynne. Don't bother yourself with introductions. But do warn him not to stay too long."

Having managed to announce a nonexistent marriage successfully, Ryan was enjoying himself. He was playing the part of a deprived and eager husband to the hilt.

Vizetelly was prompt. Ryan and Leslie had barely closed the door of the suite behind them when he knocked. Ryan opened the door to him and shook hands, then he turned and drew Leslie forward with a proprietary hand on her arm.

"No need to introduce my wife to you, is there, Mr. Vizetelly? I understand that you have memorized her face and figure so well, you can draw her from memory." His voice, usually so pleasant, was underlaid with a defensive sarcasm that Leslie had never heard before. Flushing, she put out her hand, anxious to make up for Ryan's rudeness.

Her hand was immediately drawn upward to Vizetelly's lips in a typically Gallic gesture. He was an odd-looking man, quite plump, and dressed in a rumpled pongee suit with a very long coat that emphasized his short stature. But his dark eyes were intelligent and interested, his manners seemed impeccable. Leslie greeted him courteously and asked him to sit down.

Instead, Vizetelly bowed her to a chair and turned to Ryan apologetically.

"Congratulations, sir. Naturally, had I known that Miss Gordon was your wife, I would have come to you instead of her friend, Wynne Rockwell. Also, if I had more time, I would have waited for a more convenient day to discuss this business. However, I leave for London tomorrow."

Ryan frowned. "Business? Sit down, Vizetelly, and explain the terms. You've confused me."

Vizetelly spread his hands and laughed. "There is some misunderstanding, no doubt due to the excitement of the evening. However, I am sure that you will both be delighted by my news." He sat down, smiling. "Actually, I am only an emissary, but I do feel responsible. It was on the strength of my articles and sketches that these proposals were sent to be delivered to Miss . . . Mrs. Fitzsimmons." He had caught Ryan's disapproving look. With a quick motion, he pulled a heavy envelope from his pocket and handed it to Ryan. "As the fortunate husband of the Golden Lily," he said genially, "perhaps you should see them first."

Ryan took the envelope silently and sat down. The contents were two sheets of heavy white paper covered with printing. He read them carefully. They were contracts, sent from two rival London theaters which were evidently vying for the chance to present the Golden Lily of the Confederacy on their stages. The amount of money offered was staggering. He stared at them, while a feeling of dread settled in his stomach. Leaning forward, he tossed them into Leslie's lap.

"Handsome offers," he said stiffly.

Vizetelly beamed, his dark eyes dancing quickly from Ryan's stern face to Leslie's widening eyes as she read them. "A wonderful opportunity," he pointed out. "The Southern states are dear to the hearts of the English, even in imminent defeat. You'll have sympathy as well as admiration, my dear. And packed halls from the moment you step on a stage. Your reputation is already made in England."

"So much money," Leslie breathed incredulously, "and they only ask for six weeks of my time. Can you imagine, Ryan? London must be a very rich town." She smiled at Vizetelly. "I am truly amazed at the power you have, sir. A few stories, a sketch or two, and you have these men offering a fortune to a singer who they have never heard sing!"

Flattered, Vizetelly beamed again. "They trust my judgment."

"They must," Leslie agreed, and glanced at Ryan, expecting to see amusement in his clear eyes. Instead, he looked pale and miserable. Why, he actually thought that she would go! Hurriedly, she thrust the papers into Vizetelly's hands. "Thank them, by all means, Mr. Vizetelly, and tell them that I'm sorry I cannot accept such munificent offers."

The plump jaw dropped comically. "You—you are refusing?"

"How could I not?" Leslie asked gently. "There is no exotic creature named the Golden Lily, sir, as you should know better than I, since you created the illusion. Did you truly expect me to try to impersonate your fictional character?"

"I certainly did," Vizetelly said, outraged. "Why else did you send your friend to beg me to print those stories? She said that you were extremely anxious to begin a career on the stage."

Leslie stared at him. "If you mean Mrs. Rockwell," she said finally, "I'm afraid her . . . her ambition for me has led her to deceive you. I knew nothing of her efforts."

"But she was right, my dear. You have the talent, the beauty . . ." Vizetelly turned to Ryan eagerly. "You understand the benefits, Captain. Tell your wife she must consider this deeply."

"I wouldn't dare," Ryan said comfortably. He was no longer pale and his faint smile was in place. "She's very strong-minded." He stood, a signal for Vizetelly to depart. "I regret the trouble that Mrs. Rockwell's gossip has caused you, sir."

"I don't mind gossip," Vizetelly said, rising. "It's often the spice of life. But I don't care for lies. I will have a word with Wynne before I leave the hotel." He turned at the door and looked back, past Ryan's towering body, and smiled at Leslie. "Still, it's a shame that it wasn't true. If you change your mind . . ."

"She won't," Ryan said, ushering him out. "She's as stubborn as they come."

"What a thing to say," Leslie chided as the door

closed. "Strong-minded and stubborn, both." But she was smiling.

Ryan's eyes were thoughtful as he came back and pulled her up into his arms. "Am I being selfish, Leslie? Am I holding you back from something you want to do? Why did you refuse?"

She turned her head and pressed her cheek against him, holding him tightly. Some day she would tell him what she had learned about his mother, what she had seen about an entertainer's life when Belle died, and all about the long thoughts she had been thinking since. But not tonight. Instead, she leaned back and smiled provocatively. "The clapping doesn't last," she said softly, "love does. I'll just entertain you."

His grin flashed. "An excellent thought," he said approvingly, and turned her toward the bedroom.

In bed, she opened her arms to him as he slipped in. "Just think—another wedding night," she sighed, stroking his chest. "How married we are. Who else gets married so often? We must really enjoy taking those vows. . . ." She laughed, a clear, childlike sound of amusement, at his indignant growl. "Oh, Ryan . . ." She moved over him, snuggling into the crook of his shoulder, touching his lips lightly with hers. "No bell, book and candle could make us closer, no parchment covered with names." She touched his lips again and then tentatively licked them. He smelled so delightful, and tasted even better. She settled herself more firmly against him and tasted his neck.

"Tonight," Ryan said, a trifle unsteadily, "I plan only to hold and caress you."

"Ummmm."

His hands moved down her curved back and splayed fingers over her slim buttocks. "I want to show you," he went on, "that I don't always have to gratify my desires."

"Ummmm?" She was still tasting, having moved to his chest and nuzzled a flat nipple.

"It's an appropriate time, since in your condition," Ryan sounded a bit strained, "there are bound to be days when you're tired and out of sorts. I want you to be free to tell me . . ." He groaned as her tongue flicked into his navel, and moved, rising on one elbow and sliding her away.

"To tell me," he began again, and then stopped, looking down at her in the dim light. She lay in the usual tangle of honey-gold hair, her face soft with desire, her eyes a dark blue, her lips curved in a half smile. Strands of her hair nearly covered her breasts, which now were so fascinating to him.

"Tell you what?" Her voice was very soft and lazy.

Silently, Ryan lifted the hair from her breasts and smoothed it back over her shoulders. Then he bent, his mouth seeking the gleaming roundness, the taut, pink rosettes.

Leslie drew in her breath. Her breasts were so sensitive now that the merest kiss sent living fire through her veins, funneling down to the innermost part of her being. Her fingers gently threaded through his thick hair, guiding him from one aching tip to the other. Her hips moved involuntarily as the liquid flames pooled in her loins, and Ryan's warm palm moved down, stroking her into quiescence.

Leslie grew utterly still as his fingers invaded the triangle of dark curls. The warm pads of his fingertips were alive with a subtle promise of pleasure, of an unknown ecstasy. She closed her eyes as the fingers crept further, then she drew in her breath again as they slid back up through a moist, velvety path to the apex of her thighs. They had found a tiny, fiery point that made her thighs tremble, her breath catch in her throat. She hardly noticed that his lips had left her breasts; her entire attention was fastened on that point and the delicate torture of the barely brushing fingertips. She felt poised on the edge of something wonderful, something strangely appealing. Tentatively, she tensed her buttocks and pushed ever so slightly upward, feeling the fingers slide away, feeling his lips and tongue fasten gently over the pulsating, flaming point. The explosion of pleasure caught her by surprise, made her cry out, made her body twist and tremble against his mouth, wanting more and more. . . .

In a deep excitement, Ryan moved over her, his lips covering her mouth, his tongue thrusting possessively as he parted her thighs with a knee, pressed himself into her still quivering flesh with deep sounds of erotic pleasure.

With a sigh of satisfaction, Leslie wrapped her arms around him, wriggled luxuriously against his straining loins. "I thought," she whispered breathlessly, "that you were going to show me . . ."

"Some other time," Ryan promised hoarsely, "perhaps when we are very old. . . ."

Chapter Seventeen

A COOL BREEZE TEMPTED LESLIE TO GO FAR BEYOND HER usual walk the next morning. Up past Government House, up the steps cut from solid rock that were called the Queen's Staircase, and through the leafy path toward tiny Fort Fincastle on the bluff over the town. She felt wonderful. She had slept through the night in Ryan's arms, had awakened to his kiss. And now, dressed in her smart brown suit and a tiny brown bonnet on the back of her head, she surveyed the blue and gold world below her and decided that she didn't care if she never saw it again. It was beautiful, with its trees and flowers, its clean streets and lovely houses, its blue bay. The hotel was beautiful, too, and most of the people in it pleasant, but they were all transients like she was. And Ryan was. Everyone waiting to go home, and she wanted a home, too.

Below, the light flutter of waves made the ships at the docks tug at their lines as if they were anxious to be off on the December trip. Leslie could hardly wait for the old-fashioned Southern Christmas that she knew they would have at the Lockwoods' home. She left her vantage point on the bluff with a happy sigh. Ryan had said that they would leave early and somehow find the *James Bulloch* on the way. She had every confidence in him. This time, when they arrived in Wilmington, they would be properly married. Married enough even for Ryan.

Arriving at the hotel at noon, she found Ryan waiting in the suite wearing a dark blue suit instead of the casual clothes she expected. He looked very pleased, but he frowned at her brown suit.

"Put on something appropriate for a wedding," he said, "and do so quickly. We are leaving for our meeting with the *James Bulloch*."

"What? Where? How far?" Leslie was dashing for the closet, rummaging through it, spluttering. "I haven't a thing . . ." Her hand fell on the white lace, the delicate white lace which had been mended so much. She drew it out, smiling. "Extremely appropriate, considering everything," she said, and laughed at Ryan's expression. Stripping off the brown suit, she put on the white lace. It was more fetching than ever with her newly rounded breasts. She took his arm and turned him toward the outer door.

"Now tell me. Spence didn't bring his warship in and defy the government, did he?"

Hurrying her out, Ryan laughed. "Almost. He's at Cochrane's Anchorage, nine miles east. He sent a small boat in to tell me."

"Bless him," Leslie said breathlessly, crossing the piazza. "He must know how much I need to talk to that chaplain of his. Oh, Ryan, I can hardly wait to hear all he knows!"

"And I can hardly wait to stand before him with you," Ryan replied, handing her up into the carriage. "Or have you forgotten?"

"Not for a minute," Leslie assured him, though in truth she was filled with thoughts of her father. How she wished that Ryan could meet him. All his anger and contempt for Harry Gordon would drop away at once, she was sure. Her father's character was easy to read in his face and his kindness to others. He was a strong man, not a weakling as Ryan pictured him.

The deck of the raider was considerably higher than that of the *China Pearl*. Leslie wished for her breeches and boots when she saw the rope ladder. But she went up agilely in a flutter of white lace and petticoats and stood on the deck looking, with a wildly beating heart, for a man with a chaplain's insignia.

Spence came quickly to take her hands, his fingers warm, his voice soft as he cautioned her.

"Secrecy is as necessary here as on land, Leslie. Say nothing to indicate that this is more than a friendly meeting. We three will go below together, but you will meet the chaplain alone in my cabin."

Of course. There were patriots aboard who would report even their captain for aiding the cause of an army deserter. It was only that it was hard for her to think of her father as a criminal. Head bent, she walked with Spence and Ryan down a spacious companionway and turned into a lighted passage. A door stood open into the officers' ward room.

"Ryan and I will wait here," Spence said calmly. "When you have finished your conversation, join us. My cabin is at the end of the passage."

Ryan's fingers suddenly curled protectively around

Leslie's slim hand. "I can keep my mouth shut, Spence," he said roughly. "You already know that."

Green eyes glinted beneath the cocked hat. "My ship, my rules, Fitz. She will be all right."

The look Ryan gave her as he reluctantly released her hand warmed Leslie. He wanted to share this part of her life no matter his feelings about her father. The thought gave her confidence as she swept down the hall and knocked on the door.

The door opened, exposing a luxuriously paneled and appointed cabin. A firm hand grasped her arm gently and drew her in, then the solid man in Confederate gray closed the door and stood looking at her with sudden tears in his blue eyes.

In the split second before she cried out and flung herself into his arms, Leslie saw that the tawny gold hair was now sprinkled with gray, that the firm chin she remembered was hidden beneath a silvery beard. Then she was clinging to his broad girth and crying, held tightly in the well-remembered comfort of her father's arms. Now she knew why Spence wouldn't allow Ryan to come with her. No one else should know that the chaplain on the *James Bulloch* was an army deserter.

Once Leslie calmed down, they talked for an hour. She learned that Spence's "connection" was his brother, Alan Burdette. Alan, a pacifist who abhorred war and killing, had set up an underground in Florida to help men who felt as he did. Those who still wanted to serve their country were given new papers and identities and trained for non-combatant jobs.

"None I have met are cowards," her father told her. "Many of us work on the battlegrounds and in field hospitals. The army is so disorganized now that all one must do is show up in uniform, identify yourself and go to work. No one questions your orders—they are too happy for the help. Since I studied for the ministry,

Alan decided that I should be a chaplain and had me ordained." He grinned at her. "An army chaplain on a navy ship! No one but Alan could have arranged that."

"And after the war?"

"I will be the Reverend Groover the rest of my life," her father said quietly. "The safety of us all depends on total secrecy. But I am content. I believe I have found my calling. I work now with the hopelessly wounded and the men who have lost their faith, and I hope and believe I am helping them."

"I am sure you are," Leslie said warmly, "but if only Ryan could know . . ." She stopped, seeing the adamant refusal in his eyes. "All right. I promise that I will never tell him. But will you marry us? We planned for it, though, of course, I didn't know the chaplain on Spence's ship would be you!"

Her father smiled gently. "You would give me away, Leslie. Your attitude toward me is not exactly that of a stranger. I cannot risk it. It would put Captain Burdette in extreme danger."

"I would do nothing to put either of you in danger," Leslie said passionately, "not if my life depended on it. I will treat you as only a respected new acquaintance, and Ryan will never know! In fact, he will suspect more if we do *not* marry here, for he will wonder why the chaplain refused. Please, father . . ." The ardent pleading in her blue eyes was irresistible.

"If the captain does not object, then . . ." her father began, and Leslie was gone, flying through the door and down the passage.

Slowing her pace as she neared the ward room, Leslie smoothed her hair and went in quietly.

"The Reverend Groover has agreed to marry us, Ryan."

Both men leaped to their feet, Spence frowning, spluttering words: "No, Leslie. That isn't wise . . ."

"We *have* to," Leslie said recklessly. "We've told all our friends that we are already married—for the usual reason." Reddening, she met Spence's shocked eyes squarely. "I know that you will keep that secret—as I will keep all others."

"Then, by all means, marry," Spence said hastily, and led the way to his cabin.

The chaplain, his bearded face serious, seemed to measure Ryan carefully as they were introduced, his penetrating blue eyes meeting Ryan's clear gaze and holding it for a long moment. Then he relaxed and began the short but reverent ceremony, his gaze wandering often to the bent golden head of the bride and the pink-cheeked face that was as serious as his own as she repeated the vows. But the way Ryan boomed out his firm intention of loving and cherishing Leslie "till death do us part" brought a smile that split the silvery beard.

There was no ring. At the last moment, Spence drew off a gold band with a crested seal and handed it to Ryan. It hung loosely on Leslie's slim finger but she curled her hand firmly around it and gave Spence a brilliant smile, full of gratitude and affection. He smiled back, letting go the last vestige of a dream that he knew was hopeless.

Then it was over, the bride kissed, the official papers signed, the tension eased with a glass of brandy. Ryan hurried Leslie out, reminding her that Spence was anxious to leave the anchorage. In the hall, she pulled away from him.

"I wish to thank Chaplain Groover personally for the news that he brought me, as well as the wedding," she said calmly. "I will be with you in a moment."

Entering the cabin, she shut the door behind her and embraced her father once more. "After the war," she whispered, "look for us at the big springs near the

Green Swamp. I love you very much, Father, and I am very proud of you." She kissed the bearded cheek and hugged him hard, feeling their tears mingle. "Are you happy for me?"

"I am," her father said huskily. "The man loves you, child. That's the greatest of blessings in marriage." He smoothed her hair with a gentle hand. "Go. Don't keep him waiting. . . ."

From the deck of the raider, Spence watched the *China Pearl* swing away and head back toward the port, with Ryan at the wheel and the small figure in blowing white lace close by. The Reverend Groover stood beside him, also watching.

"The worst fights between those two," Spence said quietly, "have been over—uh, her father. Ryan has never made a secret of his disgust for a cowardly deserter, and, shall we say, a negligent parent." He glanced at the chaplain with worried green eyes. "It will be a terrible temptation for Leslie to tell him the truth now. Do you think she will?"

"Never." The Reverend Groover spoke with absolute conviction. "She promised."

Spence sighed, relieved. He trusted Ryan, but the less who knew, the better. His brother Alan was very dear to him.

Aboard the *China Pearl,* Ryan put an arm around Leslie's slim waist. "I liked the Reverend Groover," he said comfortably. "Spence told me quite a bit about the man while we waited. Did you know that Groover is actually an army chaplain who works right in the field hospitals and battlegrounds? He's only filling in on the *James Bulloch* as a favor to Spence."

"Really?" Leslie made the word as carelessly admiring as she could manage. "Then you consider him a brave and dedicated man?" Oh, she was bursting to tell him! Her heart was full of love and pride for her father.

"I do," Ryan said soberly. "I should think it would take more courage to move among the enemy fire without even a pistol to defend yourself. Yet he does it every day."

Leslie looked away, biting her lower lip. "I—liked him, too," she said softly. "I'm glad he's the one who married us."

Ryan pulled her closer, laughing suddenly. "Mrs. Fitzsimmons, what in God's name prompted you to tell Spence that you were pregnant?"

"I didn't!"

"Don't beg the point."

"Well, he was going to refuse . . ." Leslie grinned wickedly, leaning closer. "You should be glad. Did you see the date he put on our marriage papers? June 20, 1864. Six months ago! Is that legal?"

"Not until the ink dries," Ryan said, and began to laugh helplessly. Spencer Burdette was a true friend.

On Christmas Eve the *China Pearl* rolled in the aftermath of a winter storm. Her sails furled and tied, her paddles thrashing, she pushed doggedly through the rough seas. Her sleek bow rose endlessly on cresting waves, plunged endlessly down the steep slopes and into another, sending tons of water washing over her decks, swirling around the boots of the men on duty.

Snug in the cabin, Leslie watched the hooded, black-clad men and thought their patience as endless as the sea. Oceans had taught them to take what came their way and make the best of it. Her glance sought the tallest figure and found Ryan looking toward the stern again. She knew that his eyes were fixed on two blurred shapes behind him, the *Nassau Belle* and the *South Star*, with Captains Latimer and Barclay in command. After a storm it was common practice to watch for a flag of distress and give aid if necessary, and the *South Star* was old and rotten. Still, after a moment, Ryan turned away, satisfied, and Leslie left the window, going back to her book.

A slow and troublesome trip, but almost over. They had hoped to arrive in Wilmington the night before and spend both Christmas Eve and Christmas with the Lockwoods. Now, it would be close to midnight before they crossed the bar. The storm and the watch over the other ships had delayed them, and the wind was still strong from the southwest, the sky heavy and lowering, threatening more rain. But at least they'd have Christmas Day with William and Helen, and the thought of it cheered Leslie. Down in the hold of the *China Pearl* there was a stack of presents, carefully chosen and gaily wrapped, bound to please Helen and her daughters. Ryan had found a case of fine sherry and a box of Cuban cigars for William. Thinking of the pleasures, Leslie looked up with a smile as Ryan entered the cabin. The smile was not returned. Ryan shook off his oilskins with a disgusted grunt.

"I don't like the looks of the night ahead," he growled. "We haven't passed one Federal ship, and at this longitude we should have passed two cordons and been within sight of the third. Something is wrong."

Leslie stared up at him for a moment and then her smile deepened. "Perhaps they have done as Helen hoped and declared a Christmas truce. That would be wonderful!"

Ryan laughed, a short, sharp sound without humor. "I wish I thought it possible. It's more likely they've drawn them in for an attack on Fort Fisher. Spence told me that it would be before the first of the year."

Leslie's smile faded. "What will you do?"

"Go in again at the south inlet," he answered bluntly. "It's all we can do. I hope Barclay makes it. It's a wonder that ship of his is still floating after a storm like that." He dropped into the chair at the desk and looked at her with eyes full of concern. "This is one trip I wish you had missed. It's hardly the weather or conditions for a woman with child."

She had never seen Ryan so worried. Rising, she slipped into his lap and put her arms around his neck. "We'll be fine," she said softly. "All three of us are Fitzsimmonses now, with the famous Fitzsimmons' luck."

His arms tightened around her. "Just the same, you'll go below early. With this sea running and the rain we'll have, visibility will be poor. If we get a surprise, I want to know that you're tucked below in safety." His darkened eyes brooded over her tenderly. "You are my life. Remember it," he quoted with a smile, and kissed her.

Wrapped in his arms, Leslie felt no fear, no foreboding. Only his warmth and his solid strength. Whatever happened, Ryan would get them through.

The sun was invisible, the only sign of its setting a deeper gloom. Leslie was below in the ward room, watching the rain pelt down through the companionway and seep through the cracks in the planking. They were approaching the inlet at the south end of the Cape Fear River, and behind them the *Nassau Belle* and the *South Star* dogged their wake.

"Too close," Ryan had commented. "They're desperate to get into calmer water, or they'd realize that three ships together make the chance of discovery too great."

Leslie herself was looking forward to the calmer water of the Cape Fear, even though the smaller Federal cruisers often ran into the river. They could chase a runner a good way before they came within range of the fort's guns, but Ryan's ship could outrun them. She dozed in the black darkness and hoped again for a Christmas truce.

An hour later the coal gas swirling in the air told her that the hatches had been covered, the binnacle shrouded. But still the ship crept, slow and wary. She dozed again in the uncomfortable chair. The time to worry was when the speed increased.

Muffled, heavy footsteps above her head alerted her. She opened her eyes sleepily as Finney's bulk dropped down the ladder and loomed in the doorway. He grabbed her arm.

"Into the hammock room, ma'am, now!" He pulled her roughly to her feet. "The bulkheads are thicker there. The captain says pick a corner and stay in it."

Stumbling as he pulled her along, Leslie protested. "Why? It hasn't started. . . ."

"We're trapped," Finney said grimly, "in the middle of half a dozen ships. And we can't turn and run for it, not with the others behind us. Just do as he said." He was gone, leaving her standing, trembling, in total darkness.

The meaning of what he had said finally sank in, and with it a deep dread. Instinct sent one slender hand protectively to the rounded curve of her belly, the other hand felt desperately along a wall to a corner. Sinking into it, she cowered and put her hands over her ears as the sudden screaming of shells split the air and the *China Pearl* surged into top speed. But not a shell struck, and the glow of the Drummond lights was dim. The ships behind them were the target! Her throat closed, thinking of the agony on those old, slow ships with the young, reckless captains, hoping for no more now than to save the lives aboard. She waited tensely, wondering if by some miracle Ryan had slipped through. The ship around her vibrated and groaned with the force of the straining engines; the rough water set the ghostly shapes of hammocks swinging wildly over her head. *Had Ryan slipped through?* With a desperate hope she crept through the darkness and grasped the cold, wet rungs of the ladder. She had to see.

The rain had stopped. Her head rose above the edge of the companionway into clear night air; her face turned forward, her straining eyes looked directly at a tremendous, bristling black hulk off the starboard bow, not a hundred yards away.

With a gasp of horror she scrambled down and fled through the door as the black night blew away in a blinding explosion of light. The first thundering salvo from the warship smashed into the bow of the *China Pearl*, throwing the ship off course and flinging Leslie into her corner. Her head hit the bulkhead sharply, her body sprawled. She pulled herself up, nausea rising in her throat as the ear-splitting scream of shells came again and she felt the shock of a solid blow. The ship reeled, turned back on course and plunged forward. Struggling to brace herself in the corner, Leslie prayed as the nightmare went on. It was a constant thunder of guns, of whistling shells and explosive blasts, and, worst of all, the repeated shuddering impacts. Men screamed and cursed on deck, hoarse cries of pain and anger.

Leslie was far beyond fear, shocked into the knowledge of true disaster. She grew strangely still, waiting for the end, wondering that the ship was still going forward and watching the glow that flickered down the companionway, the red glow of fire. The stern of the ship was taking the punishment now; she could hear the sound of glass falling after each blow. Then, with a final burst of speed and a dull explosion somewhere inside the ship, the *China Pearl* slowed and began drifting in calm water.

Leslie got to her feet as the sounds of the guns faded in the distance. As the silence grew around her, she realized that the engines had stopped. She went forward gingerly, touching the place on her head where it had struck when she fell, and felt the stickiness of blood. She wiped it off her fingers and went on, to the foot of the ladder.

"Man those masts, what's left of them! I want every rag of sail you can stretch!" Ryan's harsh shout rose above the groans and the running feet on deck. A seaman dropped down the ladder with a lantern in his hand and brushed past Leslie without a word. Grabbing a pile of bandages, he disappeared up the ladder again. Standing there, Leslie suddenly felt choked by the warm, metallic odor swirling out from the ward room. Steam. The boilers had failed, or burst. She coughed from the acrid smell and climbed up far enough to breathe fresh air.

The sails snapped overhead and filled with air, but the ship moved sluggishly, turning north. Men were carrying lanterns on the deck, their faces shocked and strained in the glow of lights as they doused the fires. The water ran slowly, spluttering on the fires, washing around the prone bodies of the wounded.

Finney's thick legs stopped between her and the scene; his hamlike hand came down for hers.

"The captain says you're to come up and come forward," he said calmly. "Watch your step, ma'am. The deck's not safe."

Trembling, Leslie climbed the rest of the rungs and held Finney's arm as he led her around the smouldering wood and debris to Ryan at the wheel. Ryan's right side was heavily bandaged with bloodstained cloth, his coat thrown carelessly over his shoulders. He put out his left hand and drew her close.

"Ryan . . . your side!"

"Sh-h-h, it's nothing. It looks much worse than it is. No bones broken. Are you all right?"

"Yes." Looking north, she stifled a startled cry. The sky was lurid with exploding light; the drum of heavy artillery rolled like distant thunder. "What is that?"

"A Yankee-style Christmas truce," Ryan said dryly. "The attack on Fort Fisher is under way. And they put an effective trap at the south end, too. They got us all." He turned to Finney. "Set the fuse, Bosun, and bring up the chest. Get Tudbury and tell him to pick five more good men. Then report back to me."

Panic hit Leslie with astounding force. The resigned tone of Ryan's voice was more frightening than the shells. Finney was gone with no more than a nod, as if he had known beforehand what he had to do. Her throat tight, Leslie managed a whisper.

"What can *I* do?" She wanted desperately to do something. The *China Pearl*, like a wounded friend, tore at her heart. Drifting with only a few scraps of sail, she barely answered the helm.

"Call on your courage," Ryan said quietly. "We're losing her, Leslie. We have no power and she's badly holed, taking on more water than we can handle. The war is over for us."

Somehow it was better to know. Leslie turned and looked back, past the dim outline of the inlet to the burning hulks of the other runner ships. Soon they would come up the river to plunder and burn the dying *China Pearl*. But if Ryan wanted her courage, she would supply it. She turned back to him.

"Everything comes to an end," she said, her voice steady. "I'm glad that I'm with you."

His left arm tightened convulsively, holding her. "You won't be," he said gruffly. "I'm sending you to Smithville with Finney in one of the small boats. You'll be taking the gold with you."

"No!" She shrieked the word, jerking away, her face contorted. "I won't leave you! Do you think me a coward?"

"I do not," Ryan answered. "I know that you would stay, through hell if necessary. But you are my only hope. You can save my treasures—my wife, my child and the gold that must support us." He was calmer, his faint smile appeared. "If I'm to survive, I must have a reason. Give me my hope, darling. Something to live for."

Leslie stared at him with a feeling of dread, sensing his iron will, fearing her own defeat. Her eyes blurred. "If we can escape, then you can. Come with us."

"If there is no one on the ship, they will hunt down the small boats," Ryan said evenly, "and I can't ask anyone else to stay. I am the captain here, Leslie. Are you going to help me, or do I lose all?"

He had won. Tears ran unheeded down her face as she met his eyes, clear and steady in the lantern light. "I will go," she said, "and I will wait. But I will never be whole again until you come to me."

Ryan's face twisted in sudden pain. "Nor will I," he said, and bent and kissed her. "I will come, my brave darling. We will have our future."

Behind them, Finney spoke gruffly. "The wounded are away in the other small boat, sir, and the rest are swimming. They'll land on the river shore. If they aren't captured, the sentinels from the fort will aid them tomorrow." He hesitated. "A small cruiser is coming through the inlet, Captain. We'd best be away."

Ryan straightened to the wheel with a muffled groan, favoring his wounded side. "We should be there. . . ." He twisted the wheel sharply as the ship's hull grated over an obstruction, shuddered and ground slowly to a halt. "There it is," he said with grim satisfaction, "the shoal I was hunting. She'll not sink until my work is done." He swung away from the wheel and took Leslie's arm. "Put the boat over on the lee side, Finney. Mrs. Fitzsimmons is ready."

Finney nodded and turned back, shouting hoarsely to the waiting, black-clad men in the waist of the ship.

At the last moment, Leslie summoned every ounce of courage, every shred of dignity. She embraced Ryan quickly, turned away and stepped into the boat without a word. Then, sitting in the bow with Finney beside her, Tudbury and five more men at the oars, she called back to Ryan with a note of panic in her voice.

"Where shall I wait for you?"

Ryan's tall figure leaned over the rail to call to her as the boat swirled away in the tide. His deep voice came faintly to her ears. "The green place . . . the one in your heart."

Leslie stared at the receding hulk of the ship as the men bent to the oars. The green place? There was nothing there. The green place was only a dream in a world of harsh reality. Bewildered, she tried to understand. Was Ryan telling her that a future for them was only to be in her heart? Was he telling her that he wouldn't survive? She whirled, staring at Finney's bearded face.

"Take me back, damn you! He's fooled me, and you knew it!" She jumped to her feet. "Take me back, or by God I'll swim!"

Finney's bearlike arms pulled her back to the seat, one wide, rough palm covered her mouth. "You'll bring the boarders down on us and that gold, too, ma'am, with that noise. I follow the captain's orders." He wasn't looking at her struggling form or paying attention to her muffled screams. His gaze was fixed on the ship in a dreadful fascination. "Pick up the pace, men," he barked suddenly. "Draw away, draw away. . . ."

Leslie's wide blue eyes stared over Finney's hand at the rapidly diminishing silhouette of the *China Pearl*. The lights of the approaching cruiser limned it sharply, yet she could see no figure moving on the decks. Where *was* Ryan? She struggled again, pushing with both hands at Finney's rock-hard arm, kicking, squirming to slide down and away. He ignored her efforts.

"Watch," he whispered gruffly, "and you'll see the reception that Fitz gives those Yanks."

The men on the cruiser had evidently seen that the *China Pearl* had run aground, and they gave the area a wide berth, anchoring off to one side. Small boats had been let down and armed men filled them. They were rowing rapidly now toward the helpless ship.

"Now," Finney said prayerfully, *"now."*

With a mighty roar the entire stern of the *China Pearl* exploded, thundering upward into the air with a shockwave that set their small boat rocking violently. Finney's hand left Leslie's face and grabbed the gunwale, steadying the boat as waves drenched them. Leslie's eyes never left the holocaust behind them; she was hypnotized by horror. A series of lesser explosions blew out to the sides, showering the water with burning timbers, adding to the brilliance of the towering column of flame. The golden light shone like a noonday sun on water around the burning ship, accenting the flailing black dots on the surface. Men were swimming for their lives, their boats overturned and fiery debris falling all around them.

Silent, motionless, Leslie watched the end of her world. She was soaked by the waves, chilled by the cold December air, conscious of nothing except the scene from hell before her. She didn't feel the heavy coat that Finney draped over her shoulders, and barely heard him speak.

"Don't give up, ma'am. Fitz will make it through if

anyone can." He waited, his bearded face growing uncertain as he saw her blank eyes. He raised his voice a trifle. "He had time to get off before she blew. And he'd try. He has a lot to live for."

Leslie's white, frozen face turned slowly. "Did Ryan blow up his own ship, Bosun?" At his nod, her face crumpled. "For God's sake, *why?*"

Finney relaxed a little. At least she wasn't struck dumb. "He had his reasons, ma'am. Foremost, to give us time to get away with no pursuers. And next was personal. He said that he'd be damned before he'd let the Yanks sack the *China Pearl*. That gunpowder was meant for the South. I laid a mighty long fuse to it, Miss Leslie. He had plenty of time to slip overboard after he put a match to that fuse. . . ." He went on talking, trying to comfort her, but his eyes were still on the scene behind them. The whole ship was burning now, the black skeletons of the masts smoking and breaking off, falling into the flames below. Off to one side the Yanks had a boat righted and were climbing into it. Suddenly, Tudbury spoke harshly to the other men at the oars.

"Pull, damn you! Do you want to spend time in a Yankee prison?"

Chapter Eighteen

IT WAS PAST NOON ON CHRISTMAS DAY WHEN FINNEY
helped Leslie down from a fisherman's cart and led her
through the gate and up the path to the Lockwood
home. He was worried. She was too silent, too pale, the
huge blue eyes still seemed to see that towering column
of flame. They had landed before dawn at Smithville;
he had paid off Tudbury and the other men, who were
glad enough to be free of Yankee justice. Then he had
hired the cart and set out for the house that Fitz had
told him to find. He had never seen the Lockwoods and
he was uncertain of their reception. He glanced at
Leslie, a white, shrunken waif in his heavy coat, her
hair tangled and damp down her back. He shrugged.
Captain's orders. He knocked firmly on the door.

Beaming, Helen opened the door, stared and
screamed.

"William! Come quickly . . . quickly!" She grasped Leslie in her arms and held her close. "Oh, my dear, my poor dear! What has happened? What horrible mishap?"

Finney edged away and found his shoulder clasped by a stout man whose pleasant face looked utterly shocked. "Come in, come in, man. You look exhausted."

Bewildered, Finney went in. It was in his tired mind that he owed Mr. Lockwood an explanation. He waited as the plump, silver-haired woman and two twittering girls marshaled Leslie up the stairs, and then turned to Lockwood and told him in a few sentences what had happened. Lockwood was pale when he finished. He asked one question.

"Do you think that Fitz could have survived?"

"I doubt it," Finney said with brutal honesty. "But I wouldn't say that to his wife. He had lost a deal of blood from a nasty wound in his side and his right arm was near useless from it. It's a long swim there to the river shore and the tide was running hard." He hesitated, looking away. "A strong man and stubborn. I'd like to think he made it. In the meantime, I'm to stay in town until Miss Leslie decides what she wants to do. I've got the captain's gold outside, hidden under some gunnysacks, and I'd like to leave it here."

Lockwood had been studying the rough man intently as he talked; now he reached out and took his hand in a firm grip. "Thank you for bringing Leslie to us," he said. "Fitz and his wife are both very dear to us. And, yes, you may leave the gold here, but only if you stay and guard it. We have a room that you can use."

Finney stared at him for a long moment. "We'll ask Miss Leslie," he said finally. "I'll do what she says. Fitz would want that."

Helen was also worried. Leslie submitted to a bath

and put on one of the dark blue skirts and white blouses she had worn before. She answered questions by saying the ship had been wrecked and Ryan had sent her ashore with Finney, but that was all. She agreed to take a nap, but when Helen peeked in a half-hour later, she was lying on the bed with her eyes open, staring at nothing. Helen went down and dragged the details from Finney, who was in the kitchen drinking brandy with William.

"Oh, dear God," she breathed when she had heard it all. "Here, give me that bottle of brandy." She turned back at the door to look at Finney with tears glistening in her eyes. "We loved him, too," she said brokenly. "I pray that by some miracle . . ." She couldn't say more. She left with the bottle and a glass in her hands.

The brandy revived Leslie enough to come down to dinner. There was little talk, since the subject heavy on their minds didn't bear talking about. But Leslie was composed. Still pale, she toyed with the food, sipped the prized tea and sat stiffly erect in her chair. When William broached the subject of Finney staying with them, she looked at Finney and nodded.

"It's kind of you," she said to William. "I would like it very much."

Afterward, clearing away, Amy whispered to her mother. "She needs to cry, Ma. She's keeping it all inside."

"I well know that," Helen retorted. "If it were one of you, I'd slap your face and bring it on. But I can't raise a hand to that suffering girl. Fitz was her world."

The dam broke when the family entered the drawing room. The room was festive with Christmas decorations. A beautiful tree held candles like tiny, burning stars and opened presents sprawled beneath it in a clutter of gay wrappings.

Leslie sat opposite the tree, her eyes caught by the

tiny flames and then by the gifts below. Something jarred her frozen mind. The gifts she had bought and packed in the ship . . .

"Your presents blew up," she said stupidly, and then turned and looked at Helen with agony in her eyes. "Oh, Ryan, Ryan . . ." She bent forward, feeling her heart ripped from her chest, the piercing pain of loss twisting and turning like a dagger. Bursting into a storm of weeping, she put her head on her knees and shook with wrenching sobs. Helen held her tightly, patting and trying to comfort her.

"That's right," she murmured, "let it out. It won't heal inside. . . ."

Later, exhausted, Leslie went with Helen to the small upstairs bedroom that she had used on her first visit. Sinking down on the edge of the bed, she looked at Helen humbly.

"I've ruined your Christmas," she said, "bringing nothing but grief. I'm sorry."

"Oh, my dear, how can you say that? You know that we love you." Helen gave way to tears herself. "If only we could help you bear it."

"You've helped," Leslie said simply, "as no one else could. I'll be all right now. It isn't over for Ryan and me. He told me never to give up on him, and I won't. If it takes a miracle, why, then we'll have one. Miracles are common with us." Her head came up, the slim jaw set stubbornly. "I will wait, and he will come to me."

"Oh, Leslie . . ." Helen looked at her helplessly. It would be better, she thought, if she would accept the loss and work through it. If Ryan had managed to get to land, he'd be here by now, of that much Helen was certain. But she couldn't bear to even hint at it. "Sleep now," she said gently. "I'm going down and fix a hot toddy for that great bear of a man of yours. Finney, isn't it? He could use some sleep himself."

In the next few days, Finney located three of the men who had swum ashore. They were able to tell him that all of the wounded and the rest of the others had been captured and taken as prisoners to the Federal ships, and were no doubt in Fort Montague by now. They had managed to elude the Yanks themselves and were pleased to receive their back pay so they could go home. None of the three, however, had seen Captain Fitzsimmons. Finney told Leslie, reluctantly.

"It proves nothing," Leslie said gently. "In the confusion that night anything could happen. He could have been captured and taken away before the others. You told me yourself, Bosun, that I shouldn't give up on him."

Finney only nodded. She had left him nothing to say.

Rumors were rampant in the town of Wilmington. The fort had held; the Federal fleet had moved offshore to regroup. But there were stories of a huge force of army troops coming by land to assist in taking Fort Fisher. People left town in droves, taking what belongings they could pack and traveling south. At dinner one night, William told them all that he had made up his mind to go, too.

"We are all going to the country," he said firmly. "The farm where Amy and Mary Ann have been staying is out of the way, a small place in the hills that may well be overlooked. We will be safer there than anywhere else."

"Finney and I will not crowd you." Leslie's voice was as firm as William's. "We have a place to go, and we're going." She glanced at Finney's startled face and smiled faintly. "A long trip, Bosun, but—captain's orders. Buy, beg, borrow or steal a wagon and we'll be on our way to the Hillsborough and the green place."

"Yes, ma'am," Finney said blankly. He didn't trust the burning, almost fanatic look in her blue eyes, the sheer determination in the carved ivory of her face. But he had heard the captain's words. He had wondered at the time what Fitz had meant by "the green place." He reckoned that he'd know when he saw it.

For the two days while Finney gathered supplies for the trip, William tried to talk Leslie out of it.

"I'm a family man," he told her, "and I recognize your condition. You may lose your child on such a hazardous, difficult trip."

"I'll not," Leslie said calmly. "I am used to rough living. Finney and I will make do."

Defeated, William turned to Finney. "You're crazy to try it, with that chest of gold and a pregnant woman. You'll be killed and robbed before you reach the Florida border."

Finney shook his head. "That won't happen, Mr. Lockwood. I've learned to be wary, and I've bartered for an Enfield for each of us, and a brace of pistols as well. No one will take us unaware."

William stared. "You expect that fragile girl to shoot a rifle?"

"She's a better shot than I am," Finney said, "but I can back her up." He went back to packing the wagon with mostly army stores. A tent and woolen blankets, a camp stove and utensils, ammunition and kerosene. There was a thriving market for those things if you had gold. He wanted to be prepared, and Leslie had told him that they would camp most of the way, and that a good deal of the land they would cross was uninhabited. "Plenty of deer and wild hogs," she had said. "You won't need much salt meat." Finney was looking forward to venison and he was fond of woods and hunting.

Even clothes could be had, Leslie discovered, if you had gold. Nothing fine, only worn but useful ginghams and light woolens. She had Finney find her an army cloak, a pair of oversized nankeen trousers and a knitted cap. She was careful to keep those items out of Helen's sight.

They left the third day, and Helen, who at last knew the magnitude of the journey and the dangers, was beside herself.

"You'll be lost in that wilderness," she mourned, "and we'll never see you again. William tells me there aren't even proper roads!" She looked up at the two of them on the spring seat of the wagon. Great, grizzled Finney, his bulk even larger in a heavy army coat, and the small, bundled figure beside him. In spite of the sizes, it was easy to see that Leslie was in command. There was a look of high pride on the fine-boned face, that same fanatic fire in her intensely blue eyes. She smiled down at Helen and reached to clasp her hand once more.

"Please, don't worry about us. I know every inch of the way. Keep well and safe until I see you again."

Finney was to say later that he had never enjoyed a trip more. The way Leslie knew was the way she had traveled with her father, and Harry Gordon had avoided towns. Only twice on the trip did they stay inside, and both times it was in a farmhouse. Other nights, they camped.

"I'd be proud to have a daughter like you," Finney told Leslie one morning, the only personal remark he made to her on the trip. "I spent a deal of time in the woods when I was a boy, and you're the handiest around a campfire I ever saw."

Leslie thanked him, but that was all. She wasn't sure that Ryan would like it if she told Finney the story of her life—and how else to explain why she had cooked over campfires for three years? These days she thought more and more about what Ryan would like when he came to her, and she meant to have a life and a place ready for him if she could.

The mules that Finney had bought were strong and healthy, but slow, and Leslie set herself to endure the snail's pace. The weather grew warmer every day, though there was still frost on the ground when she woke in the mornings. The trip gave her time to plan and dream, jostling along beside the silent Finney. The baby moved inside her and that was a marvel to hold in her thoughts like a jewel. Ryan's son. How pleased he would be!

They came at last to the edge of the Green Swamp, a month and a half from the day they had left Wilmington. She stared at the grove of oaks and magnolias where she had lived. She remembered the years only dimly, but the day that Ryan had arrived came back with a clarity that brought tears to her eyes. She could see that lean, whip-strong man with the banner of bright hair come swinging along the swale with the heavy saddle in his hand, and her sharp longing cut her like a knife. She turned away and directed Finney off to the west and through the open woods to the springs.

"Get down," she said, and clambered down herself to lead him to the edge of the springs. He shook his grizzled head in wonder.

"Clear as glass and deep enough to float the *China Pearl*," he said, and could have bitten his tongue off. But she didn't wince, only directed him to look at the land around them, the massive trees and fertile soil.

"We must pick the best place to build a house," she told him. "This is the green place where Ryan said to wait."

Finney looked at her in awed pity. This wild place for a woman alone. She was half mad in her grief. The thought of her building a house here and waiting in it forever for a long-dead husband was eerily frightening.

"Is there a town nearby?"

"A day's ride to the west," Leslie said carelessly. "We'll go there tomorrow and find a place to stay until the house is built."

Finney thought desperately of some way to dissuade her. "Best you stay in the town until the captain appears," he said, stumbling awkwardly over the words. "He'd know better about the house."

"Oh, no," Leslie said confidently. "I want it ready for him. I believe I know what will please him." Looking at Finney's worried, downcast face, she felt a sudden sympathy.

"I know that you think he's dead, Bosun," she added gently, "and even I know it's possible. But with so many prisoners taken that night from all three ships, his capture may have gone unreported. As long as there is a shred of hope, I will keep faith with him. I must, for I promised."

Finney drew a deep breath of relief. She wasn't crazy, after all, just stubborn. But she was wrong. His honest eyes met hers sadly. "I hope you're right, ma'am. But I doubt the Yank who captured the master of the *China Pearl* could have kept from crowing about it." He watched the small face change again into that carved ivory mask, the slim jaw set as she turned away.

"Nevertheless, I will build the house—in time to see that Ryan's son is born in it."

The next day they forded the Hillsborough at one of the wide, shallow rapids, the wagon's wooden wheels creaking and straining alarmingly over the rocks, and traveled west through terrain that Finney hoped never to see again. Deep sand on the high pine land and hub-deep muck in the marshes. He worked as hard as the mules, his axe ringing through the pines where they grew too thick to pass, his big shoulders straining at the back of the wagon when it stuck. In sight of the settlement of Tampa, he relaxed.

"I'll buy a saddle. I can oversee the building of the house on muleback. This wagon won't take that road again until the house is done."

"Buy two saddles," Leslie said serenely. "I'll be going along."

Finney glanced at her and then shrugged his heavy shoulders. Why mention that she'd be risking trouble by riding in her condition when he knew that she wouldn't believe it? He wasn't sure he believed it himself. It looked like Fitz's woman could do anything she put her mind to.

By inquiring of the first man they saw tilling a field, they made their way to John Tudbury's farm. The Tudburys, with two strapping sons at home, were more than willing to provide them with room and board and two laborers to swing hammers. There was a small, local sawmill, Tudbury told them, possessed of a narrow cart and a stout mule which could be used to transport lumber. He and his wife, Anna, were happy both with the extra income and pleasant company.

Settled, Leslie wrote to the Lockwoods and sent the Tudburys' address. Then, burning with energy, she pushed Finney to get on with the plans and the house.

"Cypress," she ordered, "both inside and out. It won't rot and it's pretty. Find the best builder you can and I'll draw out what I want."

By mid-April, when the news trickled in of General Lee's surrender at Appomattox, ending the War Between the States, the house was half finished. By the end of May it was done. It sat on a knoll not far from the springs, graced by a background of massive shade trees and with a sunny, cleared space for lawn and gardens. The honey tan of the cypress had been given an oil stain that made it glow with life. There was a rock fireplace and an abundance of windows. The home-made furniture and rag rugs were simple but adequate from Leslie's view. But it was small, with only two bedrooms and a room that served as both drawing room and dining room. The kitchen was a separate structure behind the house, reached by a small hall.

"To keep the heat out of the house in the summers," Leslie explained to Anna Tudbury. "Heat is hard on babies, I've heard."

Anna Tudbury was a hard-working pioneer woman, wiry and strong, full of earthy wisdom and good will. She glanced at Leslie's burdened body. "You'll stay with me until the baby is born," she said. "I know a bit about birthing. It's best to have help the first time."

"The baby will be born here," Leslie said firmly. "It's our home." In her mind, that "our" included Ryan. "I'm moving in tomorrow. Everything is ready, even a cradle."

"Then you'll have your first guest," Anna told her. "I'll not let you go through it alone. John and the boys can shift for themselves and Mr. Finney can stay with them. We won't need a man around at a time like this."

"I'm grateful to you," Leslie said quietly, pushing away a sharp pang of longing. There was a man who she wanted around desperately. In the past month and a half she had had to fight a growing fear. The war over, and still no word! Hope flared with every letter from the Lockwoods, but never a mention of Ryan. William had written that in the postwar hysteria for revenge, many a runner captain was held to be charged with piracy. "So far," he had written, "there have been no convictions. To their credit, the Yankee Navy men called as witnesses have told the truth—there were few, if any, acts of war from the runners. A certain group of politicians are vengeful. I think they'd have them all drawn and quartered if they could."

Leslie regretted the bitterness, but she drew hope even from that letter. If some men were still being held, one of them could be Ryan.

With no one around but Anna, Leslie began swimming again in the springs. June had brought a solid heat that made her heavy body uncomfortable. She stripped and bathed every day, though Anna told her that she looked like a sea cow in the water. Looking down at her bulging belly, Leslie had to agree. But it felt wonderful —until the day when she was seized by a powerful cramp that nearly drowned her. She struggled to the shore.

"Anna!"

Her scream brought Anna running. With a quick glance at the thin trail of blood drifting from between Leslie's thighs, Anna pulled her up and struggled through the mud of the bank.

"It's started," she said, panting. "I'll get you to bed. At least only your feet are dirty."

Now, why did that remind her of the dawn when Ryan found her stowed away in his cabin? Oh, yes, that time only her feet had been *clean*. Leslie laughed shakily as Anna wrapped a towel around her. "Once, on the ship," she began, then her eyes widened, her body bent. "Ryan's son," she whispered, "is as impatient as he is. . . ."

Ryan's son was born three hours later, squalling lustily.

"Healthy as they come," Anna pronounced as she cleaned him, "and louder than most. Nothing wrong with his lungs." She looked at Leslie's pale, sweating face with approval. "You never can tell about a little woman," she added. "When the time was right, you popped him out like a watermelon seed. You'll never have trouble birthing when you marry again."

Leslie closed her eyes, hiding the pain that the thoughtless remark had brought. It had hurt more than the delivery. *Oh, Ryan, Ryan. Everyone has given you up. Everyone but me.* She opened her eyes again and met Anna's gaze.

"Stop your chattering and give me my baby." She held out her arms for the bundle.

Later, watching him nurse, Leslie searched the tiny face and decided that the brow line was definitely Ryan's. The faint fuzz of light hair had a reddish tint, but other than that she could be sure of only one thing. He was altogether beautiful.

"Now," she whispered softly, "I have someone to wait with me."

Chapter Nineteen

In August, Leslie had a letter from Spence, forwarded by the Lockwoods. Spence was in England and would stay until amnesty was declared. Otherwise, along with other Southerners who had resigned from the U.S. Navy to join their own states in the conflict, he would be tried for treason. Fortunately, he had had an influential friend in Washington who had warned him of it in time for him to escape.

"I heard of the tragedy that befell the *China Pearl*," he wrote, "and William Lockwood told me of the uncertainty surrounding Fitz's disappearance. I contacted my friend in Washington and asked him to investigate the men still held in Fort Montague."

Leslie's heart leaped at that. Perhaps there would be some hint . . .

"Surprisingly," Spence wrote, "there are seamen

from the *China Pearl* still held there. There are men anxious to charge them with piracy, using the excuse that the ship was deliberately blown up as boarders approached. They are calling it an act of war. More senseless, illegal revenge!

"However, the men will be released, my friend tells me. Eyewitness accounts recently taken from the Union men who attempted to board the ship prove only that the captain was on her before the explosion took place, so they cannot charge the men. One northern senator was angry enough to have the men questioned and examined in case Fitz was among them. My friend said they had an official, detailed description of Fitz and none of them resembled him.

"I am sorry to bring you only more bad news," Spence wrote on, "but it corroborates Lockwood's opinion that Ryan was lost that night. Perhaps one of the seamen will contact you and tell you how Ryan died, and end the uncertainty. I am deeply grieved for you both, Leslie, as I am sure you know. Always, Spence."

Pale, Leslie folded the letter and laid it on the table beside her. She felt frozen and numb, the bright, cozy room around her suddenly as gray as a prison cell. That letter had been weeks on the way, weeks in which she had been full of hope without reason. For the first time she was looking down the tunnel of years ahead and there was no light at the end. *One of us without the other would be only a torn and aching half*. Ryan's words came back to her with their full meaning. Spence's letter had done what nothing else could do, torn away even the hope of Ryan's return.

I should have stayed with him, she thought dully. We should have drowned together, holding each other in our arms. She leaned back in the chair and closed her eyes. The thought of sinking slowly into oblivion in

Ryan's arms was infinitely better than this. Perhaps they would be together in some afterlife. Perhaps when she died she would find him. A vision of the deep, clear waters of the springs outside came stealing behind her closed lids. They would cool the raging pain and offer the same oblivion.

In the bedroom behind her the baby cried. Leslie rose automatically on numb legs and went in to change and feed him. Waving his arms, the baby made sucking sounds as she pinned on a dry diaper, grasped her breast greedily as she sat down to nurse him. Holding him, she traced the miniature but familiar brow line with a slender fingertip, smoothed the fine, reddish-gold hair on the throbbing little head, and knew with sad certainty that for once in her life she had been a coward. No matter how long the tunnel of empty years, she must make her way through them and love this child enough for two.

Rocking, she felt the baby's suckling gradually cease, saw his eyes close in contentment. Asleep, he looked even more like Ryan, warm against her heart. Then, from some deep place inside, a thought came. *Perhaps Spence was mistaken. Ryan could have been taken to another prison.*

Oh, God, Finney had been right. She *was* crazy. She fought against the senseless stupidity of it, tried to push the thought away. But the hope stayed. She could feel the surge of it pushing stubbornly through the miasma of grief, asserting again that Ryan was alive, that he was coming to her as he had said he would. The feeling was very strong, very sure, filling her heart.

The baby was fast asleep. She put him in his cradle, and then, with quick, decisive steps, she went out and picked up Spence's letter. Going through the short hall to the kitchen where Anna was starting the fire in the black woodstove, she reached around Anna's wiry figure and shoved the letter into the flames. Anna gave her a critical look.

"Paper makes smoke."

"That's what it should be," Leslie said, "smoke, drifting away. Insubstantial." She smiled at Anna. "I'm going down to bathe."

"Well, don't drown," Anna said crossly. "I don't swim, and I'd sure hate to have to call some man to drag your naked body out of there. Can't you wear something?"

"I have no intention of drowning," Leslie said, "so don't worry about it."

Dinner was ready, and Leslie hadn't come back from the springs. Anna stood in the doorway of the house indecisively, thinking of the baby waking with no one there, wondering if she should go down to the springs or call. Sometimes it did no good to call. That girl spent more time under the water than on top of it. She looked up as a horse came cantering toward the house from the west. A strange man sat erectly in the saddle, sweeping the scene with a glance that came gradually to rest on her. He slowed the horse and took off his slouch hat, exposing a rumpled head of chestnut hair. Clear hazel eyes looked down at her.

"Is this the Fitzsimmons' house?"

"It is," Anna said, cross again, "but she isn't around. She's down at the springs, swimming, instead of here, eating her dinner like she ought to be." She had looked toward the springs involuntarily, and the man followed the glance. He laughed.

"I'll fetch her for you." He wheeled his horse and was stopped by Anna's screech.

"I'll fetch her myself! If you want to see her, you wait here." From the way he looked, she wasn't making any impression. He looked ready to put the horse to a gallop. "It wouldn't be seemly," she added firmly. "She—well, she doesn't wear anything to swim."

A faint smile appeared on the man's rugged face. "She won't mind," he said gently, and kicked the horse into a gallop just as she had thought he would.

"Oh, Lord," Anna said helplessly to no one in particular, "well, maybe it'll teach her a lesson."

Swimming far below the surface of the crystal-clear water, Leslie's slim body arched slowly toward the surface, her tawny gold hair a rippling fan behind her. Her arms swept in long, sure strokes as she propelled herself upward, her slender legs feathered the water gracefully. Silver bubbles floated upward from her face as she let out the deep breath that she had taken before she dove. Then, as she broke the surface, she rolled and floated face up, dipping her head back to let her hair stream away from her face. Her full breasts rose and gleamed wetly in the sunlight, the ivory and gold column of her body suspended in crystal. Looking at the sky, she knew that Anna would be furious. It was past dinnertime.

A horse coughed, the kind of cough a horse makes when a blade of grass goes down the wrong way. Leslie whirled, dropping her feet and legs, sinking to neck deep. Not just a horse eating grass, but a man, standing and watching her! Blinded by the sun, she stared at the dark silhouette.

"That was the most beautiful thing I ever saw in my life," Ryan said unsteadily. "Like an underwater angel. Are you coming out or am I getting in?"

With a strangled, incoherent sound, Leslie flung herself toward him, grasped his outstretched hands and pulled her streaming body up into his arms. She was kissing him and crying, her hands frantically running over his hair, his neck, his shoulders. Touching his cheeks, she finally dropped her hands and slid them around him beneath his coat.

"It *is* you," she said brokenly, as if only her fingertips could prove it. "It really is. Oh, Ryan, I knew you would come, but how *dare* you take so long?"

The rest of them were at the house—Finney, John Tudbury and the two Tudbury sons—when Ryan and Leslie came up over the knoll, Ryan's clothes much wetter than hers. They had already known, since Ryan had stopped at the farm to ask directions, and, of course, they had told Anna. They had brought food and a couple of bottles of homemade whiskey and were set to celebrate. Anna was cooking furiously in the kitchen. She looked up as Leslie came in, taking in the sparkling, deep blue of her eyes, the pink-flushed face and the laughter lurking in the corners of a softened mouth.

"I always wondered how you'd look happy," Anna said, her own smile quirking in her sun-wrinkled face. "Don't float away, now."

Leslie laughed and hugged her, her love spilling over, her happiness a vibrant force that took in everyone. "I won't," she promised. "Where's the baby? Ryan wants to see his son."

Anna gestured toward a basket in the corner. "The poor neglected little thing is waiting for a touch of affection and a bit of mother's milk," she began, and watched Leslie snatch up the peacefully sleeping baby and leave. Anna put down her spoon and followed. She wanted to see the look on that man's face when he saw that sturdy bit of humanity.

The room was silent as the tall man bent over the bundle in Leslie's arms, then reached out and took it, holding his son like a man does, one broad palm splayed under the thickly padded bottom, the other cradling the shoulders and wobbly head. He stared into the small face with a look of awe. The blue eyes opened and blinked, the pink mouth stretched in a toothless yawn.

"Blue eyes, like yours," Ryan began as he searched the features, "and a tinge of gold in the hair . . ."

Startled by the unfamiliar deep voice, the baby stiffened in his hands; the yawning mouth opened wider. An indignant roar split the air and vibrated from the rafters. Grinning, Ryan handed him back to the comfort of his mother's arms.

"Listen to that," he said proudly. "There's a lot of Fitzsimmons in him."

Laughing, Leslie hastened into the bedroom to feed and soothe the baby. She could afford to leave Ryan in the company of the others now. Let him spin his tales and satisfy their curiosity over those bottles of whiskey. There was no long, gray tunnel of years now, only an unending panorama of sparkling blue sky and sea, of this home and the green, growing things around it.

Later, when the baby slept again and they all sat around the laden table, she told Ryan of Spence's letter. He grinned wryly.

"I was one of those seamen," he said, "and keeping very quiet about it. When the men from the cruiser picked me out of the water I was only half conscious and couldn't identify myself. Then my wound infected and I was delirious with fever for some time. By the time I recovered, the crew knew that I was to be charged with piracy. They had given me a name and claimed I was one of them." He looked at wide-eyed Finney and laughed. "In spite of having to give up the superior comforts offered to captains at Fort Montague, I was damn glad they did. It was better by far than hanging."

"But Spence said that they had a description of you,"

Leslie said, frightened again at the thought. "How did you fool them?"

"The description," Ryan said, "was detailed and accurate. But it was prepared by the only Union officers ever to see Captain Fitzsimmons in person. Remember the men who took over my ship in the Hillsborough? I was off on a hunting trip and my first mate, hoping to help me escape, claimed to be the captain himself." He glanced at John Tudbury. "A good thing, John, that I sent Ralph ashore with Finney and my wife. Had he been captured with us, I doubt even I could have persuaded those men that he wasn't the infamous Ryan Fitzsimmons. The description was perfect, right down to the mole on his left ear." He turned to Leslie. "Where is Spence's letter, darling? I'd like to see it."

"I burned it," Leslie said indignantly. "Not even Spencer Burdette had the right to tell me that you were dead!" Sudden tears filled her eyes. "It was the first time my faith failed," she added shakily, "and then, thank God, it came back, stronger than ever."

"I wish I had had the same faith," Finney said gruffly. "When Fitz walked up on Tudbury's porch I damn near died of fright. I figured I was seeing a ghost."

The laughter was a release of tension, a signal that the celebration was complete. They drifted off into the night for the long ride home. Leslie protested.

"You'll be till dawn getting there," she said, "stumbling around in the dark. We'll fix all of you places to sleep for the night."

"Sh-h-h," Anna admonished, gathering up her possessions. "If ever a couple deserved their privacy, you two do tonight. It'll not hurt us to ride along slow and think of God's miracles."

Leslie stood in the doorway until the sound of hooves

faded. Then she shut the door and turned to look at the long, lean body sprawled in the biggest chair in the house. Still thin from the long months in prison, Ryan's strong features stood out from flattened cheeks. There was a faint dusting of silver in the bright hair at his temples. But the eyes looking into hers were as clear, the faint smile as endearing. She swept toward him across the cosy, littered room, as graceful in the gingham gown as ever she had been in silk. Suddenly shy, she perched herself stiffly on his muscular thighs and looked at him questioningly.

"Are you tired?"

His arms went around her lazily and pulled her close, one hand going to the knot of golden hair to flick out the hairpins with familiar ease. "Extremely tired," he said, as the hair dropped in a silken flood over his hand, "of waiting for our friends to leave."

She leaned away from him, laughing, her eyes shining in the lamplight, her pink mouth invitingly open. She saw the sudden wave of passion darken the clear eyes, felt it ripple through the long body, then the arms around her crushed her against him so tightly that she could hardly breathe and his lips covered hers savagely.

Trembling with desire, Ryan took her mouth with deep, possessive thrusts, his hand searching her sensitive breasts with a rough urgency. Twisting in the chair, he pressed himself against her, desperate with wanting. The roughness, the sudden assault on her senses after so long, was too much. Leslie's hands strained against his chest; a whimper of alarm rose, muffled, from her throat. Instantly the pressure of his body eased.

"I'm sorry, my own darling," he murmured, and then slipped an arm beneath her thighs and rose with her, striding toward the spare bedroom.

She was no longer afraid. His quick reaction had reminded her that this man of hers was at times violently passionate but never capable of cruelty. Even when his passion ruled him, there was something inside that wouldn't allow him to hurt her. She tugged at his collar when she saw where he was taking her.

"The other room, Ryan . . ."

"Not tonight," Ryan said unsteadily, and laid her on the freshly made bed that Anna had left. "Tonight I'll not share you even with my sleeping son. You are mine, Leslie." His hands were busy with the buttons of her bodice; the dim light from the open door showed her his dark face, tense with passion. "I cannot wait," he said huskily, "to feel myself within you, to know that once again we are truly knitted together, truly one." He pushed aside her bodice and loosened camisole and buried his face between her full breasts. "I need you," he whispered, as he had once before. "I need you so much."

A wave of transcendent love rose and rippled through Leslie's veins, crested and burst into fire. Her hands flew to help him rid their bodies of the confining clothes, her kisses covered the skin she bared, her heart pounded as he swung up and over her.

"My love . . . my life . . ." Hovering over her, he arched his broad back and pressed between her quivering thighs, entering her with exquisite slowness. The hard length of him was solid within her, a radiating heat that filled her starved body with an aching joy and a promise of ecstasy. Her strong, slender arms pulled him down, wanting the weight of him crushed against her.

Ryan let out his held breath in a gusting sigh and pressed his face into her neck. "Now," he whispered, "I am home and whole again."

She moved, caressing him with that subtle rhythm that was all her own, coaxing, teasing until he could bear the sweet torture no longer. With a deep sound of male pleasure, he arched again and began the long, slow thrusts and withdrawals that sent them soaring toward peak after peak of heavenly sensation until that ultimate peak and the edge of ecstasy. Then, breathing hard, he grasped her hips in his broad palms and lifted her to him, driving in until their bodies slid tightly together and clung. Leslie felt her inner flesh lock around him, begin to ripple. They cried out together as they tumbled over the edge and down, down and down, into a pool of dark, throbbing rapture.

They couldn't sleep. Curled together, they touched and talked through the hours, questions, answers, laughter.

"It's a wonderful house; it feels like a home."

"It is a home, now. But we need a ship."

"Is there money enough left for a small steamer?"

"More than enough! Gold goes far in the South these days." She hugged him, smiling. "We'll be sailing peaceful seas and living in our green place," she quoted softly.

"Didn't I say that it would happen?"

She nodded her head on his shoulder and then left him as the baby cried. In the other bedroom she dried and fed the wailing child and rocked him to sleep. Then, coming back, she found Ryan's arms reaching for her again.

"The baby," he said suddenly, questioningly. "You haven't told me his name."

"How could I?" Snuggling against him, she sounded a trifle indignant. "Naturally, I've been waiting for his father to name him."

"Oh." Ryan lay still, thinking. Finally, he propped himself on one elbow and looked down at her. "Would you like Gordon? Gordon Fitzsimmons is a well-sounding name."

Leslie caught her breath, searching his face in the dim light. "That's the last name I would have expected you to choose," she said slowly. "Why did you?"

His broad mouth twitched, quirking up at one corner. "Because," he said solemnly, "I think it has a better ring to it than Groover Fitzsimmons."

Leslie shot up to a sitting position. "Oh, my God! You knew! Then—I did give it away, somehow. . . ."

"You didn't," he assured her, serious again, "and I never will, either. Your father did. Any man who sees you appreciates your beauty, but there are few who will ever look at you with such perfect love in their eyes." He brushed a tear from her cheek with a gentle hand. "His very heart shone over you, Leslie. How could I miss it? I wanted so badly to shake his hand and tell him that I'd been wrong, but, of course, I couldn't. But, since you've given me the opportunity to name our child for him, perhaps that will be enough."

"It's enough," she said tremulously, and collapsed over him, hugging him hard. If there had been one small cloud in the blue sky ahead, it was gone. She put her cheek on his broad chest and lay contented, listening to the strong, steady beat of his heart.

Tapestry

HISTORICAL ROMANCES

POCKET BOOKS